Other Titles by Publisher

Francis B Nyamnjoh
Stories from Abakwa
Mind Searching
The Disillusioned African
The Convert

Dibussi Tande
No Turning Back. Poems of Freedom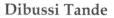

Kangsen Feka Wakai
Fragmented Melodies

Ntemfac Ofege
Namondo. Child of the Water Spirit

Emmanuel Fru Doh
Not Yet Damascus

Thomas Jing
Tale of an African Woman

Peter Wuteh Vakunta
Grassfields Stories from Cameroon

Souls
Forgotten

Francis B Nyamnjoh

Langaa Research & Publishing CIG
Mankon, Bamenda

Publisher:

Langaa Research and Publishing Common Initiative Group

P.O. Box 902 Mankon

Bamenda

North West Province

Cameroon

Langaagrp@gmail.com

www.langaapublisher.com

ISBN: 9956-558-12-5

To Souls Forgotten

1

Did I lock my door? There's no going back to make certain. The results are about to be released, and I can't move an inch from the board in front of me. Let thieves sneak in and carry away my belongings. I don't care. Knowing how I've performed is all that matters right now. It's like waiting for the verdict on a case in which the judge has wetted his beard with *matango* (palm wine) from both camps. How could I bear another major failure in this Faculty of Orthodox Law? What would I say to my parents and to all of Abehema? I'm frightened to think of all it entails.

It is strange how fast time flies. That I've been here for two years already is hard to believe. Yet nothing could be truer! Time is rapid yet stealthy, like a night storm of destructive spirits in my home village of Abehema. There, whenever the wicked elements transformed themselves into nocturnal spirits and descended into the world beyond below the surface calmness of the lake, innocent farmers and households complained and wept with bitterness for their damaged crops and roofless houses. "They have done it again, the witches!" The afflicted sought the wrath of the ancestors to descend upon the evildoers. And the village authorities always responded with deserved sympathy, chastising the wicked in order to strengthen community spirit.

To track down and punish the witches, enemies of communal peace and harmony, village authorities have employed since pre-colonial Abehema a standard procedure recognised by all. This involves watching all farms and compounds that strangely escaped the mass devastation

1

caused by mysterious storms. The owners of the unaffected farms and houses would be accused of witchcraft and punished accordingly. Generally, they would be asked to drink a concoction of *tgungha* (sasswood) from which only the guilty are said to die, and few are known to survive.

Though the white man fought hard to abolish the practice in his days, Abehema has somehow managed to maintain the administration of *tgungha*. Today, whatever the modern authorities might say, *tgungha* has done more for law and order in Abehema than the police and gendarmes stationed some hundred kilometres away in Kaizerbosch, who seldom visit the periphery except to collect poll and cattle taxes from the toiling peasant farmers and wandering Fulani herdsmen. Despite the survival of *tgungha* as a deterrent against evil, there is a general recognition by the elders that witchcraft is more rampant today than it ever was in the past. The more they fight it, the stronger and more cunning it becomes, they claim. And time flies on...

If time passed with achievement, there would be little to complain about. Nothing would seem out of turn or purpose. Time makes sense when we go along with it, and it rewards our creative efforts to make sense of it. When two years are spent doing a single programme of Orthodox Law, then something somewhere is basically wrong. Why can't something for once be right for me in this bloody university? Just what is my crime?

So far there is no sign that the authorities are to release the results in the twinkle of an eye as their notice suggests. I'm prepared to wait. I won't budge, even if it means staying here until thieves empty my perhaps unlocked room and grass grows through and over my feet. This is not the time for jesters to juggle with my academic future. It's a matter of life and death, my anchor of hope to family and village. The lecturers had better make no mistake. They have a record for making mistakes that stab students like doctored daggers. I bet I'll make a clean clear pass, clean and clear like water from the rocky springs of Kakakum. May my ancestors direct their every step and decision at this crucial moment, so the authorities may not be blind when they should see. My dear father in Heaven, tender me your hand at this hour of need, help me across the Rubicon. I pray you.

Other anxious students share this bench with me. Countless others stand close to the proclamation board – the focus of attention. Some are pacing up and down, trying to smoke or chat away their tension. For the moment the *Guillotine* is glistening. Soon after the results, students will break the glass covers of the famous results board. Male and female students shedding tears of angry disappointment will tear the result sheets into bits and pieces.

That's what happens every year, a ritual of some kind. The reaction of the authorities is also a ritual. Quite predictable, like a workman whose only tool is a hammer and to whom every problem is a nail, or a cook whose only spice is salt. Each time it happens, they replace the destroyed board with a new guillotine, and describe the students' behaviour as "irresponsible vandalism." By indulging in minor, even symbolic destruction of university property, aren't we, baptised and confirmed failures, challenging their diabolical attempts to exclude us from partaking in the sumptuous banquet that awaits all winners? In what more effective way could we show that something is amiss with our system of education?

Year before last there was a massive strike ... no, a massive attempt to strike. I was still in high school, chewing and digesting books and notes in preparation for the 'A' levels, and praying several times a day to qualify for a place in this academic beehive which I knew only by imagination. Winds of the strike blew across to us in the provinces. This is a land of great winds, winds more powerful than Radio Mimboland International. By hearsay, we learnt that students had gone on a rampage. The disorder affected the whole city, bringing many activities to a standstill. The head of state had to intervene personally to calm that about which the radio was silent. The strike had led to or coincided with, I don't know for sure, the raising of student grants. We "freshers" were grateful about the raise in student grants, if only symbolic, and dismayed by the 'chameleons' whose changing colours clashed with the students' idea of the "Genuine Intellectual." Nothing was done to repair the unhealthy student-lecturer relationship, which has worsened ever since. It is whispered here and there in the campus that our *renowned* lecturers are seeking "their noble revenge," trying to make us account for the actions of our predecessors! That's why failures, resits and further failures are so rampant. "Intellectual revenge," they say, "is nothing like the pedestrian sort we know." And how apt!

A student with copies of *Roots* for sale? I think I should buy, but MIM$300?! Rather expensive... but worthwhile. It's a journal true to its name. When students in the Faculty of Social Thought write, they make sense. They dig into Roots of issues and abhor the mediocrity we of other faculties drink like absent-minded alcoholics. Each issue of *Roots* carries a feature article on the academic atmosphere of the university. If they have any sense of timing, they should feature resit examinations this fateful month of September.

The table of contents is rich... What! The lead article is in Tougalish? Perhaps this is the beginning of the long-awaited change in this institution. Sometimes articles had to be translated into Muzungulandish to make them publishable. Isn't it ironic that the Faculty of Social Thought gave a Tougalish name to its journal? Why not "Les Racines" or something to that effect, as long as it sounds Muzungulander? What significance for us Tougalish Mimbolander students that the lead article, on examinations, is also in Tougalish? Good luck? Or bad luck as usual?

The author is a fellow student I know in person and respect. He has the gift of seeing things in another light and

4

saying them in other words. He can see through the chameleons' colours and say what lies beneath with mincingly menacing words. What a steaming conclusion! *"If the academic atmosphere in the University of Asieyam is poisoned by uproars and dins,"* Marxy Wang writes, *"it is because of the overwhelming nature of the collective frustrations of the students and the self-propagation and mystification of academics."*

Why can't our bearers-of-knowledge drop their buffoonery and turn to their illustrious counterparts in the faculty of Social Thought for inspiration? What virus is it that blunts their sense of emulation? Or is it just the old story of motivation getting strangled by excessive lust? Isn't it incomprehensible that two occupants of the same seat, nourished by the same toil and sweat, aren't able to spark each other off?

I do reproach Marxy Wang and his faculty for one thing: their tendency to take a cat-on-the-fence position when militancy ought to be the watchword. They advocate scientific neutrality and a sort of objectivity, which only strengthens and protects the very misdeeds and vices they are out to combat. What's the practical utility of such an approach? It's fear of being termed *élements dangereux*, fear of excommunication by the popes of power, that makes them criticise with their tails between their legs. I wish they would defy the authorities – speaking out clearly and boldly – instead of imprisoning change in an envelope of banality termed *l'objectivité scientifique*. If fear of the authorities is their problem, as I think, then we the downtrodden are forever doomed. Fear can breed but more fear.

I agree with Professor Moses Mahogany who died an outlaw and whose books are as feared as his ghost by those who matter. He says we need people committed to the cause of the crippled and the dribbling, the wretched and panting runners-up of life. Only people ready to fan the dying flame of the forsaken are on our side, not those who pray with their eyes open or their feet in the air, not those who use a phoney type of Holy Water that attracts the very witches they pretend to chase away. Instead of circumnavigating, I wish Marxy would tell the naked truth, which is: "If the students fail their examinations, it is because their material conditions and class interests of lecturers privilege the production and glorification of mediocrity."

The sudden rush to the guillotine is frightening. I know I should be over there too, skimming through the hangman's verdict. The thought that these may well be the results of my class that have just been pasted up increases my heartbeat. I am reassured. My neighbour on the bench returns and I lean towards her to inquire. "Ce sont les résultats de la troisième année," she says, with little enthusiasm. Then as if she had read my mind, adds, "Certe qu'ils sont catastrophiques." Yes, they will be devastating as usual, the third-year results. That's to be expected. The guillotine knows no Patience. *Catastrophique* is the Muzungulandish adjective for this enormity. Even final-year students have to spend donkey years struggling to harvest the ripe fruit that hangs over their noses and might see it snatched away at the last minute. Our learned lecturers see in them potential rivals. All must be done to discourage them.

These are the type of things that Marxy and his colleagues should air! True, they are the only persons who have attempted to fart this loud against the establishment. Should that be cause for complacency? Good thing I know him personally. I should let him know how much we count on him and his likes. With our present headaches and entanglements, we can't afford the luxury of fighting with our hands tied behind our backs in the name of science. The battle for change is long and tiresome. Marxy writes like one moulded in the furnace where great revolutionaries are forged. I feel the ox in him overflowing with energy yearning to be harnessed.

Another list has just been pasted up. This time I'm among the first to the board, but the results are for the second year students. It's always the same. A handful of rejoicers and a multitude of wailers. The mournful tears of the multitude drown the joyful cries of the successful few. My neck is next in line to be scrutinised by the guillotine. Sweating palms, soaked armpits, a racing heart. I'm about to be circumcised afresh. God forbid!

Why this feeling of loneliness despite the crowd? It chills my blood in a strange manner, like crossing a graveyard alone in the heart of the night. I've had this sort of feeling twice before. Once right before I was circumcised, and again when my younger sister died of a snakebite several years back. "Failure is not going to mean the end of the world," I try to console myself. "Don't pretend, Emmanuel Kwanga, it would be the most demolishing blow you've ever been served," continues the strange voice in me.

"Ne me pousse pas!" threatens my neighbour, a fat, bearded student of twenty-seven or so. He can't be less, can he? His casual jeans patched on both knees by an obviously disgruntled tailor, together with the faded T-shirt over them, are a common sight on campus. I'm wearing something similar, but not as patched or faded. It appears I've been leaning on him without noticing. I murmur a few words of apologetic Muzungulandish and see he is just as engulfed by his thoughts as my leaning on him. The fact that he is still sitting here means we are certainly classmates. Where has he been the whole year? I've never seen him in class. "Now that's what I call foolish, Emmanuel! How do you expect to know everyone in a class where two thousand students is a conservative estimate?" I forgive myself such silliness, naturally. My Muzungulandish neighbour is probably as distraught as I. We are each wandering in an enigmatic world of our own. This heavy feeling of gloom in me refuses to budge. It's my turn next.

I try to think of Peaphweng Mukong, my father, and of Ngonsu, my mother. I also think of my step-mothers and their children, and of my dear brothers and sisters back home. I think of the village of Abehema and its problems. I would hate to further shatter their hopes. How disappointing it would be to them for me to be thrown out of university like a penniless tenant! Abehema might finally relinquish all claims to a share of the scarce cake of *Kwang* (the good life). Can you imagine stalking your game tirelessly, then watching it walk away unharmed?

I've disappointed them before. Three years ago when I obtained my GCE 'A' level papers, the joy in the village was boundless and the feasting like at Christmas. Everybody, my parents in particular, believed the ancestors had blessed our village at last! Abehema would have a son of the soil in government, as District Officer – the biggest post they knew. When I told them I still needed to write and pass a public service examination and undergo a three-year training programme in a Public Relations School to qualify as DO, they thought I was reluctant to make them proud, to be their *Kwanga* – their light out of the tunnel. It took time, a long time to explain things to them. It was only when Kimbi, a college friend from the neighbouring village of Yenseh, added his voice to mine, that my people were at last convinced I would give all to be DO. Only it wasn't as easy as they thought. I narrowly avoided being cursed by those to whom I owe so much, those who had named me Kwanga in anticipation of *Kwang*.

I imagine the look of disappointment on Peaphweng Mukong's face, the person who has made the most sacrifices to sustain my expensive climb to the top of the academic ladder. It's been his ambition as my father to see me among the cream of the country. Everyone in Abehema has contributed in one way or another to the cultivation of this farm – Kwanga – on which they have planted their hopes for *Kwang*, convinced that one person's child is only in the

8

womb. Although no child can occupy more than one womb, from birth the child belongs to the entire community, to tend and harness for the good of all and sundry. They all stood behind me years ago, thinking that educating a child was like planting a coconut tree. Some of my people have died waiting for the harvest. I've deceived those of them still alive into thinking the crops will be ready next year. What shall I say when they come and find nothing in the farm?

My parents and Abehema would never believe me if I tell them the reason I have stayed here longer than expected is that I've been failing my examinations. Since I first set foot in school, they've known me as their unbeatable son, "the wrestler with a cat's nimbleness." Invariably they believed I would lead the class, even when I desperately clawed at anything to avoid repeating one. To reverse this image of me would be no less difficult than getting into Ngonsu's womb to be born afresh.

Oh, how I wish these learned men knew the mess into which they've pushed me. How I've become a prisoner without a crime. From a young ambitious and hopeful lad to a frustrated dropout, without the slightest transition. God forbid!

I still remember how hope embraced me when I learnt I'd made the 'A' levels. Once that miracle occurred, my problem became how to obtain a university degree in the minimum period of three years, secure a good job and begin to earn a salary for my upkeep and the sustenance of my family and my people. I built fanciful castles in the air. My father, Peaphweng Mukong, and mother, Ngonsu, built theirs. Everyone in Abehema did the same.

The night before my departure for the university, every man and woman of age had a word of advice for me. They stressed how pleased they were that I was going away to the land of greatness. "Kwanga", some chose to begin, some preferred "Emmanuel," while others used both. Their message was always the same: "One person's child is only in

9

the womb. You've outgrown the womb in which you were conceived, to prove that you are the child of the entire village, and not your parents' only. That's good, Kwanga, now go into the distant hills and hunt in the name of Abehema."

"Remember, you are our ears and eyes in that far off Great City of Nyamandem which we hear of only. It's our enormous pride to have a representative there at last. We've been ignored far too long by *Kwang*. From now on, our very own Kwanga will be at its very heart. We're grateful to you our saviour. Make us even prouder, Emmanuel."

"The Great City is full of bad youths who like to corrupt and mislead the good ones, so we hear. Beware of them! Do what we are sending you there to do, and seek no more."

"Be polite and respectful to everyone you meet, older or younger, taller or shorter. Remember: humility pays, arrogance destroys."

"Place your feet each above the other when you walk, that you might provoke no one."

"Be obedient to the teachers who are like your parents in the foreign soil where you are about to go. Do always as they say. Be nice to them, and they will be nice to you," and so on and so forth. I listened to each and every visitor with attentive patience, and tried to store everything they said, even when this seemed senseless. Some spat into my palms and asked me to rub my face with their spittle as a sign of good luck. I did that and more, and left pregnant with good will.

The gifts Ngonsu my mother received were many and varied. They consisted mainly of foodstuff, much of which I left behind because it would have cost a fortune to transport everything to Nyamandem. The very last thing my father did the night of my departure was ask his late father to intercede with the ancestors and God for me. He held out a huge brown calabash full of water fresh from the river

10

behind our compound, and prayed for God's and our ancestors' guidance and protection. He asked the heavenly forces to keep me company throughout my journey and stay in the soil of the foreign and the unknown that had invited me, and Abehema by extension. This ritual was the conclusion to the protection and fortification rite Peaphweng Ndyu the diviner-healer had performed on me four days before. The incisions he made on my arms and legs were still fresh. He had infused various lotions in them and told me to be confident: "For this will protect you against poison and the forces of evil." Peaphweng Ndyu's credibility as a diviner-healer was firmly established. Even Chief Ngain, my father's distant cousin, consulted him regularly, it was rumoured.

The journey to the Great City was long but thrilling. Beyond Kaizerbosch, our district capital where I had twice been to write the GCE "O" and "A" levels, right from Zingraftstown everything was new to me. I had never travelled as far afield, let alone farther than this regional city, which, though not half as big as Nyamandem, epitomized *Kwang* to the provincial folk. To know that the seat of wisdom which I was to experience as an academic beehive was situated right in the heart of *Kwang* itself enthused me. I wanted to miss out on no detail in the various stages of initiation. I stayed awake until our bus arrived in Nyamandem at night. A marvellous sight, a spectacular revelation. Electricity twinkled everywhere, as if the starry skies had fallen on the city, enveloping all in its blinking blanket of shadowy fulfilment. I shared the happiness of the city that night with Kimbi – the same college friend who had helped to explain to my parents and village that becoming a DO was not as easy as they imagined – and his girlfriend. All through that night the lights smiled *bienvenue* to us.

Beginning very early the following day, when the bright starry lights had gone, I began to see the Great City in its true colours. Though I had come down from the province

11

qualified for both the scholarship and university accommodation, I was only awarded the former, and this only after an unpleasant struggle. In a wink my idea of Nyamandem had changed, from a garden of blooms to a jungle where the able preached one thing and did quite another, and where corrupt practices were kept from public scrutiny because of the "civilised" belief that it was only normal for a goat to eat where it was tethered! Though the accommodation officers were supposed to give priority to students from the provinces, the sons and daughters of the rich urban influential men and women received the lodging allotments. Only a few genuinely provincial names were on the list, sprinkled like little droplets of water over a floor thick with dust. Yes, that was the other face of the Great City, the face the bright lights that first night could not conceal for long.

Today I know the Great City in and out. I now know it is far from what I saw that night two years ago. That sight was a passing illusion, the type of "cosmetic appearance" which, as Professor Moses Mahogany once wrote, "is likely to deceive the foreign tourist, but not the native who has learnt to distinguish between gold and golden, and who knows that no one ever makes any valid judgement about a country from a flying plane, from within a luxury car, or through the windows of a five-star hotel." Since then I have had to face the harsh realities of life, modern life. What room is there for change? I don't know. I don't think. I find it hard to hope anymore and hard to cope.

The Dean comes out for the third time, still in his robes as academic hangman. My heart sinks. He goes to the board. We all gather around him, each jostling to be the first to learn the truth, good or bad. He pastes up the list and rushes back to his office, like an old peasant escaping a thunderstorm. He knows his crime, he and his colleagues. They are sadists, learned sadists. That we all know! The crowd of students is thick and I find it hard to see the list clearly. There is no doubt it's catastrophic, judging from the repeated shouts of:

"C'est mauvais."

"Ouais!"

"On m'a tué."

"On est mort."

"C'est incroyable!"

"Masa, man don die!"

"They have killed us!"

One by one the students slipped away, as perplexed and shattered as they were last June. Those of us behind surge forward, anxious and each hoping to be the rare escapee from the festive blade of the dripping guillotine.

At last I come face to face with it. I've learnt through repeated consultation just where to look for my name. For tense minutes I stand there, unable to believe what I see. "Emmanuel Kwanga" is not on the list of life. I scan it over and over again, fingering each name prayerfully – despite the protest – just in case. There is no miracle. The story is over, a tragic tale of misfortune. It's been two years of delusion, two years of unfulfilled dreams of modern comfort for my people and me. Comfort which I thought was possible that night I first set eyes on this monument of *Kwang*!

As if to close the whole chapter of false hope, a gush of tears covers my eyes, blinding me to the list. My right hand forms into a fist, and with a single blow shatters the glass, before I know it. I'm wounded, but in protest. Others join in, and soon the board is beyond recognition, pieces of glass smeared with angry blood. I wipe my eyes and bandage my hand with the Bob Marley "He-who-fights-and-runs away…" T-shirt I'm wearing. Then turn homewards, to the ghettoes where I belong.

It took Emmanuel Kwanga over an hour to arrive at his little room in the ghettoes of Basfond, where he had lived two years of fruitlessness. All the way from the university campus, he behaved like a madman or a drunk. He stopped abruptly in the middle of a busy road amid people and passing cars, paying no attention to the recklessness of the many who drove with fraudulent licences. To swear at, curse or accuse the authorities in public, oblivious of the subversion that entailed, even to dare to voice personal misfortunes to no one in particular, regardless of the embarrassment it caused, wasn't all that indicative of a mind not at peace with itself? And he was indeed lucky not to have been knocked down by an impatient driver, apprehended by the security officers who strode the narrow streets with muddy feet like feasting maggots in a carcass, or assaulted by the genuinely mad and drunk.

"What!" his door was wide open, just as he had feared.

Now with the benefit of hindsight, how he wished he had damned the results and returned home to ensure the door was locked! Trembling with fear and fury, he managed to walk in. The tragedy was complete. His belongings were gone, all of them: the books, the bed, table and two chairs, the clothes and the utensils. All had vanished.

As far as he was concerned, the city and its institutions had denied him, despite his determined quest for its virtues and delights. "I'm no longer wanted here," he murmured in a voice weakened from weeping as he collapsed to the cold bare cement floor. "That's the verdict. The city has declared me an outlaw, and I know my way out. What more?"

2

The tall, imposing, grey-haired, 56-year-old Peaphweng Mukong ascended the hill like an energetic youth. He was anxious to know why Chief Ngain had ordered him to rise with the birds. What could be so urgent? Might it have to do with his request of two months ago? If so, he would count himself a lucky man indeed. Arranging a marriage to a princess was no easy thing, distant cousin of the Chief though he was. How thrilled his son Kwanga would be by such good news. The more he anticipated the fulfilment of his dream, the broader his self-gratifying smile grew. He was proud of his son at the university, and the villagers approved of his pride. It was the sort of achieved pride the ancestors considered legitimate. Which other dignitary wouldn't be proud for sending a son as far away as the Great City, to learn to understand and advance in the magic of the white man?

"Yes," he asserted deservingly, a trace of boastfulness detectable in the way he held his chest. He continued in thought: Kwanga's (he seldom called his son 'Emmanuel') joy would soon be complete. And he, Peaphweng Mukong, would be the most visible notable in the entire chiefdom. At public meetings, his stool would be placed only second to that of Chief Ngain. What more did a man want of the god of fame? Already, he was famous as father of the most learned son of the soil. Everywhere he went people introduced him first as the man whose son was to graduate in under a year, join the government and carve a place of prominence for Abehema. Every other title, such as the man with the biggest provision store in the village, or the man with the most modern compound, was secondary. If only he could get the charming Princess Tem to marry 24-year-old Kwanga, that would crown it all. His fame and satisfaction would be fathomless! And even the ancestors would nod in recognition and pride.

The deeper Peaphweng Mukong thought of it, the greater his anxiety, and the more he tackled the steepness of the hill like an agile young man. "The matter must be decided today," he concluded. "I've waited too long. It's either a yes or a no, and no amount of waiting would change a mind determined to say no."

He came to the top of the hill where the 300-metre-wide crater lake spread in front of him. From there he could make out the huts of the herdboys who took care of his friend Tangh-e-keh's cattle, amongst a host of others on the green pastures at the foot of the distant Hiseng mountains. A bit tired, he decided to relax his feet and lungs. He climbed to a smooth rock and sat down to smoke the long clay pipe he always carried in the side pocket of his thick dark coat. As he dipped his hand in to fetch the pipe and box of matches, he remembered Ravageur, the white man from faraway Muzunguland, who had given him the woollen coat four years back.

"God blessam, God bless my combi," he muttered in Pidgin-Tougalish, in the manner of the itinerant Baptist preacher he nearly became as a young man. For a while he wondered whether his good friend would ever come again. "He who used to love this lake like a witch does darkness. What an enigma he was!"

Peaphweng Mukong recalled how Ravageur used to travel alone in a powerful but battered Land Rover all the way from beyond the Great City just to see and feel Lake Abehema. Ravageur was quite unlike the villagers who had grown up in awe of the lake because of the strange stories of its strange happenings from time immemorial. He would choose to camp solo up here rather than accept accommodation from the Chief or down in the main village.

Whatever he was seeking, he never told a soul, not even Peaphweng Mukong, his trusted friend. For days he would conduct countless experiments with strange instruments of every sort and take meticulous photographs of the lake and its surroundings with his cameras. Then he would disappear, just to reappear a couple months later. Most villagers thought him a white witch, because he was antisocial, and also because he dared to stay alone around the lake at night, where few of them could stand solitude even at day. They had grown up fearing the lake because of its strangeness. They neither bathed in it, nor let their livestock drink from it. Children grew up knowing the lake was a place to worship from a distance, not to play in or seek sustenance from. Nobody knew if there were fishes in the lake because no one dared check for fear of being dragged underneath mysteriously. They had enough goats, fowls, cows and game in their hills and valleys to not want to tempt the forces of the lake with inquisitiveness about what the lake could offer beyond serving as a sacred place. This was why some villagers suspected Ravageur's intentions. Ancestral wisdom told them that wickedness does not whistle in the trees like wind.

"I wonder what that tall hairy fellow used to look for?" Peaphweng Mukong pondered aloud.

It was the very same question he had asked himself over and over without an answer. For two years Ravageur would neither mention his surname, admit to being an unusual tourist, nor reveal the truth about him as an outstanding geochemistry researcher whose interest in Lake Abehema was more than just touristic. Kwanga and Ravageur had disliked each other the very first time they met. While Kwanga had a strong and almost instinctive hatred for whites, Ravageur disapproved of his condescending and hypercritical attitude. Although Peaphweng Mukong admired his son's sense of superiority and independence, he would not have a child decide his friends and foes for him.

Secretive though the middle-aged Muzungulander was, Peaphweng Mukong had remained his friend during the two years he came and went. Ravageur used to bring him and the family (except Kwanga who was usually away) lots of little presents, 'modern things' that won them equal amounts of respect and envy from the unfortunate rest of the village. What Peaphweng Mukong could not understand was why a man who appeared that friendly, to him at least, should stay away this long without signalling his existence. What then were friends for?

"Maybe the fellow found all he was looking for," he smiled cynically, afraid to think that Kwanga might have been right after all, in protesting against his friendship with Ravageur.

"Whites are strange people, aren't they? No, not whites only." He refused to yield just yet. "People… that's it. People in general are strange and unpredictable," he smiled again, his firm kola-nut-stained teeth betraying his defiant personality.

From where he sat, Peaphweng Mukong was able to see beyond Abehema. To the right, he could perceive the village of Yenseh about fifteen kilometres away, and to the left, Tchang, a much smaller and nearer settlement. Like his village, both were along the Ring Road that linked the administrative capitals of Chuma and Tunga Divisions: the one, Kaizerbosch, about one hundred kilometres south, and the other, Alfredsburg, almost twice as far but to the north, he couldn't see. The undulating valleys and hills had always fascinated him. He admired the continuous spread they appeared to form. Like a bird, his eyes seemed to fly across until they disappeared into infinity beyond the distant hills of the neighbouring villages. The view was fantastic, even though the sun was still rising and the fog had not yet cleared fully. An absorbing and gratifying spectacle it was.

The prolonged look made him dizzy, so he stopped for fear of losing his balance and falling off the rock.

When he was through with smoking, he emptied his pipe of ash, climbed down from the rock, and stooped to dare to do the unusual – wash his hands in the sacred lake. Quickly he withdrew them. The water was abnormally hot. He was struck by the discovery. What could have left the lake boiling hot so early in the morning? What could have made it this hot, at all?

"Strange thing, this lake! It would never cease to surprise people," he muttered.

Panicked, he resolved to take the matter up with Chief Ngain once in the palace. If the boiling water was a premonition of some kind, sacrifices could be offered in time to avert impending misfortune.

He resumed his journey to the palace situated up in the mountains, after an impetuous decision to visit Tangh-e-keh's cattle in the next two days to see how the herdboys were coping. He was quite aware that his infrequent visits to the herds made a poor superintendent of him. Perhaps it was time he told his friend to replace him with younger blood, that he was getting too old for the task.

"That will have to wait just a little longer," he said. "Just the time for Kwanga to leave university and settle down to a good job with the government," he anticipated.

"Until then, Tangh-e-keh's money is still worth straining for. I won't chicken out of activity because of old age, while my son starves in a foreign land," he stressed.

Then he continued on his way, following faithfully behind his solid staff.

Although he walked away and was soon out of sight of the lake, his mind refused to leave it. He kept thinking of the mysterious mass of water and the stories that had marked its existence. He remembered what happened when he was a youth twice younger than his 'learned' son today, and shook his head confoundedly. How could anyone have predicted that memorable occurrence? Who could have stood up and sustained a convincing argument that the world beyond was more endowed with powers than ever imagined? That particular episode diffused the air of incredulity that prevailed at the time, and forever made the sceptics seal their naive lips in matters supernatural.

He recalled the incident with particular vividness. It was at the death of Chief Phwe. Everyone had assembled at the palace to witness his funeral and the enthronement of his legitimate successor, the present Chief's uncle. (Though to be more exact, he was something like a step-uncle to Chief Ngain.) There was another nephew who defined legitimacy his own way, and was ready to fight to death for the wooden throne he so coveted. The dispute was tense, and the confusion total. Though the king-makers proclaimed Ndang the chosen one, it was startling how many people still supported the rival but self-nominated candidate. How could the crisis be resolved most amicably, despite the vile shouts of war from those who by some strange logic or another believed a war could be decisive?

There was hope when some dissidents began to soften their stance on hearing Ndang declare he would rather give up than fight a war of succession. Just when the king-makers were about to seize the opportunity and seek peace, the struggle slipped out of human control into the hands of the supernatural. The world beyond took it upon itself to resolve the matter that threatened the very foundation of Abehema. Certain strange phenomena began to occur, creating concern and forcing the village to turn to those with competence in the language of signs and symbols for interpretation. The most powerful of them, a diviner-healer named Tshou (father to the renowned Peaphweng Ndyu of today), was chosen to mediate between the living and the dead, the turbulent and the calm, the foolish and the wise – between chaos and order.

Tshou interpreted all phenomenal changes. He explained the eclipse that occurred one market day, bringing instant darkness in broad daylight, as the anger of the world beyond and a glimpse of the chaos, loss and sorrow that would follow any prolonged rancour over succession. If the royal nephews preferred to divide instead of unite, he warned, there was nothing but annihilation to expect. The croaking of many toads at the same time in the night was a sign of the mass mourning that would follow, should the struggle be allowed to degenerate into war, he went on. When at night many owls hooted, Tshou saw it as a premonition of how witches would "capitalise on the dispute by *eating up* many people, and setting off chains of false and counter-accusations." The heightened sense of fear amongst the people, he suggested, was an indication that the dispute had invited far more spirits from the world beyond than was necessary for their mental health. He had an explanation for every strange event, explanations that made many afraid, and increased calls for the urgent reconciliation of the two pretenders.

Public pressure reached a proportion which even Tsam the power-monger could no longer ignore. Both contenders agreed to meet Tshou to hear and ponder over the solution he claimed the ancestors had reached. So, on the following market day, Tshou announced the proposition and invited the population to witness him seek ancestral absolution at the lake the day after. When they came to the lake the following morning, it was no longer the lake everyone knew. It had broken up to form two separate lakes – one twice the size of the other, and both quite far apart. The villagers were spellbound.

"Those stupefied faces, what could ever make me forget them?" he asked in a tremulous voice, as if he were experiencing the shock all over again. Then he continued with his recollections: The impact was immediate, felt by everyone. Even Ndang and Tsam for once forgot their differences. What they saw was both strange and frightening. When Tshou, dressed more like a magician than a diviner-healer, was satisfied that all had taken in the spectacle, he broke the silence.

He turned to the crowd, which he asked to prepare for absolution from the ancestors, guiding spirits of the soil. Absolution was necessary because, as the villagers of Abehema could see for themselves, the rashness of some of their tribesmen had greatly upset the ancestral world. All could see the way a village once united and in harmony had been torn asunder. What had happened was good neither for Abehema nor for the ancestors who had held it together. The lake was a sign of unity, which selfishness and inordinate ambition were trying to undermine. How could a house divided within face its adversaries with the oneness of voice required? How did two brothers expect to carry home huge bundles of firewood if they refused to lend each other a hand? Despite the passion for evil and chaos that threatened to split Abehema, he stressed, there was good news from the living-dead. The ancestors, though terribly hurt and disappointed, were ready to forgive and forget. With this, he called upon Ndang and Tsam to listen keenly to the message he had been instructed to deliver.

There was complete silence as Tshou took his time. Absolute quiet could be sniffed in the air. At last he resumed.

"The ancestors have asked me," he paused to clear his throat, "to tell you how they've followed your dispute with paternal interest and concern. You are like fingers of the same hand, so they say," he raised a hand with spread-out fingers to the rival princes.

"If the thumb appears fatter and more prominent, know that God wouldn't have made it so was the nature of its job not such that it required this."

He stopped speaking abruptly, to observe a buzzing bee with interest. When the bee disappeared into the grass, he stroked his rough sandy beard contemplatively, and nodded with understanding as his brows furrowed deeper as though weighing the enormity with which each word dropped from his lips.

"That the thumb is truly subordinate," he continued from where he stopped, "is evidenced by the fact that it can only coordinate if the fingers are willing to be coordinated. What this means to us is that as coordinators, we must endeavour to place group goals and concerns above our personal ambitions. For too much fat paralyses the thumb's muscles and kills its sensitivity."

He paused and took a little dark bag of cowries out of his big all-containing raffia bag. The little dark bag made a hissing sound each time he pressed it, and whenever this happened, he got it closer to his ear in order to listen more attentively. When he was through with pressing and listening, he turned to the rival nephews and the anxious population, ready to interpret.

"The ancestors have resolved the issue in this way," he began.

The crowd fell silent again. Nothing stirred, not even the grass under their feet crackled. No one wanted to miss the verdict. The good name of the village had been soiled in mud by power-mongers. Who had the ancestors decided should clean up the mess and redeem the people? This was the awaited moment, the time of reckoning. They listened.

Tshou the diviner-healer seemed deliberate in delaying the pronouncement. And the more time went by, the tenser his audience got, and the more expectant. The silence was such that one could hear the wind whisper between the gathered throng.

Ndang and Tsam virtually stopped breathing, their faces stiff as the wooden faces of masked dancers.

"Strange what the lust for power could bring out in people," muttered Peaphweng Mukong with a smile, recalling the tensest moment of that episode of many years back.

At last Tshou let the words drop from his mouth like ripe mangoes from a tree under a gentle storm.

"The ancestors have settled the issue in this way," he repeated. "Ndang would accede to the throne as Chief of Abehema, while Tsam becomes his senior notable and adviser in charge of the tributary village of Hiseng. Do you agree or do you choose to be destroyed by the wrath of our forefathers?" The ancestors sounded menacing through him, his voice signalling the retributive impatience in store for whoever dared to dissent.

To the pleasant surprise of all there gathered, Tsam was the first to voice his satisfaction with the wisdom of the ancestors.

Peaphweng Mukong recalled immediately thinking then of the biblical confrontation which the pastor of their church at the time had recounted to them barely a week before the incident. The pastor had told them of how King Solomon had found out who of two women was the true mother of a baby by offering to split the baby into two halves. Upon hearing the cruel suggestion the woman to whom the baby rightly belonged said she would rather the pretender have it than see the child killed.

The way Tsam quickly accepted the settlement was the sign of a man desperate for power. For his part, Ndang was a peaceful person, who at one point in the crisis had seriously contemplated giving up the throne in order to save Abehema and the people he truly loved. Peaphweng Mukong didn't think many of today's leaders capable of similar virtues. Ndang accepted the settlement because he loved the people, but Tsam did so for the sheer love of power.

Both having accepted the terms of the settlement, Tshou asked them to shake hands. And as they did so, the strangest thing of all happened. The village watched both lakes gradually come back to one!

If Peaphweng Mukong hadn't been personally present to see with his own eyes, he would very easily have dismissed any such story about the mysteriousness of the lake simply as "the creative imagination of a mind fed by mischief."

Gradually, however, he had come to conclude that the lake was much stranger than people were prepared to believe. He was born in Abehema, where he had grown up and settled. He had toyed around with Christianity in his childhood days, and had even contemplated becoming the pastor of their local Baptist church. All this had faded away with the winds of maturity and understanding. Now it was all something of the past. So were many other things.

"Isn't this what life is all about?" He smiled pensively.

Now he was an old man with an impressive progeny, and the great prospect of being immortalized by the extraordinary feats of his son who was in the last stages of the race after *Kwang*. Graduation from the university for Kwanga was just a matter of months. He remembered his son telling him this the last time he came home on holidays.

"The good life we've yearned for all these years is now just round the corner, ready to give us the most palatable surprise we've ever known as a village," he muttered, excited like a child promised a new dress for Christmas, or like a farmer about to harvest the first fruits off a mango tree he had planted and tended with infinite patience.

"Who would ever again accuse Abehema of not working hard enough for its share of the scarce cake of *Kwang*? Nobody! And thanks to whom?" He smiled in triumph.

Now that Peaphweng Mukong passed by, it struck him for the first time how attached to the lake his whole life had been. He wondered how many people in the village had thought seriously of what would become of Abehema without the lake, or of the lake without Abehema. The two had grown into an inseparable whole, in which it was no longer possible to distinguish between the village and the lake, the social and the geographical, the normal and the mysterious, the rational and the supernatural. All had blended together to form the marvellous mixture called life.

He quickened his pace, not wanting to miss Chief Ngain for any reason. After dealing with the palace for long, he had come to think of it as unusual in many ways, a place with a special logic of its own. Deliberate or not, at the palace things seldom went the way one expected. For this reason, he had learnt to be extra cautious by minimising his responsibility for things going wrong. For the same reason today, he was doing his utmost to be early rather than late.

Rain clouds spread over the rising sun. The promising weather of a little while ago turned dull and chilly. He buttoned his coat up to the neck to keep out the cold. His mind was still on the lake, contemplating the uncommon warmth of its water.

He was still puzzled.

"What could this mean?" he pondered.

He thought hard, but to no avail. Everything about the lake was truly irrational. Nothing about it ceased to surprise him. He would only have to tell Chief Ngain his experience. On second thought however, he asked himself, "What would he do? What really could Chief Ngain do?" To him Chief Ngain was dull-minded and too slow to act, simply the wrong man to be chief. Just not enough fire in him.

"What a strange thing legitimacy is," he thought. "What are the qualities the ancestors look for in a candidate for chiefdom? Sometimes their choice makes sense, but often the people are so disappointed with what they are given."

Chief Ngain's slackness could be seen in how long it was taking him to give Peaphweng Mukong an answer on the issue of marriage. He couldn't understand why it should take someone two months to say yes or no to such a naked request. Such a delay could be understood for a stranger in the village, but not him and his son, of all people. What was there about Kwanga and him that needed investigating, that Chief Ngain and others didn't know already? He didn't share the Chief's approach to issues at all.

"As people, we are like night and day."

He was fond of criticising Chief Ngain for committing blunders, and for lacking the endearing benevolence and diplomacy of Ndang his predecessor.

Following the death of Chief Ndang, the king-makers had named Ngain his successor. Those close to him during his youth knew he wasn't the best candidate for the post. As he, Peaphweng Mukong, would say, legitimacy was a strange thing. Choosing a chief was normally a matter for the ancestors, who then informed the living of their choice. Doubt him, protest against his style of leadership or his attitude, and you knew just what you would be up against. There was no record in the entire history of Abehema of anyone who had ever won a fight against the living-dead. Such fights were seldom started, because even fools knew they couldn't be won. This explained why Peaphweng Mukong, whatever his dissatisfaction with the Chief, could only swear and curse and bite his finger in private, but hardly ever in public where he was supposed to be modest, contained, responsible and respectful of hierarchy. For how much longer this hypocrisy would last remained a matter for conjecture. Who could foretell to what regrettable extremes a "fool" like Ngain might push even a man of goodwill like himself?

"It is all hypocrisy!" he spat, and searched in his pocket for a lobe of kola-nut which he threw into his mouth and crushed with aggression.

"Unfortunately that is also the way things are," he started a philosophical comment. "In life, hypocrisy and mediocrity seem to attract a lot more following, as people find it much easier to conform than to ask searching questions. Where our institutions are weakest and need reviewing, there we impose the strictest of taboos. Who would have imagined that Chief Ngain was going to be forgiven of his first and most grievous blunder? Yet people now behave as if all that happened was but a long painful dream. Perhaps some would even feign ignorance of the episode today!" He couldn't help a cynical smile. He would be the last person to go that far.

He remembered.

When Chief Ndang knew he would live no longer because he had been overpowered by age and a crippling disease, he sent word to invite the king-makers and other dignitaries. Among them was Ngain, son of Tsam his lustful rival, who had become a notable by taking over the leadership of Hiseng at the death of his uncle. Tsam had died just a year or two after the ancestors had settled his dispute with Ndang.

Peaphweng Mukong couldn't resist another smile to himself. He was used to such random smiles when in deep thought or when perplexed or amused by the ironies of life, smiles which could be expressive of cynicism or confusion, sympathy or joy, even sadness.

"That is the tragic side of ambition," he swore. "That he should die soon after the reward for his villainy, isn't that ironic?" he asked rhetorically, still smiling broadly. He was enjoying every bit of his reverie.

When the king-makers and other notables arrived, the dying Chief Ndang asked them to promise to accomplish certain things after he was dead. Among these was a request about the neighbouring Kingdom of Kakakum, part of which was Yenseh.

The dignitaries promised that should the Kingdom of Kakakum decide to honour Abehema in celebrating his death, their king must be entertained with four hefty *mbonghe-ti-tia* (oxen), two male and two female.

"Always remember that we must never cease to show Kakakum our gratitude for their abundant aid and assistance to us at war and in peace, during famine and in times of plenty. Never forget that when an elephant stands in an area, the patch of grass under it is safe from assault. A rat, no matter how well fed, can never rival an elephant no matter how starved. The Kakakum are the elephant and we the grass or the rat," Chief Ndang reminded his councillors.

He was a wise leader, and his words and deeds reflected his wisdom. At last, satisfied that he had settled his accounts with the living by getting the dignitaries to promise to accomplish whatever he started and settle the debts he had incurred in the name of Abehema, Ndang departed to the world of his forefathers, certain to be accepted there as well.

Chief Ndang had every reason to be worried about his life hereafter. His death was about to occur at a time when memory was still fresh of the tragic humiliation of the Chief of Tchang by his ancestors. Chief Ndze of Tchang had died without settling his accounts with the world of the living. He had lived as a greedy cheat, maliciously extorting money from his people and secretly storing it away in a hole he had bored in a bamboo on the wall in his bedroom. He seldom spent any of the money, yet he never ceased exploiting his subjects. At last he died, and relief fell upon the entire village like the first showers on the heels of a scorching dry season.

It was only when he died that Chief Ndze understood that vice was no good, and that no leader, no matter his tact, could eternally pester and prey upon his people with callous impunity. He was denied entry into the pious company of the ancestors, and for long his spirit lamented in *Msa*. The gatekeepers were firm and brutish, savagely refusing to let him in until he had settled his accounts back in Tchang. For weeks he was restless. Like a mouthy woman assaulted by her irritable husband, he wailed in pain, bitter but incapable of vindication. He knew then that there was nothing as bad as to be cursed and rejected by one's own ancestors. If only he had thought seriously of it alive, how he would have put right past wrongs!

Fortunately for him, however, one day as he wandered the gloomy uncertainty of *Msa*, Chief Ndze met a diviner-healer he knew. The diviner-healer had gone to *Msa* to recover the heart of a patient plucked off by witches out to kill the patient. *Msa*, an omnipresent mysterious world of beauty, abundance, marvels and infinite possibilities, inhabited by very wicked, hostile and vicious people known as devils, is a place visited regularly by diviner-healers in the service of hope. It is visible only to the 'cunning' who alone can visit it at anytime, anywhere, and who can conjure it to appear for the innocent to glimpse at. Possible everywhere, *Msa* is, above all, an ambivalent place where good and bad, pleasure and pain, all are intertwined. Its inhabitants are the source of admiration and envy, especially for their material abundance. *Msa* is like a market, complete with traders and buyers, a bazaar where many come but where, unfortunately, few are rewarded with clear-cut choices. To get what one wants, one must bargain and pay for it. The only currency in *Msa* is the human being, euphemistically known as 'goat' or 'fowl.' Villains tether their victims at *Msa* like goats or fowls, hoping for the best while risking the worst, as everything good or bad from *Msa* is believed to proliferate like a virus once acquired. To acquire anything, it must be paid for in full, and those who fail to honour their debts must pay with their lives. Payment once agreed cannot be revoked. *Msa* has a way of luring its victims, first with fantasies and marvels, then with the harsh reality of exploitation and contradictions. People would be completely at the mercy of *Msa*, were it not for the diviner-healers who keep its excesses in check.

"Please, do me a favour," Chief Ndze pleaded with the diviner-healer.

"Go back home to Tchang, tell my successor to enter the bedroom that was mine, count ten bamboos from the right on the wall in front of which my bed used to stand, and remove the huge pile of money I hid there."

So the diviner-healer returned to Tchang from the invisible world, bearing the message. Ndze's successor found the money just as Ndze had described. Only then was Ndze relieved of his wilderness and formally admitted by the ancestors.

So with such a story still fresh in his mind, Chief Ndang didn't want to take any chances. He wanted to be given the reception of the hero he knew he was. He had lived an austere life, committed to nothing but the welfare of his people. He had endeared himself to them by remaining as sparkling as spring water splashing on a rock on a sunny day. Abehema had realised in him its expectations of a leader, one who was capable neither of Tsam's greedy ambition nor of Ndze's ambitious greed. His self-abnegation and blunted instinct to hide in the bamboo-hole the communal wealth had been largely hailed.

Ndang dead, Ngain became chief as the ancestors would have it, and the entire village looked to him for leadership. The Kakakum, as Ndang had hoped, came up to celebrate his death. Chief Ngain failed to do as promised, despite reminders from wary notables including Peaphweng Mukong. He went out of his way to entertain the King of Kakakum with a he-goat, instead of the four *mbonghe-ti-tia* agreed, two male and two female. No one understood his behaviour, neither did he account for it. The notables shook their heads in disapproval, but made no public criticism of him, for he was sacred.

31

The death celebrations came to an end and the King of Kakakum and his group of masked dancers left for home. The day following their departure, something strange happened. Abehema witnessed yet another supernatural phenomenon. Stupefied, the villagers watched the herds of *mbonghe-ti-tia* disappear into the lake one by one. Nobody did anything to stop them, not even Chief Ngain, whose obsession with possessions was remarkable. No one was capable of doing a thing to stop the oxen, anyway. So the *mbonghe-ti-tia* disappeared into the lake, hundreds of them, chased away by a chief who had allowed greed, like weevils, to eat into the open-handedness that a position like his demanded of the occupant.

And that is how Abehema came to be without its *mbonghe-ti-tia*. Today, Kakakum is known for its fertile and attractive breed of oxen. This is nothing compared to Abehema before Chief Ngain blundered. Nowadays the villagers can only watch with envy as tourists – foreign and local – drive past to Kakakum to admire the king's oxen. Had Chief Ngain not been blinded by chronic greed, their village would still have been receiving these tourists. His lack of benevolence had cost Abehema much in tourists, forcing its searching inhabitants to content themselves with a handful of whites only, who came to admire and even dare swim in the lake, or, like Ravageur, carry out experiments in a secretive and worrying manner.

Chief Ngain only had to descend to Yenseh to see how the villagers there were sucking from the juicy fruit of *Kwang*. Then he would know just how much damage his indiscretion had caused his own subjects and chiefdom. How did he expect *Kwang* to trickle down to the people under his tactless greed and immaturity?

"Yes, immaturity. Greed is the failure to recognise the importance of sharing. In a child, this is forgivable because of the child's budding humanity, but in an adult, it's a deformity," Peaphweng Mukong asserted.

He heaved a sigh and made an effort to bury his bitterness, especially as he was approaching the palace. A man who came to the palace with a heavy mind or a bitter heart or with an ill will against the chief, such a man was likely to fall ill, and perhaps die. The palace, in principle, was a place of peace, not of harsh thoughts or foul words. So he switched his thoughts to less problematic issues, even trying to stop speculating on the subject of his invitation. He wanted to be able just to wait to be surprised by the chief. He was unable. His mind refused to stop thinking of his request to have Princess Tem marry Kwanga.

Thinking briefly of the princess, he wondered why she hadn't called at his store at the market yesterday.

"Normally, she calls round to greet me and ask after Emmanuel, as she prefers to call her would-be husband," Peaphweng Mukong forced a smile.

"Perhaps Tem didn't come down yesterday," he tried to reassure himself. "Of course, she can't have been to the market and not come to see me, could she?" he insisted.

"Anyway, I'm soon to know the truth, am I not?"

He made up his mind to find out from Tem whether or not she had visited the market. If she said yes, she would have to explain why she didn't come to salute him. He didn't want to think he was about to have an uncaring daughter-in-law. Maybe Chief Ngain was advising her against the marriage. He wondered.

"God forbid!" He tried to banish the thought from his mind.

3

The palace stood elegantly on top of one of several hills overlooking the hill of the lake, a compound of twenty, once well built but now fast dilapidating, grass-roofed houses. The footpath leading there was narrow and bushy all the way from the main village, and only got broader as one came within a stone's throw of the palace itself. In the past, when the people and their chief spoke with one voice, the path was always clean. Nobody wanted a chief with the goodness of Ndang to be bothered by dew and grass. With Chief Ngain they felt different. Once on the broader piece of road cared for by the palace women and children, it dawned on Peaphweng Mukong that he was not the first to use the bushy footpath that morning. The absence of dew on the interlocking grass should have told him that before, but he had been too embroiled in his memories to notice.

As he approached the bamboo gate of the rotting wooden fence surrounding the palace, he stopped to inspect his eyes for specks and to wear his machete across his left shoulder as was expected. He also adjusted the multicoloured cap on his head, making sure its red feather was well pointed. He coughed thrice according to custom and went through the gate, stopping briefly by an adjacent pot of medicine to dip in his right hand and touch his forehead with its potent mixture. That done, he hurried through the broad courtyard into the once beautiful and imposing conference hall, where he announced his arrival with three loud claps of hands in honour of the throne, although it was empty. His gesture reflected the belief that the throne was more important than the person who occupied it. For, as their forefathers had taught them, chiefs might pass away, but chieftaincy will forever be.

Though Chief Ngain wasn't there when he arrived, Peaphweng Mukong noticed many other notables in the conference hall.

"Hwoophweneh," he wished them good morning in a familiar manner, and sat down to join in their conversation as a young prince went into the inner palace to report his arrival.

It didn't take Peaphweng Mukong long to learn that he wasn't the only notable Chief Ngain had invited. Almost all his colleagues on the village council were there. His hopes had been raised for nothing, he thought. Had he been the sole guest, he might have continued to nurse the feeling that the invitation was to do with his request for his son to marry Princess Tem. He tried hard to mask his disappointment, for this was neither the best place nor time for feelings of dejection.

Moments later, Chief Ngain, dressed oddly in a green cattle Fulani gown, red hat and brown sandals, made his way into the hall. The notables stood up in deference until he found the throne and sat down. Then they regained their seats. Not to show this customary respect to a chief, bad as he might be, would be to question the very essence of chiefdom. This no notable was ready to dare. No one wanted to be identified with the witches who subverted the institutions and legality their forefathers had fought numerous wars and sacrificed countless nights of sleep to enshrine.

The chief cleared his throat and saluted them.

"Gheaphweneh," he shouted the traditional greeting.

"Mbeih, we've slept well your highness," murmured the notables in return, all ten of them.

"Yes, I have invited you so we may discuss what to do about last night's strange occurrence," he said, rather abruptly.

Seven notables, including Peaphweng Mukong, expressed their ignorance. They looked lost.

"Yes, of course," admitted Chief Ngain. "I'm aware that not every one of you knows about the incident, am I not? Rush me not. I have my style. Yes, you've been invited to discuss the issue, so that together we may decide how best to bail ourselves out of a brewing embarrassment. Yes, a brewing embarrassment. Those of you who happened to have attempted cleaning your faces or hands in the lake this morning should have remarked how hot the water was. Yes, how hot the water was. Quite unusual, won't you agree?"

He paused to clean his face with a royal piece of cloth handed him by one of his female attendants, nodding his head and repeatedly saying, "Yes", in an irritating and silly manner. He was sweating like an imbecile caught stealing from a neighbour's kitchen by a stern foster-father.

Peaphweng Mukong nodded with understanding. He had guessed rightly that something was the matter, from the unusual warmth of the water of the lake. "When you grow up, marry and get old in the same village, you come to have a fair picture of the way things work, and can anticipate dysfunctions even before they occur," he prided himself in his thoughts.

"Isn't it somehow abnormal that Chief Ngain should sweat in such chilly, unsmiling weather?" Peaphweng Mukong wondered. He managed one of his sardonic but discreet grins, and listened on.

"Yes, we must examine the situation critically and act promptly, to nip danger in the bud. It is essential, very very essential indeed, that we behave as a body, with solidarity of purpose. As we say, united we stand, provided ... no, divided we fall."

"There is a story which the King of Kakakum told me during Ndang's funeral. Yes, which the King of Kakakum told me. I've shared it with no one until now. Aren't you fortunate? Yes, it's the story of an old man who was about to die. He assembled all ten of his children, whom he sent into the forest with instructions to fetch firewood, yes. When they returned, he asked them to tie the wood together, and then, yes, and then asked each to try breaking the bundle. No one could, not even the strongest of them. Yes. He then ordered them to untie the bundle, and to attempt breaking a single piece of wood each, using their hands as before. This, they found much easier to do, much easier to do.

"Yes, when they had broken all the wood into smaller pieces, he told them the morale behind his lesson. 'If', he said, 'after my death you decide each to go his own way, you shall all perish as the pieces of wood you've just crushed,' he told them. 'If you stay united, you shall be as firm as the bundle you couldn't break.' That, my noble councillors, that is the power of togetherness, yes" he commented, using his bloodshot eyes to sample their reaction.

The councillors' faces didn't betray their thoughts or feelings, which were quite cynical. He, not they, needed coaching on the importance of unity! By telling them a story on unity, wasn't he in a way shooting himself in the foot? And who else but a fool like him would fail to notice a boomerang so apparent? This was what the notables thought and felt, individually, each unaware that the others were thinking in similar ways.

"However," Chief Ngain continued unsuspectingly, "before we agree on a line of action, yes, I must first of all tell you what has happened. We all know Ardo Buba, Chief of the Cattle Fulani, don't we?" he asked and, not waiting for an obvious answer, went on. "He is no more, yes, no more." His voice was heavy, slow and deliberate – one of the rare times it couldn't be described as thunderous.

The notables remained expressionless. He was disappointed, for he had hoped they would show immediate sorrow and concern. He took out the piece of cloth from his Fulani gown – an irritating departure from the elaborately designed, Kakakum-decorated and Kakakum-woven gowns that Ndang used to be admired for – and cleaned his face again. It wasn't hot because the morning was dull and sunless, yet he sweated as if a blacksmith was at work in a furnace on the ceiling directly above him. No notable appeared surprised by the fact that he was sweating.

Chief Ngain sent an attendant for his pipe, which he lit and started to smoke. Then he resumed talking to the notables who were quite stunned by his sudden decision to smoke again, after giving up for almost a year.

"Yes, it's a pity, a great pity indeed, won't you agree?" He murmured, forcing more tobacco into the huge earthenware pipe, decorated with white and red beads on the exterior.

"It is a great pity that such an important, yes, such a kind and responsible person should die as miserably as this. Like a rat! A rat! Pathetic, won't you say?"

He took a deep smoke of his pipe and began to puff little round balls into the air, much to his own admiration. On their part, the notables were impatient with his detected lack of seriousness or a clear sense of purpose. He resumed.

"Ardo Buba was discovered floating on the boiling lake by Princess Tem as she returned from the market last evening. Yes, discovered by Princess Tem."

Peaphweng Mukong's heart jumped at the mention of the princess. So she was in the market after all? He shook his head, quite puzzled by her strange behaviour. Now he could no longer resist the suspicion that her father was advising her to stay away from him.

How scandalous! He vowed never to forgive the chief if this indeed turned out to be his game.

"After the meeting, I shall ask to know what he has decided concerning my request," he resolved. "I think I ought to make him understand that he's shilly-shallied for far too long, and that my patience is fast running out," he threatened, regrettably in anger.

The sooner he knew the Chief's mind, the better. No amount of waiting would change a thing, especially if Chief Ngain had made up his wicked mind to ignore his request. To Peaphweng Mukong the chief was a queer, greedy, jealous, unpredictable leader, who on dying would, like Chief Ndze, remain at the crossroads. Their values and beliefs were like water and fire. In truth, the only thing Peaphweng Mukong thought linked the two of them, the unfortunate fact of being distant blood relations aside, were the ancestral rites and rituals. He was aware that even this form of solidarity was in jeopardy, because of the Chief's greed and stubborn disregard for advice.

For a while Peaphweng Mukong tried to temper his thoughts, lest he be cursed for thinking evil of the Chief as bearer of the ancestral spear of leadership. On second thought, he decided to contemplate the whole idea of legitimacy all over again, and, perhaps, resolve his predicament forever. On the one hand, pushed by the belief that what the living-dead had agreed upon must never be questioned he felt he had a duty to respect Chief Ngain. On the other hand, he wondered what prevented an ancestral recantation of legitimacy from a man who, in his decisions and actions, seldom bore in mind the people. This couldn't be right! There must be something phoney somewhere He couldn't reconcile Ngain's malevolence with the magnanimity and benevolence of the living-dead. For the first time ever, he decided enough was enough. He wouldn't be subdued any longer by a chief blamed without exception for ruthless and irresponsible behaviour, amongst other vices.

He was firm. "Today our two families will either be bonded for life, or forever kept asunder," he swore, then pulled himself together and listened.

Chief Ngain was still speaking, going round and round the same point. Rambling was more the word.

"Bullshit," said Peaphweng Mukong, to his hearing only. He wondered, "If he has nothing to say, why can't he let us alone? Why force us to rise with the birds, only to play games with us? My stomach has started to rumble with hunger after all, and the sooner I'm on my way back home the better."

His mouth watered as he thought of the warm loaves of fufu-corn he was sure to find waiting on his dining table. "Whose turn is it to cook today?" He tried in vain to remember which of his three wives had the duty of cooking for him that day. Whoever it was, it didn't matter, he concluded. As long as there was enough beef in the sauce, and everything was well cooked.

"Once Princess Tem brought me the sad tidings," Chief Ngain babbled on, "I sent four of my retainers to take good care of the corpse. Yes, take good care of the corpse. Then I sent for you my councillors. I'm pleased with your response, and ready for your valuable suggestions as to what must be done," he said, fidgeting with his pipe. "Yes, the floor is yours for advice," he added, then leaned back on his throne, and puffed more grey balls of smoke into the air.

The meanders created by the smoke, as it traveled toward the bamboo ceiling, offered him a lovely spectacle. The notables, from whom he waited to hear, thought he was being childish, every single one of them.

By all standards, Chief Ngain wasn't an orator, and couldn't have presented his case more tactlessly. Diplomacy and oratory were the two qualities he most needed to curb the surging scepticism in his notables.

Silence fell on the hall. For a long time no one said anything, for none knew where the chief was heading. Though he had spoken at length on the matter already, the notables still couldn't say what for sure he was all about. No one ignored the fact that he wouldn't normally seek advice if he thought he could do it alone without risking much. The way Chief Ngain treated them was little different from how they as fathers dealt with their children. His absolute ways had forced them to use long wooden spoons when eating with him, as they would normally do with perfect strangers.

To their knowledge, no stranger could be any worse than Chief Ngain, who despite several years as their leader had remained an enigma. He had chosen to deal with them from a distance, as if he were a leper. Seldom did he seek their advice, and when he did, there was sure to be a trap somewhere that he was desperate to avoid. On several occasions the villagers had been molested by the police and gendarmes for dodging the modern authorities in matters of tax, because Chief Ngain had chosen to channel into pockets and cheap beer, the tax-money he collected from them. On other occasions the village had narrowly avoided war, provoked by a leader who preferred to crow alone like an only cock. Today the notables were all using long wooden spoons to eat with the Chief they had tolerated for a long period.

Peaphweng Mukong wasn't alone in wondering why sometimes the person the ancestors selected for chief turned out to be in such disharmony with the rest of the society. The other notables were equally perplexed. They had always been, but since so many taboos forbade the open discussion of their political institutions, no one could say who else was under the same thinking cap. They had been born into the belief that it was wrong to think or wish evil of the one whom the living-dead had judged fit to rule. Vivid were their memories of instances where the ancestral definition of legitimacy didn't always tie with their outlook. Though too scared to share their worries with one another, their bitter experiences with Chief Ngain had pushed them each to question the whole idea of ancestral infallibility, and the right of the dead to determine the affairs of the living. If the ancestors were that concerned about Abehema and its welfare, if they really had the people at heart, they wouldn't be that soft on dissenters like Tsam, nor that wicked by

41

selecting greed and chaos in the person of Ngain to lead Abehema.

When no one spoke, Chief Ngain decided that the best way to extract a response would be to address his question to one notable after another, thus making sure each one had to reply in turn. Even then, the notables showed they weren't ready to be dragged into something they barely understood. There were many unanswered questions. For instance, Chief Ngain hadn't convinced them about what Ardo Buba could have been doing at the lake when he drowned. Ardo Buba lived several hills away from the lake, and was a less than infrequent visitor to the palace.

Another question hanging was why Chief Ngain appeared so concerned with the death of a chief who had his own people? Why was he trying to act as if he was more of a chief than Ardo Buba had been? Why was he weeping more than the owner of the corpse? The notables all thought Ardo Buba should be buried by his Cattle Fulani people, whom he had probably endeared himself to with good deeds and benevolence.

These curious aspects, along with Chief Ngain's strange countenance, reinforced their suspicion that something was amiss. Despite the feeling, none of them was bold enough to stand up and tell the Chief what he thought, or of the critical remarks they were making to one another, but only in whispers.

Admittedly, some thought that even to dare to discuss Chief Ngain's misdeeds in private was quite an achievement, for they had never ventured that far before. They were to be shocked by the challenge Peaphweng Mukong was prepared to launch, which was unprecedented from anyone who wasn't a pretender to the throne, nor a close blood relation.

After careful consideration of the matter, and inspired by the critical whispers of his fellow notables, Peaphweng Mukong concluded that the best answer to Chief Ngain was not silence. It was necessary for them to make the chief understand that they failed to see things his way, and that if in the past they had chosen to turn a blind eye on some of his outrages, it wasn't because they didn't know that something was wrong. Sometimes people chose to endure discomfort, just for the sake of peace and harmony. So Peaphweng Mukong stood up and asked to be allowed to speak. The chief readily granted him the floor, expecting to be supported, naturally.

"Before saying what I have to say," Peaphweng Mukong began, wetting his lips with his tongue, "I would like to make it clear that I speak only for myself, and not in the name of every councillor," he pointed out, unconscious of the distraction he caused by playing with the bunch of keys in the pocket of his coat.

Chief Ngain drew his attention to the unpleasant noise. Peaphweng Mukong mumbled a few words of apology and proceeded to make his point.

"With that clarification made, I can now say what I have to say. I must thank his highness for even thinking of inviting us to consider the sudden death of Ardo Buba with him. May Ardo's soul rest in perfect peace."

"May he rest in peace." The other notables agreed, much to the pleasure of Peaphweng Mukong, who didn't expect them to join him.

"It is indeed reassuring to be reminded that we are still councillors, although we might have felt abandoned many a time before," he continued, encouraged.

"The chief's story about the Kakakum man and his children reminds me of a saying we know too well: that none of our hands no matter how gifted, can tie a bundle of firewood unassisted by the other. We also have a saying that no man is ever too hardhearted to abandon his family for good, and another that a crime is never too serious to be forgiven.

"I must thank his highness for giving us the floor to say how, were we in his place, we would like this issue resolved. My suggestion is the following: Because we know so little about the circumstances under which Ardo Buba was drowned, I dare say it is very difficult, if not impossible, for me to suggest any precise line of action. However, I do think there are certain precautionary moves that must be taken.

"The first thing we must do is to send someone to Kaizerbosch, the divisional headquarters for modern government, to alert the police and the gendarmes to Ardo Buba's death.

"Also, we must let his subjects know what has befallen their leader, if your highness hasn't done so already. It is the right of the Cattle Fulani people to know of the death of their leader in time, so they can bury him with dignity and ceremony. They would never forgive us if we denied them the right to know of the death in good time. They may be strangers in our land, but as grazers they are a community. We wouldn't want their ancestors to curse them when they are not at fault, would we? As we are well aware, it isn't impossible for Ardo Buba's soul to be denied entry into the world of his forefathers because he wasn't buried with honours and in time.

"Regarding our own customs, none of us, I think, needs reminding about the taboo which forbids us from burying another people's chief.

"From what your highness has told us so far, we can't say for sure if Ardo Buba died a natural death, was killed, or killed himself. And no one needs reminding, either, that we never bury suicides.

"So the other thing I suggest we do is invite a diviner to tell us what is at stake in all that has happened. Perhaps the lake has been desecrated and needs purification. Who but a diviner can say?

"And talking of divination, I wonder why Peaphweng Ndyu the renowned diviner isn't amongst us this morning. Perhaps the other notables have remarked his absence too, and like myself are curious to know whether Peaphweng Ndyu was away, as we know he travels much and is often out divining in foreign lands, or whether he turned down the royal invitation, or was simply not invited for one royal reason or another?"

He turned to the other councillors, as if to seek support. They affirmed by shaking their heads, implying that they too would like to know why the diviner, a fellow councillor, was absent.

Satisfied he wasn't alone in expecting Peaphweng Ndyu to be there, Peaphweng Mukong went on to suggest in what way the diviner's presence would have helped.

"If he were here with us," he speculated, "we wouldn't leave this conference hall without knowledge of what is at stake.

"I have spoken. Let anyone correct me if I have erred."

With these last words, he pulled up his baggy trousers to the level of his knees and sat down.

The notables were unanimous in applauding Peaphweng Mukong. Although at the beginning he declared he was going to speak for himself only, his speech had touched on everything they would have said. And they appreciated his insight and understanding of the ways of the land. Some of them even stood up and echoed all the points he had made, his example seeming to have unzipped their mouths.

It was imperative for Chief Ngain to invite Peaphweng Ndyu the diviner-healer, to determine the cause of Ardo Buba's death, and to find out if the lake had been desecrated.

It was their urgent desire that the modern authorities at Kaizerbosch be told about this death, for they didn't want the village to be dragged into a conflict it hadn't bargained for.

Abehema had had enough ignominy already, and should stomach no further shame. Not if this could be avoided through responsible and timely behaviour.

The mosquito that gets entangled in a spider's web pays for all the blood it has sucked. He who invites the devil home must be ready to sacrifice his soul. No one provokes a python without knowing how to contain its venom.

Chief Ngain lit his pipe a second time. His hands shivered slightly as he struck the match, and the notables noted this in silence. When he had smoked for a while, he cleared his throat and replied to his councillors.

"Yes, yes … yes. I have listened to the suggestions you have to make," he said, trying hard to sound composed. "What you have said is good indeed, but I have something better to say. Better. I have very tangible reasons why I don't think the plan of action you have put forward is the best."

At this juncture he eyed Peaphweng Mukong who shifted with unease on the bamboo bench, which he shared with five other notables. Peaphweng Mukong disliked the way Chief Ngain was using his piercing, bloodshot owlish eyes to infuse a feeling of guilt into him. As long as he believed in the virtue of his position, Peaphweng Mukong would not be subdued by bewitching gazes.

"First of all!" Chief Ngain all of a sudden shouted, startling all the notables except Peaphweng Mukong who had decided not to lower his eyes.

"First of all I must spell out that I don't share your belief in Peaphweng Ndyu's divining powers," he proceeded in a loud and quarrelsome voice.

"Yes, you don't mean to say you ignore the fact that he transforms himself into a bee … and goes from compound to compound overhearing people's private conversations and domestic conflicts, with the intention of using them later in his so-called divination?

"Or that every time people disagree over one thing or the other, he comes intruding with supposed solutions which are in fact just the fruit of his eavesdropping and rumour-mongering?

"How dare you suggest that a chief of my standing should descend so low in a matter of this importance? Was the late Ardo Buba so insignificant for his death to be interpreted by a diviner with Ndyu's credibility? No, no, no! Yes, a thousand times no!"

In a tone not less rancorous, he proceeded to oppose yet another suggestion made by Peaphweng Mukong and reiterated by others.

"Yes, secondly, secondly yes I'm not in favour of sending someone to report the death to the authorities in Kaizerbosch either. Yes, not at all in favour. They would never accept that we had no hand in Ardo Buba's death. Yes, to be found floating on a boiling lake isn't a common happening, is it? Yes, and the police and the gendarmes only easily accept what is common, not the unusual. Yes, not the unusual.

"An extraordinary death as this, yes, as this, is likely to be investigated by the police and gendarmes for ages. They would question and question so much so that a child born yesterday can mature, age, and perhaps die, yes, leaving them questioning!

"They are odious, the police and gendarmes! Yes, yes … yes! You are no strangers to the cunning employed by these so-called modern makers of peace in their ridiculous craving to supplant traditional keepers of the peace like us, are you? Yes, they do not operate in the same manner we do, yes, or that our forefathers did. The more you try to help them, the more they come after you, yes, doing all they can to impeach you and to put you in jail. No!"

He shook his head vigorously in negation, to indicate the rigour of his contempt for the modern makers of peace.

"Thirdly, yes, thirdly, we must take upon ourselves the duty of burying Ardo Buba. Yes, burying Ardo Buba. This is because, as he told me himself, his people never agreed with him nor obeyed his orders. They were like fire and water, which don't see eyeball to eyeball. Yes, if we fail to give him a burial therefore, he is bound to rot away like a rat. Yes, like a rat. And we don't want that, do we? … Like a rat!

"That I can assure you! Yes, for none of his subjects would bury someone they hated, yes, whom they accused of conniving with the modern collectors of the Cattle Tax to steal their cattle from them, steal their cattle from them. His death is sure to be greeted by his people with a sigh of relief!

"So rest your scruples, yes, and do a dead man a last service for which his soul will forever be grateful. Would you my dear notables, would you allow the corpse to rot and smell unbearably like a rotten rat, or would you command respect from both the dead and the living, yes, command respect from the dead and living through endearing deeds of responsibility?"

These last words were uttered in a soft, almost pleading voice.

There was a brief moment of silence, as the notables dissected Chief Ngain's cacophony. From the manner in which he spoke and the reasons he gave for wanting things his way, none of them was left in doubt that he was somehow implicated in Ardo Buba's death. This prospect alone forced some of them to tremble with fear and wrath.

Why was Chief Ngain so wicked? They wondered, one and all. What must Abehema have done wrong to the ancestors, to be entrusted with a chief that bad?

Unable to whisper without Chief Ngain eavesdropping, they asked him to allow them some time to decide how to respond. So they went out to deliberate amongst themselves.

When they entered the conference hall again, they told him that Peaphweng Mukong was their spokesman, and that anything he said would be said on behalf of them all.

Thus agreed, Peaphweng Mukong stood up, a grim expression on his bearded face. He beat his coarse index finger twice and shook his head rather vengefully. Then he spoke out.

"We are agreed that whoever shakes hands with the devil must go alone. Let him drag no one along," he said, looking directly across at Chief Ngain, who sat at the opposite end of the hall studying the bamboo ceiling as if seeing it for the first time. "The evil of the wrongdoer must not enter someone else's house."

"The reasons you have given are not convincing, so we say 'No' three times," Peaphweng Mukong told the chief, quite indifferent to the need to be respectful of authority.

"It is strange that you should suddenly doubt Peaphweng Ndyu's competence, when all along you've invited him to solve domestic rows among your wives, or between them and yourself. Today, he isn't competent because it has to do with the death of Ardo Buba! We disagree with you," he insisted.

"If you suddenly disapprove of him," Peaphweng Mukong argued, "why not send for the renowned Wabuah of Kakakum, a diviner whose renown is worldwide?"

Chief Ngain was amazed by Peaphweng Mukong's utterance, the like of which he had never heard before. Was this arrogant wizard possessed or what? Who did he take himself for, daring to scrutinize royal words and deeds in such outrageous fashion? What did a man like this stand to gain by sabotaging the sanctity of the chief's authority and person? Could Princess Tem be at the root of this?

While Chief Ngain searched his mind for an explanation, Peaphweng Mukong raged on, exacerbating the sabotage, embittering the Chief even more.

"Yet you haven't even mentioned him!" exclaimed Peaphweng Mukong, referring to Wabuah of Kakakum.

"You must have your own reasons for disapproving of divination, apart from your claim that Ndyu is incompetent, which you know isn't true.

"On the other hand, we don't see why you should be afraid to tell the makers of modern peace about the accidental death of Ardo Buba. If you genuinely take it for an accident as we do, there is no reason why we should hide the death from the police and gendarmes. You have reported other matters to them before.

"We have always tilled and toiled hard to pay our taxes, haven't we? And why should we be petrified of the urban peacemakers? Why should we not look at them in the face? Are we the tax collectors who instead of handing over the money they collect to our masters in the city, prefer to pocket it or bamboo-hole it as if it belonged to them?"

The more Peaphweng Mukong spoke, the greater his disregard for Chief Ngain's sacred personality.

He paused for a while to blow his nose and clear his throat, and then told Chief Ngain of the conclusion reached by himself and his peers.

"However," he began, "we have decided upon what plan of action to adopt. The ten of us, here present.

"We have agreed to do exactly what you say we mustn't do. So we will consult the diviners, Peaphweng Ndyu and Wabuah. Divination is the backbone of our society, and a leader who questions this needs to offer sacrifice to appease the ancestors that appointed him to the position he now is abusing.

"We will inform Ardo Buba's people of his death, and ask them to come and collect his corpse for a dignified burial. To take upon the shoulders of Abehema the prerogative of burying the chief of others is to assume that a cock can crow freely in a foreign land. We hold it to be true that no matter how much a leader might have wronged his people, they can always pretend to forget his atrocities and give him a decent burial. To treat a corpse with contempt is to be ignorant of what constitutes life in a person. Unless, of course, Ardo Buba committed suicide.

"Finally, we think that the right thing to do is to send someone to alert the modern authorities in Kaizerbosch that the Abehema-based leader of the Cattle Fulani is dead. This, we feel, is behaving correctly," he sounded triumphant.

"Have I spoken well, *leaders* of Abehema?" Peaphweng Mukong asked his fellow notables before regaining his seat, stressing the word 'leaders'.

Like before, the notables each showed approval by hitting his right hand against his knee, for no one, by custom, would clap for or applaud someone else the conventional way in the presence of the throne. He was a good speaker, and they praised him for it. Above all, they appreciated the fact that he had referred to them as "leaders of Abehema", and wished that it might send the right message to Chief Ngain: that they had agreed to say "No!" to their role as stooges and to become genuine partners in leadership.

Chief Ngain was sweating profusely, and cared little about his piece of cloth any longer. He glared at Peaphweng Mukong like a predator, his bloodshot eyes famished. Peaphweng Mukong was determined not to care any longer. He had the mandate of his peers. What else could bring more security than to know your voice was the voice of the people? Who wouldn't move mountains with the whole village united behind you?

The embittered Chief Ngain ground his teeth for a while before blasting out at last.

"Yes, since you have decided to ignore the advice of your leader, go ahead and act the way it pleases you to act!" He thundered his admonition.

"Do not, yes, do not say I never warned you, when Abehema suddenly begins to fall asunder like the toes and fingers of a leper!" he castigated, then paused to smoke his pipe. After which he took a deep breath and said:

"On second thought, yes, yes, on second thought no leader wants to see his people perish just like that, without him lifting a finger to help them. Yes, no leader. That is why I'm giving you until this evening to think carefully about the position you have taken on this issue. Yes, if by midnight I have heard from none of you, I would ask my retainers to proceed with the burial of Ardo Buba, whom I know to be a dear, friendly and responsible leader, whose remains I can't bear to see eaten by dogs!"

He put out his pipe and gave it to one of his attendants who had stood by him all through the meeting, to take back to the inner palace where it belonged. Then he looked up again at the notables who were bent on rubbing his crown in the mud.

"The rest of you may go," said he, all of a sudden, without the traditional offer of raffia wine and kola nuts that should normally have graced the meeting, however young the day. How could a man with such disregard for protocol convince anyone he cared a damn about the ways of his forefathers? the notables wondered.

"Yes, the rest of you may go," Chief Ngain reiterated, "I would like Peaphweng Mukong to stay behind for another matter. Yes, another matter that is in no way connected to Ardo Buba's accidental death."

He didn't need to explain any further, for it was no secret to anyone in the village that Peaphweng Mukong was seeking to have his son married to Princess Tem. Though there were some notables who didn't see why Peaphweng Mukong insisted on Princess Tem, who was neither the most beautiful nor the most well behaved girl in the village. To these notables, it was not unlikely that Peaphweng Mukong might be nursing a dream of Kwanga his son becoming not only the modern leader that he was sure to be by virtue of his high education, but also the future chief of Abehema by virtue of marriage to Princess Tem.

With his peers gone, Peaphweng Mukong suddenly felt alone and vulnerable. Almost immediately he regretted having accepted to stay. The heated confrontation with Chief Ngain had made him more sceptical than ever of securing the Princess Tem for Kwanga. Perhaps he ought to let fate take control of his son's life? Then Kwanga would marry the girl the ancestors had chosen and smeared with camwood for him. It was always dangerous to attempt too much to shape the course of things, he reasoned. "What the ancestors have ordained, how can any man put asunder and live in peace?"

In his desperation to choose life's course for Kwanga, wasn't there the risk he might jeopardise the very bliss his son sought by choosing the wrong course altogether? That was his fear, so he echoed his earlier resolve to make today the very last time he was discussing marriage with Chief Ngain. If nothing positive came of it, he might well forget about Princess Tem, and just let things take their natural course. With that, he composed himself and waited for Chief Ngain to return from the inner palace and say why he had been asked to stay behind.

Chief Ngain re-entered the hall, followed by a young male attendant who was carrying a calabash of raffia wine, a bowl of kola-nuts, and a medium-size bag of raffia. The young man placed the items on the floor next to the throne, and was ordered to leave.

Peaphweng Mukong thought, "So there was wine and kola-nuts after all, and Ngain had chosen not to welcome the notables the way tradition demanded?" His stomach churned at such callous disregard for the ways of the land. "Terrible man," he whispered.

Chief Ngain offered him some raffia wine in a cup made of the horn of an antelope, but which he declined to drink. The time for wine had come and gone unattended, he told himself. He wouldn't drink the bit the chief recommended, nor would he accept the lobe of kola-nut the chief tendered him. He was apprehensive. There was every reason to be. Intuitively, he felt he had to be most careful about the chief's friendly gestures. He was thinking fast. He failed to see any decent reason why Chief Ngain would wait till the others were gone to introduce wine and kola-nuts. Wouldn't a thoughtful, caring and well intentioned leader have served his councillors wine even before telling them why they had been invited? For this reason and more, Peaphweng Mukong remained suspicious, and when he would neither be made to eat nor drink, Chief Ngain offered to shake hands with him, as some sort of reconciliation. He declined, reminding the chief of the taboo that prohibited anyone from shaking hands with his royal highness. So when Chief Ngain could not succeed in making Peaphweng Mukong do what he wanted, he resorted to words.

"Yes, you are a very very admirable person indeed, my ideal of a notable," he told Peaphweng Mukong. "You have proven your worth, yes, proven your worth, and I'm very ready to reward you." He sneezed.

"I have carefully thought over your request to have the Princess Tem for your son. It is a most singular pride for me and the village, to have my daughter marry a promising and intelligent fellow like your Kwanga. There is one thing, one thing I ask of you in return.

"Yes, for this marriage to be possible, you must accept to relieve, yes, to relieve me of the terrible embarrassment my councillors, under your active encouragement, are about to plunge me in! Do you accept the terms of my offer?" He sounded quite desperate.

Peaphweng Mukong's "No" was prompt and firm. There was no question of shaking hands with the devil. His peers would never forgive him, let alone the ancestors whom he believed had thrown their weight behind him along with the other notables. He had been elected to serve his people. It was his duty to save them in their hour of need.

Why was Chief Ngain so willing to bribe him even with his daughter if he was not guilty of Ardo Buba's death? Would he, Peaphweng Mukong, not be struck dead by lightning if he compromised with evil to destroy the harmony of the land? The ancestors had a thousand ways of putting the village to the test, and providing Abehema with a wicked chief might just have been one of these ways. It was not for Peaphweng Mukong to turn down the responsibility the ancestors were assigning him through his peers. No! Abehema had seen in him a leader, and he had to prove himself worthy of their confidence. So he echoed his "No". Then he stood up and walked out, without looking back.

The infuriated Chief Ngain rushed to stop him, but his bulk and gown were too heavy for him to walk faster. So Peaphweng Mukong slipped out of the conference hall in time to avoid being retained. Chief Ngain threatened and cursed, but the notable didn't stop to look back even once. He just kept going, knowing that henceforth he would have to visit Wabuah of Kakakum for amulets, lotions, and herbs, to protect himself against the witchcraft of Chief Ngain.

Henceforth, it was going to be a fight not between Chief Ngain and the other notables, but one between the chief and Peaphweng Mukong or between their vital forces, with the village as partisan onlookers.

Just who was going to wear the crown of victory in the end was a matter for the living-dead to decide. They were already fast at work, and their verdict only a matter of time.

4

Emmanuel Kwanga sprang out of bed like *Kuogk*, the ferocious mourner and masked dancer of Abehema. For a brief while, he danced around the floor like a hunter enveloped by a raging swam of honeybees. Confused and wet with sweat, he staggered about in a subconscious attempt to locate the light switch. He was shaken, and trembled all over. Groping, he found the switch at last and turned it on. The sudden brightness of the powerful fluorescent bulb caused Patience to awake with a start, and sent hundreds of frightened cockroaches racing for refuge in the cragged crevices lining the walls. A couple of baby rats abandoned a packet of biscuits on the table and escaped to their underground hideout.

"What's going on?" Patience complained, her tongue grumpy and aggressive, and the rest of her not quite awake. "What is the matter with you? Switch off the lights!" she protested further, squinting. "I haven't slept enough!"

Emmanuel was too frightened to pay attention to Patience. In his semiconscious state her voice sounded faint and faraway, as if from someone stranded in the muddy potholes across the road.

Finding it hard to get back to sleep, Patience, still muttering her dissatisfaction, turned around to face him. She rubbed her eyes to attune them to the brightness, then looked to see what he was doing up in the middle of the night. Emmanuel's expression must have transformed her aggression into instant concern, for she jumped out of bed and sat by him at the table.

"What is the problem with you?" she asked, bringing her chair nearer to his. "Why are you not in bed?" she added, feeling his forehead and chest for signs of fever and headache. "Tell me..."

Patience looked concerned and worried. She had always cared for Emmanuel, although she sometimes hated herself for continuing to fill his calabash of holes with the precious water of her love and care.

"That's the power of love," many of her friends had whispered to her. They recounted their own experiences to show she was not alone in being taken advantage of by "such ungrateful pigs" that men are.

Her best friend Desire, a young woman experienced with men, had told her just to pray and hope for change in her Emmanuel, and not to delude herself that changing boyfriends and hunting for Mr Right might make things better. "A bird in the hand is worth two in the bush," Desire had told her. "And all male birds are the same, at the end of the day. They perch only long enough to harvest pleasure, and woe betides those of us who are not smart enough to harness them while it lasts. They are all the same, men! The ones you meet for the first time are just as bad, if not much worse than those you've dumped or been dumped by!" Desire had come to the conclusion that, like fantasies, men were hopelessly boring when experienced in reality.

In light of her own past disappointments Patience took Desire's words to heart and learned to accommodate Emmanuel despite his mountains of faults. Now her attachment to him had grown so strong she couldn't imagine life without him, nauseating though he often was.

Emmanuel made an effort to answer her, but couldn't find the words. He seemed too scared to speak.

She placed her arms round him and peered into his eyes. She could see and feel the fright in him, but what had caused it? With her eyes, she made a quick survey of the poorly fitted apologies for windows. Both were intact, implying no one had broken in. Could he have been bitten by a snake, or threatened by one of the scores of rats that daily challenged her right to live in peace in the perforated rooms she rented? There was no mark on him to suggest either. Perhaps it was a nightmare? The longer Emmanuel stayed mute, the more she speculated, and the greater her frustration.

"Speak to me, would you! Say something. Tell me what is bothering you. Is it a bad dream? Please, please – won't you say something?" Patience implored in vain. Unable to bring Emmanuel to words, Patience simply cuddled him, hoping her tenderness might calm his shock, whatever had caused it.

It occurred to her that a prayer might help. So she recited a Hail Mary, an Our Father, and a Glory Be. Then she started to sing a soothing melody – a folk tune from Camp-Kupeh, her village of birth. So caught up by her singing, she didn't notice when Emmanuel fell asleep, in her arms.

Patience was early to rise, as was her habit. She took a quick bath and put on a trendy dress, ready for the office, although it was only 5 o'clock and work didn't start until eight. She had a full-time job as typist at the General Secretariat of the Ministry for National Development, but she was also a part-time student at the Come-Try-Again Evening School (COTAES) situated at Quartier Kongosa, not far from where they lived. It was her custom to rise early, take a bath and prepare for work, then settle down to revise her lessons and do her assignments for three hours or so, before leaving for the office.

With this routine, Patience was seldom punctually at work. She had little to fear from a boss who rarely came to the office before midday, or from Betty (nicknamed 'weaver-bird'), her exceptionally understanding and talkative colleague.

Emmanuel was the one person who found Patience's early hours particularly disturbing – at odds with his concept of cohabitation, and a nuisance to his idea of a good night's sleep after an evening out consuming lethal brews with fellow dropouts. He had complained repeatedly about her unusual hours, but Patience had told him point blank she would not sacrifice her studies for anything, and that she didn't give up hours of sleep each night for the love of it. She was determined to have her Advanced Levels one day, God willing, and would not be dissuaded, not even by three previous unsuccessful attempts. With the GCE she had decided to stick like a tick and would not lighten her grip until she could feel the blood of life and opportunity swell her arteries.

Though Emmanuel did not want Patience to think he was unsympathetic to her zeal to achieve, he could not stop complaining. At one point, Patience was so incensed: she thought she could do without him. She gave him the choice between accepting her as she was, and respecting her freedom to please herself, or moving out to hunt for accommodation elsewhere. The second choice was no choice at all, as far as Emmanuel was concerned. No one ignored the Herculean difficulties involved in finding someone to live with in the city, especially when, like him, one belonged to that group of people the urbanites referred to as 'pests' or 'parasites,' desperately clinging to a city that clearly had no business with the likes of them.

Not wanting to be thrown out of a shanty into the gutters, Emmanuel tried to suppress his selfish instincts, to complain less when Patience's aggressive alarm clock screeched at 4.30 am and the fluorescent bulb erupted in response. It wasn't an easy concession to make, but then, he couldn't have his cake and eat it too.

This morning, however, Patience decided to make an exception, given last night's episode. She chose not to disturb Emmanuel, who was still wheezing like an asthmatic, by doing her studies in the other room, where there was neither a table nor a comfortable substitute. She solved the problem by moving both chairs from the bedroom, so she could sit on one while the other served as a study desk.

From the pile of books in an old carton under the bed, she selected a textbook and an exercise book, both on the European History of International Relations. This evening's class at COTAES being one on history, she wanted to prepare thoroughly, to be able to answer any question the lecturer might ask. He was an arrogant second-year student from the Department of Modern History at the University of Asieyam, who took delight in bombarding his students with difficult questions, then sitting back to laugh cheekily as if he were God's greatest gift to the world. She opened the textbook to the chapter that dealt with the Six-Day War of 1967 between Israel and Egypt, and started to read.

In tonight's class at COTAES, Patience was determined not to be the dumb girl she often felt she was. She had cultivated a special interest in the messy politics and violent history of the Middle East since her first year at secondary school, and she believed she could answer any question about the region without having to refer to the textbook. She knew how the conflict between the Israelis and Palestinians had originated, and how historians and political commentators were agreed that neither terrorism nor arrogant intransigence would settle their differences and unite them in peace as good neighbours. She could explain the controversy that had surrounded the Camp David Accord, which, though enticing Egypt and Israel to an historic shake of hands, had alienated the former from the rest of the Arab community and fuelled more feelings of tension and mistrust in the Middle East. She could even lecture the class (if only that boasting bastard would let her) on how the black African states had initially expressed solidarity with their Arab counterparts by distancing themselves diplomatically from Israel, and by each swearing in the name of Allah never to backslide or to behave like two-faced witches.

If asked to forecast the future of Middle Eastern affairs, as the lecturer loved to do, Patience thought she might not be so confident in her answer. She defended her ignorance by claiming that such a question could only call for conjecture, not facts, in any case. History wasn't about guesswork, but about events, real events – dead and buried, she had been told. At the same time, this being a subject dear to her, she would not like to give up just like that.

She stopped reading for a while and pursued the discussion in her mind. The question was partly answered by what academics had said already, that for there to be any peace, there must be no terrorism and no intransigence. Only genuine concern for human life, not guns and bullets or slings and stones, could realise the dream of Israeli and Palestinian children to share the same playgrounds with happiness and goodwill. "The force of argument must lord over the argument of force," she had read somewhere.

Suppose the belligerent nations were to decline the suggested abandonment of current tactics? Then the world might be doomed! Terrorism might get worse, so would the victimisation of thousands of innocent people! Some of the warring leaders, in their desperation to foil their foes, might lose their minds and become infatuated with nuclear or chemical weapons, the very deadliest of man's inventions! And God alone knows what might ensue. Suppose Israel, India, Pakistan, North Korea, Iraq, Iran and China were to join ranks with those that produced and stockpiled such lethal weapons already. The risk of a mad dog doing something savage or of machines simply getting ballistic would be so many times greater!

Patience was too frightened to pursue the thought, so she returned to her reading and tried not to speculate any further on the issue.

After studying for an hour, she lost concentration. She tried to employ a technique she learnt several years ago in secondary school, known as 'cramming', but it didn't work. Her mind kept going back to last night, and to Emmanuel.

She wondered what could have made him so terrified. Had he dreamt one of his awful dreams again? Like when he dreamt he was leading a nationwide student strike, and security forces arrested him and dumped him into River Nasaga along with many others as food for crocodiles and hippopotami? Or another in which he joined a conspiracy to assassinate the entire staff of his former university but was caught and given shock treatment, and when that failed to bring subservience, he was lynched and his parents tortured and imprisoned for life? How about the most ridiculous of them all, a dream in which he launched a political party of his own promising social renewal and a clean sweep with popular slogans, only to be abandoned by his own followers soon after, accusing him of poisonous naiveté?

She had noticed signs of insanity in Emmanuel. He was paranoid about everything. Worried, she had advised him to consult a doctor, any doctor, modern or traditional. That was after they had lived together for three months.

Emmanuel did not take her seriously. He did not believe her when she told him he often cried out in his dreams and walked in his sleep, and that nearly all her friends had complained of his aggressive bullishness. Neither did he admit that his bitterness over his relegation from the university was attaining manic proportions, and that he was allowing his illusions about reforming the educational system to interfere unduly with his need to survive.

Over eight months, Patience had seen Emmanuel's dismissal from the university turn him against society. He didn't see merit in anything or anyone anymore. Glimmers in his face faded as he saw his hopes squandered. It was like watching life being sucked from a being. Patience felt he was stretching his pessimism and cynicism too far. She feared the price of his insubordination. In her opinion,

Emmanuel was too blinded by his anger and too naive in the way he fought back to end up any better than a disgruntled and embittered loser. Others animated by similar dreams of transforming Mimboland had failed as surely as he would. The malpractices, inequalities, and impunities he abhorred were far too entrenched to be undone by unstructured anger. Let alone overnight by the rash and powerless volcanoes of immaturity!

With a yawn Patience closed the textbook, stood up, stretched herself and peeped into the bedroom, saying to herself in pidgin, "Ma Mami ye. Na which day dis sufa go finish, no?"

Emmanuel was still asleep.

She decided against waking him, though anxious to hear what he remembered about last night.

She would prepare breakfast instead, she thought, striking a match to light the stove, which stood on an elevation of bricks next to the narrow window. When the Chinese stove refused to light, she picked it up and shook it to establish the problem: very little kerosene left.

"Masa! Dis small ting di drink kerosene like fish di drink wata!" she exclaimed, bringing her hand to her mouth as she realised she shouldn't have spoken that loud.

Under the bed, hidden from peeping neighbours was a five-litre plastic container marked 'SHELL', which she used to shell away her kerosene. As she went to collect it, she was relieved to see Emmanuel still snoring away, despite her noise with the stove. "Tank God, like yi go jump for ma head like dog weh rabbies don catch am." She smiled.

Back in the outer room, Patience lit the stove, placed over it a blackened frying pan containing twice used groundnut oil, and started peeling mildly ripe plantains to make *dohdoh*. She would then fry some eggs. She and Emmanuel loved having *dohdoh* and fried eggs with tea for breakfast.

It was only when Patience was almost finished eating her breakfast that Emmanuel woke up. He called out to her in the way a child calls out to its mother. Patience appeared in the bedroom, a cup of tea in her hand, and sat by him on the bed.

"Are you alright?" she asked with tenderness, bringing her left hand to Emmanuel's forehead to feel again for fever. She could see he was worn out.

Emmanuel nodded.

"I'm fine," he added faintly.

"I don worry sautee." She sometimes forgot that Emmanuel disliked speaking pidgin, especially with her.

"I'm okay," he yawned and stretched his hands, trying to gather momentum to get out of bed. The will was there, but his alcohol-rich body was taking its time as usual.

"Why don't you get ready for breakfast, before the tea water gets cold," insisted Patience, gently pulling him out of bed.

"What's for breakfast?" he asked, as if the answer would determine whether he got up or not. He sounded as undecided as a mosquito hovering over a potential victim watching it closely.

"*Dohdoh*," Patience said softly. She was like a mother trying to bribe her pampered child out of bed.

"I've had my share already," she added, at the same time as she followed Emmanuel's hand to a slight swelling on his right leg, probably bitten by a bedbug, a mosquito or both.

It was a familiar sight, so Patience didn't comment.

Emmanuel got up and decided to go for a bath instead of just washing his face and cleaning his mouth, before settling down to replenish his growling stomach. To raise the temperature of the cold water in the bathing bucket on the veranda, he used some of the hot water Patience had boiled to brew tea. His claim that cold baths or showers increased his chances of catching a cold did not convince

Patience who saw it as another attempt to justify his weakness and lack of drive. On his way to the bathroom, situated behind the shanty, Emmanuel felt an urgent need to answer nature's call. He placed the bucket carefully by the side of the wall of wood and mud thinly covered with cement and rushed back inside to collect some toilet paper.

"Sorry, I finished it this morning," Patience told him when he wanted to know where the toilet paper he couldn't find was hiding.

Emmanuel was tense, and doing his best to control the load at the neck of his anus.

"I don't know why we are always running out of the stuff!" he stamped the floor. "Something that doesn't cost anything!" he grumbled, giving the impression anyone could afford toilet paper, even the wretched and the unemployed like himself.

He squeezed his bottom together to force the waste back up into his bowels. Once the waste retreated, it was virtually impossible to impose ejection, meaning he was constrained from enjoying his breakfast for a while.

"It's not the money, it's the time," Patience noted. "I keep intending to buy it, but..."

Emmanuel interrupted.

"How can you lack time to buy something sold everywhere, even by hawkers along the pavements and roadsides?" he challenged.

"Na wosai for dis house they writam say na me must buy toilet paper?" retorted Patience, in pidgin, with rising temper.

It was true that if you let a man climb on you every time, he invariably grew to think his rightful place was on top! Why did men always spit on women, and ride them ruthlessly as if they were stubborn horses?

Emmanuel could sense a storm gathering, and he was in no mood to undergo further cross-examination as to why he didn't do something to help her out with the domestic chores and financial burdens. Instead of challenging her to reclaim his responsibilities as breadwinner, he chose to drink around town and sleep into the day like distinguished mediocrity blessed with servants to provide servitude round the clock. Not ready to begin the day with a quarrel, he pre-empted her.

"Before going to the office, leave behind money for as much toilet paper as you want, and I will buy it from the Small-No-Be-Sick store down on Famlanawa Road," he volunteered. "For now, can I take a page or two out of the *Looking Glass* you brought back with you yesterday?" he asked, knowing full well Patience bought no newspaper she didn't intend to use for her Civics and National Affairs course at COTAES.

Why dis man bad heart so eh? She wondered. Why can't he see my resumption of studies only a week after the last disastrous attempt, as my unstoppable resolve to make the GCE? What makes him think these papers are useless?

"You better use pieces of the cement bag in which I brought the plantains back from Wololo Market on Saturday," she told him, trying to mask her anger. And silently added to herself, "You probably use dry banana leaves at home in Abehema, so I suppose the cement bag is quite an improvement! He really ought to be ashamed of himself, this villager!" She cursed him quietly. Depending on a woman even for petty things like soap and toilet paper! How many men did he know in the city who were housed and fed free of charge by women? Why was he so thick-skinned? Or was he simply pretending not to be affected by her criticisms? And the biting sarcasm of her friends and relatives? Even their newest neighbour, the divorced Madame Jeannette Mvodo, had complained bitterly.

"Patience," Madame Jeannette Mvodo had called her a couple of weeks ago, about a month after moving in with three kwashiorkor triplets. She had just had the misfortune of burying a present and former husband on the same day, both of whom had died in mysterious car accidents, knocked down by taxis in two different locations in Nyamandem at the same time. "Do you think it's proper for you to be milked like this? Is it fear of not having another man that makes you slave for him like a zombie? Don't you know what beauty you carry? Please, don't let him molest you as if you were an *Evu*. I've been through one such relationship myself. Believe me when I say that loving ungrateful bastards is painful. Instead of appreciating you, they go around boasting to their friends about how cheap we women are! You should hear some of the filth they belch in public after a bottle! Bastards! Swines!" Madame Jeannette Mvodo had complained with venom.

Patience remembered promising her to talk with Emmanuel. Should he refuse to cooperate this time, she would call it a day. She would throw him out into the gutter that shimmered with decaying refuse, urine and rainwater, to be swept away into oblivion. The truth of the matter, though, was that after recently calling off of an engagement to a terribly unfaithful fiancé who repeatedly flattered her that she was the very oxygen he breathed, Patience had cultivated cynicism about figments of a Mr Right. Men to her were like a plantation of blighted cocoa pods, each competing to outdo the other in blight.

Speaking to Madame Jeannette Mvodo, Patience could see herself carrying through on her imagined threat with ease and without guilt, but now, two weeks later, she hadn't talked with Emmanuel the way she had promised. Here he was, still towering over her, and perhaps boasting to his friends about it! Why couldn't she confront him? Was it a spell he had cast on her? Was it that he was good in bed? Or was it simply her fear of falling from the frying pan into the fire that held her back?

There were moments when, like now, she was determined to put an end to the nonsense. This couldn't go on, whatever it was! She mustn't continue treating him like an egg she feared might drop! Tonight, after work and classes, she would talk to him, provided he wasn't too drunk to listen.

Emmanuel ignored Patience's suggestion to use the pieces of cement bag. She couldn't be serious, wanting him to cement his bottom! He took two pages of the *Looking Glass* and threw them out the window, to pick them up once he was outside again. Patience noticed nothing as she sat in the outer room contemplating their relationship. He walked by her with a piece of cement bag ostentatiously displayed in his hand.

"Who the hell is there?" Madame Jeannette Mvodo protested as Emmanuel tried to force open the door of the bathroom that was also the lavatory.

Emmanuel heard the splash of water and knew this woman he hated so, this she-devil with massive breasts and giant buttocks, was bathing. Passing out urine was one thing, but a bath, particularly by her, was more than time consuming! Attending to all the folds and segments of her massive bulk was not something done in a hurry.

"Damn it!" He swore and kicked the feeble door, forcing its aluminium cover to bend inwards. If he waited a minute longer, he would do it on himself. His greasy forehead formed wrinkles of despair.

"Couldn't you wait a second? It seems you stood spying on me go back to the house, so you could slip in and besiege the toilet," he accused. "Bulky idiot," he added. "Don't say you didn't see my bathing bucket standing there, wicked woman!"

He spat, partly because of the awful smell of the lavatory, and partly to show his contempt for Madame Jeannette Mvodo. He was most irritated, especially as the urge to empty his bowels returned and intensified. His tear glands also threatened to burst. He could imagine his father criticizing him and saying crying was fit only for mothers, sisters and little ones.

"Don't you ever speak to me like that again," retorted Madame Jeannette Mvodo, gathering fury. Then she farted thunderously, making the lavatory quiver.

She was grateful for the opportunity to give the pest a wind of her mind. For the past couple of weeks she had waited for Emmanuel to cross her path, so she could splash venom on him in a way he would never forget.

"Don't you ever dare, you hear me?" she echoed with vehemence. "Imbecile! I'm not the class of women you can talk to anyhow, you hear? Beggar-idiot! Aren't you ashamed to run away from university and hide behind the skirt of a struggling girl five years your junior?" She lashed out. "Good for nothing monkey!" Then followed with: "Who told a primitive villager like you to come to the city where you don't belong?"

She was enjoying her punches. "If you want your food served in bed, pack and go back to your primitive village, wherever that is! If you think you can refuse work and live off my sister like a leech, we are going to peel you off her! We don't want natives like you in the city. Take your witchcraft back to the village with you, you hear?"

Emmanuel was perplexed by her use of the word 'sister' and by her solidarity with Patience, a person she barely knew.

What eluded him was the fact that many women tend to consider one another sisters, whether or not they share the same parents or hail from the same community. They share a common experience of inadequate access to power and privilege (structurally at least), which bonds them together. A common sense of victimhood is as thick as blood, and women recognise and find that handy in struggles against injustices informed by male prejudices. Madame Jeannette Mvodo was Muzungulandish and native Nyamandem, and Patience Mimbolander from the coastal forest village of

Camp-Kupeh, but their cultural and linguistic differences did not stop Jeanette from thinking of Patience as her sister. Neither did the disparity in their ages.

There are times when even a rash person surprises us with uncharacteristic calm and composure. People's actions are difficult to predict, and often familiarity or intimacy does not make the task easier. A human being is like an octopus with enigmatic tentacles, each unique and capricious, so that understanding the one does not necessarily facilitate understanding of another, or of the same in subsequent situations.

Emmanuel received Madame Jeannette Mvodo's insults quietly, without uttering a single word of riposte. He knew an argument with her could lead nowhere. He had hated her the very first day she came to inspect the two rooms that, together with Patience's, formed the shanty their Nyamandem landlord called a house, and for which he charged exorbitant rents. He could tell this woman was a troublemaker from the savage scar above her defective left eye, and given the mysterious circumstances in which she had lost two husbands, he had decided to keep his distance. Patience had found her interesting and ignored his advice about not making friends with a witch and not falling prey to cheap friendship.

He accused Patience of washing their dirty linen in public, instead of seeking to iron out their differences in private. Hadn't her parents brought her up to see wisdom in the saying that the tear of the homestead meanders into the ear? She had berated him before friends and foes and turned his name into a scandal in the neighbourhood. Would that change him? Did she believe he could be pressured into compromising his principles? In his book, such illusions could mean only one thing. That she still didn't know the Emmanuel with whom she had lived for eight months! She and her gossiping gang were wasting their time.

When he couldn't stand Madame Jeannette Mvodo anymore, he simply turned and walked away, determined not to start the day with a quarrel. Unaware he had gone, she, bent on stripping him naked with ridicule, continued brawling from within the stinking bathroom, punctuating her discourse with thunderous farts. "He-goat stench!" she shouted, then farted. "Even if you drink all the perfume in Nyamandem, you'll never smell better!" She spat.

Still plagued by the waste in him, Emmanuel struggled across the muddy road to a compound with several lavatories. His need was too urgent to stop to ask permission from the inhabitants of the compound. Moreover, there was no one outside whom he could ask. One of the four lavatories was open. He sneaked straight in, and once he had targeted the little round hole properly, deposited his waste. He cleaned himself with the *Looking Glass* – which to his delight contained a picture of the vice chancellor of the university – and was out again before anyone could accuse him of trespassing. The feeling of double relief that followed the dumping was most pleasurable. He felt like the captain of a ship who had successfully disposed of tons of toxic chemicals off the African coast, at little or no charge.

Unlike villagers, city dwellers kept their latrines under lock and key most of the time. Perhaps a careless tenant or a visiting relation from the village had forgotten to lock the lavatory Emmanuel had just used. To him, it was this strong tendency in the city to idealise greed and private property that made the city stink with filth and ugliness. With a bit of humility, there was so much a city, even one as great as Nyamandem, could borrow from even as remote a village as Abehema. Arrogance had connived with ignorance to stifle humility in city dwellers and their authorities.

Had the mayor ever asked himself why, when he couldn't avoid driving through the ghettoes, the wheels of his Mercedes Benz were smeared with a stinking mixture of mud, decaying refuse, urine and excrement? Or did he always avoid the stench by shutting his car windows? Didn't the mayor's driver complain about the pungent aroma that filled the air whenever he tried cleaning the wheels of the limousine? And where did the mess he cleaned off the limousine end up? Vicious cycle!

There was no question. The city was a masterpiece of insalubrity. Emmanuel's quarrel was with those who apportioned blame to the wrong people. What was to be expected of frustrated strangers or homeless urbanites, the mad and sane alike, with nowhere else to go to answer the urgent calls of nature? Were they to blame for doing it on the pavements and pitches, or behind bars, in motor parks and other public places? And where would he who pointed the accusing finger say they should have gone, to the rivers or the bushes in the wilderness? He smiled to himself, like a nude madman at the city centre unable to understand why only little children dared to look his direction.

Perhaps urban authorities could repost, not without evidence, that being a dirty city in a way has its uses. For one thing, what would residents, those in the ghettoes most especially, do without the refuse-mountains that littered streets without names, serving as signposts and points of reference? And what government could cope with the extra calls on the state wallet if every urbanite were up and kicking and chasing away death daily, because of overly improved sanitary conditions? Emmanuel was at his cynical best.

When he returned to the bathroom, Madame Jeannette Mvodo had finished and was gone. She had left some excrement at the mouth of the toilet, which he forced in irritably with some water from his bucket. Then he set his bucket of now cold water down, closed the door firmly and started to undo his trousers.

My tea must be cold by now too, he thought. "I will have to heat it up again, or make a new cup altogether. I love my tea hot." When Patience had a flask, things were fine. Then that cousin of hers borrowed it for good! What a greedy fellow, Martin! As selfish as a lake with no outlet!

Martin was another person he hated, knowing Martin didn't think much of him either. He was tired of overhearing Martin call him 'an opportunist', 'a louse', and 'an accident seeking attention.' How could Patience allow herself to be poisoned by such gossip, malice and jealousy?

Whatever people said, whatever Emmanuel sometimes thought, Patience was a wonderful young woman, and he loved her immensely, in his own way. He didn't express his love the 'romantic' way with flowery but empty rhetoric. His idea of love was different, old-fashioned maybe, or simply too repressed to be associated with how love had come to be identified in the city.

In his view, the city was full of men who had learnt to talk left but act right. They said all the right things to women, but in their actions, they did all the wrong things. He simply would not pretend like they did so comfortably. He knew of men who would kneel before a woman and kiss her toes with chants of 'I love you darling' and litanies of 'You are my sweetheart, my honey, my butter … my sunshine, my all', when they didn't mean a word of it. He took determined exception to messing Africa up with Muzunguland misunderstood.

He would rather be honest with himself and with Patience, even at the risk of being called names, than live a lie, saying things he didn't mean, doing things he didn't feel, and promising what he couldn't deliver. His very own Peaphweng Mukong and the team of elders who had initiated him and his cohorts into the ways of the land in Abehema had instructed him on how a man loves, a lesson he was determined to heed. He would not necessarily love Patience more by pretending to help out in the kitchen, to

73

sweep and dust round the house, to go ashopping for groceries. Love runs deeper than appearances. To love a woman was to respect established norms and not change direction with the wind. To earn being taken seriously, to prove your worth. How could you say you loved a woman if you were fickle-minded vis-à-vis every passing sensation sheepishly borrowed from the ways of others? To love a woman was not to lose your balls to the vicissitudes of changing times.

To love a woman was to be convinced you care for her, to consider and treat her as an integral part of your life, to protect her and offer her guidance. To love a woman was to stay firm, to be the rock of continuity on which she stands to reproduce order that has withstood the test of time. That was what he understood by loving a woman. And he knew his idea of love was the same as his father's or his father's father's. His mother's too.

In this way, he was convinced he loved Patience dearly, which was what mattered, not what others thought or said behind his back. Love to him was a matter of the heart, a story told in feelings, not something to be tamtammed in stadiums and marketplaces, recited like the rosary, or tattooed on the forehead. He had come to compare love to the knickers of a married woman, to be hidden from all eyes but the husband's.

He was honest when he claimed there was little he could do without Patience, and he was grateful for all she had done to enhance him. Ever since that fateful evening eight months ago, when she appeared from nowhere to reassure him that life was still worth living, Patience had kept strong her support for Emmanuel through the thick and thin of the city. It was only of late that Patience entertained bad advice from envious friends and nosy gossips. Why had she begun tuning into such evil influence? And why did she seem less than keen to shake it off?

His love life was not a thing Emmanuel discussed with others, so he was not in a position to learn that two wrongs do not make a right. If men were saying a lot of nice mushy-mushy things to women and deviating in action, how did Emmanuel help the cause? By putting his money where his mouth was, some would have thought. By deciding not to say the lovely things Patience needed to glow in their relationship, wasn't he running away from his responsibilities? He may be smart in realising the deception that characterizes most relationships, but wasn't he wrong in letting this affect his own? He had identified a problem, but how did he help solve it? Wasn't it defeatist simply being cynical about things?

What would happen if God told his rural folks one day: "I send down rain but lazy farmers don't take advantage of it to cultivate their farms. So henceforth, I shall send no more rain down to the earth"? Wouldn't everyone perish? Because he knows much better, God still sends down rain even with all those lazy farmers about, probably with the hope that the lazy ones would look at the harvest of the few hardworking ones and learn from them. In the same way, Emmanuel should have considered rising above the myopia of his village folks and their forefathers on the one hand and the rhetoric of his city peers on the other to become a beacon of hope for Patience. After all, he did sympathise with women which was why he didn't want to deceive them in the first place. He ought to come out boldly for them, express his love the romantic way and set about bringing back to the soul of relationships the dignity and depth of womanhood.

As Emmanuel bathed, his mind went back to last night. He remembered having a nightmare and felt he must have screamed, and jumped out of bed or sleepwalked, as Patience had said he did whenever he had a bad dream. Why didn't she ask him about it then, as soon as he woke up this morning? Perhaps she was waiting for him to return from the bathroom? He lifted the bucket and poured the remaining water over his head, dried himself with the towel Patience had used earlier and returned to the house.

Last night was still top on Patience's mind, though she waited patiently for the right moment to ask Emmanuel about it. She was half lying on the bed and half listening to the news bulletin being read over the radio, while Emmanuel finished breakfasting in the other room. Something in the news caught her attention. She leaped out of bed into her slippers and rushed to the blinded doorway separating the two rooms.

Emmanuel looked up from breakfast and saw a delighted Patience in the doorway, the curtains pushed to one side.

"What's up?" he asked, slightly nervous.

"There's no work today," replied Patience, her eyes brilliant with delight.

"Why?" he sounded indifferent.

"The radio says so."

Emmanuel was surprised.

"Is that reason why there should be no work?" He replied with a sardonic laugh, clearly amused by her simplistic response.

Patience failed to take offence, she was quite used to his overbearing I-know-all attitude. When terribly annoyed, she sometimes came close to asking, "If you knew that much, how come you never made it at university?"

"President Longstay is so pleased with the performance of the national football squad at the African Nations Cup that he has declared a nationwide public holiday," she explained. "I'm delighted, as you can see," she added, pushing the curtains farther away from her. "It couldn't have come at a better time, for I'm really not in the mood for work today."

She danced about the room to the pulsating tune of the bikutsi music that followed the newscast, then changed her outfit, settling for something more casual and indoors – a homemade, heavily embroidered orange gown that gave her a maternal look.

Emmanuel sat in front of the large mirror that stood on the table, a pair of scissors in his right hand. He wanted to trim the edges of his beard, but not shave it as Patience and others preferred. Despite complaints that his long dreadlocks had teamed up with the bush on his chin to give the impression of a madman, he had refused to cut it off.

Now, as he contemplated which strands of his crisp, spongy beard to prune, he felt angry that Patience and other civil servants should attach so much meaning to a day off work, while he had been forced by the University of Asieyam to languish in inactivity. He loathed idleness, and didn't believe in holidays. This, like many of his values, was an aspect of his personality that few of his recent acquaintances even recognised, let alone shared.

Those who criticised him for not working were quite unaware of the degree to which he was personally tormented by the idleness the university had imposed on him. His entire life had been a shining example of hard work and the determination to excel.

He could recall how, by the age of ten, he was already quite used to his father's plantations of Arabica and Robusta coffee and to his mother's farm of assorted food crops, of which his diligent and conscientious tending won him the admiration of his parents and the jealousy of his half brothers and sisters. As a student he had worked round the clock, because of his firm belief that studying was the right way to achieve the grace and happiness the villagers of Abehema had decided to seek through him. They had watched him tread with the care and hope of a market woman carrying a basket of eggs down a slippery path on a rainy day. To be suddenly thrust off the narrow meanders of the path his people had chosen and glorified was most paralysing.

The University of Asieyam had paralysed his ambitions in the same way that the heartless witches of Abehema had crippled his half-brother six years ago. Who would not protest on seeing seventeen years of unrelenting toil and quest for self-betterment, and for the betterment of his kith and kin, forced down the drain? How many people would have the courage after such a tragedy to go searching for food in garbage cans, just because life, any life at all, regardless of quality, was worth preserving? Who goes hunting for an elephant to settle for a rat at the end of the day?

He doubted if his critics, Patience included, ever really stepped into his battered shoes the way they claimed. He was sure they wouldn't criticise him in the same merciless way if they made a genuine effort to understand the hell his life had become. They wouldn't allow their impatience and prejudices to get the better of them, and they surely wouldn't insinuate that he was mad and all what not. He wondered how many of the most vociferous of them would have survived a similar disaster. How shrewd, he acknowledged, was Shakespeare when he wrote that everyone could master grief except the afflicted!

He looked at the mirror and saw the reflection of Patience's exciting and rounded figure on the bed.

"If that makes you so happy," he started in the form of a question, referring to the public holiday, "then you better send President Longstay a letter of appreciation and support, so he can decree many more in future. I only wish one was able to decree oneself out of more pressing problems." He meant to be tongue-in-cheek, and when Patience didn't interrupt him with a counter-punch, he went on.

"By the way," he said, satisfied with the dubious radiance of his dark image, "tell me why your sudden change of mood? Aren't you the same person who a short while ago was all dressed up for work? You weren't anticipating the holiday, were you?"

Initially, Patience read nothing into his words or tone.

"No, I anticipated nothing," said she, shaking her head in negation. "The Minister didn't know either. He would have told me if he did. He lets slip many things official before these are finally released to the public, to the likes of you," she stressed with the pride of the privileged personal assistant to a master of indiscretion that she was.

On second thought she added: "What do you mean 'your sudden change of mood?'", looking at Emmanuel through the back of his head. "Is the civil service my parents' fields, or is it my private business, where I should work without Sabbath yet find no cause to complain? With the government, who gets paid more for working harder than others, that you would want me to strain without relent?"

Looking at her reflection in the mirror, Emmanuel could see she was pretty worked up.

"With your current practice of being hours late for work each day, don't you think having public holidays as well is taking too much for the owner not to notice?" he asked, touching his chin lightly with the tip of the scissors. "I wonder how many of you in the civil service do remember that your efforts are supposed to be the laxative our country needs to purge its bowels of the wastes of underdevelopment?" he added. "Your civil service is the tombstone on the grave of hope in Mimboland," he castigated, then opened his mouth widely to inspect his teeth in the mirror, noting with dissatisfaction the thick layers of plaque between them. He remembered cleaning his teeth better with chewing sticks and solutions of wood ash as a child in Abehema, than he was able to do now in the city with modern brushes and pastes. Another illusion of progress, he cursed.

"That's why you ought to join the civil service, to know it from within," Patience began, her intention being to use the opportunity to persuade Emmanuel yet again of the need to take up a job. She had always insisted it was better to be an uncivil servant, than not work at all.

"If you were a *fonctionnaire* – civil servant I mean," she corrected herself apologetically, recalling his bitter distaste for the corruption of Tougalish with Muzungulandish words and phrases. "As a civil servant or functionary, I'm not alone in dodging work. I'm not even amongst the artful dodgers. To be one, one has to be up there, not down here," she used her hand to point up the ceiling and down the floor, echoing her meaning that the pacesetters of all practices good and evil within the civil service came from its upper rather than its lower ranks.

"If you are critical of me, then what would you say of my boss who is seldom in the office, and who spends far more time ploughing his mistresses than moulding the nation or bringing up his own children? Or of those civil servants on sick leave all year long, too sick to do *ngomnawork*, but not sick enough to abandon their private pursuits or to earn their salaries? And the doctors who encourage them with false medical certificates and vows of hypocrisy, what would you say of them? As a hunter, you must learn not to misdirect your bullets."

"You talk of me joining the civil service as if it's just a matter of walking into the labour office and shouting: 'Open Sesame!' You know as well as I do that things aren't that easy in this Godforsaken country."

Emmanuel was full of steam. He was fed up with her constant insinuations that made him appear as if he hated to work or to earn a living.

"I love working and hate holidays, that I've told you a million times before!"

He turned and faced her.

"As I have said before as well, no work is work for me unless by doing it I can satisfy the aspirations of my parents and people back home in the village. They haven't invested their subsistence in me all these years for me to content myself with half a loaf in the city! Nor did they send me out hunting to come back home with empty hands! They never dreamt of building an empire of avarice for Kwanga alone, nor of a spring where none but I could fetch drinking water. Their dream has never been the same as the dream of a rich couple trying to mould an heir out of a dunce and only child. Rather, theirs has been the dream of a community in search of a better life for itself by planting its ears and eyes in the city of abundance. It's not been merely a question of having me stand firmly on my feet, but of having me stand tall so they may use me as their ladder up the festive tree of abundance promised them on Freedom Day. They, like your own people, I believe, have a saying that captures this conviviality superbly: 'one person's child is only in the womb.'"

He said these words so emotionally, that she thought he might burst into tears, something he rarely did in her presence, perhaps for fear of losing some of his supposed manliness.

He challenged: "You who persist in making me feel guilty for not working. Where have you found a job of the type I have just described? Tell me," he insisted, poking the scissors menacingly in her direction.

"You have to try, keep trying," replied Patience. "If you don't look, no job will come knocking on your door, will it? The answer lies in seeking, remember? Ask, seek, and knock, so the Bible says. And remember," she was deliberate. "Half a loaf is better than none."

She paused briefly, then added, "I appreciate the way you feel for your parents, your people, your village. We all do, don't we? Is there any of us who would hesitate to make our families, communities and friends part of our success, if we could? Most of these feelings are dreams, things we would all like to do for our relations, our home village, if the means were there. Should we cease living each time we cannot realise our big dreams?"

To her, there was little to be gained by lamenting over misfortunes, at least not the way Emmanuel did. She preferred a boyfriend who did not become undone by the tragic punctuations in life, someone who would not hesitate to do even the menial jobs of house boy, garbage man or truck pusher while plotting his next steps forward.

Emmanuel sighed and clacked his tongue several times, to express his exasperation with Patience's stubborn point of view, the way a spoilt child would deflect criticism. Although she got the message, she did not stop speaking as she often had in the past. Whenever he was overpowered by the force of her argument, or simply uninterested in what she had to say, Emmanuel would switch off by clicking his tongue and sighing disgust. And should she defy him and continue with her unpalatable utterances, he would start to sulk, get wild like a rattlesnake, plunge into a lengthy monologue that made him even madder, or simply pick up his faded second-hand Levi's jeans jacket and leave home, to go drinking with fellow dropouts or with friendly civil servants who knew him well enough not to pepper their generosity with sermons and moralisations.

Although jobless and penniless, Emmanuel hated nothing as much as pity. He would not hesitate to strike back at any person who tried to insinuate that, as a drowning man, he ought to cling to anything. He had even declined offers of drinks from certain persons he knew whom he believed were just out to ridicule him, to soak his beard in a muddy pool of stagnant water, to mock him behind his back. Even though he was exceptionally tolerant with Patience, so he thought, there was a certain point beyond which he could bear no further insults, not even from her. And that she knew well enough.

Patience was bent on making her point. She would not be put off just yet by fear of exceeding her bounds. So she pretended to ignore Emmanuel's irritation and threatening looks.

"Tell me about the job advertised by Hotel Charles de Gaulle," she began, moving to the edge of the bed closest to the table, a grim look on her face, "Won't you consider applying for it? Receptionist sounds like a good job, don't you think? And Charles de Gaulle is just not any hotel, is it?"

If he was serious, she thought, if he had any conscience at all, he would jump on this opportunity and apply before the deadline in two weeks. He knew she was suffering, that stretching her meagre earnings to cover her family back home and provide for him as well was a feat few women in this age and time would even dream of performing, didn't he? And didn't the fact that she had reminded him God knows how many times already suggest to him that she wanted a change of attitude on his part, or else?

Emmanuel could see that Patience would never cease to bother him. That the job affair was top-most on her mind nothing could mask. He was equally adamant.

"I have told you my mind on the matter several times before. I even did so just now. Didn't I, Patience?" His irritation was almost getting out of hand.

She nodded.

"Why then do you keep asking me the same stale question every time?"

In a slow and deliberate voice, he added, "If you are fed up with housing me, you better say so and cease using the job to coat your real purpose. Because you insist, let me repeat what I've said many times before: cleaning cups and serving drinks is not what my parents bargained for when they sent me to school. Moreover, it wouldn't bring them the betterment they've toiled and sweated for years to have! Imagine me cleaning plates and serving drinks! Forcing myself to smile politely and say thanks every time someone drops a coin! Coins stolen from the public wallet most of the time. God forbid!"

This was Emmanuel at his stubborn best, an attitude that evidenced his weakness, not his strength.

"If you don't know," he continued, "my people hold me in high esteem back home, and won't bear to see me stoop so low for so little! Until I was dropped out of the race for greatness at the academic beehive, my parents thought of me as a potential district officer, not as a cleaner-of-hotels! Never! I'd rather be a herdsman for a rich cattle owner like Mr Tangh-e-keh or Ardo Buba back home in Abehema. It isn't because I have been thrown out of that damn university that you or anyone else should think you can make a zombie of me. I know what is good for me, and will not be treated without respect by anyone, for whatever reason!"

He thundered so much that Patience started to tremble.

"So, as I say, you can–"

"Stop it, Emmanuel! Stop it!"

Patience burst into tears, unable to stand his words any longer or push him any further. With tears meandering down her cheeks, eroding some of her makeup in the process, she asked, "What do you mean, if I'm fed up with you?"

She pursued. "Who has said I am fed up with you? Why does a thing like that cross your mind, unless that's what you are planning to do yourself? Perhaps you're telling me that you've found a better girl than me. If that's what you want to say, say so, and stop beating about the bush! Don't think I can't survive without a boyfriend. Did you find one here when we first met? So go right ahead and do as you please! I shan't die because of that!" she shouted between her sobs, low in self-confidence, a plight that made her vulnerable to such opportunism that Emmanuel was currently exhibiting. "I'll not tie a cord round your neck in order to keep you tethered to me! You are not a goat, you are fr–"

Emmanuel couldn't stand her shouting anymore. "Stop that, Patience! Stop before I do something we are both going to regret!" he yelled.

He was mad with fury, and his eyes were like two over-yeasted brown puffballs dipped in red oil. In typical fashion, he pounded the wooden table repeatedly with his fisted right hand, and stamped the floor with his right foot simultaneously, for impact.

Patience stopped speaking abruptly, like an incomplete tape-recording. She didn't want to stretch her luck, for any fight between them was bound to be a mismatch as usual, with Emmanuel battering and bruising her brutishly. She could go any number of rounds with him, as long as the confrontation was limited to subtle persuasion or thunderous rebukes. Whenever he ran out of words, as was the case now, she was better off keeping her distance and keeping her mouth shut.

As always when their arguments degenerated to a level where physical confrontation became a real possibility, Patience began to brood. Now she was asking herself for the thousandth time the rationale of having as a boyfriend someone who was a perennial liability, a health hazard, a threat to her life. Like in past soul-searchings, her feeling of can't-do-without-him seemed always to overpower her vindictiveness, or simply, to blunt her determination to change him for mutual good. Some of her friends had come to explain her almost incomprehensible attachment to him, with the suggestion that Emmanuel was using charms and amulets of especial potency – *tobo-asi* – to blind her to reality and to keep alive her infatuation for him. And Patience was sometimes tempted to take these allegations seriously, although she never asked Emmanuel about them.

Despite his decision not to start his day with a quarrel or a fight, Emmanuel felt as if Madame Jeannette Mvodo and

Patience had conspired to drag him into a confrontation willy-nilly. Even if he hadn't exactly succeeded in avoiding a quarrel, he would not be drawn into a fight.

"I'm not in the mood for any further discussions," he roared. "And let me not hear a single word from you again," he warned, pulling his left ear to stress his point. "Just leave me alone!" He had a way of having his way.

He would have liked to go out drinking, but the day was still too early for any serious engagement with beer. Notwithstanding the fact that it was a public holiday, the bars wouldn't get rowdy until midday. He heaved a protracted sigh and took a deep breath of the air contaminated by the stench that emanated from the latrine behind the building, then turned back to the mirror and started to trim his beard.

Patience stood up and went out to clean her face. She returned to the wardrobe where she reapplied some makeup and adjusted her finely plaited hair, using the little mirror in her crocodile-skin handbag. When she was through, she changed into a much smarter outfit and put on a matching pair of high heels. A woman must dress well, mud or no mud.

"I'm going to visit my cousin Martin, at Carrefour Sorcière," she said curtly.

Emmanuel did not respond.

She picked up her handbag and wore it over her left shoulder. Then, as she walked past him on her way out, added, "I hope this gives you time to sort yourself out."

Emmanuel was worried by Patience's worsening attitude towards him. The change in her wasn't abrupt, but the suspicion that things might reach their elastic limit one day was firm in him right from the day they first met. The city was hostile to him and quite naturally, he had developed a sixth sense to cope with every nasty eventuality. For eight months, they had lived together in what he insisted on thinking of as peace and domestic harmony. Now, as he reviewed their past together, Emmanuel thought that though there had been disagreements over the issue of work before, Patience's tone was never as sharp and uncaring as it had grown to be of late. Today, deep down in his heart of hearts, he was convinced she was consciously biting and blowing in the same way that rats used to bite and blow his fingers when, as a little boy growing up in Abehema, he would go to bed forgetting to wash his hands after the evening meal.

For long he had pondered the gradual unfolding of Patience's worries over material well-being and the problems of a jobless boyfriend. Who was behind her latest upsurge of criticism? Where had her relaxed approach disappeared to all of a sudden? Convinced that where there was smoke there was bound to be a fire nearby, he ran through Patience's list of friends and acquaintances like a diviner-healer hunting for witches and wizards. It was evident that the "campaign" to force him into the gutter had a powerful new impetus. Who was the face behind the mask? Who was this new instigator that Patience was so ready to listen to? Could it be the one-eyed witch with whom he almost quarrelled this morning? He couldn't say for sure, but he would keep his eyes and ears open until the virus was traced and disciplined.

Just in case things got worse, he needed a plan of action that would save him from any public disgrace by Patience. If things came to the very worst, he figured he would have to move in temporarily with one of his male associates, before deciding permanently on what best to do with himself. To allow his head to be shaven with a snail's shell, and by a woman for that matter, simply because she cooked for him and offered him shelter and sex, was something he would never tolerate, something his father never tolerated as a young man nor as the elder that Peaphweng Mukong now was.

"Move in with a man," he muttered, as if in disbelief.

He knew this was easier said than done. The unfortunate truth was that city men, no matter how friendly they might appear to be on the surface, were basically less inclined to offer help and support to people of the same gender. They could drink together, discuss women, plan and commit mischief together as friends or associates, but only as long as each had a contribution to make towards keeping things in gear. Unlike their village counterparts, city men tended to be less understanding, less helpful and less sympathetic to the plight of their fellows. At heart, most were wedded to greed.

While a woman like Patience whom he had never met before quite readily offered to take him in, upon hearing his sad story of relegation and burglary, Emmanuel believed that few men from the city, not even those who claimed to be friends, would have made a similar gesture. His view was that city men preferred to spend their time, money and effort chasing after women and promising them heaven on earth, to fishing their fellows out of difficulties.

He particularly remembered his bitter experience with Kimbi, a person whom he would never have dreamt could disappoint him. It was this very Kimbi, his college mate and closest friend from the neighbouring village of Yenseh, whose behaviour had shocked Emmanuel beyond measure. Hailing from the same area, Kimbi was naturally the first person he had turned to when the going got tough that fateful evening eight months ago. Kimbi's reason for being unable to provide temporary accommodation was that Kimbi's new girlfriend, unlike the previous one, was more liberated and consequently less tolerant of Kimbi sharing his bed with another bloke. Kimbi had mentioned something about being gay, but Emmanuel had been too angry to give that a second thought.

Now, as he thought back on what happened that day when everything seemed like an endless sea of gloom and disappointment, Emmanuel couldn't withhold his feeling of hate towards Kimbi's new girlfriend, and towards what he saw as her borrowed ways and values. He couldn't help thinking of her as one of those who spent valuable time devouring cheap fiction produced for the ears and eyes of Muzungulanders, and trying to behave as though the realities depicted therein were just as applicable in Mother Africa. He detested her for thinking badly of his quest for shelter. He hated Kimbi even more for betraying their friendship and for disregarding Kakakum's tradition of good neighbourliness with Abehema.

Emmanuel would never forget the day the doors of the University of Asieyam were slammed in his face and all his belongings stolen. That was the day he marvelled most about many things in life, especially about the mysterious nature of hope and love. For it was also on that day of failures and despairs, when he discovered another dimension of love and hope, the one in the other and the other in the one. The epitome of both virtues was Patience, and looking back to that fateful day, he didn't think anyone else could have offered him any more reason not to take his life than did Patience.

That evening, finally disappointed by those he had all along thought to be his friends, Emmanuel gave up and started to roam the streets, sometimes not at all conscious of where he was going, who he was, or what in particular he sought. His experiences for the day had been totally confounding, and there were moments when he actually felt mad. Thoughts of the examinations and years of futility at the university tortured his mind. He couldn't bring himself to accept that the doors of that prestigious institution had shut him out forever. He shuddered to think of the implications, and the thought that university education was over for him pierced his heart like a thousand spears. Unlike the sons and daughters of his richer compatriots, unlike female students with irresistible thighs and other commodities to market amongst the rich and powerful, he couldn't be evacuated to a university in Muzunguland for redemption. His only hope had been Asieyam, but now that he had been flushed out in disgrace...

Darkness was fast approaching, but Emmanuel had no idea yet where to lay his head for the night. He felt like an innocent boy stranded with a huge bundle of firewood in the heart of an evil forest, deceived and abandoned to lament alone by witches. He didn't know what to do. He hungered and thirsted, his lips had cracked and his saliva tasted like raw bitterleaf; but there was not a cent on him, and little else he could do to calm his growling stomach. Without much choice, he continued to roam the streets, committing himself to the forces beyond and their henchmen below, but not succeeding to avail himself in any way.

Then, in the depth of the night, as he walked through the Carrefour Louis XIV for the hundredth time, the sacred sound of religious singing and drumming filtered into his ears from a distance. He stopped to make out where the sweet music was coming from, and reluctantly walked in that direction, suddenly aware that the music might be serving an evil purpose. Stories abounded of how urban witches used common religious symbols and rituals to trap the innocent into their sinister lairs of destruction and crooked enrichment through gruesome ritual murders and bumper harvests of body parts.

He soon came to a big hall that towered amid a delicate string of half-upright and half-crumbling shanties. For a moment he hesitated, then plucked up his courage and walked in, careful not to cause a stir and not to soil the tiles with the mud on his feet. This was indeed the place of the singing and drumming. There were lots of people sitting with Bibles wide open, listening and reading along with their young perspiring pastor of infinite charisma, who alternately intoned songs and read from a Bible on an altar on the side of which a giant cross of red wood had been carved.

Emmanuel took a brief nervous look around, and felt at once enchanted by the superabundance of the religious. The hall was filled beyond capacity, but just to his left salvation could be found in a bench that wasn't as saturated as the rest. He moved there and managed to make its jolly occupants create space enough for him to perch. Then the bench became so tied that a man farted loudly, attracting a chuckle or two from his immediate neighbours, but not distracting other pilgrims in progress. The house of God is never too full, Christ was right! Sitting next to him was a plumb young woman in a flowery blue kaba who neither participated in the singing nor in the reading. And just by looking at her, he could guess this must be her first time too.

The pastor was sharp at denouncing the low ebbs to which moral values had fallen in society. He castigated public authorities openly, for failing to assume their responsibilities and for making matters worse if and when they weren't simply at the forefront of the messiness that had become the order of the day. Girls were denounced for skimpy dressing, and men for not being able to turn a blind eye. None seemed good enough by the standards of his new church, and salvation was possible only for those who joined him to crusade against a world of rampant vices. Everyone had lost their soul to one vice or the other. Even traditional values and cultures that had served his followers for centuries were to be condemned and set ablaze for being of the devil. The future was reserved for a group of chosen few only: brothers and sisters in Christ, the truly born-again. Every word that dropped from his mouth was greeted with a profusion of: "Praise the Lord!", "Christ is great!", "Alleluia!", "Amen!", "In Jesus name", and a lot more than Emmanuel could remember.

When the service was over and the congregation of born-again Christians had dispersed, Emmanuel found himself alone with the young woman who had sat closest to him, and whose charm he had not failed to notice. She appeared to be praying, but like a Catholic. For what had she come there then? To find out what this fresh wind of religious fever was all about? That wouldn't be strange, for many people were curious, himself included. In any case he felt an urge to speak to her, to tell her how desperate he was, but the fear in him was stronger. What if she stormed out, accusing him of evil and sin? He feared, sensitive to the fanaticism for which the city's religious zealots were notorious. For a minute or two, he closed his eyes firmly in prayer to his forefathers and to God, a blend his father had encouraged him to use for rapid and better results.

While he was still in prayer, the girl stood up to go. Were it not for the sound of her shoes Emmanuel would not have interrupted his prayer to open his eyes and see what was going on, and what a chance he would have missed! He cleared his throat, to make her turn round. She did, but he was too choked by fear and insecurity to say a word. As he contemplated how best to tell her his problem, she took the initiative.

"Aren't you going home yet?" she asked, swinging her handbag of crocodile skin as if to dissipate the embarrassment of speaking to a total stranger first, as a woman.

With a smile she added in a beautiful voice, "Do you think it's how long we pray that matters?"

Emmanuel felt much better, now that she had spoken first. No woman would stop to speak to you if she wasn't interested, he thought, deciding to give it a go. Nothing ventured, nothing gained. He felt encouraged, but still perspired profusely.

"Courage, courage," he could hear the voice in his mind urging him on. He hesitated, doubting the sincerity of the voice.

Then, like a parachutist attempting his first jump, he looked away from her, and whispered timidly, "I don't have anywhere to go."

"Did I hear you well?" she asked. "What do you mean you have nowhere to go?" She looked quite surprised and sceptical.

So Emmanuel told his tale, all of it, giving all the details he thought necessary to gain her sympathy.

When she had heard the entire story, she asked him for his name.

"Emmanuel Kwanga," he whispered, tense and anxious in his anticipation of the magic words 'come with me'.

"Patience is mine," she said, trying to scrutinise Emmanuel who seldom looked up at her from where he sat. She could see that his shoes were covered in mud and that his faded Levi's jeans trousers were soiled too. It was his face she wanted as witness, for mud was part of daily life in the city, something even the very rich could not avoid entirely.

Then a miracle happened. After scrutinising him for a while, Patience offered to take Emmanuel home to her place for the night. Overwhelmed with joy, he jumped with the intention of embracing her, but stopped abruptly, as a voice in him warned against counting his chicks before they hatched. Cautious then of overreaction, he simply thanked her, and together they walked home. She gave him food to eat and beer to drink, after which she gave him a mat to sleep on in the room that served as her kitchen and parlour.

That was how Emmanuel and Patience had met eight months before, a meeting, which he took as confirmation of what his mother was fond of telling him about life.

"Things," Ngonsu was used to saying, "don't always happen the way we would expect them to happen. When you want your life to turn one way, it defies you and turns another, and when you are desolate and expect nothing out of life, a glimmer of hope appears from nowhere!"

Yes, Patience was the glimmer of hope from nowhere to an Emmanuel shattered by life with a will of its own. That was eight months today. How or when they fell in love is another story, more complicated in the telling.

Barely a week after their chance meeting, something happened which Emmanuel was sure would close the doors of hope in his face again. He received a bitter letter from Kimbi, lambasting him for all sorts of things. In a very mocking tone, the letter called Emmanuel 'High and Mighty', 'the meanest human being God created since Adam', and accused him of seeking to destroy Kimbi's love life with gossip and rumour: 'What you told Maureen, my former girlfriend, about me was relayed to me in detail by her. Instead of marring my character, you only succeeded in showing yourself for what you are – a contemptible slot.' In the letter, Kimbi boasted: 'With me, you shall always remain the inferior party, no matter how hard you work to mar my reputation. The inferiority complex that has taken possession of your soul will keep you strutting after me like a fly round a mound of cow-dung: You will never succeed to move me, you idiot.' It ended with a warning: 'The Jealousy that is driving you mad will be the death of you. I shall meet with you someday when we can square the deal. Until then, keep your jealous nose off my back, and my affairs. You contemptible son-of-a-bitch!'

Emmanuel feared the worst after Patience had read the letter, but was delighted when her only reaction was to shake her head and say: 'And you say this Kibi or whatever you call him is your f-r-i-e-n-d?'

After eight months of living together, all Patience's friends and relations knew and would say mockingly behind her back was that she had auctioned her heart to 'a penniless, jobless, wayfaring, crazy Rastafarian-type university dropout'. And with insinuations that she herself must be crazy, because this happened barely months after she had dumped from her home village of Camp-Kupeh a man of substance twice her age – the type to make a woman truly feel 'mon mari est capable'. Richard was a customs officer led by multiple sources of easy money into believing that wealth could buy love – 'I've got the cash, I can sleep with any woman I like' – even when he was most unfaithful to the woman he claimed he loved and wanted as wife: 'What else does she want? Don't I give her money?' Whether or not it was proper for her to fall so low 'into the arms of a barefooted beggar without a compass in life', had remained a matter of controversy amongst those who believed Patience's welfare and happiness to be their business.

5

Emmanuel sat in the kitchen-parlour wrapped in thoughts about the past, some of which were sweet and inviting, but most of which were bitter. Living in the past wasn't the answer to his current concerns, he thought. No sooner did this occur to him, than he became more restive and upset. He became scared as well. What chemical reaction within him could have caused such unpleasant alterations in his temperament? He could neither bear memories of things past and gone, nor reflect on this morning's disagreement with Patience, nor recall the awful nightmare he had last night. He stood up and went into the bedroom to look at the mirror again. His grasshopper eyes were even more inflated with anger.

He went to the bed and sat down, his head buried in his palms. The nightmare was now at the centre of his mind. He wanted to interpret it in peace with no Patience around to bother him about such menial jobs as washing cups and serving drinks to the rich and filthy.

How did it all start? He strained in thought, searching for the clue that would lead him to the bulk of it. At last he found the loose end of the thread of events, which he started to follow in an effort to trace the path of events between the time he dined with Patience and when he was frightened out of bed by the nightmare. This way of finding out was his best bet for a detailed and consistent account of what happened.

Emmanuel reconstructed mentally the events leading to the nightmare as follows:

Patience and he returned home from the movies quite early last night. They'd just watched a film on apartheid titled *Amok*, that portrayed the passions of black South Africans in such moving detail and depth that they began to doubt the idea of a greater hell for them. They had an early dinner and played cards for a short while before going to bed. Patience was the first to fall asleep, after he told her he wasn't in the mood to make love. Silence reigned in the room as Emmanuel digested the day's activities mentally, a silence broken only by the momentary movements of foraging rats and cockroaches, or the noise of thirsty mosquitoes. (Whenever these creatures were quiet, he could hear himself breathe.) Patience slept like a tombstone, probably exhausted after a hectic day.

What were these thoughts about? Where did they start or end? With both hands, Emmanuel explored the thick bush on his head, as with fuming impatience he attempted to wake his defective memory. Finally his memory awoke, though only to a certain extent at first. He remembered what his thoughts were about, but tried in vain to know when he might have stopped thinking. Perhaps he must have thought until he fell asleep.

Then the nightmare.

Abehema was at the centre of it all. He saw it in his sleep as if through a television screen hanging on the ceiling. It was so terrible, and looked so real. On this screen Abehema was projected in its entirety. There was a journalist who kept commenting that this was the village of Abehema, as if Emmanuel needed a commentary to recognise his place of birth! Emmanuel ignored the journalist and watched the screen keenly, reading meaning of his own out of the projected symbols.

The scene that followed on the screen was the mysterious Lake Abehema, two-sided mirror between the living and the dead. It looked muddy as if trampled upon by cattle, and it was slightly bigger than Emmanuel knew it to be. What must have happened to soil the sparkling lake with mud in this way, making it impossible for the villagers to use its waters as their mirror anymore? He couldn't say what this meant, but just as he was trying to think, yet another projection was made on the screen.

Two masked spirits appeared on opposite sides of the lake, and stood glaring across at each other. Each had a spear in his left hand, and a warrior's machete in a scabbard that hung over the left shoulder. There was a very large group of people at one side of the lake, midway between the masked spirits. As this projection became clearer, Emmanuel recognised the people to be the villagers of Abehema.

Virtually everyone was there – he saw his brothers and sisters, and his mother and half-mothers. They were all there in the group, innocent and cheerful in their misery. Where was his father? He flashed his eyes through the group and failed to find Peaphweng Mukong. He concluded his father wasn't there. In fact, he would easily have picked his father out, for he was a tall man, about the same height as the taller of the masked spirits. Equally absent was Chief Ngain. Emmanuel wondered where the chief had disappeared to. What sense could an assembly like that make without these two? He watched on, anxious but patient.

All of a sudden the masked spirits began to exchange horrifying shrieks, each in its own peculiar manner. The villagers were scared. In consternation they watched the masked spirits draw their machetes and cut repeatedly into the water of the lake. Emmanuel couldn't understand the meaning of their violence and was tense with fear. He started to sweat all over. As the masked spirits continued to cut into the water and to shriek, an object emerged for a split second at the far end of the lake, but disappeared into the water again. The shorter of the masked spirits was faster. It noticed the object, and acted with the speed of lightning. It drew its spear and threw it at the spot where the object had just disappeared. How precise spirits are! That portion of the lake became red with blood. The lake was in commotion.

The water moved as it would in a violent storm. The villagers became sad and started to weep. Emmanuel saw his mother, his half-mothers, and his brothers and sisters weep. It was a pity to see the instant gloom, which the masked spirit's triumph over the object had cast on the villagers.

Even the other masked spirit seemed to disapprove of what had happened. It shrieked more than ever before. It drowned its machete and spear, and held its head of wood mournfully with both hands. For its part, the masked killer spirit was quite unperturbed. Instead, it stopped shrieking and started a wild triumphant laugh that stung with cruelty. The people abandoned their neutral position, and rallied behind the taller masked spirit, and, together, they watched the turbulent water.

Gradually the agitation died down. A body emerged and floated on the water. The people were keen to see what would happen. In this body was the spear that had pierced it to death. As the body floated towards the killer masked spirit, its identity became clearer to the petrified onlookers. At first it looked like a strange animal, but it turned out to be a black cat. Emmanuel's hair stood on end. What could have pushed this masked spirit to kill so sacred an animal as a black cat? And as if killing it wasn't strange enough, the masked spirit fished out the dead cat and ate it raw, growling and grunting as some of the thick dark red blood dripped in to colour the violated lake further.

Overcome by the abomination, the people followed the taller masked spirit back to the village, still deep in mourning for the black cat. The action of the killer masked spirit was a clear indictment of their future happiness and tranquillity. They wondered if they had a future anymore. If killing a black cat was a sign of great misfortune to come, what more of eating the killed cat over the lake, sacred residence of the ancestors and forces beyond contemplation? Beyond imagination! Grief without measure!

For a whole day the villagers would not stop weeping. The taller masked spirit that led them home did all in its powers to lighten the thickness of evil, but even it knew there was no cause for hope.

Emmanuel found himself crying heavily too, crying in harmony with his people, for even in a dream there was no question that the misfortunes of Abehema were his just as well. He didn't know when for sure the taller masked spirit vanished and his father featured in its place, but he knew what happened after that. And it was disastrous. At the same time that his father was busy calming the people, and assuring them that a sacrifice here and a sacrifice there would appease the enraged ancestors, two white men disguised as Kakakum warriors appeared from nowhere and charged towards the crowd with hand grenades. Or was it some sort of research equipment, which he mistook for hand grenades? He couldn't quite say, but none of the villagers noticed the white men racing in their direction. Not wanting to take any chances, Emmanuel tried to scream his father's name, and to alert the gathering that danger was round the corner. His voice wouldn't come out!

At the point that Emmanuel tried in vain to warn his people, there was a total blackout, so the screen went off as a result. What he didn't know, however, was that although his voice had failed to respond to his attempts to scream in the dream, he indeed did scream out in his sleep. The scream, together with the fear created in him by the nightmare, had made him jump out of bed in the night.

Emmanuel was most depressed by the nightmare. He decided he must go home to Abehema as soon as he could afford to pay his way there. Too scared of how his parents might react to news of his relegation, he had stayed on in the city ever since the university closed its doors to him. Now that the nightmare seemed to indicate the safety of his parents and people was at stake, he would rather go home and bear their wrath and disappointment.

Because the matter was heavy, and he wasn't sure she would understand him, Emmanuel decided against telling Patience about his nightmare. He would lie if she insisted on knowing what forced him out of bed last night. He justified his decision with the argument that, hailing from a different part of Mimboland than he did, Patience had enormous cultural differences, differences which were a barrier to their sharing a common meaning on certain culturally specific occurrences.

He remembered how he had once almost laughed his lungs out when Patience told him that in the forest village of Camp-Kupeh where she was born, there was no central authority, and that each family head took care of his immediate dependents in matters of communal decisions and action. Unable to imagine a community where everyone was his own little chief, Emmanuel had retorted rather playfully, "Little wonder you are constantly forgetting your place as the weaker sex." The slap she gave him on the back as a result should have taught him to be more respectful to the principles of equality and participation.

After the distressing nightmare, Emmanuel badly wanted to go back to Abehema to tell his parents and people the truth of what he had seen. He felt they were entitled to know everything that had happened to him. For eight months, he had kept away from them, afraid to go home because he didn't want them to curse him for the relegation. Now he believed he was being naive, for, sooner or later, they were sure to find out somehow. Wasn't it wiser to take the bull by the horns, rather than have them find out through distorted versions by Kimbi perhaps? It was for this reason that his mind was now firm about returning to Abehema. He must be a man! It was just possible that the treacherous Kimbi might have spilt the beans already.

"If Kimbi wants me off his affairs, I want him off mine!" Emmanuel swore. "He would have to explain who authorised him to meddle in my affairs, if he has been running his foul mouth with my people."

The more he pondered on his failures, the more confident Emmanuel became that his parents and Abehema would eventually understand that the modern world was far more of a delusion than their simplicity and innocence had permitted them to discover. It was essential for them to understand the true nature of the *Kwang* after which they blindly aspired. They lived in the past with demoded ideas about education and opportunities. Though they weren't entirely to blame for their misconceptions of the changing circumstances, the cities and towns had tended to monopolise the race for civilisation, and to deny villages such as Abehema the right to share in the fruits of progress.

The time had come for the villagers to know the truth. The time had passed when a minimum of schooling was enough to qualify anyone for modern office and benefits. Schooling had become like a farm of which no one was sure what to expect: you may work so many ridges, plant your best seeds and expect a very handsome harvest, but be rewarded with a most disappointing yield, just as had happened with Abehema and him, their seed. In other instances, you may work just a few beds, plant just a few seeds and even forget to tend, yet be pleasantly surprised with a bumper harvest. It was their right to know that the tree of modern abundance was a retreating mirage with which they could never catch up. The belief that *Kwang* was something worth pursuing was a dangerous illusion which circumstances had forced upon the villagers of Abehema, and which he, henceforth, thought it his duty to dissipate.

Emmanuel stood up and went to the table for a biscuit. The rats had been nibbling at the package, and there wasn't a single biscuit they hadn't contaminated. However, he managed to scrape the contaminated bits off three of them, which he ate with a glass of water. When he was through, he got back into bed, tired and drowsy from the review of his nightmare. Knowing that Patience was unlikely to be back before lunchtime, he looked forward to three hours of sleep. Once in bed he didn't take long to start snoring.

Though he slept for more than three hours, Patience wasn't yet back when he awoke. Perhaps Martin had asked her to stay behind and help him with his domestic chores. That was the unavoidable problem of visiting a cousin who preferred vicious gossip and meddling in the affairs of others to having a girlfriend or wife to cater to his cooking, cleaning and washing. In any case, Emmanuel was angry. Martin's problems were not his problems, and Martin didn't have to solve them by inconveniencing him or his Patience.

What bothered Emmanuel was the fact that Patience had overstayed her time at Carrefour Sorcière. By staying out so long, what did she think he was going to have for lunch? Weren't working women supposed to use public holidays and weekends to cook their husbands or lovers special dishes? What then was she overstaying at Martin's for? Was it his fault that Martin didn't have a girlfriend or wife?

To Emmanuel's thinking, Patience's attitude towards him had changed too much. Gone were those early days when she used to pamper him like an egg, in fact, when she would have jumped into a lake of fire if he had but ordered her to.

"Strange the way love comes and goes," he muttered with a sigh, pregnant with a bruised ego.

Deciding he wasn't going to sit indoors and sulk like a nursing mother, he cleaned his face with a glass of water, used the mirror to ensure his dreadlocks were sufficiently unkempt and that his discoloured Bob Marley *"He-who-fights-and-runs-away..."* T-shirt was well tucked into his faded Levi's jeans, and finally left for Les Connoisseurs, a nearby bar, to drink his anger and frustrations away, God willing.

103

6

O nce out of the house, Emmanuel changed his mind about where to go for a drink. He wanted somewhere free of certain kinds of people, where he could have a beer without having to answer rude questions about his torn jeans and scruffy shoes, or about the bush on his head and the whereabouts of his jaws and chin. The idea was to go where there was no segregation based on the size of the wallet, or on how many ties and socks, shoes and suits, shirts and underpants a man could boast about having. Although he shunned bars and machines that served status rather than people, Emmanuel wanted somewhere with machines of a different kind. Like his fellow dropouts and the underpaid-overworked underlings in the civil service, he loved playing fruit machines. They were like one-armed bandits who, unlike politicians and top civil servants, were limited in their capacity to grab and retain forever, and once in a while sure to disgorge the excess coins for the lucky winners to transform into bottles of beer and subsequently into urine.

There weren't that many drinking places in the city that suited this description. Emmanuel knew only of Eldorado, situated at the very heart of decrepit Ohala south-west of the busy commercial centre, and of L'Alimentation Des Oubliités, the most frequented bar in Basfond, the mosquito-ridden marshy dwelling south-east of the university, where he had lived like a frog for two years as a student. Corrupt and inefficient though lecturers were, massive failures at Asieyam by the students that peopled Basfond like maggots in the belly of a rotten elephant half abandoned by lions and vultures couldn't fully be explained without factoring in the mosquito and rampant malaria.

The second quarter was much closer to Kongosa where Emmanuel and Patience lived. His memories of Eldorado weren't that friendly, especially after what had happened to him some time before, when he followed a prostitute home from there and was molested by her pimp and his pockets emptied, just because he had tried to do what most students did: run away without paying for her services. Since that incident, he preferred going to the swamps, where he felt much more secure despite the stinking pools of water and the mosquitoes and their buzzing unphilharmonic orchestra. He remembered Kimbi's failed attempt at composing a song titled *Mosquito Net*:
"What is this mosquito
That doesn't know rest?
Music, music, music, always
Music too dangerous for siesta
That is my pay for tolerance
I see a net as top priority
Mosquito: Music for money for net for friend?"

Even Kimbi's girlfriend did not like the song, an instant flop. And so he never managed the money for a net.

Emmanuel's mind thus made up about where to go, at the crossroads, instead of continuing straight across to Les Connoisseurs at the other side of the street as was initially his idea, he turned left and started off towards the university, on a tarred road that seemed to have more potholes than it did tar.

Emmanuel passed jubilant crowds of people, mostly young men and women on their way to the airport to accord the national football squad a rapturous welcome. Some sang and danced and drank, some relived the tense moments of the nations cup finals, and others shouted the names of individual players they considered deserved presidential decoration. Local musicians commissioned to reproduce commissioned compositions by national superstars in praise of the squad animated the crowds. They seemed very proud of their team:

"Our players are Rhinos!" some shouted intermittently, "indomitable Rhinos that go from strength to strength! The indomitable Rhinos – irresistible aphrodisiacs of football!"

And in a songlike manner others echoed, "The Rhino is king of the jungle. It feeds on the eagle, scares the elephant and leopards, and renders the lion invisible. The Rhino is ours."

Others were quite happy just screaming:

"Nothing is impossible with Mimboland! Long Live the Rhinos!"

"We win at will!"

"Not everyone can be Rhino!"

"Longstay + Rhinos = Mimboland! Vive les Grandes Ambitions!"

Their patriotic hilarity translated their feelings of intimacy and oneness with their squad, the veritable heroes of the nation.

In typical fashion, Emmanuel was indifferent, cynical, in fact. He had never liked football, and showed great distaste for the way it was being turned into a national religion. He had a peculiar way of seeing football and alcohol as one and the same thing, sometimes even daring to compare it directly with Manawa, a famous beer nicknamed 'Brainwasher'. He was of the opinion that politicians used football too often to blindfold the masses to matters of critical public interest. Where others saw in football great potential for national unity and integration, Emmanuel tended to see it essentially as a dangerous, derailing, mass hysteria drug. His was a point of view which even his closest friends didn't share, and which he dared not air in public, for fear of being lynched. Even Patience was not with him on this, being the fanatical supporter of the national Rhinos that she was.

Within five minutes of the university, Emmanuel noticed a group of soldiers, heavily armed with machine guns, tear gas and water cannons. Surprised and wondering what could possibly be amiss on a day set aside for football jubilation, he hesitated like a praying mantis, pondering whether or not to proceed.

His animosity towards the authorities was unequivocal, but so was his fear of soldiers, a fear exacerbated by the atrocious stories he had heard, and the way he had actually seen soldiers molest purported champions of disorder (as the leaders of student strikes and demonstrations were known). Personally, he had never been preyed upon by a soldier, but he had witnessed several nasty confrontations between the army and striking students. Confrontations in which the students were seldom victorious, but the principle of which they cherished too much to give up strikes and demonstrations altogether. The students believed justice so important a virtue that they didn't mind shedding tears and blood of sorrow and pain now and again, just to keep hope alive.

Emmanuel literally tightened his belt and feigned courage. He inspected the contents of his wallet to see if his identification papers were intact. To him, such documents were to the forces of law and order what traps were to hunters in Abehema. His national identity card was there, the national party membership card (slightly defaced after being mistakenly washed along with his pair of jeans), and his expired student card as well. Only the poll tax ticket for the current year was absent, because he hadn't paid any.

Although relegated, he had continued to use his student card to benefit from privileges reserved for students. With the expired card, he had managed to escape the notorious vigilance of many a fussy policeman and gendarme, and had deceived the local tax-collector of

Kongosa. In doing this, Emmanuel was not unaware of the saying that a man might crook and plunder the state with impunity for ninety-nine days, and be caught unawares on the hundredth and squeezed to disgorge all he ever swallowed in greed. Only in his case, Emmanuel didn't believe he was to blame for doing what he did, or for not doing what he didn't. For, so he reasoned, no one for whom stealing is only an alternative to starvation ought ever to be accused of theft, let alone punished.

This self-exoneration did not diminish his phobia for soldiers and men of force in general. He could denounce injustice with vehemence and criticise the powerful with words poisonous as the python's bile, but he shuddered at the mere contemplation of torture, or the prospect of having to physically settle a dispute. His power was mainly verbal, but to tell the truth, few who had heard Emmanuel bark were aware he couldn't bite, nor that his aggressive appearance was merely a cover. Now, he felt thankful that no one he knew was there to marvel at the goose pimples he had developed at the mere sight of soldiers.

As he stood contemplating whether to proceed or to turn around and bolt, Emmanuel could hear his heart thump like the sound of a pestle in a mortar of maize. He felt the wetness of his armpits with his hands, and cleaned the sweat off his face with the bottom end of his Bob Marley T-shirt which bore the famous words: *He who fights and runs away, lives to fight another day.*

Even snakes, his phobia from childhood, were only half as frightening as men in camouflage. If the authorities were out to track down tax-defaulters as he guessed, why choose a public holiday? And why bring the army out of their seclusion to take over from the police and gendarmes? Further still, why come to the university instead of the quarters? No, tax evasion as a reason didn't hold water. The matter must be something other than taxes.

He pursued his mental attempts to explain the presence of the soldiers:

What was it that had brought machine-gun-carrying soldiers to the university premises? Strikes? How could that be when everyone seemed so quiet, so peaceful, in such celebratory mood with the indomitable Rhinos of football?

Hunger strikes maybe, but this was certainly not the sort of atmosphere he had come to associate with student demonstrations.

Perhaps the soldiers were there to put out a fire before it was started? Possibly. Perhaps suspecting an outburst of cholera, the university authorities had appealed to these military doctors to use their hypersensitive feelers in identifying disgruntled stomachs for purging, before the entire campus became infested with running stomachs.

Pretty confident this guess was the right one, Emmanuel quickly twisted his student card, which he threw into the filthy gutter nearby, then watched it as it was soaked by trapped rainwater. When the card had sunk to the bottom of the gutter and he could no longer see it because of the filth on the surface, a strange feeling of loss gripped him. He felt hopeless, like a child who had lost both parents in a sudden disaster. In a way, the drowning of his card was like the final nail in the coffin of his aspirations, and in the ever-soaring dreams of his folks. It was as if he had said adieu to all illusions of expectations of *Kwang*.

His reason for destroying the card was different. He didn't want to get himself into trouble, for, expired though the card was, there was always the risk that the soldiers might mistake him for a genuine student, just as the police and gendarmes had done in the past. And how could he tell that the result might not be evil this time? Ninety-nine days for the defaulter, one day for the torturer…

With dubious steps Emmanuel advanced. He hadn't gone beyond fifty metres when one of the soldiers noticed him.

"Depêches-toi, faignant!" the soldier clattered gruffly.

Emmanuel hurried towards them, knowing from hearsay that the golden rule with soldiers was obedience, total obedience.

The soldier who had ordered him to come forward was embroiled in a heated exchange with a querulous market woman on her way to the city centre with a staggering head load of assorted vegetables, and whom the soldier was accusing in military Muzungulandish of trespassing.

"Vois moi la vieille-là. She wants to teach me my job or what? I'll show her that no one treats me in this manner! Oui, personne! Même mon père au village! And she dares to speak to me in her vernacular? Faignante, imbécile, chienne!"

So the soldier clattered like thunder, at the top of his hoarse, beer-eroded voice. He was a tall dark handsome man with a full moustache and sideburns.

The woman would not take his accusations lying down, and retorted in the language of the soil.

"*Eláng á zut!* [Look at your anus!]" she insulted him. "I've used this road to the city ever since I was a young girl with budding breasts. How dare you ask me to alter my path today, at 60! What's gone wrong with your generation? Where has all the respect gone? You see your grandma struggling with a load this heavy, and instead of supporting her attempts to inject some comfort into her life, you stop her and start wasting her time? Tell me the master you are serving, and I'll tell him to spank your bottom. Naughty boy, thrash your little bottom well! Dog!"

She spat. "'Sold-ate', sold-ate my head," she mocked. "Invisible ant! *Abé a ne mvé bilé* [Ugly as a pot of medicine]," she spat again. "Tell me, how many wars have you fought, Mr Sold-ate? Over women, yes. Over *odontol*, yes. Is this what makes a sold-ate – *odontol* and women?" She spat at him, shouting, "*Yén má mebí ma!* [Look at this mound of shit]."

Then she brought down the huge basin from her head, as if to say: 'today na today, we go see who be who!'

"Even Atangana, the great warrior – and may the almighty Atangana curse you and your entire family and village! *Me kúp wá zaá á nyól!* [May you be covered with leprosy!] Even he that fought real wars against the white man, not battles over women and *odontol* like you pigs do for big pay, even he would never have blocked my path to the market! And you, son of a rabies- and scabies-infested dog!" She interrupted her tirade with a cough.

The old woman was infuriated by the soldier's inability to communicate with her in the language of the soil, and the soldier in turn was accusing her of pretending not to speak Muzungulandish, the language of *commandement*. Although neither understood the other's language, they continued to use hostile words and to throw abuse at each other.

Meanwhile another soldier took charge of Emmanuel.

"Vos pièces, monsieur!" Emmanuel was ordered with sternness of tone.

He presented his national identity card and his party membership card, worn out though the latter was. Despite his determination to be courageous, his hand trembled like a dry twig in a soft wind.

"C-c-c'est t-t-tout?" stuttered the grumpy soldier, eyeing Emmanuel with the suspiciousness of a doubting watchdog by training.

"Où est l-l-la-a carte d'étu-u-u-d-d-d-iante?" he specified what he wanted, adjusting the beret on his head.

Emmanuel thanked his stars. He was right to have disposed of his old student card, for it would certainly have incriminated him, whatever it was the soldiers were looking for.

"I don't have a student card, I'm not a student," he replied, trying not to sound tense.

"P-p-parlez Mm-muu-zzzu-ngulandais!" the soldier stammered. "J-j-je n-ne c-c-compr-pr-prend pas Tougalais," he pulled a wry rebuking face, his stammers worsened when he heard Emmanuel's Tougalish, which was as irritating to him as the sound of a mosquito during siesta.

Knowing too well not to take offence with a soldier, and one that stammered for that matter, Emmanuel translated his response into Muzungulandish.

"Je n'ai pas une carte d'étudiant," he said with apologetic politeness. "Parce que je ne suis pas étudiant, chef." He slipped in the 'sir' with the hope of placating the soldier, for it was known that junior and rankless members of the forces cherished being addressed as 'chef' by peace-loving civilians.

"Et q-q-qu'est-ce que t-t-tu viens f-f-faire ici?" The soldier wanted to know what the hell Emmanuel was doing around the university, not being a student.

Either this fellow was pretending, or he had just arrived in the city from a battalion somewhere in the provinces, or he was simply under the grip of *odontol*. For there was no soldier in the city who didn't know that the university campus wasn't any less accessible to the public as it was to students. Who didn't know, for instance, of the taxi men, truck pushers and hawkers who took their meals at the university restaurant as if they were students? Or of the light- and medium-weights around town who habitually spent forbidden nights with their mistresses in student hostels? Emmanuel thought, either this light-skinned fellow who spoke Muzungulandish with a northern accent, was new in the city, drunk or putting on a show.

"I was just passing," he said, but recollecting himself in time, furnished a Muzungulandish translation. "J'étais en train de suivre mon chemin, chef."

He hadn't the courage to ask the soldier why a road had been built through the university, if it was never intended for public use, or why, that being the case, was it that the public could use the very road most of the times without having to answer questions.

"P-p-pers-s-s-sonne n'entre ici qui n-n-n-n'est pas ét-t-tudiant," the soldier informed him. "Donc r-r-ret-t-tournez alors l-l-là d-d-d'où tu v-v-viens!" he belched.

Emmanuel made an about turn and disappeared down the road, thinking himself most fortunate to have escaped. He pitied the old market woman as he departed, and wondered what they might do to her. Couldn't they see she meant it when she claimed ignorance of Muzungulandish? Suppose he was genuinely blank in Muzungulandish himself, what would they have done to him? Punished him for speaking Tougalish instead of Muzungulandish?

"And to think we are a bilingual Mimboland, bilingual in Muzungulandish and Tougalish! What a joke!" he cursed. "Poor old woman, poor language of the soil, poor everything but Muzungulandish!" he muttered, and kept racing until he was well out of sight and danger. And that wasn't until he reached Les Connoisseurs, the bar he had turned down nearly an hour ago, for idiosyncratic reasons.

Les Connoisseurs was unusually crowded this afternoon, but being a public holiday, the functionaries had joined the professional idlers earlier than usual in pursuance of bottled happiness. Everyone seemed in praise of the national football squad, for defending the country's international pride and integrity, and there were various brands of national music to blast joy and feelings of achievement into everyone.

As Emmanuel picked his way through the elated celebrants, he recalled what Professor Moses Mahogany once remarked about football many years before in a similar celebration. It was an observation the authorities didn't find flattering, but which was readily published abroad. The professor had dared to write, like the madman many thought he was: "If every one of us in office could perform similar feats with selflessness and patriotic goodwill, or if only we could toil half as hard for the country and not our lustful purses or abysmal appetites, wouldn't life be better off for the miserable peasants and urban scavengers whom we the well-off seem to want to forget all too easily? And wouldn't celebration become something permanent, deep-rooted and meaningful for all and sundry? And would anyone, no matter how critical and difficult to please, have cause for thinking that the people were merely brainwashed now and again with satanic rites and volatile dreams?" It is rumoured that President Longstay had immediately taken up an alias – The Indomitable Rhino of Politics – as if cosmetic surgery alone was largely sufficient to make of him a convert to the virtues and visions propagated by Professor Moses Mahogany. The Professor had of course lambasted the President for power without responsibility, and for toying around with the dignity and aspirations of Mimbolanders. "We are a nation sentenced to silence by your fear of the power of words," he was said to have told the President in an open letter.

Emmanuel heaved a sigh.

"Little wonder he didn't live for long," he said of Professor Moses Mahogany, the controversial subversive found dead mysteriously at his home, with a shattered skull, a missing brain and missing genitals.

At the counter Emmanuel bought himself a Manawa with money withdrawn the day before from Patience's wallet without her permission. He stood and gulped two mouthfuls with a belch before thinking of a place to sit. The beer replenished his energy and restored his composure, but still he needed to sit and rest his legs after racing like a hare. He looked around for an unsaturated bench or a spare crate, hoping to be lucky. Close to the door were two young men he hadn't noticed as he walked in, but with whom he remembered having attended the same secondary school a few years back. They smiled. He smiled back before going to join them. Though there was virtually no sitting space left, they managed to compress themselves so Emmanuel was able to fit in. Some drinkers sharing the bench complained, but none of the three did as much as cough in response.

Pius and George were delighted to meet up with him.

"Long time no see," they said, each offering to shake hands.

"Yeah, long time no see," Emmanuel replied, shaking hands with both. "Yeah men, delighted to meet you guys again. Very delighted."

For a while his eyes flirted with both faces, before fastening themselves on Pius, the bulkier of the two.

"I dare say you've changed quite a lot," he remarked. "You must be living like a minister, Pius!"

On hearing the remark, George looked away in an effort to suppress a chuckle. He was used to comments about how fat his friend had grown, but each time this song was sung, he would take a closer look at Pius' double chin, segmented neck, and executive belly as if he were seeing everything for the first time, then he would burst out laughing, thereby forcing Pius to sulk and protest bitterly. This time, however, he didn't want to provoke his friend by laughing out loud. The image of Pius as a pig would not leave his mind.

Pius, however, had no qualms about his bulk.

"Yes," he admitted. "Everyone says that, although I don't think I've changed that much. I won't mind growing fatter actually, because bulk isn't a burden to me. I play football, volleyball, basketball, tennis – you name it. I swim, I dance and I putdown – things some slim guys like this mosquito," he pointed at George who exploded in laughter, "face immense difficulties doing."

Pius paused to light a cigarette, a mischievous smile on his face. Emmanuel noticed the gold lighter, but kept his disapproval for such 'extravagance' to himself.

"You've changed as well," Pius remarked of Emmanuel, with a puff. "You never used to have a beard, and your hair was never so long and twisted. I can see you've caught the Rastafarian mania."

They laughed, all three of them. Then clicking the sides of their bottles and saying 'cheers' to one another, they each drank a mouthful. Pius and George drank Manawa as well.

"Tell me, men," began Pius, wetting his lips and rubbing his hands like a village child about to devour his beefiest rice and stew on Christmas day. "Are you still marking time in Asieyam, or have you managed to sail across the Devil's Triangle?"

He had to shout because the noise in the bar at this moment was such that they couldn't hear one another otherwise. Everyone else seemed to be discussing the exalting feats of the national football squad. They screamed away at the top of their voices. Even the blast of the music was overwhelmed by the football euphoria that reigned in the crowded bar.

Emmanuel had no alternative but to shout back.

"No, men, things were damn too tough for me."

He didn't take Pius's question amiss, because no one with any idea of the difficulties facing students at the University of Asieyam would find their failures a laughing matter.

"I burnt my mandate last year," Emmanuel confessed, using a common slang among the students to say that he was expelled for academic reasons. He was trying to sound light-hearted, because he hated the fake tears of sympathy that urbanites were so fond of, and which made them appear like crocodiles in disguise.

"Just as I thought," said Pius, shaking his head in sympathy. "Never heard of a university half as frustrating as Asieyam, where thousands fall through the cracks despite valiant attempts to absorb wisdom like blotting paper does ink."

Emmanuel felt Pius was avoiding his eyes. Funny guy this, he thought. Avoiding my eyes as if he were in any way responsible for my failures. I feel like asking him to stop behaving as a guilty sorcerer, like someone who has betrayed a friend, or worse still, sold his family to the devil for money! Does he think I am going to eat him up for knowing I lost my place at the university? This was the problem with people in the city, always masking the true nature of their feelings and thoughts. They're never really bold enough to say: 'Here am I in my true colours,' with a take-it-or-leave-it attitude. Emmanuel felt irritated with Pius for showing unease about a bundle he didn't help tie, or poison he neither concocted nor administered. That was what he found difficult to understand in urbanites, their abysmal hypocrisy!

"Do you remember what happened to me at the Science Faculty?" Pius managed to ask, fingering the mouth of his bottle.

"How can I?" Emmanuel expressed surprise. "I didn't even know you had registered in Asieyam. I thought…"

"Yes, I did," Pius didn't let Emmanuel finish. He pulled his finger out of the bottle with a puff, and took a sip of Manawa.

"Yes," he said in a thin and shallow voice. "When after the first year I discovered things were not really working in my favour, it dawned on me that I might just be able to make it in neighbouring Kuti. My parents were interested when I sought their opinion, and the money was there for them to spend. Things have gone wonderfully well for me since then. I even topped the Dean's list this year," he boasted. "Could I ever have passed my exams as a student in the University of Asieyam, let alone lead the class? No way!"

"I agree with you that Asieyam is an academic nightmare, a dangerous beehive. The burial ground for our futures."

What Pius said was enough to revive Emmanuel's feelings of jealousy and self-pity. He saw the story as confirmation of his disadvantaged situation, and of the injustices inherent in society. Here was a fellow student with an alternative solution to the problems caused by the University of Asieyam. Pius' parents had the money, and that was why Pius was able to escape the academic hangman's noose at Asieyam. How could the offspring of misery and poverty succeed in a civilisation that has room only for the corrupt, for ill-gotten wealth, and for success narrowly defined around the individual purged of every relationship with others? How could his own parents, mere peasants, be expected to perform miracles with the faded tokens paid them yearly for tons of bags of coffee cultivated with every single sweating muscle and sacrifice in the villagers? So he felt jealous, not so much because he disliked Pius as a person, but because of the advantage Pius had over him through no extra personal effort, an advantage he didn't think Pius deserved, particularly as he believed his peasant parents to be just as hardworking as (if not more than) Pius' parents, who were civil servants based in the city.

Emmanuel pulled himself out of the bitterness of his thoughts to listen to what George who, apart from his momentary chuckles, had so far sipped his Manawa in quiet like a real Mimbolander. To sip one's beer quietly and to pick one's way through a society inflamed by problems of every kind was, in Emmanuel's view, to behave typically like a Mimbolander, to condone the nationwide sorcery and shady charm of troublemakers. Mimbolanders, as far as he was concerned, went about their inactivities unquestioningly like a people hypnotised or numbed by repression. To him it seemed far more difficult to run a family than to govern Mimbolanders, which would explain why the top of the top often behaved as absentee landlords, visiting the country only once in a while to give orders and harvest afresh.

George started in a deep voice the volume of a tamtam, his hands clasped firmly round his bottle of Manawa, like someone afraid to lose an addiction.

"I often wonder about the situation at Asieyam. Things there are such that instead of weeping, I feel like laughing cynically," he chuckled, desperately trying to wear a serious face, which, it was clear, wasn't one of his strong points.

Emmanuel could see that George had a lot on his mind.

"I don't know who is making a fool of whom there at Asieyam," George wondered. "Do the lecturers make fools of the students or do the students make fools of the lecturers? Can any of you answer?" He sounded like a school teacher quizzing his pupils.

"The lecturers, of course!" Pius shouted instinctively. "No question about that. You shouldn't even ask, you just should know," he echoed, his voice vibrant and high-pitched.

This was a passionate dimension of Pius that Emmanuel was seeing for the first time and that made him wonder if he hadn't been too sensitive earlier when he thought Pius was being hypocritical towards him. "It is the lecturers who frustrate the students, and who constantly make the students feel mentally handicapped, as if they had no brains but water in their heads," Pius concluded with vehemence.

"What do you think?" George turned to Emmanuel.

"Basically the same as Pius," Emmanuel told him. "I believe the lecturers are driven, by jealousy and lack of self-confidence, to frustrate students whom they see as rivals in all domains, academic in particular. It all stems from the dubious idea of the scarce cake my folks call *Kwang* – the good life which, as you know, is so enticing that whoever tastes of it is no longer in a hurry to give others a chance. We are quite aware of the abyss of discord down which such satanic greed can plunge our society. Imagine what would happen if we all started struggling and biting the ears off one another's head, either because they've sliced off far too much for themselves, or because others have dared to ask us for a piece too! Where two brothers fight over the *gari* their mother left them, the ants are sure to rejoice over what is bound to spill. Unfortunately in our case, any fight is likely to be so bloody that even the ants would be poisoned by the bad blood running in all our veins!"

"That is well put, Emmanuel, well put, which makes me all the more surprised that a Brainy chap like you should be thrown out of where the best brains should be," George commended, raising his bottle to propose a toast. "Cheers! à votre santé!" he shouted. "I agree with you both," he went on, feeling buoyant and tipsy, after drinking only three-quarters of his Manawa.

Those who drank Manawa were aware of its high alcohol level. It wasn't for nothing that Manawa had been nicknamed 'Brainwasher'.

Not fully satisfied, George asked: "Don't you think that the massive failures at Asieyam are indicative of the incompetence of the lecturers as well, and that lecturers might in fact feel ridiculed by the high incidence of student failure?"

"Nonsense! That's total nonsense! I disagree completely," Emmanuel interrupted, impatient with George's reasoning. "You make it sound as if the students are more interested in exposing the incompetence of the lecturers than in passing their exams. Also, you make it look as though someone else besides the lecturers evaluates the work of the students." He protested, hitting his lap with the bottom of the bottle he held, and winced at the resultant pain.

At first George felt Emmanuel was merely being intolerant with a different point of view. After more discussion, he still thought Emmanuel might be missing out on some of the subtleties of the situation. For a couple minutes the three drank in silence, until Emmanuel recalled his confrontation with the soldiers.

"Tell me," he began, placing his bottle of Manawa down between his legs in a very protective manner. "Where are you two putting up here in the city?" he asked. "I suppose your parents still live and work in Zingraftstown?"

"Yes," said George, "mine are teaching at the same Government High School where they've always taught, in Konama. In fact, they are due to celebrate their silver jubilee as seasoned teachers in May next year," he chuckled. "Here, I'm putting up with a cousin of mine who works at the Ministry of Economics and Debts, where Pius and I met by chance three days back."

As for Pius, his story fitted Emmanuel's stereotype perfectly. "It's about two years since my dad was promoted to the post of Provincial Delegate for National Development, and transferred to work in Sopposburg," he said. "So it's quite a long time since I was last in Zingraftstown. However, I'm here in Nyamandem just for a brief while with my dad, who wants to push a few buttons so I can be granted a government scholarship. I have an excellent academic record, and my dad doesn't see why he should fund my studies from savings while less qualified calves are fattened with the public milk. He and I are staying at Le-Quartier-des-Chiens-Méchants, with an uncle of mine who was recently appointed Deputy Minister for Economics and Debts. We hope to be here for a couple of days more."

Emmanuel didn't let his jealousy and sentiment of wretchedness subvert his real intention for wanting to know where in the city Pius and George resided.

"Did you pass through the university on your way here then? Or did you come through the other way?" he asked them.

"Actually, we came straight from the ministry, where Pius and I planned to meet and decide where to go for this drink we are having." George thought Emmanuel was simply being curious.

"I remember the taxi man explaining to some female Muzungulandish students why he couldn't take them to Cité de Asieyam. He mentioned something about roadblocks, and how outsiders were being debarred from the area. Didn't you hear, George?" Pius asked his friend who shook his head to say no.

"Why do you ask, anyway? Is something wrong at Asieyam?" Pius turned to Emmanuel.

"Yes, I think so," replied Emmanuel, proceeding to explain. "It wasn't really my idea to come here today for a drink. I had planned to go to L'Alimentation des Oubliées in the swamps of Basfond to meet some friends. Just as I climbed the elevation leading to the plateau where the academic beehive is, I saw a group of soldiers armed to the teeth like some tribal warriors about to surprise their neighbours with an attack. At first I hesitated, but on second thought, I asked myself: 'What has a disabled person to fear from the keepers of republican peace? What has an aborted baby to fear from a mutilated or dismembered corpse? Would a tree of normal height frighten the wine tapper who fell off the tallest palm in the forest without breaking a limb?'

"So I took a step forward, using temerity to drown my cowardice, allowing myself to be noticed and summoned for interrogation by those not so humble servants of the republic. They asked me to identify myself, which I did with no more than two cards – the national and the party. At first, the guardians of the peace didn't seem satisfied. They wanted, or rather, would have loved to know I was a student. They asked for my student card, which I told them I didn't have. That's why I believe they are on the look out for certain types of students, but exactly what type, I can't say for sure."

"I suspect a strike in the incubator," George conjectured.

"Perhaps something to do with the recent influx of subversive literature from abroad, more specifically from Muzunguland," suggested Pius, the look of an insider written all over his face. "Uncle Kaawmsa was telling my dad and me yesterday that certain Muzunguland-based subversives are trying to use the students to fish for trouble in the serenity of our seas and rivers. He said these guys are jealous to see the administration succeed so well, and would like to sabotage all its attempts at the equitable distribution of the fruits of progress. They are keen, said he, on soiling our face in the mud and destroying our image as the paradise island of Africa. If the Dark Continent was blind as some claimed, Uncle Kaawmsa asserted, Mimboland was there to serve as seer, and nobody would deprive the administration of making Africa great through its vision. And no effort would be spared in crushing the angels of darkness and stagnation! No, not with the benediction of our masters above! He went on and on but that was basically his point. I suspect the presence of soldiers at Asieyam might have to do with that."

"Didn't they ask you any leading questions?" inquired George, an anxious look on his face.

"You didn't notice anything more, agitating students for example?" asked Pius.

"No, but for the clattering soldiers, the place seemed as quiet as a graveyard," replied Emmanuel. "There was an old market woman as well, but she was just like me, simply on her way to sell her vegetables. I didn't see any students, which is why I hesitated to think there is a strike."

"I don't think so either," said Pius, shaking his head. "If there was a strike, we would hear the uproarious students even from here. I am inclined to take seriously what Uncle Kaawmsa told dad and me yesterday. Perhaps the soldiers have received word that the subversives abroad are using certain students to spread unpalatable tracts and have come out in their numbers to purge the campus with a timely laxative."

"I'd rather we stop discussing such sensitive issues," George suggested, his countenance showing some discomfort. "There's always the risk one might be mistaken for ... you know."

"Savez vous à qui vous avez affaire?" Pius asked the notorious question often asked by or about spies. "You can't be too sure, can you?" he laughed. "I may well be the ears and eyes of Longstay amongst friends, and who knows who else?"

Although Emmanuel disagreed, he kept the fact to himself. So the conversation drifted away from the University of Asieyam and other issues they knew to be sensitive.

Emmanuel asked Pius for his Kuti address. "One never knows," he added, watching Pius scribble the address on the label peeled off the bottle of Manawa. "It isn't impossible that I find myself in Kuti someday."

George also scribbled his address on a similar piece of paper, and handed it over to him saying, "You are welcome anytime to visit me." The address was: State Training Regional Institute for Kid Educators (STRIKE), G.R.A., Kanda.

Emmanuel thanked both of them, and promised to write as soon as possible.

Pius and George offered him a couple of beers each, and he was grateful to stay and drink with them, because he wanted to forget his problems for a while, to ease himself of cumbersome thoughts and bad memories. The Brainwasher did just that to him. It unburdened his head, emptied the dustbin of his heart, and gave him the gay buoyancy of a jubilant swallow. Time ticked away fast as the three of them became more and more alcoholic (the gear in which to be, as wished by all, here and there in high office, throughout Mimboland). The barman provided them with excellent music, the latest Makossa, Makassi, Bikutsi and Kassav in town, which together with the beer, brought many a beleaguered heart temporary respite. Some danced to celebrate the illusion of success, others danced to forget it. A loyal and dutiful citizen, the proprietor of Les Connoisseurs! That he switched off the music despite the vociferous protest, in order to listen to the 3 p.m. news bulletin in Tougalish, was proof of his subservient patriotism.

When people drink, they need no such thing as broadcast news, alcohol being news of a kind in itself. However, that didn't stop the crowd in the bar from hearing that President Longstay was leaving the country the following day with a village of thirty attendants for a prolonged private visit to Muzunguland, or that tonight he and the first lady planned to receive and honour the conquering Rhinos after their brilliant performance at the Nations Cup.

This was followed by shouts of: 'Bon Voyage Monsieur le Président. Nous vous aimons à mort', 'Allez-les Rhinos', 'L'impossible n'est pas Mimbolandais', 'Nous sommes Vainqueurs', 'Vive les Rhinos', 'Vive le Président', from those of the excited drinkers who understood Tougalish a bit. Others reminded President Longstay, as if he were at the bar listening to them, of the need for more public holidays and for alcohol that would cost even less than its current giveaway prices. "With even cheaper beer, we would all say farewell to Odontol and other primitive brews," one shouted, to the amusement of most of the listeners. Some wondered why the national football team could not win championships on a weekly basis, so the number of football holidays could multiply, especially with the understanding president they had, who could stand up in the stadium and declare a holiday, without having to bother about the fuss of actually signing it first. It is strange how alcohol can induce momentary creativity. With the brief news bulletin over, the proprietor turned off the radio and his customers resumed their drinking and dancing to the thrilling sound of the latest from Muzunguland in Mimbolander and Caribbean music.

Emmanuel's mind was back on the news (trying to make head and tail of it). To say that the news was brief didn't mean it lacked its normal features of gloom, or that the usual extravaganza on the banalities of President Longstay and his wife were absent. As ever, there was something about plane crashes or hijacks in the North, floods, earthquakes and famine in the South, terrorism and intransigence in the Middle East, war nearby, racism in southern Africa, and superpower whisperings round the globe. There were the normal stories about staggering oil tankers in the Gulf, blackouts in world trading centres, and drastic falls in the prices of coffee and cocoa and cotton.

Whenever he heard of coffee in the news, Emmanuel would think of his parents and the people of Abehema, toiling away as hard as ever under the Arabica and Robusta, and watching the crops flourish with love and rural dreams. How little say they had in deciding the faded tokens they got in return! He was sure Abehema wouldn't believe him, if he told them that some of the people who decided prices or consumed coffee as a finished product, had no idea what a coffee plant looked like. Not that they should, some would say, since money is the king and great dictator on this and other matters. Heaving a sigh of frustration, he resumed his drinking, hoping thereby to curb his dejection.

Pius and George vanished quite unceremoniously. Emmanuel understood perfectly why they couldn't have left otherwise. They went chasing after two pretty girls who had come into the bar only briefly and, for whatever reason, had decided against having a drink at Les Connoisseurs. Who would argue, Emmanuel wondered, that it wasn't proper for these young men, both dressed up in expensive Muzungulander gear, to chase after two pretty girls, equally fanciful in their foreign outfits? Who would blame anyone for taking advantage of the opportunities Nyamandem offered its citizens to be modern and happy?

"The only thing which baffles me," he shouted, quite inattentive to the fact that others might perceive him to be loony. "Yes, the only thing that baffles is how Pius and George and many others in their class do manage to survive the oppressive scorch of the sun in their Muzungulander paraphernalia," he smiled cynically, just as his father would, albeit more consumed by jealousy than his father.

"Perhaps I would come to understand if I were able to afford similar outfits of my own. Then I would know what one feels like in a suit of wool under this tropical furnace." He smiled again, ignoring the inquisitive concern of a worried middle-aged man who sat next to him.

In a way Emmanuel was pleased Pius and George had left. He could sit quietly and sip the beer they had provided. He felt the side-pocket of his jeans. The addresses they had scribbled for him were there, quite secure. He was grateful his mates had given these to him before they disappeared. Somehow he had the feeling he might need to use Pius' address sooner or later, though he couldn't say why he felt that way.

When frustrated and confused, desperate for hope yet almost drowned by uncertainties, one tends to make ungrounded prophecies every now and again. That was the case with Emmanuel who, contrary to what he and others thought and said, was not entirely devoid of academic hope. In his heart of hearts, his relegation had not quite extinguished all glimmers of hope, yet.

With his partners gone, Emmanuel wasn't in a hurry to go home. He wasn't hungry anymore, and his beer was there to keep him occupied until it was late enough to go home and get to bed. All he wanted was to sit and sip in peace, and perhaps hope that someone he knew would walk into the bar and keep him company. Drinking was best when done in company, not alone. Doing it alone could be as dull and boring as a rich man opening a bottle of champagne in solitude. Time was flying like a *Mabuh* bearing a message of war between two chiefdoms. He wasn't bothered, he wasn't a mother anxious to get home and suckle her baby, or a woman desperate to please and keep her man with delicious dishes.

His buttocks virtually glued to the bench, Emmanuel abandoned himself to beer and music. With hallucinatory eyes he watched others do the same. He wasn't someone who easily got drunk, but Manawa wasn't a beer for amateurs either. He kept sneaking out through the back door to empty his bladder at an open space between two buildings, where there was no toilet, but which stank of a mixture of excrement, urine and dripping condoms. Each time he sneaked out and started to urinate, he unsettled a large colony of festive flies and drowned an ant or two.

He finished the Manawa Pius and George had left him, and bought himself two more. Of the MIM$1000 he had secretly 'withdrawn' from Patience's wallet, only 350 were left. He decided he would save 250 for the next day, and buy himself some roasted beef – *soya* – with the rest.

Outside the bar, under a stunted mango tree, stood a poorly constructed shade, where a charcoal dark young man had started barbecuing beef for sale. Emmanuel staggered out, attracted by the delicious smell and the fresh night air that had now enveloped this part of the city. He stretched out his hands and performed a brief muscle exercise, cracking his fingers. Then, taking care to cross the delicate bridge of wood over the gutter that separated the bar from the street, he made his way to the mango tree where there were many people buying or munching.

A young man by the name of Oumarou operated this particular spot that had become popular for its excellent barbecues. He had come here a year before, escaping the fratricide in his native Warzone. On arrival, Oumarou had done a variety of odd jobs to earn himself money enough to start a barbecue business. He had roamed the streets as a beggar, sold charms and amulets to the ambitious and the forsaken, sung and drummed Warzoner folk tunes for the amusement of obliging citizens, and done an apprenticeship under the renowned barbecue experts of the famous 'Ministère de Soya' at Quartier Haoussa. Once satisfied that he had made enough money to stand on his own feet, Oumarou had negotiated for this spot with the proprietor of Les Connoisseurs (after carefully eliminating all other possibilities).

And who could say that he hadn't made the right decision? Hadn't he made enough money to rent a hut where he could lay his head and pray for peace back home in Warzone? And wasn't this a great improvement on his previous situation, when as a fresh refugee he could only feed from garbage cans and sleep in front of shops at the city centre, or at the railway station and motor parks, like a madman? Above all, wasn't he contemplating marriage with a beautiful young refugee from Warzone, an Arab like himself, with whom he was now living together at Quartier Haoussa, after knowing each other for three months? And who could say there wasn't hope for him, and for Warzone his beloved country, or for all his brothers and sisters? So Oumarou sold his beef with hope, the very hope that had stuck with him during his darkest hours, and given him cause to smile again.

"Coupe-moi la viande de MIM$100," Emmanuel told Oumarou, trying to keep his balance. His legs were no longer quite reliable.

"Qui est celui ci?" complained a fellow buyer. "Vous ne voyez pas que Oumarou est en train de nous servir?" The tall fellow brandished an empty bottle of Manpasman reproachfully, looking drunk enough to be dangerous.

Emmanuel was not afraid, being equally under the inspiration of their common source of courage. "If he is serving you, in what way does that stop me from placing an order?" he retorted in Tougalish, his language of convenience and comfort.

"C'est un Tougalais," remarked the tall fellow, much to the laughter of his companions, a woman and three men.

"What has being a Tougalish Mimbolander got to do with it?" Emmanuel was disgusted.

"Ils sont comme ça, les Tougalais, toujours à gauche," said the tall fellow, ignoring Emmanuel. His comment brought further laughter from his friends.

"And frogs – how are they?" Emmanuel felt really provoked. Frustrated by the fact that his attacker was totally blank in Tougalish, he added spitefully: "Dites moi, comment sont les crapauds, les grenouilles?" He didn't know which word stood for frogs and which for toads, so he used both.

He was only laughed at. The tall fellow ridiculed his Muzungulandish.

"Il parle le Muzungulandais comme un Wami," he said.

"And you, do you speak Tougalish – even Pidgin-Tougalish?" Emmanuel challenged.

"Le Tougalish c'est quoi?" laughed the tall fellow. "C'est une langue ça?" he mocked. "Et même si c'était une langue valable, est-ce que toi tu parles le Tougalish même? N'est-ce pas c'est le Tougalish de la poubelle que tu parles, mon frère?"

With this the fellow turned to Oumarou who was asking to know if he wanted powdery pepper and 'démarreur' (a purported aphrodisiac) added to the beef sliced into little pieces for him and his friends.

"Oui, mon frère," replied the tall fellow, kissing the woman in the group. "Beaucoup. Les oignons aussi. Et mettez nous un peu plus de *mbangala* là eh."

After expressing his need for much hot pepper, 'démarreur', onions, and roasted genitals, the man said of Emmanuel: "Et mon frère le Tougalish ci, il veut la viande de MIM$100 eh."

The woman giggled, and together they walked to a waiting taxi on the other side of the road, which they drove off, still poking fun at Emmanuel.

"A mere taxi man – an idiot," Emmanuel muttered with contempt.

"Oui, monsieur?" Oumarou turned to Emmanuel, who appeared deep in thought. "Vous voulez la viande pour combien monsieur?" he asked, cleaning his trenchant knife with a greasy towel that hung over a nail pierced into a stick on the wall of zinc behind him.

"Cent dollars!" Emmanuel screamed. "N'est-ce pas j'ai bien dit cent dollars!" He was irritated.

"Il n'y a pas la viande de cent dollars. La viande c'est à partir de deux cents."

Oumarou thought he recognised a troublemaker in Emmanuel, one of those idlers in Kongosa who would like to eat meat even though they hadn't the money to pay for it. Without the beard, Oumarou could have sworn by Allah that Emmanuel was the rogue who ambushed and attempted to rob him of an evening's sales a couple months ago. He reproached Emmanuel for wasting his time, and turned to serve another customer.

"Coupe alors pour deux cents," Emmanuel consented. "Mais il faut que ça soit grand eh," he warned.

Oumarou was already cutting for a less fussy customer.

"Attendez," he told Emmanuel.

When he was through with the young woman he was serving, he cut a piece and sliced it for Emmanuel.

"What's this!" Emmanuel exclaimed, rejecting the beef he had been offered. "C'est tout? Pour deux cents? Non! Si vous n'ajoutez pas, je n'accepte pas!" He threatened. "Do you think I pick this money?" he asked, sincerely shocked. "MIM$200 isn't a small sum, eh."

Oumarou was furious. He snatched the plate away from Emmanuel and emptied its contents back to the lot in front of him. Then picking up his knife, he asked Emmanuel to leave.

People assembled to listen to Oumarou raging away in a mixture of broken Muzungulandish and Arabic. He folded his trousers up to his lap and showed them the multiple scars on his legs and lap. "These are scars inflicted by the war in my country," he told them. "These two here," he showed them the scar on his left arm and the other above his right jaw, "these were actually stabbings from my brother's knife, my brother who was fighting for one faction and I was fighting for another."

He shook his head in sadness.

"So tell this man not to provoke me, for I've seen red. I've even drunk my brother's blood! If he doesn't go away before I count five, I swear in the name of Allah that he'll see fire!" With these words, he flashed his knife angrily, and made a desperate surge forward to reach Emmanuel. He was prevented.

An elderly woman – the very one who earlier at the University of Asieyam he had witnessed giving a soldier a bit of her mind, who had interrupted her journey home to find out what the shouting was all about – pulled Emmanuel aside and advised him to disappear if he valued his throat.

"These people don't joke with the knife," she warned. "They stab, and stab to kill. Go away," she insisted, pulling the reluctant Emmanuel away from the scene.

"Get back in there or whatever. We don't want to see blood," she said, leaving him at the mouth of the bar, before continuing her way.

So Emmanuel staggered into Les Connoisseurs again, retrieved the remainder of his beer from the back of the bench, emptied it into his throat, and struggled out once more, this time heading for home. Apart from the bar and the immediate vicinity, it was dark everywhere. Going home wasn't easy, even though Patience's shanty was only a stone's throw away. He negotiated the narrow corners and filthy gutters with difficulty.

By the time he reached home, he was wet up to the knees, and his trousers stank of excrement. His third fall had happened when he was nearly home. He stumbled over an exposed water pipe and fell into the compound where he went to empty his bowels in the morning, making such a noise that a dog and her puppies began to bark. Managing to stand up again, he wiped his hands and felt his bruised legs, then bolted like a blind man with haemorrhoids.

He arrived at the shanty panting and still pursued by the dogs. In panic he felt for the door, bruising his head against the roughness of the wall in the process. Once inside with the dogs closed out, not quite realising the full extent of his injuries, he didn't bother to look for iodine which was somewhere in Patience's wardrobe. He fell into the bed where Patience was already asleep, not even bothering to take off his wet shoes and trousers. Lying beside her, his head throbbed, his eyes whirled and his whole body spoke pain.

7

They both took their places at the makeshift dining table in the kitchen-parlour. The savoury smell of *Ekwang* brought saliva to Emmanuel's mouth and made him all the more impatient with Patience's inclination for protocol. Generally, he never approved of the strange table manners she constantly sought to impose on him, manners whose origins were as foreign to Africa as were the knife, fork and napkin that provoked his bitter opposition to her etiquette. The fact that she compelled him to eat with knife and fork foods he felt more comfortable eating with his fingers unnerved him most of the time. If he was ready to go along to get along with her once in a while, he certainly wasn't giving her a signal to ride him like a horse on the issue.

This particular dish was his favourite, the cultural dish of Camp-Kupeh, her home village. Like many other traditional things in the southern parts of the country – the very first zones to be penetrated and impregnated by civilising whiteness in colonial times – *Ekwang* had been a victim of corroding Muzungulander ways of doing things. Unlike Abehema, which was far away in the north-western hinterlands, Camp-Kupeh was a coastal forest settlement, and as such, had been more exposed to the storms of superiority that blew from across the Atlantic. So while in Abehema much was still done the way it had always been done, Camp-Kupeh had lost almost all of its original practices and values, including the way *Ekwang* used to be eaten, that is, with the fingers.

Patience didn't cook *Ekwang* often, because its preparation was difficult and time consuming. She always cooked it to celebrate a particularly happy moment, or to overcome a very trying experience. Today's was the fifth in over a quarter of a year, and Emmanuel still had to be told why she had prepared it. The people of Camp-Kupeh were known far and wide for their *Ekwang*, which allegedly was always prepared with the incantation: 'go come back, come no go', intended to entice love and loved ones. Patience had recounted to him how her ancestors had had to visit the world beyond down below Mount Kupeh to steal the recipe from the kitchen of the formidable queen of witches.

Despite her tale, Emmanuel didn't think of Patience as one who had much faith in ancestors or in traditional beliefs about the origin of things. The fact that she laughed mockingly whenever she repeated the tale was ample proof of his viewpoint. She was one of many who firmly believed that to know or to show commitment towards anything traditional and distinctively local was to stake all they had gained in terms of civilisation and the global. They were keener on modernising their traditions than on indigenising their modern views and ways. So the further they kept themselves away from the superstitious savagery and barbaric primitivity of their disgraced forefathers, the better they thought were their chances of becoming part of a civilised world.

"How do you like the food?" Patience asked Emmanuel as soon as they started to eat.

"You should know what I think of your go-come-back-come-no-go by now, shouldn't you?" Emmanuel retorted, tired of being asked the same old question every time he sat down to eat something she cooked.

"I know" Patience replied. "Why can't you just repeat what you've told me before spontaneously? Why must you be overly conscious of overdoing everything? Why are you always so tense when it comes to showing love?"

She paused briefly to scrutinise him, then added, sulking, "You can keep trying to hide your feelings. And I'll keep reminding you that as a woman, I make my feelings known. I love hearing nice things about myself, even from a boyfriend who behaves like a village chief."

Then she lowered her voice, stretched her hand out and touched his arm, saying, "Emmanuel, you must stop treating me as if I'm a banana stump or a pleasure machine."

Her gentle and piercing voice made Emmanuel feel guilty, but he pretended otherwise. "Haven't I always shown you my love and care, in my own clumsy way at least?" he countered, sounding like someone created after God had lost his magic formula for romantics.

"You've shown me that you love or care for a blanket and a food flask. And you are indeed right about being clumsy!" Patience applied more salt to his fresh wounds of guilt.

Her tongue sharp and aggressive, she withdrew her hand abruptly.

"What else have you done?" she challenged. "Remind me since I am so forgetful," She mocked.

She gazed at him spitefully, her fork stuck in her food, and her hands in a tug of war over the table napkin. When he continued to eat as if he wasn't listening to her, she stormed even louder: "All that matters is your greedy self, your stomach, your lusts! Pleasure harvester, that's all you are! Or is there more? Eh? Eh? You delight in not being tender, even when that seems the only thing a man like you could possibly offer. That's the whole problem with you men," her mind flashed back at her severed relationship with Richard, her ex-fiancé, "thinking that we are there just to be hurt and used." Staring into his eyes, she added, "You complain about the city milking the village like a cow, but you forget that men milk women just as much. Are women not your cows?"

Her anger had brought her to the brink of tears.

"We are not going to replace eating with talking, are we?"

Touched, lost for words or both, Emmanuel was out to appease. He didn't want Patience to continue in the same vein, lest things degenerate into a quarrel, something he didn't wish to be dragged into on a hot Sunday afternoon.

"I really like this meal, and would like some peace to enjoy it. Marvellous, your cooking has always been," he told her. "After eight months, there ought to be no doubt how well I love your cooking, looks, your all."

He leaned forward to kiss her on the cheek, but she backed away, still sulking. He stood up and went round to her, still feeling guilty.

"Let me repeat what I have said countless times before: I love your cooking, always have." He was being diplomatic. "And I love a lot more."

Patience gave him a stern stare.

"I really do, and always will," he repeated, still trying to embrace her. She still wouldn't let him.

Finally, after much pleading on his part, Patience gave in, and showed her forgiveness.

"I love you, and I love your food forever and ever" he kissed her on the cheek, and made the sign of the cross.

"Amen," she joked and giggled.

"Then may our catering Father Longstay deliver us eternal ladles and spoons," he stretched the humour.

"And grant even the jobless their daily bread," Patience laughed, stuffing his mouth with *Ekwang* to prevent him from corrupting the Lord's Prayer further.

"You don't hope to go to Heaven when you die, do you?" she giggled again. "You can't, even if you try. The gates of Heaven are armed with the best bouncers to keep gatecrashers at bear. Imagine that you were last seen in a place of worship over eight months ago! And that wasn't even under normal circumstances! You thought of the church only when you were stranded, homeless. Pagan you are ... the Devil's claws!"

"If I miss going to Heaven because I'm pagan, what shall Miss Blasphemy and Hypocrisy miss it for?" He laughed a long and mocking laugh.

"In any case, no more of this," he said, succumbing yet to another spoonful from his merciless Patience.

"Enough of this joking!"

Patience was ready with another spoonful, which he tried to resist saying, "You don't want to take me seriously. You complain of love blankets and food flasks. You joke when you shouldn't and are serious when you should be joking. Then you blame me for not understanding women!"

"Who is joking?" she feigned seriousness.

"Do you mean that you accept my proposal?"

"What proposal?"

"The one you know," Emmanuel smiled.

"You see, who is joking with whom?" she pretended to be disappointed.

Emmanuel asked Patience to stand up, and after sitting in her place he made her sit on his lap. She loved it. He thought that she looked especially beautiful this Sunday afternoon, and felt an upsurge of feeling for her. He couldn't resist whispering something sweet into her ear, and the way her eyes brightened with pleasure brought him pride and reassurance. Even if the University of Asieyam and academics had waved him a final farewell, Emmanuel thought, his Patience wasn't quite so ready to play him a similar trick, despite the instigations she was receiving. This he could read from her eyes. And what could be more reassuring than that? Patience was his and he was determined to be hers for as long as she wanted him and him her.

It was more than a week now since his bitter exchange with Madame Jeannette Mvodo and since Patience threatened to throw him out if he didn't change his attitude on getting a job. His meeting with Pius and George, his abortive attempt to buy roasted beef from Oumarou, together with other factors, had pushed him to re-examine his hard-line position on the issue. Since then he had repeatedly asked himself:

If the city could afford to smile upon Oumarou, a mere refugee with a blotted past and without a future in war torn Warzone, what more of him, a rightful national of Mimboland? Was he that forsaken that even the wretched dregs of war such as Oumarou could ridicule him? He had also thought seriously about the prospect of going to study in Kuti, and had decided to discuss the matter with Peaphweng Mukong, after, of course, recounting his Asieyam misadventure from start to finish. He had even enquired already, and had found out that not every student who went to study in Kuti was from rich parents or on scholarship. Some born and bred in poverty had made it to Kuti, chiefly because the value of the Kuti currency in the black market was very low. In fact, so low that with barely a couple of hundred thousand MIM dollars, a careful student could study comfortably for a year. This was an inspiring piece of news he wished he had come by five months ago. It was never too late to study, especially for a person with a glowing ambition like his. After a few mental calculations, he was able to establish how much money he might need. If he could work for a year, he reckoned he just might save enough money for a three-year stay at the National University of Kuti, the nearest by foot and lorry from Abehema through Alfredsburg or Kaizerbosch.

"I have some good news for you, Patience," he announced.

"And what may that be?" she expected nothing dramatic.

"I've decided to find a job, no matter what job," he told her. "Not as receptionist though," he hastened to qualify. "The problem is that I can't be a receptionist and

140

avoid thinking of myself as doormat to the same haughty fiends who signed my death warrant at Asieyam. I just cannot bear the thought of me as usher or facilitator to debauchery. Any other job would suit me for now, while the search for something better continues. I apologise if my announcement fails to satisfy your expectations."

There was no need for him to be apologetic. The mere fact that he had overcome his disinclination to work overjoyed Patience. She jumped up and pulled him off his seat and kissed and embraced him deeply and warmly. The eating was temporarily suspended, as Patience dramatised her gratitude. Satisfied, they resumed eating, and started feeding each other alternately.

For the first time in recent weeks, they both felt how sweet love could be, when there were no barriers or ill feelings to temper it. Emmanuel for one was at last convinced that all anyone really needed was to discover the right person and the right attitude, and love would be sweeter than the honey Peaphweng Mukong used to hide away for emergency medicinal purposes, and which as a child Emmanuel couldn't avoid stealing, no matter how hard he tried to be the good boy. Now he felt there was every reason for his relationship with Patience to blossom.

Their meal over, Patience asked Emmanuel into the bedroom. She was still to tell him her reason for cooking *Ekwang*, although he had now forgotten all about it. Instead, he was trying to call her attention to the fact that she might be late for the Camp-Kupeh Cultural and Development Association (CAKUCDA) meeting, which she attended every Sunday afternoon as a matter of primary patriotism. She said there was something she had to talk to him about, something that couldn't wait. So they went into the bedroom and sat face to face on the bed. They were both anxious: Patience to tell her tale, and Emmanuel to hear the story that couldn't wait.

"I had a most disturbing dream last night," Patience began rather abruptly.

Emmanuel's heart sank. Not another nightmare, he thought, quite tense.

"I couldn't tell you about it this morning because I was in a hurry to go to Sunday mass." Her sudden change of countenance almost frightened him.

"What about?" He wore a worried face. He was becoming quite scared of dreams.

"It is most terrifying," said she in tears. "It was a very horrifying dream."

If simply thinking of the dream could make Patience shed tears, Emmanuel didn't know what to expect. But he couldn't bear her weeping the way she did, so he did his best to cheer her up, and encouraged her until she was able to recount her dream with only intermittent outbursts of tears.

"I dreamt we had a baby," Patience resumed her narration.

"Which is a good thing," he interrupted with a sigh of relief.

"Yes, but that isn't the whole dream, is it?" She was slightly irritated.

"Sorry, go on," he apologized tensely.

"I will, if you promise not to interrupt again," Patience said. She paused for a while and gazed at Emmanuel until she was satisfied he was ready to listen, then continued.

"It was a terrible dream. It was your idea that we go to your home village of Abehema, to present our baby to your parents and people. At first I hesitated, but eventually I gave in when you said that going to Abehema was the only way I could come to be accepted by your people. I was ready to convince your parents that I'm the type of woman they would love to be their daughter-in-law. We bought a lot of presents for your family – soap, kerosene, cooking utensils and so on. These items we took with us. We also carried certain essentials for ourselves and for the baby, enough of everything to keep us going for the couple of weeks that was our intention to be there. When we arrived, there was no Abehema to be found."

"What! Did I hear you well?" he couldn't believe his ears. "What did you say?"

"Em-m-a, Em-m-a, Emmanuel. T-h-e-r-e w-a-s n-o A-b-e-he-m-a t-o b-e f-o-u-n-d," she spelled it out a second time, unable to stop weeping.

"Yes, Abehema was nowhere... nowhere. At first I wouldn't believe you, but from your sincere and innocent countenance, I knew you weren't pulling my leg. So I accepted that the village of Abehema had actually existed. In its place was an extensive sea of water. You made me understand that the lake by which your village was known must have over flooded its banks to drown the entire village. Your parents were nowhere to be found either. In fact, there was no sign of life. And all we could conclude was that everyone must have perished in the flood. There was nothing for us to do. But for our baby, we might have made one desperate move or another.

"When we could no longer weep, we decided to come back here and alert the authorities that something strange had happened in your village. At first no one would take us seriously. Some of the authorities we contacted didn't even know where Abehema was. They doubted our sanity with questions such as: 'Vous êtes fous ou quoi?'; 'Où est Abehema? Vous dites que c'est un village ici au Mimboland?'

"Eventually, though, they came to take us more seriously. So a national commission was set up to investigate the tragedy. At this point the dream fizzled out. I've been unable to interpret it, though I'm so horrified."

Patience was troubled. "All through mass this morning, I thought of it, but was quite unable to make head or tail out of the dream."

For a while Emmanuel sat deep in thought, his head buried in his palms. When at last he looked up, all he said was, "I don't have an interpretation for your dream either."

He hated to make her more disturbed by recounting his nightmare of a week ago. Standing up and moving towards the mirror on the table, he said, "You better leave for your meeting now, if you don't want to be fined for late-coming. I may have an interpretation ready by the time you come home."

He went back to her on the bed and said, almost in a whisper, "All will be fine. There's nothing to fear." Then kissing her briefly on the cheek, he helped her up.

Patience took a glass of water out to the verandah where she cleaned her face. She returned to the bedroom and freshened up with makeup and perfume, and was ready for CAKUCDA, her crocodile-skin handbag hanging over her left shoulder.

"Just one brief question before you go," Emmanuel stopped and pulled her back to the bed.

He cleared his throat and mustered the courage he needed, and asked her, "Are you pregnant, or was it just in the dream?"

"I don't know for sure," replied Patience with a smile. "I suspect I am. Why do you ask? Does it frighten you?" She eyed him with cunning.

"Me? Frightened? What is there to be frightened of?" Emmanuel tried to play the tough guy.

"No! Not fright, but just to have the pleasure of knowing that fatherhood is round the corner." He bent forward and kissed her.

"For how long do you think you've been in this state?" he asked as he escorted her out of the room, his voice slightly tremulous.

"Just over a month maybe," she smiled again. "Remember the day you forced me to drink that Manawa stuff of yours that hit me on the head like a hammer?"

Emmanuel nodded.

"I think that was the day it happened."

"And you've kept it from me all this while?" he feigned disbelief. "Such good news? You can be so secretive!"

"What would you have done?" she challenged, but not with an intention to hurt. "It isn't too late to start buying the clothing, if that's what you mean." She giggled.

"Not at all," he replied with a smile. "I'll walk you to a taxi," he volunteered, closing the door behind them.

Together, hand in hand, they walked to the road, something they couldn't remember when they last did.

8

"**P**atience," Emmanuel murmured, as soon as Patience had showered and come to bed beside him.

"I've thought a lot about the dream you narrated to me this afternoon, and about others I've had before, and strongly feel that I ought to go home to Abehema and see if all is well. Dreams generally do not reflect reality, but sometimes they do. Some dreams tell us certain things before they actually come to pass. And just in case these dreams we've had are signals of any kind, I've decided to go home. If anything were to happen I'd want to be with my people before it does.

"Already I feel overburdened with guilt, especially for clinging on here in the city when I should have returned to face them with the bitter truth about my years of futility in Asieyam. And unless I go home to explain things and apologise to my parents and people, I won't be at peace with my conscience."

Patience felt the dejection in his tone, and was sorry for him. What she didn't know was that her dream, like his nightmare the week before, had awakened his fears and emotions of insecurity. It had also brought back, in an even stronger form, his pessimism and inclination to see his mishaps as intended consequences of conspiracies by the powerful against him and his downtrodden folks. The more he saw the dreams as strange and unusual, the stronger his instinct that Abehema was in grave danger.

As usual, Patience exceedingly understood. She cheered him up with words of optimism, and cuddled him.

"That's what I thought of suggesting," she whispered. "I didn't know how you might take it," she added, holding him tighter. "I fully agree that you should go home and see what things are like with your family and people. I'm glad you've finally decided not to let the bitter experiences at Asieyam continue to blur your vision. As I've always maintained, it's no use lying to your parents because they would find out anyways, and because it gives the impression that you think you are to blame for what happened. I'm confident your parents will understand, and that you will be forgiven. So don't let any of this bother you anymore. At least, don't let it continue to numb you."

Comforting though Patience tried to be, Emmanuel couldn't quite avoid feeling guilty. His conscience was so assailing that he buried his face in her bosom, choked by tears, an emotion he rarely expressed in her presence.

Stroking his beard Patience said, "As soon as you have found out and everything is alright, do come back to me." She said slowly. "I've started missing you even before you are gone."

"Me too," he managed to whisper, bringing her closer. "I'll come back as soon as I can. There's no need staying long in the village if all is well."

Then, still thinking of his village and its problems, he said, "I remember reading somewhere that villages are inhabited by the dead and dying, and that no one with any future would go to settle forever in one. Forward-looking urbanites might pay their home villages a courtesy visit now and again to obtain cheap food, bury dying relatives, or offer sacrifices to disgruntled ancestors. They stay for a day or two, perhaps for a week at most, then disappear to the city again, where they can claim to come from this or that village, from the safe distance of the insulation offered by modern worldviews and expectations."

He paused briefly before remarking, as if it had just occurred to him: "Isn't this true of Abehema? Don't our dreams smell of death and dying? And have I not been away from my poor folks for God knows how long, chasing after a civilisation that is chasing me away?" His voice was muffled by sobs he couldn't withhold any more. Hard masculine tears rolled stealthily down his cheeks and were sucked in by his beard.

Patience felt the wetness with her hand but said nothing.

Still sobbing Emmanuel said, "I will shave it tomorrow," referring to his beard. "The dreadlocks as well," he added. "That too is coming down tomorrow." Stroking his beard as if for the last time, he concluded, "My parents must recognise me as the son they saw off to the so-called Great City. And above all, I don't want to frighten our son when he is born."

Then he fell silent, as Patience thought hard. Where on earth could he have got the idea that their child would be a son, hardly four weeks into her pregnancy? Neither of them spoke again until they were overtaken by slumber.

9

It was the third day since Chief Ngain had been arrested by the gendarmes and bundled into a van. Nothing had been heard of him, apart from the fact that he was being held at the Gendarmerie in Kaizerbosch. The village of Abehema had no idea whether he was going to be tried in court or released. According to the modern law of Mimboland, a gift from Muzunguland, Chief Ngain was considered guilty of the murder of Ardo Buba until he could ably prove otherwise. In the past, when there was no such thing as civilised law from Muzunguland, the village of Abehema would have approached the case from an entirely different angle. The village authorities would never have started with the assumption that a suspect was guilty until he could prove his innocence. The suspect's freedom was guaranteed until his guilt had been established beyond reasonable doubt. They would never have trampled upon an individual on the basis of suspicion and hearsay alone. Rather, they would work day and night without relent, meticulously gathering evidence from witnesses and through divination, until there was enough to warrant a loss of liberty. How things are always changing for the worse, in the name of civilisation!

Abehema had been three days without a leader. No one thought it a healthy thing to deprive the human body of the head that coordinates its activities. What use was a hand without the thumb? The villagers believed strongly that, just as the thumb wasn't capable of much without the fingers, so too were the fingers useless without the thumb. Finding a thumb to coordinate the activities of Abehema thus became an urgent problem for the anxious fingers of the village.

Nothing would move well, no one would sleep with soundness and peace of mind, until the leadership crisis was resolved. Abehema needed a leader of some kind to settle its accounts with the ancestors, and to keep life's train on the rails while Chief Ngain awaited trial in Kaizerbosch. Much had happened to bring disharmony between the people and the world of their ancestors. Abehema desperately needed someone on whom to confer authority, and whom they could ask to bridge the critical gap between the living and the dead.

So the notables decided to hold an emergency meeting at the marketplace, which they preferred to the palace purely on the grounds of security. No one was ready to risk his life by holding a meeting in the deserted palace of a wicked chief. Who could say what potent medicines he had buried at the entrance to the palace, or in his conference hall, to kill anyone who visited his lair while he was away? The ancestors had been right in advocating the use of long ladles when dishing out of the same earthenware pot as the devil. Just as the ancestors had warned, a pot too hot to handle suffers from a broken mouth.

The notables responded promptly. Those who came early grouped themselves together in front of Peaphweng Mukong's market-house, chosen for the meeting because it was the most spacious in the market. The other structures were little huts of thatch, where women and children displayed their foodstuffs and liquor for sale on market days. A majority of the notables were traditionally dressed in locally woven, elaborately embroidered, multicoloured gowns, an indication of the importance and respect they attached to the occasion. Peaphweng Mukong, who was among the early arrivals, was also dressed traditionally, but it was public knowledge that he felt more attached to his winter coat, which everyone knew through repeated reminders that Ravageur the Muzungulander, his white friend, had given him. It was certain that as soon as the meeting was over, Peaphweng Mukong would replace his gown with the coat, which he had brought along in a big raffia bag.

He asked the notables to drink the beer of their choice from his off-licence. Nothing was as prestigious to the men of Abehema as beer brewed in the cities. City beer offered them much-needed respite from the monotony of the local corn brew, *Kang*, which to them was definitely inferior to what came from the city in bottles firmly capped. There was the famous story of a white anthropologist who had trekked for days to study the heart of the kingdom of Kakakum, and who had been stunned to find city beer in a village that seemed almost entirely removed from civilisation. He was said to have remarked, "In Mimboland, beer is a thousand times more pervading than the government's messages of development and unity. It even refreshes parts that have never before been penetrated by car, radio or President Longstay's pervasive photos."

When all the notables had come and had each had something to drink (most enjoyed drinking Manpasman, which they called 'king-size' or 'chomeur'), Peaphweng Mukong ordered his store-boy out, and turned the market-house into a temporary meeting place. Once everyone was in, the door was shut and bolted. The meeting began.

Top of the agenda was the election of an interim head to coordinate the efforts of the notables. The issue didn't pose great difficulties, though its position on the agenda might have suggested it would. Peaphweng Mukong was nominated and became head by acclamation. For not only was he a distant cousin of wicked Chief Ngain and therefore of some royal blood, he was also the most popular among the common folk. The election done, the meeting continued under his chairmanship. He thanked his fellow notables for giving him the opportunity to serve his village during a time of need. He promised to sacrifice body and soul for Abehema, should it come to that. Reminding his peers that a trying time called for men with a dedicated sense of patriotism, he invited them to pledge their love and unflinching commitment to Abehema. He was applauded and reassured.

"Let's then get onto the crucial issue of the day," Peaphweng Mukong told the notables, his election speech done. "We know that Chief Ngain is locked up in Kaizerbosch in connection with Ardo Buba's death. We equally know that telling the gendarmes about Ardo Buba's death was, to the best of our knowledge, the most appropriate way of saving our people from ignominy. We also know that this episode has distanced our ancestors from us. That is what we have to act fast to undo. Restore the traditional harmony of this vital relationship, and do so fast should be our ardent concern for the moment. We can't say precisely in what way Chief Ngain was involved in desecrating the land he was supposed to sanctify. To find out, we must work hand in hand with two diviners – our very own Peaphweng Ndyu, whom I couldn't invite to attend this meeting because he had travelled, and Wabuah of Kakakum. How best do you think we should proceed?" Peaphweng Mukong asked, pausing for an answer as his eyes flashed round the room.

It was clear that he looked embarrassed in his embroidered gown. If he had to be leader, he must learn to wear what traditional leaders were used to wearing, not the winter coat from Ravageur, his good white Muzungulander friend.

The notables didn't tarry with their suggestions. They appeared to have expected the question. Some suggested they contact Wabuah of Kakakum straightaway, for the sake of credibility. They argued that Chief Ngain and the outside world would disbelieve any divination by Peaphweng Ndyu, who was most likely to be seen as an ally of the notables. Others thought otherwise. They believed there was nothing wrong with asking Peaphweng Ndyu to divine for the village. No one ignored Peaphweng Ndyu's competence as a diviner, nor the wisdom he had inherited from his father who preceded and initiated him into divination. Moreover, the need for divination was primarily to restore internal harmony, not really to convince the outside world, as some saw it.

Peaphweng Mukong didn't face any difficulty bridging the two points of view.

"I respect your concern and wise suggestions," he told them. "Your viewpoints are indeed complementary. So, why don't we seek indisputable credibility by consulting both diviners, and then comparing their findings? I'm pretty certain that should the findings of these two agree, even our staunchest enemies would be humbled. If you don't object, we can listen to Peaphweng Ndyu's divination tomorrow, and to Wabuah's the day after. Meanwhile we must send someone down to Yenseh to ask Wabuah up to Abehema for an emergency. What do you have to say about that, peers?" he asked, respectfully.

The accord was unanimous. The notables applauded Peaphweng Mukong once more. None of them regretted having participated in making him leader. He was the right man for Abehema in its hour of need. So far he had shown himself equal to the task. Though this was only a beginning, there was no reason to think things wouldn't continue the way they had started. The notables agreed to meet in the evening of the following day to listen to Peaphweng Ndyu's divination. Meanwhile, each and every one swore to say nothing about the just concluded meeting once outside the market-house. It was also agreed that Phwe, a young man who was practising long-distance running in preparation for recruitment into the national army, should race to Yenseh early in the morning and tell Wabuah that Abehema was desperate for his services. Then the notables shook hands with one another and parted, each wending his way home.

Peaphweng Mukong handed the keys back to the store-boy, who took control again. He had an important thing to do before retiring for the day. If Peaphweng Ndyu had to divine for Abehema tomorrow, he needed to be informed on time, so he could prepare adequately. The message was too important to send any of his children to deliver it. Hoping to meet the diviner at home, Peaphweng Mukong decided to go there himself. Before setting out to climb the long tiresome hills, Peaphweng Mukong changed out of the cumbersome gown he had worn purposefully for the meeting, into the winter coat he had brought along in his raffia bag.

10

It was late in the night when Peaphweng Mukong left the diviner's compound for home. He was satisfied, but had had to wait for long because Peaphweng Ndyu wasn't at home when he arrived. The diviner was a committed son of the soil, ever ready to sacrifice his personal pursuits for public goals. Like many other men of goodwill in Abehema, Peaphweng Mukong had a lot of admiration for this man, the very epitome of humility. When Peaphweng Ndyu returned and found the notable waiting, he apologised at length for not being there to welcome the dignitary, and readily agreed to postpone a scheduled trip to Tchang to attend to his people. He knew a son in need was a son indeed.

Though it was pitch dark, Peaphweng Mukong refused the offer of a torch. He insisted he knew his way home well enough to arrive at his compound safe and sound. Peaphweng Ndyu lived up in the hills, far away from the main settlement in the valley where Peaphweng Mukong and the greater half of the village lived. Though people had complained that his compound was too isolated, the diviner rejected all arguments to join the rest of the village and live together as one.

"The fingers of the hand are not the same in length," he would rationalise with a sly look on his wrinkled oblong face. Then, chewing the tobacco he always carried in his mouth except when eating, he would explain himself, spitting at random: "I serve the village better up here than I would if I were down there in the valley with you. I'm like the clairvoyant dog that guards a compound at night from ghosts and men of evil. Without me you in the village would not see or hear the invisible spirits that haunt Abehema every night."

Whenever the bald-headed Peaphweng Ndyu put his argument thus, it was difficult for anyone to continue accusing him of bull-headedness. They could understand the importance of a socialised clairvoyant, someone with the power to see, hear and speak the language of witches at night when evil reigned supreme and the world of the living was most vulnerable, then alert the authorities at dawn. How could the witches be tracked down and sanctioned, if everyone of goodwill were blind and deaf at night?

Somewhere on his way home, Peaphweng Mukong realised how difficult it was to keep to the footpath. He wandered off it too often, and staggered like a drunkard. He didn't think the problem might in part be the alcohol he had drunk, even though he had done something foolish by drinking beer and raffia wine indiscriminately. In any case, he regretted turning down the torch, and he had gone too far from the diviner's compound to return for it. He would rather struggle on, and so he kept going, on faltering feet. He felt something unusual about the footpath, which he had known all his life. He didn't want to believe he was imagining things, or that the alcohol he had taken might be playing tricks on him. Instead he thought, as always, that, having spent all his life in Abehema, he could tell by instinct when something was wrong. And so his feeling that the path tonight was definitely unusual grew.

"Where is this strange rock from?" Peaphweng Mukong wondered aloud, when all of a sudden he hit himself against something hard. Like someone in a trance, he felt the hugeness of the rock stretch across his path, covering the bush beyond. He didn't know this path to have rocks as huge as the one obstructing his passage at the moment. "This can't be an ordinary rock," he muttered, most perplexed. Unable to find his way round the mysterious rock, and his legs beginning to melt as if they were made of wax, Peaphweng Mukong collapsed. He didn't feel quite himself, and couldn't say what was going on. The earth seemed to spin with extraordinary velocity, and he had the impression he was swinging and swaying like a sparrow in a storm. It was like a dream, a strange waking dream taking place somewhere between his conscious and unconscious selves.

In the unusual state he now found himself, Peaphweng Mukong's mind started racing strangely. Forgotten horrors and mysterious imaginings sprang to life like mushrooms in a graveyard, assuming the vicious elegance of an evil forest on a hillside. The distorted phantoms he visualised were either trying to lure him or to frighten him with their enormities. He lost courage and composure. He began to palpitate like a rain-beaten dog. The apparitions were indeed gruesome and nauseous, and the convulsions they caused shattering.

At one point he felt himself transported out of Abehema on a piercing bed of thorns and barbed wire, to an abyss of chilling darkness that smelt of death and the dying. A monstrosity with the face and hands of a human galloped up to him, clacking his teeth with fear and threatening to cut his throat with a trenchant knife of steel. Petrified, he attempted to scream, but was incapable. Shocked and bewildered by his impending loss of blood to the vile vampires that surrounded him with thirsty mugs, he closed his eyes in a desperate quest for salvation. The idea was to evoke his ancestors and God to come to his rescue. Because the forces of evil had already taken control of his mind, his words of prayer remained an unharnessed idea in his unconscious. There had to be a way of escaping the satanic rites in progress, the wanton shedding of innocent blood! These emotional battles were taking place in his subconsciousness, but looked so real to him.

When he finally regained consciousness, Peaphweng Mukong found himself feeling the iron ring on the third finger of his left hand. Wabuah, the Kakakum diviner-healer, had prepared this ring for Peaphweng Mukong's protection against every evil, including the seasoned sorcery of Chief Ngain. Convinced that the ring on his hand had joined forces with God and his ancestors to exorcise the evil spirits that had come in all forms and shapes to challenge him and seek his lifeblood, Peaphweng Mukong recited the magic incantations Wabuah had instructed him to say whenever he felt himself in difficulties.

He then tried his legs and attempted to rise. It was easy, his strength had returned, though he still panted from fear and exhaustion. He tried to feel the rock, but it was gone, dumping him a few metres away from the footpath. Peaphweng Mukong felt around the immediate vicinity, but there was no rock half as large as the one he was certain had blocked his passage. "I said it, didn't I?" he whispered, as if in triumph. "I said this was not an ordinary rock, but someone trying to play games with me." He heaved a sigh and resumed his journey, thankful to Wabuah and the ancestors, and thankful to God above.

Suddenly the skies began to rumble with thunder. Peaphweng Mukong quickened his pace. He prayed to reach home in time to avoid the impending downpour. The flash of lightning helped him as much as it menaced. Whenever there was a stroke of lightning, he tried to make a mental sketch of the meanders of the footpath. He wasn't always successful. Sometimes the stroke was so overwhelming it caused him to fall instead. The situation grew worse as the storm developed. Mustering courage, he kept going, repeatedly whispering to the ancestors to intercede with God on his behalf. "Tomorrow's meeting would be a failure should anything happen to me," he thought, regretting he had come himself or at least alone to invite Peaphweng Ndyu. He was sure one of his sons would have run up the hills, informed the diviner, and returned home long before it was fully dark. This wasn't the sort of hour for a man his age to be struggling unaccompanied along a footpath this remote. What if, having failed to block his path with the rock, the witches appeared as a lion or leopard to frighten him and steal his soul? He absent-mindedly touched for comfort the potent ring Wabuah had prepared for him.

He murmured a few more words of prayer as well. "Fathers of Abehema, do not let anything evil befall me before dawn. The people are in need of my services, my selfless services," he prayed. "I'm not fighting for any personal glories," he assured the ancestors and God. "Everything I do, I do for Abehema. I am for life not death, to make not mar. I need your blessings. Abehema yearns for forgiveness, love and hope."

The rain didn't start lightly as it often did. Rather, there was a sudden torrential downpour as if Lucifer had torn the skies apart with a razor. Soon Peaphweng Mukong was soaked to the bones. His winter coat was heavy on him, and his baggy trousers stuck to his skin in the manner of ticks. He was angry about what was happening, though he blamed no one for it, not even himself. To him, this was all part of the sacrifice, the inevitable price he had to pay for being 'a man of the people'. Hope kept him going. He staggered and fell with Christly similitude, but wasn't deterred. As he shivered with cold, it occurred to him that a fever might develop that could hinder his presiding over tomorrow's divination. "God forbid!"

Rainwater roared through the gullies like stampeded cattle. The thunder groaned in the manner of replenished oxen. The lightning flashed like the machete of *Bli*, the Kakakum mourner-masked spirit. Peaphweng Mukong was as meek as a lamb, picking his way with hope through an enormous mountain of impediments. His mind was torturing itself with conflicting thoughts. But it felt good he could think at all, for thinking served as an outlet for the frustrating tensions that were mounting in him. He thought of the lake in particular, and wondered just how much it would overflow in the morning. The prospect worried him. "Should it continue raining at this rate," he told himself, "it wouldn't be impossible for the swelling lake to swallow up the entire village." The ancestors had to forbid this. It was their sacred duty to protect Abehema from harm, all harm – whether by external or internal agents.

It happened so fast. Lightning flashed. The heavens roared. The earth shook. The ferocious storm lifted and smashed Peaphweng Mukong against a huge tree trunk. Unconsciousness beneath the tree, blood oozed from his bruises.

When Peaphweng Mukong regained consciousness, he was astonished to find himself at home in bed with Ngonsu, his eldest wife, mother of his oldest son and pride, Kwanga. It was incredible He couldn't believe it. How did it come about? His first reaction was to inspect himself. There was no sign of bruises anywhere on his body. Neither did he feel any pain. There was the strong smell of lavender on the ring he wore. Wabuah had explained that would happen every time the ring was actively protecting him against evil forces. What were these evil forces, which had decided to attack him at such a critical period in the life of his village? Why was he in bed with Ngonsu, when all he could remember was being lifted up and slammed down by the storm, on his way home from Peaphweng Ndyu's compound? He was more than dismayed. He just couldn't understand a thing. He shook his wife to wake her. Perhaps she could throw some light on the mystery.

Ngonsu was simply stunned by her husband's bizarre story. She found it hard to believe. Although witchcraft was part of daily life in Abehema, stories such as the one he was recounting were too unusual to be accepted just like that. To believe in witchcraft did not mean one was impervious to ordinary logic. It meant ordinary logic plus. There was nothing on him to confirm the fable he wanted to force down her throat. If he was certain he hadn't just dreamt it, why hadn't he greeted her with the bizarre story as soon as he returned home? Why had he behaved at first as if nothing unusual had happened, only to wake her up a few hours later with a story this strange? Ngonsu nearly stopped her husband midway through his tale, to ask him to go back to sleep and cease dreaming strange dreams. How did he expect her to believe his fabrication about the rock, the torrential rain, the storm, the lightning, the smash, and the bruises? Everyone in the valley, she was sure, could bear her out, that it had neither rained nor thundered nor stormed that night. From where did he get his story? Was he sure he hadn't had too much to drink? Why were there no signs of his alleged bruises? As far as Ngonsu was concerned, either her husband had had a confounding dream, or he had been confounded to the point of hallucination by too much alcohol. No explanation short of this could make sense to her or anyone else.

Peaphweng Mukong himself didn't know what to make of his experience. He knew what he had gone through, but now all seemed like a mystery to him. When in the morning his neighbours confirmed there had not been as much as a drop of rain that night, and that there was neither a storm nor thunder nor lightning, Peaphweng Mukong asked Ngonsu not to mention a word of what he had told her to anyone. This wasn't the sort of thing Ngonsu would naturally have liked to discuss with others. It sounded too farfetched and would make her look ridiculous. So for one of the rare times in her life, she didn't find a secret such an impossible thing to keep.

Peaphweng Mukong remained puzzled by what he was positive had happened. The experience was too heavy to brush aside. He believed it was premonitory of impending terror. Whether personal or collective he couldn't say, nor could he tell how or when it was going to strike. He decided he must tell Wabuah of his experience when he came to divine the day after tomorrow. There was no doubt in his mind that, were it not for the ring Wabuah had cooked with potent herbs and roots for him, Abehema would have been telling a different story about him. Instead of trying to doubt his story, Ngonsu would have been mourning over his corpse! The evil forces, whoever they were, had tried him and found a nut impossible to crack.

11

Peaphweng Ndyu's divination was long and exciting. It was also his most elaborate as far as the notables could recollect, which made him all the more credible.

He used the sophisticated technique of combining cowries with the stiff sharp quills of the porcupine to unmask hidden causes and effects. This was a clear sign of the maturity he had attained in his field. Perhaps the day might come when he would be able to shake hands in public with Wabuah of Kakakum as a professional equal. Becoming a good diviner was like planting an avocado seedling and watching it grow. It thrived on patience, attention, and constant practice. There was no need for hurry, because hurrying usually makes the child break a calabash of water, and earn maternal smacks in place of thanks. His vocation was one that called for reflection and precaution before every step. No child runs who has not learnt first to walk. Though he looked forward to that day when his name would be mentioned together with Wabuah's, Peaphweng Ndyu was careful not to spoil the soup with too much salt.

Meanwhile, the notables watched Peaphweng Ndyu manipulate his divination kit with great anxiety. They were thirsty for knowledge of the facts surrounding Ardo Buba's strange death.

The room fell silent when Peaphweng Ndyu indicated he was ready to tell them his findings. The atmosphere was tense. The only thing that reminded him of his audience being alive was their breathing, which filtered through from the other side of the room where they sat with expectant stiffness. He raised his head and sent a brief and searching look through the group of notables in front of him.

His eyes alighted on Peaphweng Mukong's face and were greeted with a warm smile. Peaphweng Mukong understood the message, so he stood up and assured the diviner that everyone was ready to hear him.

Peaphweng Ndyu thanked Peaphweng Mukong and saluted the notables. He said he was glad to be of service to his village and promised to say nothing but what his divination was able to reveal. For he, as they knew already, wasn't the type who divined for fame or material benefit. It was his humble duty to say what he saw, and not what he wanted or was expected to see. This important clarification made, he plunged into his divination ritual. The notables followed with keen interest.

A preliminary shaking, pouring, listening and at times conversing with his divination paraphernalia gave Peaphweng Ndyu something to say to the tense notables.

"My dear notables," he began, caressing his baldness with one hand, and manipulating his kit with the other. "What my divination has revealed is shocking and bizarre. It is something bound to fill you with consternation, just as it has done to me. My instruments are by no means mistaken about who killed Ardo Buba. They have told me everything concerning this sad issue. It is your place to know every detail of it."

He paused to fetch a dark little bag made of human hair, which he shook and pressed as he recounted his divination results. The bag made a hissing sound from time to time, and Peaphweng Ndyu listened very keenly before he said anything.

"A pot too hot suffers a broken mouth," he began with a popular proverb.

The notables sat up, all ears.

"My quills and cowries all point to one thing: that Chief Ngain coveted Ardo Buba's cattle. He wanted to have them for himself, in order to sell them and become a rich leader like his counterparts elsewhere. So he thought of how best he could do this, without compromising his dignity or risking his position and prestige. He knew Ardo Buba wasn't the type of person he could easily pocket. In the language of my profession, he found Ardo Buba to be *well cooked*. Therefore, in order to succeed, he devised a highly sophisticated scheme into which he hoped to drag Ardo Buba. He succeeded. This scheme didn't include death by any means. My quills and cowries are firm on that. Chief Ngain never intended to kill Ardo Buba. What interested him was to impregnate Ardo Buba with fear and anxiety. For, he thought, once he had succeeded in doing this, having his way with Ardo Buba would be just a matter of course."

Peaphweng Ndyu paused to read the questions in the air.

"What was this scheme of his? You are all asking. I can see you're curious and anxious to know. Rest assured, for my quills and cowries have found everything out for you. Just let me consult my prompter."

Again he paused to shake and press his dark human-hair bag, which made the hissing sound over and over again. Every time this happened, he brought the bag closer to his ear and kept shaking and pressing. At last he spoke again, using another popular proverb to introduce what he had to say.

"It was by sucking more blood than it needed that the mosquito got crushed. Three days before Ardo Buba was found floating on the lake, Chief Ngain had sent Princess Tem to deliver a little package of kola-nuts to him. These weren't ordinary kola-nuts by any means. All fifteen in the package were smeared with some medicine. Whoever ate them would do as the chief willed. Ardo Buba fell headlong into the trap, for he very much loved to eat kola-nuts, as did his subjects, in accordance with their culture. As soon as he ate a lobe, he began to say and do things beyond his control. Chief Ngain had taken control of his mind and body."

Peaphweng Mukong was thankful his ancestors had prevented him from being victimized as well. He wondered what would have become of him and Abehema had Chief Ngain succeeded in making him eat the treated kola-nuts as well. He shuddered as his mind wandered back to the recent dramatic confrontation between himself and Chief Ngain. "It's true that no medicine, no matter how strong, can be stronger than the blessings of the ancestors," he reminded himself. What of last night? Wasn't it possible that Chief Ngain had succeeded after all? Why had he lost his senses to the extent that he had become totally unaware of what actually happened to him? He heaved a heavy sigh and listened to the diviner.

"The very first thing Chief Ngain did was to make Ardo Buba wander out of his home far away in the Hiseng hills, towards our mysterious lake very late at night. Ardo Buba wandered around the lake like a forsaken calf or a somnambulist, quite oblivious of the risks he ran by being out alone by the lake in the heart of the night, a time when only spirits and fortified men are free to move about or venture around a lake which none of us has mastered. It was cold and there was a heavy storm. Though he knew where he was, Ardo Buba didn't know what had brought him there. His heart beat faster as the storm intensified. There was thunder and lightning as well. In fact, it was a time of night when no ordinary person with only two eyes would venture out just like that. Ardo Buba could hear strange noises coming from the lake. Overcome by fear, he climbed up one of the trees that surrounded the lake, hoping that the noises would soon subside. He was mistaken. The noises only grew in intensity and the lake became stranger than we have ever known it.

"Ardo Buba couldn't believe his eyes. He saw someone climb out of the lake on what appeared to be the longest bamboo ladder in existence. This strange person, who was extremely tall and covered from head to toe in white calico, held a little calabash in his left hand and an ox-horn cup in his right hand. Once on the bank of the lake, he flashed his eyes around suspiciously. Convinced perhaps that no one was watching, he began to carry the water of the lake with the cup and to fill the calabash. Ardo Buba was stunned to see that though so small, the calabash wouldn't fill. It continued to gulp, until all the water of the lake had been drained into it. The strange person then corked the calabash and hid it somewhere in the grass. Then he climbed down the ladder into a village that mysteriously sprang up like a group of mushrooms, where a while before there had been nothing but lake.

"For a while Ardo Buba didn't know what to do. Then an idea struck him. He came down from the tree and took a timid look into the strange village. It was bustling with life. People moved up and down in what looked like a marketplace. Perhaps it was their market day. Ardo Buba wondered why these strange people should prefer a nocturnal market under moonlight. What if he found the frightful stranger's little calabash, uncorked it, and poured the water into the village down below? Without hesitating, but with the absent-mindedness that is typical of those under a spell, he rushed for the calabash and did just that. The lake re-emerged, but the result was catastrophic. Chief Ngain's charm must have gone to sleep. Or rather, the ancestors must have said enough is enough. They weren't prepared to have as chief someone who behaved irresponsibly, and made mockery of a sacred place. In a wink, a fierce swarm of honey bees emerged from the lake and stung Ardo Buba to death. His swollen dead body fell into the water, from which it was eventually retrieved by Chief Ngain's palace guards and hidden away.

"That's the end of my divination," he concluded rather abruptly. "We all know what has happened since then, don't we?" He asked as he began to assemble his paraphernalia. His smile was triumphant, and rightly so. He had just proven that he was capable of the greatness that only men determined and endowed with a high sense of mission and achievement could attain.

Peaphweng Mukong was the first to recover from the spell the strange story had cast on everyone. He rubbed his eyes vigorously as if to chase away sleep, and stretched out his body. Every notable felt sorry for Peaphweng Mukong anyway. For almost a week he had worked like a donkey to hold the village together under the current crisis, defying hunger and fatigue. The sooner the ordeal was over, the better for him. Not only would the village reward him handsomely, but even more importantly, he would regain the pleasure that derives from a life of peace, quiet and domestic harmony. Meanwhile he thanked Peaphweng Ndyu the diviner for his patriotism and excellent piece of divination. Then he reminded Peaphweng Ndyu of the saying that the obedient child, unlike the headstrong child who stands to lose his fortune to the faithful servant, would always inherit what his parents had willed for him. He also thanked the diviner who was sharing his expertise with Abehema's neighbours who wanted his services, for, "one person's child is only in the womb".

Peaphweng Ndyu went home a satisfied man, to contemplate his trip to Tchang, where many patients were waiting anxiously to be cured of their misfortunes or retrieved from *Msa*, the world beyond of the devil, with luring attractions and risky offers. The divination hadn't taken as long as he had thought it might, leaving him with ample time to reach Tchang and satisfy his clients there as well. His was the life of the typical diviner who seldom slept in peace or at his own home. Society was sick and needed constant attention, and he was pleased to know his services were appreciated wherever he visited. It didn't surprise many that Peaphweng Ndyu had opted to stay celibate all his life, for as he said whenever the question was raised, "Mine would be the freest woman in the neighbourhood, a passion fruit for every man's pleasure but mine." He was too busy to be of conjugal use to any woman however placid.

As Peaphweng Ndyu went home, the notables stayed behind to agree on the next steps to follow. Peaphweng Mukong told them to wait until they had heard Wabuah's version of divination as well. Then, and only then, would they be in a position to assess the situation, and decide how best to go about appeasing their incensed ancestors. He also told them he had personally seen to it that Phwe, the young man who was aspiring to the national army, started his marathon early enough to deliver their message to Wabuah in time. Hopefully, Wabuah would be around tomorrow morning at the latest. So the next divination session was set for the evening of the following day. The notables dispersed for home, shocked but convinced by Peaphweng Ndyu's revelation. Would Wabuah of Kakakum confirm or differ? That was the question in every mind as the notables left for home.

12

If someone mischievous had suggested that Peaphweng
Ndyu and Wabuah of Kakakum had met and decided
upon what to say before being invited to divine, not one
notable would have doubted him. Wabuah's version of
what had happened was word for word what Peaphweng
Ndyu had said. The only difference was that Peaphweng
Ndyu had used Abehema as his language of divination,
while Wabuah had divined in Kakakum. The notables
commanded perfect knowledge of both languages. On
second thought, however, there was really no reason to
suspect the two diviners had met, because the notables knew
that Wabuah had come directly from Yenseh earlier that
same day, and that Peaphweng Ndyu had left straight for
Tchang the day before. Since Yenseh and Tchang were to the
left and right of Abehema, the notables reasoned, there was
no way the paths of the two diviners could have crossed.
Thus the only conclusion they drew was that things had
happened in exactly the way both men had divined.

The most spectacular and almost magical aspect of his
divination was when Wabuah invited the notables to take
turns looking into his divination earthenware bowl, or the
little magic pot as they called it thereafter.

This bowl contained very clean and clear spring
water, capable of projecting the reflection of whoever stood
to look into it. That wasn't what happened, or so the
notables alleged. Instead of reflections of themselves, they
claimed they saw Ardo Buba from the time he started to
wander about to when he was violently stung to death by
the swarm of honeybees. The bowl of water also showed
Chief Ngain giving orders to his retainers on what to do

with Ardo Buba's corpse. No wonder Wabuah of Kakakum was known all over the territory. His divination wasn't the type to leave anyone in doubt, not even Chief Ngain, had he been present. It was the type of divination to silence all those who claimed that diviners and healers were all liars and swindlers whose only interest was to try to earn a living off others' hard work and sweat through deception and opportunism.

The notables had prepared a reward for him, but by the time he had finished divining, they regretted they hadn't thought of something more than just a goat and two cocks. Wabuah was happy with what he got. As long as it was nothing but a free gift, he was satisfied. His grandfather had warned him against divining for payment, cash or kind. If he had so far remained successful, it was largely because he had heeded the warning. The power to divine cannot be bought or sold. Though Wabuah wondered if Toubegh, his second son, whose current interest in divination was considerable, would continue in the same vein or opt to follow the disturbing wind of change blowing in from the cities. He had learnt of a new breed of charlatans. They were going around the cities, claiming to cure every ailment including madness, and to be capable of divining the past, the present and the future. The quest for money would make people claim the impossible, which worried him deeply. If Toubegh chose to falter in the same manner, he, Wabuah, would not be there to weep with him over the disastrous consequences of the betrayal of a noble profession.

Before Wabuah left Abehema for Yenseh, he asked to have a word in private with Peaphweng Mukong. So both men excused themselves from the notables and went out for a tête-à-tête.

"I've asked to speak to you alone because there are certain things that are best discussed in private," Wabuah told Peaphweng Mukong, once they were safely out of earshot. "I've chosen to talk to you because you appear to be the eye, ear and mind which Abehema badly needs at this uncertain moment of darkness. I can smell danger in the air like a rotten egg, and unless you perform extraordinary feats and fast, it might be too late to avert an eruption of evil beyond the powers of your village and people. The rest of the world might just have to tell a different story, should nothing happen to forestall what I see brewing. As a diviner, what my eyes can't see during the day, they can't miss at night. For the past five nights or so, I've slept in my bed in Yenseh to see all that has happened here in Abehema. This village of yours is moving in turbulent and worrying ways. You need to see the way it stirs at night, rife with witches who seem bent on bringing Abehema untold suffering and destruction. They've shaken hands with the devils of *Msa* and have been rewarded with death wrapped in fresh banana leaves like kola-nuts of peace!" He heaved a sigh of profound sadness and shook his head disappointedly.

"As for Chief Ngain," Wabuah clicked his tongue to show dismay, getting even closer to Peaphweng Mukong, as if to make amply sure no one else was listening. "As for Chief Ngain, it is no lie that he is a most wicked man. His evil way whistles. Two nights ago I watched his evil spirit fly all the way from faraway Kaizerbosch where he is detained to torment you at night. The ring you were wearing had just signalled me that something was about to happen to the person I had asked it to protect. Immediately, I got out of bed and started to burn lavender and make incantations. When I had assured myself you were going to come out of his trickery unhurt, I lay back and watched him waste his time. He transformed himself into a rock, thunder, lightning, storm and rain, but to no avail. You were lucky you had my protection because you didn't forget to put on your ring. Also, your hands were empty and free of guilt. Like I say, if nothing is done to appease the ancestors in time, a rotten egg is going to explode with a stench that Abehema has never known before. My advice to you is this: Do not let the witches untie the bundle they are bringing back from *Msa*. It bears not life but death. Beware! That is it now. We may go back in, so I may salute the others and leave for home," he said and started to move in, but was held back by Peaphweng Mukong, who looked more worried than ever.

"Please don't go away just yet," Peaphweng Mukong pleaded in a childlike manner. "We are desperate for your clairvoyance and assistance, so stay here and protect us. What you say leaves me convinced that nothing is impossible with you. You can read the future of Abehema for us. Elaborate on what misfortunes you say await us, and tell us how we can act to avert them." He was almost in tears.

"I wouldn't tell you a lie, my dear friend. My divination has its limits. There are things I can do and things I can't. I'm not like the new generation of charlatans in the cities great and small, who claim to cure, heal, divine, tell fortunes, prevent misfortunes, invite riches and kill death, all at once. If Toubegh, my son who has shown quite an early interest in this calling which I inherited from my grandfather, chooses to tell falsehoods in order to earn money as they do in the cities, that will be his funeral. For I wouldn't be there when my forefathers in the land beyond began to query him for killing a noble vocation. Isn't it amazing the unethical extremes to which certain people may descend just to earn a hot Mim dollar! In any case, modesty is my watchword, just as it was my grandfather's who preceded me in this great profession." He suddenly realised he had let himself be carried away by the strong, almost possessive emotions he felt for his métier.

"To cut a long story short," he said, blowing his nostrils after sneezing from snuffing, "all I can attempt to do is predict from a study of past and present happenings, what the future might hold. I can't say for sure. To the best of my knowledge, dreams can foretell the future with far more precision than any diviner can pretend to. I don't know how my counterparts in the cities manage, but what I tell you is the truth. Fortunately I'm not one of those who claim omniscience of any kind. I'm very sorry I can't be of further help." He was resolute.

They both went in again. Wabuah saluted the notables and took his leave. Peaphweng Mukong did his best to avoid looking dejected. It was a dangerous sign of weakness for a leader to betray muddle-headedness at crucial moments such as this. So he mustered courage and coordinated the evening's discussions on what steps had to be taken to appease the ancestors and repair the land.

By midnight the notables had come to a consensus. They had decided to take two goats, a dark one and a spotted one, a white cock, and two large calabashes of raffia wine and a block of camwood to the lake to perform the purification sacrifice to the ancestors. The time was also agreed upon. Since the desecration had taken place at night, they would offer their sacrifice at night as well. This was to be done the following day, which was known as *Tu-éviene* in Abehema, and which was also the market day – exactly a week after what had happened. Those who argued for more time to make elaborate preparations were defeated. Time was fast running out, and the sooner they acted, the better for the people. They were reminded of the fact that the harvest season was nearly over. August, the Moon-of-Wetness, was in its twentieth day already, and Abehema was anxious to restore oneness with the world of the forefathers and mothers before the feast of Harvest Thanksgiving scheduled for September 1st. With this sense of urgency, the notables agreed on how and when to purify the desecrated land. Hopefully by Friday morning, Abehema would be a peaceful, sacred and harmonious land once again.

The day's meeting had been unusually but understandably long. Some anxious wives and children had come to fetch their husbands and fathers. They were forced to stay out in the market square while the notables rounded off the deliberations. Among them was Ngonsu, Peaphweng Mukong's senior wife and proud mother to Kwanga, the pride of Abehema at university in the Great City. She carried an old, topless, Kaizerland-made hurricane lamp in one hand, and a bamboo umbrella in the other. It was her week to cook for and sleep with her husband, which was why she had come to take him home. The night was bitterly cold, and the women shivered as the cold penetrated their bare bosoms. They gathered round Ngonsu to chat and keep warm by her lamp. The wind threatened to extinguish the flame, which they were trying so hard to keep alive.

For their part, the children in rags and nakedness defied the cold as often they did, to play hide-and-seek in the marketplace and keep their blood warm and healthy. They sang and danced with innocent joy, and filled their watching mothers with maternal pride and fantasies. The children were young and bustling with energy. Their mothers could see them succeeding where they had failed, or remembered where they had been forgotten. Looking into the future through their children, the mothers could visualise themselves as grandparents enjoying the material benefits they didn't have now. Their diligent and committed progeny were sure to make them available with time. In their children they had planted their grains of hope, which they were determined to guard just as they guarded their farms against witches and wild animals. Because this made them hopeful, they were happy, and because they were happy, they refused to be hurt by the biting cold, mothers and children alike. So they waited on, the children singing with vibrant voices, stamping the ground with innocent determination and persistence, and the mothers did not let the embittered thoughts of the overburdened peasant women that they were interfere with their dreams of a brighter tomorrow.

When the notables finally came out of Peaphweng Mukong's market-house, they looked exhausted. Those who found their wives or children waiting for them felt proud, and those who found no one waiting to take them home felt angry and hurt, even though some of them lived so far away that it was demanding too much for their wives and children to travel all that distance in the cold, at night to find out what had gone wrong. Everyone knew that at night Abehema was dominated by sorcery and evil, and only the very *cooked* or fortified could venture out without jeopardy. Peaphweng Mukong thanked Ngonsu for her care and concern, and followed her home, even though they groped most of the way because the wind eventually overpowered the flame of her topless lamp.

Peaphweng Mukong was pleased to find that the fufu corn and njama-njama (huckleberry) his wife served him was still warm. Ngonsu had stored it in a hot pot of water to keep it warm. He had always admired her foresightedness and initiative. Even though his was a society where men believed that having a wife was like standing on soldier ants, Peaphweng Mukong had not found Ngonsu a difficult woman at all, but for the fact that she tended to gossip. He was intrigued why some men never ceased generalising about how it was impossible to live peaceably with women. He could boast, though very few men believed him, that for two decades and more he had not had a serious quarrel with the mother of the son who had brought him pride, and who was soon to be the first big modern personality that Abehema had ever produced. He was sure that only a woman like Ngonsu could have given him a son like Kwanga. She deserved her place as senior wife, and he was quite pleased to know that, as such, she was well respected by his other wives and the women folk of Abehema.

He ate fast and went to bed, but he couldn't sleep.

His mind was full of thoughts, strange and normal, wild and tamed. How he envied Ngonsu who slept so imperturbably beside him! He wondered why the world was such a strange and complex place. Why were experiences so different even between people who shared the same worlds, the same culture, the same house, the same bed, and even the same breath at times? Just why did some people suffer more than others? He didn't appear to find ready answers to his puzzles, so he simply sighed in heavy resignation.

"Perhaps these differences are what make the world what it is, an empty experience even at the best of times." He wondered if the world would still be one without its contradictions and complexities, without the profound emptiness at the heart of its celebrated achievements, without the deaths of the lives it inspired, and without the lives of the deaths it induced.

Peaphweng Mukong tried hard to stop thinking and start sleeping. Each time he made an effort to close his eyes, a thought came forcing its way through like a bulldozer on the Ring Road that linked Abehema strategically with the villages of Tchang and Yenseh of Kakakum, and with the world beyond.

"That's the way with thoughts," he muttered. "Impossible to tame or direct. So obstinate, thoughts!"

Just when he had almost succeeded in falling asleep, another thought invaded. This time about his son Kwanga. The activities of the past three days had made him think less about him. The idea of finding a wife for Kwanga had been superceded by the need to be patriotic to his home village and people. He didn't regret it, though he wondered what his son could be doing at the moment. He knew all must be well with Kwanga though he hadn't seen or heard from him for a very long time. He could read his son like a book. He knew for instance that Kwanga would seldom write home unless in serious financial difficulties, needing the urgent auctioning of several bags of coffee to back-door dealers.

"I wonder if all school children bother their parents about money the way Kwanga has done me through the years. He has eaten through my pockets like a rat! And for seventeen years I've lived like the divine pauper, cursed from birth by the gods of *Kwang*," he yawned, bringing his hand to his mouth. "For seventeen years, every drop of sweat I've sweated and every muscle I've pulled has been for Kwanga. How parasitical students are! My only consolation is the fact that he is doing well – that we haven't sweated and toiled for nothing."

Peaphweng Mukong wished he could advise Kwanga to stay away from Abehema until the current tensions had eased. To come home now when things were so uncertain would be risky. What he wanted least of all was to have Kwanga dragged into a brawl that could perhaps disturb the last few months of his university studies. He wanted to start serving the coco-yams he had cooked patiently for seventeen years. Thinking of which, Peaphweng Mukong nearly exclaimed at the awfully long time it took to start harvesting the white man's system of education.

Just how was he going to let Kwanga know that this wasn't the right time for him to come home to Abehema, should Kwanga have plans of coming? He thought for long.

Then he remembered what his father once told him as a young man. Once, when his father was going on a long journey, he told him to keep in touch through his dreams. "Should anyone fall ill," his father had told him, "ensure that you make me dream of it by thinking concurrently of the ill person, his illness and the need for me to know about it. You should avoid all interfering thoughts until you are overtaken by sleep." Peaphweng Mukong could recollect practising this technique once. And when his father returned home, he declared that his sudden return had been prompted by a dream about his daughter bitten by a snake. This for sure was true! And indeed, a viper had bitten Peaphweng Mukong's younger sister, at the age of nine, when their father had been away, and he had wished their father were around to take care of matters.

So Peaphweng Mukong decided to use the same technique to prevent Kwanga from coming home, if he had intentions of doing so. He had some reservations though. As far as he could recollect, this technique had only been used to make people return home for an emergency. He wasn't sure it would work in his case – to prevent Kwanga from coming home. It was worth a try, as it was by means of trial and error that people came by new knowledge. On that positive note, he thought of the turmoil Abehema was going through, of Kwanga and of his intention to keep Kwanga away from the scene until normalcy returned, and also of the fact that he wanted Kwanga to concentrate on his studies in order to top his class as he had always done. He succeeded in making these thoughts preoccupy his mind until he finally fell asleep.

13

The driver sped as if chased by the angel of death. He drove with the reckless abandon of the heavy consumer of marijuana that some thought him to be. The highway linking Nyamandem and Zingraftstown was in a good state. In fact, it had just been tarred and renamed *l'Express*. Well-built roads can either be used for good or for bad. This driver had opted for speed, a decision that worried some of his passengers who believed their lives to be in jeopardy. Emmanuel Kwanga, who was uncomfortably seated between the driver and a bulky gendarme officer, felt particularly endangered. He was thinking, philosophically:

"Ours is a double-faced tragedy. The danger is persistent, regardless of the perfect or imperfect state of our roads. When shall we stop blaming the roads for ghastly accidents? When are we going to be honest enough to admit the fault is in us? We simply use the roads to foster our very inadequacies."

His questioning was interrupted when he felt the driver's elbow on his shinbone for the umpteenth time. "And he doesn't even care to say sorry," Emmanuel, sitting astride the gearbox, complained silently, as the nonchalant driver raced on.

Deciding it a waste of time to pick a quarrel with an impolite idiot, Emmanuel resumed his reflections.

"Three months ago when Patience and I took a decrepit bus for Mbangolok to visit Desiree her best friend – who, let down by modern doctors, and gone to see traditional healers in the Basaang country – we were forced to walk the rest of the way, about fifteen kilometres, because the chap who drove the bus had no driver's licence, and was apprehended by the traffic police. Patience told me of someone who, a week or two before, was persuading her to procure herself a licence before eventually learning to drive, even going so far as to boast how he had had his licence five months before he could move a car! And on national radio the other day, an official of one of the provincial offices of the Ministry of Transport lamented: "'From the time the only franking machine was stolen from our office, I knew the number of fake driving documents would increase in the province. We have still not recovered this machine.'"

"Just how could I be sure that this thickset imbecile at the steering wheel, who is throwing all caution to the wind, has ever presented himself for a driving test? And this pregnant gendarme to the right, fat as a dead toad and perspiring like a beaten wrestler, sees nothing wrong! How can he when he has been blinded by his own corrupt practices? The driver reached an understanding with him way back at the station, by the terms of which the gendarme would be ferried to Zingraftstown – if he is fortunate enough to arrive alive – free of charge, provided he protects the driver from the traffic police and gendarmes that line the highway with checkpoints like soldier ants. Because of this connivance, every group of soldier ants we meet, like those we've already passed, are going to pretend that all is in order with this Toyota bus, that the vehicle is roadworthy, the driver's documents up-to-date, the bus not overloaded They will also pretend none of us lacks tax tickets nor identity cards, and that they are being civil with travellers anxious to arrive in Zingraftstown in good time to attend to their businesses. If we are stopped at all, it isn't because the officers want to know if the driver has a rich and handy first-aid kit, but because the 'Chef' in the bus might want to exchange a word or two in broken Muzungulandish with the 'Chefs' outside. And so goes the spiral of danger, perpetuated by the very forces elected to free us from it.

"Yet, the traffic police and gendarmes are told in no uncertain terms by the rule book and dubious bosses: 'Your role is to check overloading and test alcohol and marijuana in drivers and the road worthiness of every vehicle in front of you.'"

Emmanuel's mind flashed back at a shocking story he heard recently at L'Alimentation Des Oubliées, the most popular bar in Basfond, where he lived in Nyamandem. The storyteller, obviously drunk, had narrated the event in ludicrous style, but what Emmanuel had managed to piece together was the story of a traffic policeman who had allowed his greed to venture too far.

"One morning a taximan on his way to the city centre in Nyamandem, encountered at a checkpoint a policeman who asked to see his car documents. After seeing the documents which were all in order, the policeman, obviously disappointed at finding nothing to hang onto, asked the taximan, 'Is it papers that I am going to eat today? Give me some money to quench my thirst.' The taximan gave him a MIM$1000 note and asked for change, which the policeman refused to give. The taximan drove off in anger."

"Pregnant with greed, like they all are," Emmanuel remembered thinking of the policeman.

"On his way back, the taximan was carrying an overload. Still angry at the policeman for refusing to give his change, the taximan prepared another MIM$1000 note in anticipation. At the same checkpoint, the same policeman came forward and asked him to present the papers of the car. Pretending as if he had never met the taximan in his life, the policeman charged him for 'endangering the lives of ordinary Mimbolanders by overloading his car' and asked for MIM$1000. The taximan gave and drove off cursing: 'what you ask for is what you get'." What an ominous statement. Emmanuel had anticipated the worst upon hearing this, knowing from experience exactly what would befall whom if such a statement were uttered in his native Abehema.

"As soon as the policeman pocketed the money, it turned into a little chick, and started making 'poin poin' sounds from within his pocket. He did everything to free himself of the chick, but it would neither leave his pocket nor stop poin-poining to his utter embarrassment." At this point of the story, Emmanuel had imagined the policeman cursing himself, 'Les choses qui arrivent aux autres commencent déjà à m'arriver'.

"The policeman opened his eyes in extreme fear, fell down in front of his colleagues and narrated how a taximan had given him a MIM$1000 note that transformed itself into a chick that would not leave his pocket nor stop its poin poin sounds. He said he had done everything to free himself of the chick, but all in vain. The colleagues said they couldn't help him. He must sort himself out." A case of when the chips are down, solidarity flies through the window, Emmanuel had thought of the daily partners in crime of the beleaguered policeman.

"The policeman boarded a taxi in pursuit of the taximan who had given him the money that was turning his life upside down. Finally, the policeman caught up with the taximan at a bar and threatened to shoot him if he did not take back his money. The taximan replied in a calm mysterious voice, 'You asked for the money, which I gave you. Do what you want with it, but leave me in peace.'" Emmanuel had known this was coming. Ninety nine days for the thief, one day for the master.

"Failing to convince the taximan otherwise, the policeman went to see a marabout, hoping he would fight his case out in the world of invisible forces from which the taximan was obviously drawing. Even before he had crossed the door, the marabout told the policeman not to waste his time, for 'the money that you were given at the checkpoint was no ordinary money. You need to sacrifice at least five persons to be able to survive.'" Emmanuel remembered thinking that a diviner-healer who confesses upfront in this way must be a genuine one. He feared for the worst.

"The policeman tried sacrificing his mother, but she was well protected. He tried his father, but he was well fortified. He even tried his own children, but God was on their side. He was stranded like a reed in mid flood. He looked up. He looked down. He sweated, perplexed. Finally, he went home to think further about his predicament. The next day his wife, his children and his neighbours found him dead, killed by a chick hatched in corruption. Poin poin... poin poin... the chick was walking all over the corpse, excreting here and there."

What a frightful story. Emmanuel took a deep breath, heaved a sigh and clicked his tongue in amazement. To him the moral of the story was clear: Those who eat with greed run the risk of eating themselves and their favourite dish out of existence.

"When one is caught up in a mess like this, without much real choice, all that is left for one to do is commit one's self to fate: what must be must be," he sighed again.

The gendarme, who thought that Emmanuel was complaining about the sluggish way he sat, gathered his mass together and even sent an arm out of the window in order to create a little more room for the poor fellow. Emmanuel certainly didn't like the way he was being squeezed as if he hadn't paid the full fare. He had been asked, not in words but in callous indifference to his feelings and desires, to choose between comfort and Zingraftstown, as if he hadn't paid enough to be taken to Zingraftstown in comfort.

The most ironic thing about it all, Emmanuel thought, was that though the driving left much to be desired, only some of the passengers agreed with him when he suggested the driver should slow down and drive more responsibly. Others even dared to reproach the driver for not going fast enough! And they almost ate an elderly woman alive for calling the driver's attention to the fact that people don't have spare lives in the same way buses have spare tyres.

Disgusted with such diabolic indifference to human life, Emmanuel recoiled once more into his mental cocoon. What was all this hurrying for? He was deeply perturbed. Was this a race against time, or was it a flight away from death? If the latter, he feared very much that the end result might be counterproductive. For mysterious death had a thousand hands and moved in a hundred footpaths. Death was capable of coming stealthily behind your back, or surprising you with a sudden swift dive. In the twinkle of an eye, it could snatch you away in front of relatives and friends, just as the hawk might grab the chick, or it could torment you for ages, like mother hen would the juicy toad chosen for supper. It could smear you with poisonous saliva, and swallow you alive the way the python does its prey. It could crush your bones with the savagery of the lion and wolf down your flesh. Or it could humble you with the might and impunity of tropicalised dictatorship.

Death could be massive as well, coming in the likeness of wars, famine, earthquakes, floods, hurricanes and epidemics, to wipe out entire villages, cities or nations. Above all, death was painful, very painful. To the living and the dying alike. Death wasn't unaware of this fact, which might explain why it behaved like a cunning outcast constantly sneaking into the community under various disguises to make new friends and mar their bliss. Unfortunately, very few medicine men could prevent the contraction of such volatile and lethal friendship with death, because they couldn't predict with whom death would shake hands next. Few ever discovered death's true nature before it struck like lightning, and even fewer learned from the tragic deaths of others. Being of a million faces, death was quite impossible to pin down!

However cunning death was, Emmanuel was certain about one thing. "Death," he reminded himself, "is common to everyone, rich and poor, young and old, man and woman, master and servant. Some might be buried nameless without headstones in shallow graves hurriedly dug, some abandoned to vultures in battlefields, or dumped in rivers and seas as food for fish, crocodiles and hippopotami, some reduced to ashes for want of graves, while some are embalmed and laid to rest in expensive tombs of gold and silver, but the fundamental phenomenon stays the same and is known as Death. Does it matter whether we are buried decently or eaten by scavengers? What happens to those buried in tombs and coffins of gold and silver, or to those buried in bamboo coffins and shallow graves without headstones? Who goes where after death?"

Emmanuel was most intrigued by the question of death, and felt like going on and on.

"When I move about Nyamandem," he continued, his eyes closed lightly, "I'm stunned by the display of wealth in burying the dead. The most spectacular investment in the dead is at the city centre itself, at a square nicknamed *Vallée-de-la-Mort* (Valley-of-Death) which dates as far back as the colonial era, when the Muzungulander had the special mission of civilising this part of Mimboland. There, right in the heart of the city as if to remind everyone of the great price Muzunguland had to pay in the demanding process of cultivating Africans from solely emotional creatures into varying degrees of rational beings, is an extensive graveyard with beautiful tombstones and engravings, surrounded by a giant black fence of spiky iron rods. The graves, which are buried in floral decorations, contain the glorious remains of every Muzungulander who died teaching *La Marseillaise* or fighting in the malaria-ridden darkness of 'savage barbarism'. Though we cannot avoid these graves, the dead who lie in them are not necessarily less dead than the 'barbaric savages' whose flesh and blood fertilised and watered the delicate tree of civilised barbarism. In the eyes of Muzunguland and some of us who swear by Muzungulander civilisation, they might indeed look great. To the tortured and deprived bulk of Mimbolanders, in particular the homeless housed by the Valley-of-Death, buried rich and well means they shall forever be seen as harbingers of a nightmare that came to stay. Does it really matter how we are buried after death? Isn't the ultimate question whether or not the soldiers of civilised savagery, like the peasants they dismembered, were conquered by death in the end? Or are we that vain to invest so much only for the glory that would be ours in a world where we are no more?"

Everyone in the bus chatted except the driver who clung to the steering wheel as if possessed by the demons of speed, the gendarme who was dozing after smoking five cigarettes, the old woman who looked prayerful, and Emmanuel who was buried in his thoughts. Emmanuel, who considered himself a man of ideas, was less than enticed by the uninspiring chatters and banters of the other passengers. Judging from the sort of things they were going on and on about, what he termed '*njakritalk*' (impolite conversations), Emmanuel wouldn't have paid a cent to partake. Although sympathetic with the downtrodden and indeed one of them, he hated '*njakris*' (uncouth people), and often sought to distance himself from any. He would rather identify with men of great intellect and ideas, even with ordinary folks of good cheer, than with the champions of coarseness. The latter were just like pigs that scattered refuse heaps, swam in the stinking gutters with rustic contentment, and picked at harmless worms with misdirected aggression. To avoid being dragged into any *njakrism* therefore, Emmanuel kept his eyes closed and pretended to be asleep. In this way, he could overhear the others as he pleased without feeling obliged to contribute in order to keep the wheel of rawness turning.

Patience's charm and elegance kept lurking in his mind. What a nostalgic feeling of amour this gave him! It was barely a couple of hours since they had separated. Yet he felt as if he hadn't seen her for ages. Their parting had been a painful one, the final farewell most especially. He was on the brink of tears, and had Patience, in tears, not turned away as soon as she did, he would have done what he hated doing in her presence in public – cried. He wasn't at all happy to be going away from her, not now that she was pregnant and their living together was actually beginning to take shape: to be meaningful, replenishing, wonderful. He knew he had to go, because his heart was heavy for Abehema. He had decided to go home, and she had agreed with him. It was important for him to seek oneness with his folks back home, by explaining his failures and asking to be forgiven where he had transgressed. He owed Abehema the truth about his Cross to Calvary, and had also decided to tell his parents about Patience.

He turned down an invitation to review his speculation as to how Peaphweng Mukong and Ngonsu might react when he told them about Patience and his intention to marry her. Instead, he welcomed the memory of Marxy Wang, author of last September's article about the unholy relationship between students and lecturers at the University of Asieyam. After reading the fascinating and passionate article in *Roots* that fateful day at the university nearly a year ago, Emmanuel had intended to meet Marxy Wang for a discussion which he hoped might contribute towards finding viable solutions to the plight of students in Asieyam. Because of his relegation and subsequent hardships, he couldn't meet Marxy until six months later.

The young adult he met by chance at the Ministry of Education and Fundamental Studies (MINEFUNDS) was a very changed Marxy Wang. Emmanuel would have missed him completely had a secretary not called the name just when he was about to turn away. How the man had changed physically! Flat as a banana leaf six months ago, Marxy Wang had grown incredibly bigger. His jaws had assumed the roundness of a pumpkin, and his belly had started to swell like yeasted dough. His lips seemed to have grown thinner and his mouth wider, while his forehead and nose shone with a fresh oiliness that Emmanuel had never noticed before. Perhaps Marxy Wang was married. Many men were known to fatten up on getting married.

Emmanuel had gone into the office, introduced himself, and asked to talk to Marxy Wang outside in the corridor, thinking the latter was visiting the ministry just like him.

He was mistaken. The change in Marxy Wang had been more than physical. Not only had he graduated from Asieyam with *Mention Bien* (First Class) in Social Thought, but Marxy Wang had also obtained a job in MINEFUNDS as Assistant Chief of Service for Quality and Tranquility in Higher Education. When Emmanuel heard this, he thought the job couldn't have fallen into better hands. So joyous and confident was he that he nearly screamed and started to sing the anthem of student solidarity. There too he was mistaken, and had he shouted: "Hurrah! The students are vindicated at last!", he might have been bundled out and dumped in an incinerator by the Clean City Company.

He realised with utter bewilderment that Marxy Wang had shed his fundamental beliefs and ideas, like a tree in the dry season! These had all undergone radical transformation. Almost overnight, Marxy Wang had ceased to be the fervent revolutionary that his article, dressing and comportment had all portrayed him to be. He had become a stone-faced reactionary, who like the classic musician in Abehema of yesteryear, saw nothing wrong with singing the praises of the very institutions and lecturers he had bitterly denounced barely six months before.

At first he would not even recognise Emmanuel, then he would not discuss with him, nor would he admit to writing the article from which Emmanuel was quoting profusely. When Emmanuel showed him a copy of *Roots*, Marxy Wang made a frenzied attempt to snatch it. When he didn't succeed, he started to threaten:

"You are not supposed to have this," he said, his jaws quivering like the liver of a freshly slaughtered cow. "All the copies of that edition were banned, seized and burnt six months ago, if you don't know! Let them not catch you with that," he warned sternly, a you-will-see-fire glare in his eyes.

Emmanuel honestly hadn't heard of the ban, and now that Marxy Wang had told him, his determination to stick to his copy increased.

"Better let me have it," Marxy Wang continued, attempting to snatch the crumpled journal once more.

Emmanuel wouldn't let him.

So Marxy Wang said breathlessly, "For your own safety, force it down the latrine once you get home. If the security forces catch you with it, you are gone!" He collapsed into his chair and switched on a fan by the wall, turning it off again when papers from his congested table started flying all over the room.

Just then the Chief of Service, his boss, came in. Marxy Wang shifted uncomfortably in his chair and started to adjust his necktie and search for his handkerchief, all at once. He was tense, but didn't want his boss to notice it. Trying to sound normal, and wishing he could speak in Pidgin-Tougalish so his boss might not catch a word of it, he explained to Emmanuel that he hadn't been serious when he wrote the article.

"I was naive then," he defended himself. "Now I know that there is no cause for complaint," he added. "Les étudiants aiment faire du bruit pour rien," he said in Muzungulandish as if to appease his boss who didn't seem to know a word of Tougalish, and who was beginning to feel like the subject of a conspiracy.

"You students don't seem to realise how much the Government is doing for you," Marxy Wang reprimanded.

Angered, Emmanuel bluntly denied being a student, then stormed out of the office, vowing never again to have anything to do with Marxy Wang.

This encounter with Marxy Wang had kept Emmanuel thinking for long. He couldn't say he knew what to make of it, but he was clear it emphasised the need to take what others wrote or said with a bale of salt. If Marxy Wang's behaviour was anything to go by, it was now clear to Emmanuel that the most vociferous critics of a system were not necessarily those who had the public good at heart. Some, like Marxy Wang, might make the loud impassioned noises that gave them access to journals and the media, and that endeared them to the public ear, yet when it came to actually delivering the goods, their chronic dissembling became apparent, and their true motives thus unmasked! Such opportunists, once their personal situation had improved and they were able to enjoy the amenities, the lack of which had pushed them into anti-establishmentarianism, would immediately disown their radical statements and lip-service concern for the forgotten. Now he understood why, despite having the most PhDs as ministers, the current government of President Longstay was the most inefficient and the most corrupt in living memory. Little wonder some cynics had corrupted the PhD to mean: 'Permanent Head Damage', as the ignorance of academics in government seems to 'Pile Higher and Deeper', making them excel in nothing more than 'Phenomenal Dumbness' and 'Pulling Him/Her Down' who has anything better to contribute to national development. This experience with Marxy Wang in particular had hardened Emmanuel's deafness to all declarations of intent by the powerful, and had enhanced his doubting-Thomas attitude to politicians and academics.

14

Emmanuel didn't notice when they drove across the Nagasang, though he would very much have loved to be alive to the spectacle of driving across the bridge which was said to have replaced Donaperim as the longest in the country. Like many other new things, there was a story about *le Pont de Maturité* (the Maturity Bridge), as it was called. It was whispered here and there, and widely believed, that the white engineer who built the bridge would not have succeeded, had he not promised the *mammywatas* (mermaids) who inhabit the river that he would die upon completion of the Herculean construction. It was said that the grave at the southern end of the bridge belonged to the white engineer who had died just as he promised he would.

Though Emmanuel didn't know what to believe, those who spread the story had drawn their own conclusions. According to them, the white man and the black man both have witchcraft, but differ as to how they employ their witchcraft. The white man uses his witchcraft to develop himself and his society, by accomplishing engineering feats, such as the impossible two-kilometre-long Maturity Bridge. He has a ruthless sense of direction and purpose, and will work with meticulous stubbornness until his target is met. On the other hand, so the tale-bearers claimed, the black man uses his witchcraft to self-destruct or to inflame ill-feeling and despondency through the greedy obstruction of communal progress. Where he can, the black man would strive to be the only cock to crow in the kingdom, because he believes that no success is worth having if collective. Ultimately he betrays his own community and builds an empire of greed and solitude. If the black man is the laughing stock of the world, the tale-bearers concluded, he is largely to blame for choosing to defecate on a footpath he uses daily. Why should he blame someone else for the stench?

The bus arrived at Pakeneng, a roadside settlement midway through the six-hour journey from Nyamandem to Zingraftstown, an hour earlier than normal. There was a brief stopover for the passengers to buy something to eat from the ever-busy village market. Emmanuel didn't feel like eating, so he stayed in the vehicle with the elderly woman who was avoiding food to avoid being sick. She hated the smell of petrol, and was quite convinced that nothing she ate would stay in her bowels.

The driver bought himself roasted plantains and plums together with the boiled head of a monkey to eat while he drove, but was persuaded by the gendarme to accompany him for a quick bottle of Manawa in one of the village off-licences steaming with thirsty passengers. By the time they were through, every other person had returned and was waiting for them in the bus.

They were soon on the move again, with the driver struggling to improve the speed of the past two hours. Emmanuel began to think that the speeding couldn't be for nothing. He would be surprised if the driver didn't have a date with one of the beautiful young victims of college life in Zingraftstown, who were forced to roam the streets at night and in broad daylight, harvesting for rents, maintenance and tuition. The driver was racing like someone who didn't want to be late for the 3 p.m. movies that female students loved attending with boyfriends or casual partners. Even then, Emmanuel thought, why hurry this much? It was only 11.30, wasn't it? Looking at his wrist, Emmanuel noticed that the driver wasn't wearing a watch. The car clock was not working properly either – it was an hour ahead! Could this explain why the driver was racing this much? He decided to find out.

"Dat time correct?" Emmanuel asked, pointing to the car clock. "Yi be like say fast." He spoke in Pidgin-Tougalish, the commonest language amongst Tougalish Mimbolanders, but which he rarely spoke.

"Yi fast," agreed the driver in Pidgin-Tougalish as well. "One hour for before," he added, forcing a big piece of plantain into his mouth. "I be check say dem don cot your tongue," he said with a full mouth, giving Emmanuel a sly searching look. "Weti you woman watch talk?" he asked with a chuckle, more interested in poking fun at Emmanuel who was wearing Patience's little watch, than in knowing the time.

Emmanuel was irritated, but decided to ignore the provocation. He had found out what he wanted to know, that the fellow wasn't driving at breakneck speed because of any mistaken notion of time. He wasn't keen on getting involved in any further exchange of words with the driver, for that would only multiply the risk of a fatal accident, on a road that already smelled of death. So he politely told the driver the time, and said he wasn't being anti-social or anything, but just didn't feel well enough to get conversational. His excuse was accepted, and he was grateful for it.

The other passengers resumed chatting and bantering, their stomachs full. A couple of them wanted to know why Emmanuel hadn't bought himself some food. Was his problem money, or fear of being served the meat of a horse, cat or dog? Rumours abounded that the villagers killed pets to make quick money from travellers. It was said that the highway had dehumanised Pakeneng more than helped it, and that the manic craving for profit it had instilled in the villagers had corrupted them beyond redemption. Baby monkeys and chimpanzees were allegedly trapped and cooked alive for medicinal purposes for travelling businessmen and politicians who paid dearly for the delicacies. To Emmanuel, these were just rumours, quite unsubstantiated. No one had been caught red-handed selling horses, cats, dogs and baby monkeys and chimpanzees in Pakeneng. What if the rumours were true? Was it a secret that dogs and cats were eaten for medicinal purposes in certain parts of Mimboland? And that the high and mighty of Nyamandem particularly cherished dogs, cats and monkey brains for their occult practises? Wasn't the trafficking of ground human flesh big business for *Ndolé* (bitter leaf dish) among specialist restaurateurs in the big cities of Nyamandem and Sawang? The only problem might be if the people of Pakeneng pretended the meat was beef, which to Emmanuel's understanding seemed to be what the rumour-mongers implied. In any case, he explained to them that it wasn't because the meat was suspect that he hadn't gone to eat. Nor was his problem money, Patience having provided enough of it to take him right to Abehema. He simply wasn't hungry.

With that explanation Emmanuel closed his eyes again and wandered away in the world of his thoughts, which took him back to Nyamandem where he paid a brief visit to Patience's office. What could she be doing at this moment? Probably trying to clear her desk to go home for the midday break? He imagined she must have slept throughout the morning shift, especially as their lengthy discussion last night made them go to bed very late. Moreover, she had already caught the pregnancy syndrome, with the consequence that her moods had become as capricious as a chameleon's colours. He recalled how she threw up in the taxi that took them to the bus station, just as they drove past a stinking refuse dump before which stood a scavenging naked madman with a nodding erection. Normally it wouldn't have bothered her, but the conception had made her ridiculously sensitive. He reckoned she would take some time to acclimatise, to temper her fuss about the sordidness of Nyamandem. He was proud of her and the child she carried in her womb, and felt optimistic that his parents would accept and love them both. "One person's child is only in the womb," they had never tired of telling him, as a way of imbuing him with respect for elders and parents beyond his own, and for the children of others. This was their turn to practice what they had preached to him since his infant years.

For Ngonsu his mother, he could swear even without prior consultation that she would welcome the baby like a jewel. His worry was Peaphweng Mukong, whose hard-line attitude might need some watering down, and who could indeed be a hard nut to crack when approached at the wrong moment. He had prepared a diplomatic argument, one he intended to rehearse until he got to Abehema. In brief, the idea was to persuade his father to see a woman as a woman, irrespective of whether she came from Abehema or from far-off Camp-Kupeh. He could remember Peaphweng Mukong mentioning something about him getting married when he went home last. It had ended there, without the old man indicating whether or not he had a particular girl in mind. This had led Emmanuel to speculate that his father might have mentioned marriage simply to know his attitude towards it, and that maybe Peaphweng Mukong wasn't too fussy about whom he got married to after all. Emmanuel wondered what his shrewd father must have discovered from their brief conversation. He sincerely hoped he hadn't betrayed any particular inclination for the local girls, which could be used as an argument against Patience. He only hoped his discussions with his parents would be plain-sailing, for he could neither imagine himself disobeying them nor getting married to anyone else but Patience.

Emmanuel was forced out of his reverie by a loud explosion. He opened his eyes in shocked surprise, wondering what was happening. He felt a sharp pain in his left leg as the driver franticly searched for the right gear. The bus seemed out of control, as it skidded and zigzagged across the highway with little impact from the driver's desperate swinging and swaying of the steering wheel. Each time there was a left swing Emmanuel bore the crushing bulk of the gendarme, and the piercing elbow of the driver at every change of gear. The perspiring driver applied the brakes repeatedly, but there was little effect because the bus was going down a steep hill.

The passengers were hysterical. They screamed and cursed with every swing and sway.

"Na tyre!" shouted the driver. "Na back tyre explode. I sure," he explained, urging the passengers not to panic.

At last he managed to bring the bus to a halt at the bottom of the hill, fortunate that there was no traffic when the explosion occurred. Everyone jumped out, sweating and panicky, having missed death by an inch. The elderly woman made the sign of the cross and murmured a prayer to Saint Jude, saint of difficult and hopeless cases. Emmanuel stared vainly into the distance, disbelieving his luck. The gendarme smoked a cigarette and thought of the mother of his children back in Nyamandem. The driver crushed a fat lobe of kola-nut between his teeth saying, "God no di sleep." Even those who had urged him to keep accelerating were quite shaken. They had all come within a hair's-breadth of death, and now knew it wasn't so abstract a concept, or something meant for others only.

Someone started singing Black Roger's famous 'La route ne tue pas'. Others followed, some singing along, some humming. 'The road does not kill. It is us road users who kill. The road is there to help us develop, travel well, communicate better, and not to kill. Our clumsiness as drivers, pedestrians and riders kills. Let's be careful. La route ne tue pas. Mais c'est nous qui tuons.' The song had taken on a whole new relevance, as it dawned on the passengers that death through careless driving was a price anyone could pay.

When the driver had fully recovered from the shock, he climbed to the carriage of the bus and untied the spare tyre, to replace the one that had exploded. Then he settled down to work, assisted by two of the male passengers who happened to be mechanics by profession. Some of the passengers watched the three at work, some broke up into little groups of twos and threes, while others kept to themselves. All minds were occupied with thoughts of the accident that had nearly happened. Many who hadn't seriously contemplated it before, now began to wonder if the saying that 'no one can die another's death' wasn't true after all.

The elderly woman looked around and saw Emmanuel sitting on a stone a few metres away from the bus. She walked up to him, attracted by his aloofness and likeability in his well-kempt well-cut hair and cleanly shaved youthful face.

"Would you like to sit down?" Emmanuel asked, creating space for her on the stone.

"Tank you, ma pikin," the elderly woman replied in the language of the Tougalish Mimbolander masses, Pidgin-Tougalish. "Make God bless you and your family plenty."

She laid a handkerchief over the stone before sitting.

"I no want dirty dis ma fine fine clothes," she said of her dress, with a smile. "Yi be new, as you see." She told him it wasn't Mimbowax or Kutiwax, but Real Guaranteed Muzunguland Wax. Her daughter bought it for her two days ago. The loins that went with this gown were right there on top of the vehicle in her travelling bag, which was also new. And to think that the driver didn't want to give her the chance to look happy Sunday next in the clothes her daughter had bought for her! "Papa God for Heaven no fit gree dat one."   "Where is your daughter?" Emmanuel asked, becoming interested in the elderly woman.

"Yi dey for Nyamandem. Yi marry some boy pikin whe dey like you so." She told him. "They tell me for come visit them, but when I get there, I find the place too big for my like, and I deny for stay even for one week!"

She paused and looked at Emmanuel intently for a while.

"You like Nyamandem? You di stay for there?"

"I've been there for nearly three years," he replied. "I agree with you that it's a very big place and could be quite frustrating to someone who hasn't learnt to live there." He raised his head and looked at her as if to add, "especially for villagers like you."

"I don't tink say I fit ever learn for live in dat city," she said, then proceeded to say that she honestly did not find Nyamandem at all familiar. Too many cars, too many houses, too many idle people. Too many thieves as well, who could actually slash your head off without you noticing! She told him how the fowls she had brought for Marxy and Flore were stolen even before they could eat them – stolen in broad daylight. And that, despite the problems she had with the gendarmes and the police transporting the fowls. "See me bad luck. I waste ma moni for buy craze paper dem for fowl, only for thief man dem for thievam chop!"

"Yes," Emmanuel concorded. "That's the city," he added pensively. "Did you say Marxy?"

"Yes," said she. "You know yi?" She could guess the name rang a bell from Emmanuel's excited countenance. "If you dey for university, you go don hear yi name," She affirmed. Flore her daughter had said he was very popular, Marxy Wang. And what a lucky young man too! At his age was already a big man where he worked. "I go for he work place, I see plenty people, some old pass yi like two, three time. All man na dasso 'Sar, Sar', 'Chef, Chef' for yi." There was little more a mother could expect of a son-in-law. Marxy had started young and well, and his star will surely light his way to the top. As far as she was concerned, only the sky could limit a young man with such an early start.

She certainly was proud of her son-in-law, and went on and on about how great and lucky he was. She even forgot she had asked Emmanuel a question, or that he might have something to say which could either confirm or question her esteem for Marxy Wang.

Speaking of Flore, her daughter, she said, "When you born girl yi get goodluck, you sabi for day one." She said she came from Massajeng in Tunga Division, where for a long time there was no maternity. Labouring women had to be rushed to Alfredsburg the divisional capital, situated far up in the foggy mountains. Flore was the first child ever to be delivered in the Massajeng Maternity twenty years ago. "Na first pikin dem born am for white man hospital. Na dat one I di call am lucky!"

Emmanuel was thinking: "Without this tyre puncture, how would I have known this granny was not as likeable as she appeared? That she and her daughter were probably the primary motivators of Marxy's departure from the search for betterment in Asieyam? With a mother-in-law this ambitious, and a wife with the opportunism of Flore, no man of principle no matter how rigid could stay forever committed. I wish Marxy had explained the situation in this way, instead of pretending naivety!"

The old woman was still speaking, as if to herself. She said she saw Marxy as the River Tunga and Flore as the women of her village. In the rainy season as this, the Tunga swelled until it overflowed its banks. And when it subsided the village women would come out with baskets, to pick up fish and crabs left behind in their farms in the valleys. Flore tried the university and failed, Marxy tried and succeeded. Why should not the latter benefit the former? "Ma heart glad plenty for dem." She made the sign of the cross and praised the Lord.

Emmanuel stood up and walked away, lying he was going to ease himself. But the truth was that he felt disgusted with the vaunting, talkative old woman. He went farther up the hill and entered the bush where he found a stone and sat alone. Would Ngonsu his mother boast the way this woman

201

was doing, were she in the skin of this old woman? How did this old woman expect Marxy's parents to react, if they were to find out that she and her daughter were simply out to mine their son? Would Patience's parents behave like this in future if he were to become a rich man some day? Would they connect Patience to him like a pipeline to an oil well? He didn't think he would stomach that, not after what his own parents had gone through for his sake. He would not have their birthright stolen by the Jacobs of marriage.

He continued turning the matter over in his mind until he heard the sound of hooting. So he stood up and went back to the bus. The tire replaced, the passengers occupied their places once more and the journey resumed.

For the first fifty kilometres, the speed was moderate, but when the withdrawal symptoms became unbearable, the driver was repossessed by the angel of death, and started speeding like mad again.

This time he had managed to repair the car stereo, so there was music as well. The passengers appreciated it, for music kept their minds off thoughts of fatality. The musical piece was a famous composition by the veteran Tala André-Marie, one Radio Mimboland International had adopted as the signature tune before every news bulletin. Everyone, including Flore's mother, hummed along with it, although the words were in Muzungulandish, a language few of them ordinarily would warm up to speak, given their pride in Tougalish values, both imagined and real.

"Some man fit tell me weti yi dey talk for dis song?" Flore's mother appealed to no one in particular, although Emmanuel had a feeling she would have called him by name, had she been modest enough to find out. There must be at least one of them who understood the language, which Marxy, her son-in-law, spoke "like say dem born yi for Muzunguland," she boasted, much to Emmanuel's disgust.

"Wait till you next meet your son-in-law," replied one of the mechanics with a bitterness of tone that was meant to hurt. "Moi na pas parler Muzungulandaise eh!" he added, generating laughter at the back of the bus.

"Sorry, if ma mouth don slide for some place, make wona excuse me," Flore's mother apologised. "God bless wena, ma pikin dem," she made the sign of the cross with Catholic dedication. Then she asked the passenger directly in front of her to call Emmanuel's attention.

"Ma pikin," she said with a broad smile, "you fit tell me weti Tala di sing for Muzunguland talk?" Her teeth were brownish but all intact. She was one of those elderly people whose age was hard to tell from the number of teeth alone.

Emmanuel didn't answer her. Instead he turned to the gendarme, who shifted uncomfortably on his seat.

"What are you looking at me for?" the gendarme vaunted. "When they say you should learn Muzungulandish, you think they are doing you a disservice. Now your mama wants to know something, and there's none of you who can explain it to her."

Emmanuel resisted an urge to challenge the gendarme, preferring to have the last laugh.

"I'll tell you, Mama," said the gendarme, abandoning an attempt to turn round and face the person who was about to benefit from his knowledge of Muzungulandish.

"Tank you, Sar," replied Flore's mother.

There was silence as the gendarme waited for the driver to rewind the tape. When it started playing again, his translation began.

"The song, Mama, is titled 'I'm Going to the Land of Milk and Honey', and has been around for a long time."

Emmanuel could see the gendarme didn't mean to stop at a straightforward translation, but to embellish. He felt like telling the gendarme off for deliberately mistranslating the title of the song, but was dissuaded by his phobia for men in camouflage.

"Tala is a great songwriter, Mama," the gendarme continued. He seemed to have reminded himself what the song was all about, and started to follow the tape less and less.

"In the song he asks a farmer the following question: 'Farmer, where are you going, all dressed up in your best outfit, even wearing a trendy hat and polished shoes? Where are you going, far away from the village where you've lived in peaceful harmony with nature, cultivating coffee and feeling jolly happy?' To which the farmer replies: 'I'm going to the big Great City, the big Great Capital City which I've heard so much about'." He paused for a cigarette, pretty satisfied with his effort.

"It's one thing to speak Muzungulandish, and another to try to translate it into Pidgin-Tougalish," he confessed.

Even Emmanuel seemed contented with the paraphrasing so far, although he still couldn't understand why the gendarme deliberately substituted certain key words with his own creation.

"Mama," the gendarme continued, "Tala asks the students a similar question. He says: 'Student, where are you going, freshly dressed up in your uniform, your fashionable trousers pressed so well? Where are you going with this triumphant look on your face, leaving behind your country, your beautiful village?' To which the student replies: 'I'm going to the big Great City, the big Great Capital City which I've heard so much about. I'll travel all the way through various villages and towns to look for a better life at the big Great City, the Capital I've heard so much about'.

"Are you enjoying it, Mama?" asked the gendarme, full of himself. Flore's mother assented, and he continued. "Tala is my number one musician, after Manu. The two of them are the real ambassadors of our music abroad. They are the only two whose music has been given the stamp of approval by the white man."

Emmanuel wished the gendarme would go on with the embellished paraphrasing, and stop making silly comments.

"Tala invites the girls as well and asks the following question: 'Young woman, where are you going with your beautifully plaited hair, looking so self-conscious? Where are you going on this long broad highway that disappears to the South, a country unknown to us?' To which the young woman replies: 'I'm going to the big Great City, the big Great Capital City of which I've heard so much'." The Gendarme smiled contentedly. With a bit more practice, he could change jobs easily, he thought, graduating from the regime of obeying without questions, to the civility of interpretation.

"Finally to the driver," he began again, looking at the driver out of the corner of his eye. "Finally to the driver, Tala asks the same question: 'Driver, where are you going with your bus splashed with mud and loaded to the brink, looking totally exhausted? Where are you going under this burning sun, speeding past rivers, mountains and valleys at top speed?' To which the driver replies: 'I'm going to the big Great City, the big Great Capital City which I have heard so much about. I'm driving through villages and towns from north to south, until the big Great City, to look for a better life'.

"Then Tala, like a remarkable judge and champion of the right to move about freely, concludes by saying: 'Farmer, student, young woman and driver, you are free to seek the land of your dream, to look for your betterment in daily life with every passing moment of every day! Go seek the land of your dream!'"

The gendarme was applauded by everyone except the driver, who didn't appear to have paid much attention to what was being said, and Emmanuel, who felt the gendarme had wilfully deprived his audience of the full richness of meaning in Tala André-Marie's classic composition.

Emmanuel's anger was coupled with pity for his fellow passengers who were gullible in their illiteracy. How, he thought sadly, could such disadvantaged folks ever find out the truth in the written word, if the literate few with sharper ears and keener eyes chose to lie to them all the time?

"Tank you plenty, Sar," said Flore's mother warmly, her eyes rich with appreciation. She said of all those people, the farmer was the only one for whom she did not think the city was the right place. What would a farmer go to seek in the city, if not only to sell their crops and return to their farm? The student, the young woman and the driver, what would they live in the village for? What could the village offer them? Her son-in-law went to the city and had succeeded. She thanked God for that. Her daughter didn't quite succeed personally. Thank God Marxy was there for her to lean on. As for her, she belonged with the farmer, and her place was in the village. Flore and Marxy invited her to the city, but she found the place impossible to stay. That's why she was rushing home helter-skelter, like a farmer seeking shelter from an impending rainstorm. So to tell you the truth, the city wasn't for people like her. The city was for young blood. She went on for ten minutes, until one of the mechanics who said he was "utterly pissed off", and boiling with anger, told her to "shut her trap".

15

They arrived at Zingraftstown at 1.25 p.m. There was a dwarfish young girl waiting for the driver at the bus station. Emmanuel's immediate impression of her was typically negative. He did not approve of her makeup, which he in his typically judgemental fashion thought was exaggerated and enhanced instead of diminished her bad looks. Her trousers were too tight and made her bottom jut out, with the effect that she walked with legs astride like a dog infested with scabies or a man with an inflated scrotum. The passengers watched the driver and her walk hand in hand into a taxi and off. Some couldn't help laughing.

"Is that the *crichi* (terribly ugly woman) he almost sacrificed our lives for?" mocked one of the mechanics, sampling Muzungulander pop music tapes, which a teenage hawker was carrying around for sale.

"Let those who say beauty is relative, tell me what beauty there is in that *crichi*, with a leprous face burnt in patches by bleaching creams like *Ambi* and *Nku-cream?*" the other echoed, picking up Michael Jackson's famous *Thriller*, which he had always wanted to own.

Emmanuel had little time to spend in Zingraftstown. To stay there any longer than he did would have meant missing both of the lorries that plied the road linking the divisional capitals of Kaizerbosch and Alfredsburg via Abehema. Though the bus he caught was in a most deplorable state, he was lucky to have got it at all. In the rainy season when roads are so bad and drivers so unprepared to risk ventures into the periphery, one must be exceedingly lucky to travel even in dilapidated lorries.

The Zingraftstown-Kaizerbosch road was as deplorable as the bus that transported Emmanuel. It was untarred, slippery and muddy, and as curly and dangerous as a meandering python. Driving suddenly ceased to be a one-man show, as the passengers were all invited to pull, push and lift. For once Emmanuel wished the Nyamandem-Zingraftstown driver was present to taste the less glittering phase of a gold coin. That thickset risk, he thought of the driver, bitter as he was throughout the journey to Zingraftstown, might in fact depart from this world without knowing that not all which glittered was gold. By sticking to the cities, intra- and inter-urban drivers were indeed in paradise, envied by their counterparts of the beleaguered hinterlands.

There was a lot of pushing and pulling to do, so the passengers kept jumping out of and into the bus until Kaizerbosch finally showed its dull dark face. They arrived there at 9.15 p.m., all exhausted and covered with mud, but thankful their 80-kilometre ordeal was finally over, temporarily so at least. After handshakes with one another, the passengers began to disperse on foot. Being a little town, there was hardly any need for taxi services in Kaizerbosch. In fact, the town had only two main streets, which linked the market centre to the court and administrative station on the one hand, and to the hospital and prison on the other.

None of the streets was tarred, although everyone could see they once were. For certain patches of the skin-thick tar coating given them since the pre-independence days of multiparty politics, had, quite surprisingly, resisted the eroding force of administrative vehicles or dilapidated commercial lorries, and the shoes of urbanites or the toughened feet of bare footed rural counterparts and the trotting hooves of cattle. It was like a reminder that the past, no matter how ugly, cannot be forgotten even when we think we must, believe we can or feel we have.

It suddenly occurred to Emmanuel that he hadn't made his mind up yet where to pass the night before resuming his journey tomorrow. There were two possibilities. Mr Tangh-e-keh, the rich cattle breeder, friend and part-time employer of Peaphweng Mukong, lived not far away from the bus station. Emmanuel was pretty certain Tangh-e-keh and family would admit him even in the middle of the night, because of the strong ties that had developed between their two families over the past four years that his father had superintended the herdboys who took care of Mr Tangh-e-keh's hundreds of cattle in Abehema. Another person to whom he could go was a secondary school friend of his who had failed to make the 'O' Levels and had turned to coffee farming as a last resort. Ewe, as his friend was known, lived rather far away. Exhausted and famished, Emmanuel settled for Tangh-e-keh, the man who insisted on being prefixed 'Mister', and whose amiable profile was unfortunately marred by a chronic tendency for greed and thrift.

First, Emmanuel had to go and find out whether the two lorry drivers – Okeleke and Ndiko – had planned any journey to Alfredsburg in the morning, knowing his only chance of getting to Abehema rested with them. If they weren't going, either because they lacked enough passengers or because the roads were too bad, he would have to stick around until things got better. For it was a long time since he last did the hundred kilometres or so by foot. Neither of their lorries was parked where he had always found them in the past, but knowing where Okeleke lived, he went there to check. Okeleke wasn't in either, nor was his lorry.

On his way to Mr Tangh-e-keh's compound, Emmanuel wondered why he kept seeing people in little conspiratorial gatherings: what had happened or was happening to the people of Kaizerbosch? Had the whole town decided to take up gossip as a profession? Why were the beer parlours and bars so unusually empty? Had the

Jehovah witnesses predicted the end of the world again? Given they had, was this the way to react to news about the imminent end of the world? Wouldn't they rather drink, feast, dance and do everything mundane for one great last time, just to nip the best bite out of life before losing it forever? Whatever was the matter, he knew that Mr Tangh-e-keh would tell him the truth, so he quickened his pace and ascended the small hill that led to Tang-e-keh's exclusive residence.

Mr Tangh-e-keh wasn't at home, but his three wives and twelve children were. What struck Emmanuel, however, was the fact that they were all weeping like mourners. He found a place for his bag, whispered greetings in Abehema, which they all understood. No one answered, not even the children who would ordinarily have rushed to him shouting "welcome", and asking for biscuits and sweets.

Perhaps they expected him to join in and weep along with them, he wondered. How could that be? How could he bring himself to weep with no cause? Was it enough to weep just because others were weeping? He sat and stared at them with perplexity, wondering what disaster could have befallen Kaizerbosch, and hoping that Mr Tangh-e-keh would return to tell him what was going on, or that his wives might change their minds and let him share the reason for their grief.

Mr Tangh-e-keh didn't return before the exhausted and famished Emmanuel fell asleep despite himself. Neither did his wives and children stop weeping. Only slumber rescued Emmanuel from the conspiracy of mourning in Kaizerbosch that night.

16

Mr Tangh-e-keh heard a scream and rushed into the third bedroom from the parlour, torch in hand. He flashed the light and saw Emmanuel whom he preferred calling Kwanga, just like Peaphweng Mukong did, sitting on the bed head in palms, quivering like a reed in a flooded valley.

"Are you all right?" he asked, wondering what must have happened.

Kwanga raised his head.

"Yes," he whispered, trying to pull himself together.

The torchlight made his strained and itchy eyes water. He guessed he must have been dreaming, though he couldn't remember what about.

"Did I disturb you?" he asked Mr Tangh-e-keh, who was still standing over him, flashing the torchlight directly into his eyes like a dubious policeman.

"I'm sorry if I screamed," he apologised with a constricted yawn. "It happens to me often, bad dreams." He interrupted himself, embarrassed by the thunderous rumbling in his stomach.

"Did my wives give you food to eat?" Mr Tangh-e-keh reacted to the grumbles.

Kwanga shook his head sideways. "Everyone was busy when I arrived," he added, more concerned with the prospect that the starved worms in his stomach might start nibbling at the walls of his intestines than with his own hunger as such. He hadn't known until now that he could go without food for nearly twenty-four hours and still be alive and talking.

"Something seemed gravely wrong when–" he continued, but was cut short by the chime of the old Kaizerland grandfather clock, which hung delicately on the wall above the parlour door like a protective medicine pot. It was chiming the hour of three.

Mr Tangh-e-keh invited him to the parlour, gave him a bowl of water to clean his tired face, and asked if he'd like something to eat.

"There's fufu corn and *njama-njama* left over from last evening, which I can wake one of the women to warm for you," he proposed, sitting down with comfort on one of the four large, modern chairs he had bought recently in Zingraftstown after decades of persistent persuasion by the mothers of his children.

"There is bread as well, if you prefer something light and fast. You can have it with the tea in that flask on top of the cupboard," he pointed with his left hand, which Kwanga remembered had a finger less than the other. Kwanga didn't remember Mr Tangh-e-keh ever saying what happened to his finger. This was because he was most sensitive about the missing finger, and would, if someone absolutely insisted on knowing, prefer to lie, rather than tell the truth about the knife attack on him eight years ago by three Fulani youths who caught him red-handed sneaking away with ten of their cattle at night. Amongst the Fulani, his reputation was that of a man you shake hands with and check afterwards how many fingers you have left.Kwanga thanked him and opted for the bread and tea. For now all he wanted was something to calm the worms and steady his bowels. He fetched the red thermos flask, which he couldn't help noticing was made in The People's Republic of China – a name which always amused him, since he wasn't aware of the existence of republics of animals anywhere in the world. The bread was local but the flour Muzungulander, and the tea made in Nbuma (a farming town thirty kilometres east of Alfredsburg). The sugar, milk, cups and spoons were all

Muzungulander. Only the appetite and the belly were Mimbolander and Abehema.

Mr Tangh-e-keh watched Kwanga eat, a worried expression on his face. He seemed to want to say something, but didn't quite know how or where to begin. For five minutes only the sound of chewing and sipping could be heard. Kwanga could feel the tension in the atmosphere. Twice he looked up, but had the impression that Mr Tangh-e-keh was avoiding his eyes. This made his mind boil with questions. He could almost feel the psychological battle going on in the mind of his host: To say or not say? How to say or not to say?

Unable to bear the tension anymore, Kwanga broke the ice.

"Sorry I disturbed your sleep," he apologised again in Abehema to Mr Tangh-e-keh who was trying to suppress a yawn.

"Don't worry about the yawn," said Mr Tangh-e-keh. "I wasn't sleeping when you screamed, just brooding," he added. "How can one sleep with all this confusion – this turmoil and uncertainty beating in the air like bats thirsty for blood?" he asked rhetorically.

He could see that Kwanga was still ignorant, and was relieved none of his wives or children had spilled the beans. He was also aware of the extremely delicate nature of his task, and thought he needed all the tact and diplomacy he could muster to break the bad news to his friend's son. With his left hand he contemplated his baldness for a while, as he planned what next to say.

"Remember that the door of my house is as open to you today as it has been in the past," he told Kwanga. "One person's child is only in the womb. The son of a good friend is a son. He cannot allow your corpse to be savaged by dogs and vultures."

These were famous sayings, which Kwanga knew to be common amongst urbanites and villagers alike, but his mind was focused on Mr Tangh-e-keh's earlier ominous allusion to bats and blood. Where could he be heading? What was on his mind? Just what had happened? Kwanga felt lost as these questions crowded his mind.

"I'm grateful for your kindness," he said after a while, a respectful grin on his face. "I've always told my father of your generosity and caring attitude," he added, his conservative impression of Mr Tangh-e-keh as an epitome of greed and avarice quite unshaken.

What use are riches to a miser? Kwanga wondered, thinking back to the number of times his host would not give him even a cent for transport, and how he would wish Mr Tangh-e-keh were dead and his cattle sold to help poor students or miserable villagers. Countless were the times he had wished his father into giving up on Mr Tangh-e-keh who was a master of exploitation in the name of friendship.

"He'll be pleased to hear I stayed the night over with you," he said of his father, though aware of how much nonsense Peaphweng Mukong had stomached from the arrogant Mr Tangh-e-keh, just to see his son through education.

"He always insists I stay a day or two with you on my way to or from Abehema," he added, knowing that his father would not insist if he didn't think that Mr Tangh-e-keh might be moved by such a show of friendship to perform a rare act of generosity.

Kwanga paused and bit his fingernail like a child about to ask its parents for an awkward favour.

"I'm sorry I can't stay as long as I would like to," he said, still biting his nail. "The reason being that I'm only rushing home to see if all is well with Peaphweng Mukong your friend, the family and everyone in Abehema. It's been ages since I last went home, so I'm anxious to find out whether or not they are all in good health." He waited in vain for his host to interrupt him.

"I suppose Okeleke and Ndiko still ply the road? I didn't see their lorries at the station when I arrived, but I won't want to miss them. Have you any message for me to take along to my father?"

Kwanga felt more at home speaking to him in Abehema than in Pidgin-Tougalish. Although Kaizerbosch by birth, Mr Tangh-e-keh was well travelled and had learnt to speak many other languages in the region, some of which, like Abehema, he spoke almost without an accent.

The change of countenance was sudden and unmistakable. Mr Tangh-e-keh could hide his dejection no more. At first Kwanga thought it must be something he had said, but he was wrong. The intensified sadness on Mr Tangh-e-keh's face only added to Kwanga's suspicion that something deeply unhappy had occurred in Kaizerbosch. What for sure this something was, he still had to be told.

"I may not know what and why," he thought, "but I feel as I always do whenever chaos threatens order, or whenever my hopes are about to be dashed, like that fateful day at the University of Asieyam. I know it from the thumping of my heart, just like a dog, cat or horse knows when an earthquake is about to occur, or when someone close to them is about to die."

His mind went back to the little groups he saw on arrival, and to Mr Tangh-e-keh's wives and children who wouldn't stop weeping. How could something not be wrong? Why should Mr Tangh-e-keh, a man usually buoyant and happy, wear such a gloomy face unless something really devastating had occurred?

Kwanga looked at the clock, and wished he had the time to stay and see for himself whatever it was that had broken the normal rhythm of life in Kaizerbosch. He knew he had to go. Duty was beckoning him to Abehema, the duty of a *Kwanga* – the modern son of the soil – that he had accepted to be. He had to go home and see his parents and people, for there was a heavy load on his mind that needed to be taken out before it was too late.

He went over his plan once more in his mind, knowing that with a bit of luck, he would be in Abehema by 1 p.m. that day:

"First, I must tell them the truth about the mirage of Asieyam. Bitter though truth is, it can be lethal when discovered by those to whom one has lied all along. And since it always ends up being discovered, however hard we may try to conceal it, I have decided that it is preferable to swallow a bitter pill from the outset than to face a stormy catastrophe in the long run. I know it won't be easy to make them understand, but I must do my utmost. Success comes by trying, and he that ventures nothing gains nothing. When they finally realise it isn't my fault that I was relegated from the academic beehive of Asieyam, I will then introduce Patience.

"As far as she is concerned, I can't predict what my father's reaction will be when he hears what I have to say. I do hope for the best. I'm learning to hope for the best again, ever since I reconciled with Patience. All the same, I still shudder at the mere thought of Peaphweng Mukong turning Patience down. I wonder what I will do if that happens. Would I contest him if he decided against her? I honestly don't know, and definitely do not want things to come to that. For it would be a most awkward thing, to have to choose between the person one loves and one's parents who love one. I'm certain most will depend on how well I weave my story, which is why I'm doing all this rehearsing.

"Suppose I tell him that I respect him, Abehema and all its values, goals and beliefs, which I do, but that I still would like to choose my own wife, what is his reaction likely to be? Difficult to say. He should know, as I suppose he does, that I no longer fully belong to the village in the same way as they who live there. The path I have followed has placed me midway between Abehema and its values on the

216

one hand, and Kwang and what it stands for on the other. After all, weren't they the ones who named me Kwanga? Perhaps he would pursue this view of me to its logical end, after I've told him how helpful Patience has been to me for nearly a year. And I can see him softening his intolerance, and finally, giving me his permission and blessings. What an excellent compromise that would be! It would mean that Patience and I can be united both in church under Christ, and in my father's shrine under the ancestors. A marriage of tradition and kwang, results in a couple superior to both, and can certainly not be reduced to either without losing some of its richness. The Church would ask us to place the ring on each other's finger. And the village would honour us with a drink of raffia wine from Peaphweng Mukong's horn cup, and Mama Ngonsu, together with the other women of the village, would ask us to kneel down in front of them and be smeared with camwood and herbal oils pregnant with fertility. What a double blessing! To have both Christ and ancestors intercede for God's help for us would certainly bring more peace to matrimony than anyone could ever hope for. And if Patience insists on civil marriage because she wants to earn a little more money as a civil servant with conjugal responsibilities, we could seek the mayor's benediction as well!"

Mr Tangh-e-keh shook his head in disagreement with a voice within him. Kwanga interrupted his thoughts and focused his eyes on his host, his ears anxious with expectancy.

Mr. Tangh-e-keh absent-mindedly drummed his fingers against the armrests of the new modern chair. Then stopped suddenly. He planted his feet firmly and in a slow, sad but decided voice, Mr Tangh-e-keh broke his silence.

"I would rather you stay here with us, Kwanga," he said, supporting his head with both hands, and looking really worn out. "There is something wrong at the moment with Abehema and the entire neighbourhood. For now you are safer here in Kaizerbosch." He was firm.

"What is wrong?" Kwanga asked in a tremulous voice, a current of chill wriggling through his body and resulting in goose pimples. "I don't understand what you mean," he said, and moved closer to his host, whose head was now between his hands like a crumbling building sustained by poles about to give way themselves.

"Nothing is clear yet," he whispered. "Nothing," he tried to reassure Kwanga, whose hands were trembling. Then telling himself "now or never", he raised his head and looked at Kwanga squarely in the face.

"It is said there is a poisonous gas emission around Abehema, which is judged to be very dangerous," he said, then paused and watched Kwanga for a while. "Until we have detailed information, the District Officer has prohibited any movement in that dir–" he yawned.

"Is there news whether people have been harmed?" Kwanga was anxious for his family and folks. Thoughts were racing in his head like a stampeded herd of cattle struggling along the edge of a dangerous cliff.

"Be calm, Kwanga, be calm my son," Mr Tangh-e-keh said, patting him reassuringly on the shoulder. "So far no news, just rumours. That's all we have to go by. Don't mind the weeping, wailing and mourning. People are what they are. They are understandably apprehensive, but their reactions so far are not based on any concrete piece of evidence. All one can really do now is pray and hope that nothing of what we hear and fear is happening in Abehema, Yenseh and Tchang. May God forbid it happening to us! May our ancestors squash whatever it is in its shell!"

He cleared his throat, opened the window briefly and spat a lump out into the darkness. The lump must have dropped on a toad, which protested by croaking. Mr Tangh-e-keh returned to his seat, and a few minutes later it started to rain lightly.

"We'd better go back to bed and snatch some sleep," he suggested, trying very hard to stay awake. "Today promises to be a tense and emotional day, as all eyes turn towards Abehema, with hope that someone else might turn up to confirm or deny what is said to be going on there. That's what we've been doing since yesterday morning, fishing for news. We are all anxious, dead worried." With that, he left his chair and started towards his bedroom, when Kwanga stopped him.

"Just one more question, please," Kwanga pleaded.

"Ask it," he replied curtly, scratching between his thighs with pleasure, his eyes half closed.

"Who brought news of the poisonous gas?"

"A mukala."

"A white man?"

"Two white men, one Muzungulander in the name of Ravageur and another who called himself Vanunu, but who wouldn't say his country."

"Ravageur!" Kwanga's reaction was sharp. "Did you say Ravageur?" He couldn't believe his ears. "What was he doing there?" he added with suspicious curiosity.

"Isn't that a strange question to ask?" replied Mr Tangh-e-keh, forcing a stale smile. "Do you not know that mukalas are always touring, that they have a strange inclination for lakes and parks, and that there is a lake at Abehema and a game reserve at Kakakum River, the village beyond Yenseh?" He was quite unaware of the fact that Kwanga had known and distrusted Ravageur for a long time, especially his dubious fondness of Lake Abehema and suspicious friendship with Peaphweng Mukong.

"I know." Kwanga agreed, still intuitively suspicious, but choosing not to bother his host any more than was absolutely necessary for the time being. He didn't cease to wonder why Ravageur of all people should suddenly return to Abehema after so long. Could it be that Ravageur had gone back to resume his secret experiments in the lake?

Kwanga's fears were surging and he wished he could get more information there and then.

"Then why ask, if you know?" Mr Tangh-e-keh sounded half asleep.

"Surely it isn't anything disastrous. If it were deadly, Ravageur and this Vanunu fellow wouldn't be here to tell you the story, would they?" He was pensive, self-reassuring. "Unless they planted the gas themselves, then ran away," he pondered. Why would they bother to tell anyone in that case?" He didn't know what to think.

Mr Tangh-e-keh made one last effort to stay awake, and told Kwanga to stand up and come forward. Then asking him to hold up his left hand, he ordered: "Look at your hand Kwanga." And after a brief pause, he asked, "Are all your fingers the same?"

"No, why?"

"What makes them different?"

"Some are longer and bigger than others."

"Well done," said Mr Tangh-e-keh. "Let's get some sleep," he added.

17

Mr Tangh-e-keh and Kwanga had just washed their hands to start eating their first meal of the day, when word reached them of an escapee from the area said to be affected by the poisonous gas. On hearing the news, Mr Tangh-e-keh snatched up his keys and was soon wrestling with the reluctant engine of his battered Land Rover, bought off a retiring Tougalish archaeologist a decade before. Kwanga, despite being famished, joined him. Terribly frustrated by the scarcity of information from the deeply inaccessible allegedly affected region beyond Kaizerbosch, Kwanga's real hunger was for anything but food.

When the engine would not start, he asked Kwanga and his children to push the car to the top of the slope from where he could roll down to start with speed in the second gear. The trick worked, and soon the car was gasping along the puddled street that led to the Kaizerbosch General Hospital. Both men were keen to see and hear for themselves whether or not Ravageur and Vanunu meant what they said about a poisonous gas in Yenseh, Abehema and Tchang. If yes, they wanted to know whether the gas had caused any harm to life, human and animal. The embargo the District Officer had placed on travel to the region had made them helplessly dependent on hearsay. This was their very first opportunity to know a little more and perhaps, to decide in consequence whether or not to defy the travel ban.

The day was dreary after last night's rain. And the weepers crowding the streets made things even drearier. It looked as if everyone in Kaizerbosch had evacuated their houses to fill the streets and the market square. If only a mysterious loudspeaker would announce that it was all a hoax, that Ravageur and Vanunu had raised a false alarm, and that everybody could return home in peace, knowing their kin and kith in the remote villages of Yenseh, Abehema and Tchang were safe and sound. Life could continue as normal.

The last time Mr Tangh-e-keh saw a crowd this thick was on the day of the referendum twenty-six years ago, when everyone was pulled out of their houses, to say 'Yes' or 'No' to white and black ballot boxes – the white standing for unification with the Muzungulander Mimboland, and the black for a union with Kuti. Mr Tangh-e-keh remembered his late father voting black, and when asked why by patriots who thought he had betrayed their cause, had replied rather amusingly, but in earnest, "Don't you know that white is a very delicate colour to handle? White gets dirty too easily, and being a father with many children and grandchildren, I can't always ensure their hands are clean every time they come rushing for a cuddle. That's way I voted black. And as for those of you who voted white, wait until it has lost its sparkle! Then you'd wish you had been wiser!" A truly remarkable man, Mr Tangh-e-keh's father. His tragic death under mysterious circumstances a month after the referendum came as a great blow to his family and people. Thinking of his father all of a sudden, Mr Tangh-e-keh wondered if he was about to receive yet another blow. "God forbid," he whispered, and continued steering and encouraging the car that seemed slower than a tortoise.

The main entrance to the hospital was full of worried men, women in tears and children up in arms. There were people from every corner of the division, including the nomadic Fulanis. It was so crowded that Mr Tangh-e-keh was forced to turn back and park a long way away from the hospital. Then together with Kwanga, he fought his way through the thickness into the even thicker premises. The wailers didn't have much to tell about the latest developments, but that didn't stop them showing how they felt.

"They are crying because their hearts tell them to," Mr Tangh-e-keh told Kwanga, after alerting a sobbing Fulani mother that the baby in her hands was bawling for milk.

Seeing the Fulani reminded Mr Tangh-e-keh of his herds in Abehema, and made him even more anxious to find out what exactly was happening. He couldn't imagine himself without his cattle. How could he when he had spent so much time, money and ingenuity accumulating them! He feared for them. He feared in case the story about the gas was true. There was no doubt in his mind that cattle and other animals in the wild would be the first victims of any poisonous gas in the air. For while people could confine themselves to the safety of their huts and houses, the cattle lived in the open, more exposed to primitive hazards and malevolent forces. These animals, apart from the fact that they grazed in the open pastures, also lacked the faculties to organise urgent self-protection in the same way humans would. All this bothered him immensely. To have lived in austerity for forty years and more, saving everything for the future, and be faced with the sudden prospect of losing it all frightened him beyond measure.

He and Kwanga made their way through the crowd, until they got to the Danger Ward, where the person they had come to see and hear was reported to be. The nurse on duty, who had already turned away every "inquisitive monkey" except the District Officer and Chiefs of Police and the Gendarmerie, let them in because she was an intimate friend of Mr Tangh-e-keh (as were many other women, married and single).

It wasn't surprising that Mr Tangh-e-keh, known to be so stingy, was a popular man in town. His father had been a great politician since the days of the Kaizerlanders, and naturally, Mr Tangh-e-keh shared some of the fame. He added to that his personal breakthrough, in the world of cattle, a world long monopolised by the Fulanis. For these reasons he was popular, his greed notwithstanding. With women he was less greedy, which was what they liked most in him. So if a woman failed to notice his handsome face, she couldn't avoid his distinctive baldness, the prominence of his stomach and his bulging pockets.

He was often found eating grilled beef and drinking cheap Muzunguland wine with women, but seldom did he extend this generosity to men, unless of course he was caught red-handed with someone else's wife. Then he would try to be open-handed to the husband, more in an effort to bribe to stop a scandal than because he believed in generosity for the sake of it. He hadn't lost his finger just to be kind to men.

The nurse offered them seats, but Mr Tangh-e-keh preferred to sit beside the patient on the bed, at whom he took a quick look and decided his situation wasn't critical. The nurse went out of the room, leaving the two men alone with Mathias the patient and closing the window where some people were trying to peep in. This brought more shouts of protest and accusations of discrimination, but she wasn't bothered. She seemed quite used to being shouted at in this manner.

Mr Tangh-e-keh fetched a large handkerchief from his trouser pocket, which he used to mop his face and palms, anxious like a rich criminal awaiting the verdict of an incorruptible judge, a rarity in Mimboland.

Apart from a few bruises on his arms and legs, the patient looked physically normal. Before Mr Tangh-e-keh found the courage to ask his first question, the nurse returned with a glass of medicine for the patient. It was a darkish liquid that looked more like the concoction of a herbalist than any modern medicine Kwanga had seen. The patient winced as he drank it.

"It is more bitter than bitterleaf," he complained. "Are you sure this is from a doctor, and not a medicine man?" he sought to be reassured.

The nurse said nothing, but looked pleased he had taken it. It was indeed a concoction by a local herbalist, and she knew just how disgusting the stuff tasted.

"It will do you good, so says the doctor," she told him with a smile. Then warning Mr Tangh-e-keh and Kwanga not to bother Mathias with too many questions, she went out again, this time to her office next door.

Mr Tangh-e-keh sympathized with the patient whom he recognised as a worker at the Yenseh Health Centre.

"Mathias," he began, mopping his baldness with the wet handkerchief he held. "We are very sorry a thing like this should befall you. Whatever it is they say is going on in Tchang, Abehema and Yenseh. The wind makes noise as it blows, but the bits and pieces we've picked up so far make little sense. So I would be very grateful if you tell us what has actually happened, what you've been through, seen or heard. We are famished for news."

He was being tactful, despite his reputation as a businessman with an inflated ego who enjoyed trampling on others to monopolise the harvest from the tree of abundant profit.

"I can't pretend to know what is actually going on myself," said Mathias in a faint and strained voice, as if his lungs were hurt. "At least I know what I've just gone through," he added with a cough that forced foam out of his mouth, which he cleaned with the back of his hand.

"We are listening, Mathias," replied Mr Tangh-e-keh, adjusting his position on the bed, in order to protect his face from the coughing.

"You know I work as a laboratory technician at the Yenseh Health Centre, don't you?"

Mathias was really being menaced by the cough, and every time he coughed, foam filled his mouth. The back of his left hand was wet with foam, so Kwanga suggested he use the towel that hung at the head of the bed. He did, and subsequently coughed onto it directly.

"I know that very well," replied Mr Tangh-e-keh, slightly impatient. He wanted Mathias to go straight to the tale of strangeness. He was equally aware that he couldn't bully Mathias or dictate the pace of the narration.

"As early as 4 o'clock this morning I set out for Yenseh where I live and work."

Mathias supported his head with his right hand, which was in turn supported by the pillow. This helped reduce the coughing and enable him tell his story with fewer interruptions.

"I must say I heard nothing about a poisonous gas before my departure from Kaizerbosch this morning. I wouldn't have ventured out there, had I known or suspected something might be wrong. As it happened, I mounted my Suzuki 125 and started off for the long – and what turned out to be ghastly – ride."

Apparently, the travel ban by the District Officer had escaped Mathias, who must have gone to bed pretty early as well, to have missed the street wailings. Kaizerbosch being a town without a radio station and without phones, it was quite understandable how that could have happened, as news and administrative instructions tended to circulate a lot more by foot and word of mouth, like rumour did. The Police and Gendarmerie could man the motorable roads with checkpoints, but not the myriads of footpaths in and out of Kaizerbosch. Kwanga made a mental note of this possibility.

"Last Monday I came here to iron out a few matters in the family, and to round off the death celebration of my father-in-law, who as you probably know, died three weeks ago from thunder sent by an enemy. Everything was okay then. By 5 o'clock this morning I was already descending the delicate hills above the village of Tchang. It was biting cold, so I stopped riding for a while and put on a thick overcoat. Also I tied a scarf round my neck and slightly over my mouth, to keep myself warm. Then I resumed my journey, riding with care because I was also transporting a calabash of palm oil, which the diviner-healer Wabuah of Kakakum asked me to purchase for him here in Kaizerbosch."

Kwanga lit up when he heard of Wabuah of Kakakum, the most renowned of all the diviner-healers in the region. He knew him to be a friend of his father's, and to be well respected in Abehema.

"I rode past Tchang when it was just beginning to be daylight. Somewhere between Tchang and Abehema, things began to be abnormal. The first thing I came across was a dead hare. It was unusually fat, inflated I should say, and lay by the side of the road. Uncommon as it was to find game lying dead, I thought it must have been assaulted by hunters who, probably outsmarted, had failed to continue chasing the hare. What an unusual place for an animal to escape to, the motor road! I thought. I couldn't resist the temptation to pick it up. I tied it behind my machine and continued my journey, pleased with my fortune, and knowing my family would live like the wife and children of a big man for at least a week.

"Not very far away from the first scene, I saw another hare, which I also picked up, using the same argument to justify my action. When a little farther I saw an antelope lying in the middle of the road, my mind started to work. I began to doubt my luck and wonder if I wasn't about to fall into a carefully prepared trap of some kind or other." He coughed, violently, and Kwanga adjusted his pillows.

He resumed. "So I slowed down (in speed), and wondered how I could possibly explain what I was seeing, or rather, what I thought I was seeing. Luck doesn't mean the absence of sense, you know," Mathias commented, looking up at Mr Tangh-e-keh who listened with pensive keenness.

"Nor does luck mean the excessive extension of one's credulity," he continued.

"So when I also came across a dead python with a half-swallowed dog sticking out of its mouth, I simply untied the two hares and threw them back into the bush. It was only then that I noticed the surrounding silence. There were no flies buzzing round the dead game. Even the insects of the bushes and the habitual morning chorus of songbirds were absent..." Mathias was again interrupted by his cough. He shook as the fear revisited him.

"My greatest shock came when just at the top of the hill, at the boundary between Tchang and Abehema, I saw three corpses lying miserably across the road, their tongues sticking out and lined by foam. There were no flies on the dead. A pungent smell hit my nostrils, and irritated my entrails. To me, the end of the world had come. Before I knew more, I had fainted." Even now, Mathias' face bore the shock of his experience.

"I can't say by what magic I rode back to Kaizerbosch, or what inspired me to drink some of the palm oil I was taking to the diviner-healer. I've been told that the oil must have been what saved my life. I also know that this ring specially prepared for me by Wabuah of Kakakum, a ring that has saved me several times before, must have come to my aid one way or another." He touched his dark iron ring fondly and with conviction.

"When I regained a bit of consciousness, I felt hollow and nauseated within, as if someone had set fire to my intestines, heart and lungs. In fact, my entrails burnt with pain as if a jar of concentrated acid had been poured on them. I was greatly weakened, and this foam you see whenever I cough started right there. The air was thick and stuffy. Breathing was almost impossible. Even more so when I had to wrap the scarf over my nose to avoid the most repulsive stench that filled the air." His eyes spelt the hell he had been through, hell that seemed to have possessed him in the form of a strange cough.

"When I started back to Kaizerbosch, I didn't know what I was doing. All I felt was this urge to turn back, to venture no further. There was absolute silence ... everywhere. It was as if the world had been undone and deadened, even the sky. I was afraid as anyone could be, and as good as dead myself. Do you think, Mr Tangh-e-keh, that after an experience like that I can still doubt the existence of God or the goodwill of my ancestors?" Mathias asked rhetorically, struggling with another bout of coughing.

"I would be a madman or a dunce not to recognise the might of these forces in keeping me at bay of all the evil things that come my way daily. It is so easy to take things for granted when life is normal." He answered his own question, his face full of determination and showing his eternal gratitude for the opportunity the experience had offered him to re-examine his life.

At this juncture the nurse charged into the ward and told the visitors their time was up. The patient had gone through a traumatic experience and needed proper rest. As she explained, not even the doctors understood yet what could be wrong with Mathias's organs, and until a proper diagnosis was conducted, the severity of his condition remained a matter for conjecture.

"I'm afraid his situation may well be more critical than it looks," she expressed concern. She invited Mr Tangh-e-keh to her office next door, where she knew nobody could overhear them. There, she repeated her criticism of the hospital management, one he had heard several times before in his cozy den.

"You know we are a poor and forgotten hospital," she whispered, even though there was no one around who she feared might eavesdrop on behalf of the authorities. She had learnt to be wary, and to take no chances. One could never be too careful with the authorities who behaved like a hundred-headed monster full of eyes and ears.

"As a hospital, we lack the most basic equipment and drugs, not to mention the sort of equipment and experience to deal with something as new, as strange and as deadly as this."

With a cynical smile she mocked, "Our hospital is general only in name. You know that, don't you? It lacks even common aspirin for headaches. And were this thing Mathias reports to turn into a disaster, heaven alone knows how we are going to cope. It is because no one knows what to do that the doctor in charge of this ward has strongly advised me against letting every inquisitive monkey in to aggravate Mathias's condition with questions. So you ought to think yourself really privileged to have been allowed in," she smiled broadly, and touched his nose with a cheeky finger pregnant with meaning.

He showed his gratitude by pinching her breast playfully, then whispering her reward into her ear.

"Tell me, do you think it's wise of the D.O. to stop people from going to find out what is actually happening?" asked the nurse, pulling herself away and getting serious and dutiful again.

Mr Tangh-e-keh shook his head to show that he didn't think so. Then added, "What if people are dying or have died in great numbers? Who will bury them or stop more from dying, if we are not allowed to go there? I think it's a grave mistake on his part. But then, he is the government." He was embittered by the prospect that such delays might affect his chances of rescuing his cattle, in case what Mathias had told them happened to be more widespread. "Let's only hope that what Mathias recounts is specific to what he saw, and not a disaster of greater magnitude. Else the whole population could be wiped out just like that," she clicked her fingers, opening the door to let her friend out.

Mr Tangh-e-keh formally thanked Mathias and the nurse, and told Kwanga to remind him to have one of his wives bring some food over for Mathias. Then accompanied by Kwanga, he left the ward and struggled through a reinforced crowd of wailers whom the police were desperately trying to keep under control.

That very evening Kwanga made his first attempt to slip through the barriers imposed by the D.O. He needed to find out the fate of his people and home village of Abehema, situated some hundred kilometres away. Every shortcut he knew, every footpath he attempted, was blocked by gun carrying no-nonsense gendarmes and soldiers, with strict instructions to send back anyone who dared. Despite his phobia for men in uniform, he tried creeping through the bushes and outrunning the forces of law and order. Each time he was detected, tortured, and sent back fleeing. Finally, he gave up, and retired in tears to nurse the bruises he had sustained.

18

It was midnight. Kwanga was lying awake in bed, tears in his eyes, unable to fall asleep. Except for Mr Tangh-e-keh who had gone to an appointment with the nurse, everyone else in the house was in bed as well, worried like Kwanga and perhaps asleep. His mind was reliving every moment of the day that had just gone by, making him feel the real impact of all he had heard, seen and attempted. The day's experiences had broken his spirits and left him lonely and lost. His nostalgia for Abehema and his family was surging like *gari* in a bowl of water. After all he had heard and seen, would he ever find them alive? More tears came, more memories, and thoughts of suicide. Why stay alive he thought, if everyone related to him seemed to be dying like sacrificial fowls, or like flies poisoned by a heap of cow dung.

"Who could have imagined what I heard this evening," he marvelled. "How pathetic that the boy who recounted his sad experiences no longer has anyone to lead him through the narrow path of life. And he is barely in secondary school, only fourteen! What becomes of him in an educational system where even children with total parental support seldom cross the Rubicon? His father, a self-made man, how could death snatch him just before his song of victory? Why couldn't the forces of evil wait just a year or two, enough time for him to accumulate a little something for his family and dependants? I can't really bring myself to believe that Captain Tsemsi is dead. Judging from that story his son told, and the way he told it, what reason have I to doubt his death?

"As Tam told us this evening at the hospital when we called for the second time (thanks to the nurse who would risk anything to please Mr Tangh-e-keh), his father, Captain Tsemsi, was on holiday, one he decided to spend with his family at his home village of Yenseh. Captain Tsemsi drove all the way from Nyamandem where he worked, to Kaizerbosch in his brand-new tropicalised second-hand Peugeot 504 ordered from Muzunguland. Because of the exceedingly bad state of the roads, he left his car in Kaizerbosch, and hired a four-wheel-drive Land Rover to take him and his family through the slip and slide of the deplorable road to his home village. This was on Wednesday. And as fate would have it, he insisted on going to Yenseh despite attempts by friends to make him stay the night in Kaizerbosch. He wouldn't even let them persuade him with a party in his honour. How true it is that when your time comes, nothing can stop it!

"They had gone to bed noticing nothing, like any normal day. Death struck as the family slept, sharp and brusque. Everyone in a family of eight perished but Tam. Like he said, they were all in bed when it began, not very long after his father returned from drinking with the local dignitaries at the market square. What first attracted his attention was an odd, dry smell – a terrible smell, like a rotten egg. Then there was the crying of his three-year-old sister. Tam left his bed and went over to where she lay, crying and snoring in a very abnormal way. Though he would not say what made her cry out so, he could sense that his sister was very hot, and that her heartbeat was faster than normal. Tam himself was feeling hot, as if his body were cooking from within. He went into his parent's bedroom to fetch some anti-fever tablets and inform them of what was up. On his way in, he met his father coming out, complaining of feeling uncomfortable, as if being choked. Tam told him about his sister and his own discomfort. Captain Tsemsi told him where to find the drug, and asked him to proceed with the administration while he went out for a breath of fresh air and to relieve himself. Tam never saw his sister alive again. Not that the aspirin he brought back would have saved her life, come to think of it, but he would have liked to feel he had tried to do something to rescue her. Instead, when he returned she was already dead. As he sobbed over the innocent little corpse in his arms, his other brothers and sisters began to scream hysterically. Panicked, he left the corpse on the bed and rushed around the house in confused madness, examining his other brothers and sisters. Their situation was critical, certainly beyond his naivety and incompetence. Perhaps it would be better to alert the expert attention of his mother, he thought rather belatedly. His mother wasn't in her bedroom anymore when he stormed in. Then he remembered that his father had not yet returned either. What could have happened to him? He rushed out to see.

"How shocked Tam must have been by what he saw! The innocence with which he recounted his experience told me that his traumas were still to come. He still thought of it as a rather unusual dream. I could see that when he finally comes to think of it in real terms, and to imagine the implications of his being left alone in a jungle where the scramble after *Kwang* seems to have replaced all other values and reduced everyone into ruthless pretentious embodiments of lust and greed, he might wish he had died with his family.

"In Tam's case, like in mine nearly a year ago, I'm not being unduly pessimistic. Isn't everyone's worldview shaped by their particular experience of the society and circumstances into which they were born? And if my society had set itself the goal to mould an optimist of me, would it have subjected me to such despicable tribulations? Would it have disappointed my parents and people in this way? So unabashedly? Folks who it now appears (God forbid it to be true!) have died without a taste of the *Kwang* for which they

234

sought all their lives – the very *Kwang* promised all and sundry at the dawn of Mimboland independence? No one delights in being pessimistic. Everyone likes the good side of life! We are all bound to lose faith when each time we dip our hook into a river of fish, all we catch is an old spiky boot.

"Tam saw his parents on the grass outside their house. His mother lay dead over his father's corpse, their mouths white with foam. He touched both of them. Their blood had gone cold already. As tears clouded his eyes, he made a desperate dash back into the house to save his younger ones, his only hope. He was too late for this. All of them were dead, dead and gone. He was alone in the world. Could he believe himself and what he was going through? Perhaps he was simply dreaming. He remembered what his grandfather told him once, that sometimes dreams could just be as true as real life. His grandfather had even told him the story of how one of his daughters died and was allegedly seen roaming the paths of the village weeks after her funeral. She was even alleged to have surprised her husband in the act of making love with another woman on their matrimonial bed. As a result of the growing feeling that this could be a dream, Tam decided to find out what things looked like outside their own compound. 'I went across to our neighbour's house to see if they were okay, but they were all dead. At the next compound, I tried to open the doors, but these were bolted from within, with no sign of life.' All along, Tam was like someone in a deep dream, someone hypnotised by the cruel jokes of life. 'If I am to die, let me die running for life', he told himself.

"Once on the motor road, Tam turned left and walked feebly in the direction of the Yenseh Health Centre, partly because he wanted to inform the village nurse of what had happened, and also because many people resided thereabouts, it would be good to know if something similar had occurred beyond his neighbourhood. Tam never went that far. He collapsed a hundred metres from their house, choked by the substance that smelt like rotten eggs. In fact, he said the air was so polluted with such an odour that the only way he avoided taking in so much of it was by pulling his jumper over his mouth and nostrils. He realised he was bleeding profusely from his nose, and that his mouth was becoming very foamy. And he felt as if a bag of cement had been placed on his chest to make breathing difficult.

"As he lay dying, he remembered the only prayer he had succeeded in learning off by heart in primary school, that is in addition to the Lord's Prayer that was obligatory: Lord, I have sinned and come short of thy glory: forgive me and call me back to thyself. May thy will be done. Through Jesus Christ my saviour I pray. Amen.

"Minutes later, Tam heard the faint sound of a motorcycle from the direction of Kakakum River. He struggled to his feet and fell across the road, wanting to be noticed and carried to the Health Centre. The rider stopped when his headlights flashed on Tam, picked him up and managed to seat him on the motorcycle, then resumed his desperate journey in search of salvation. This helpful man, wearing a helmet (which must have kept him going) was equally in pain. He had lost his wife and two children in a similar manner, and was rushing to Kaizerbosch to alert the administrative authorities of the bizarre goings-on, the mysterious whisk that was striking humans dead like flies. Little did this 'good Samaritan' know that not only were the authorities well informed, they had chosen the course of inaction over timely intervention to save human life!

"From the way these two described what they saw, there is little or nothing to hope for. The cold hand of death has gone epidemic, and I have no reason for stubbornly deluding myself that my family and village have been spared the slashing fangs of the vampires of 'modern' death.

Kwanga wiped his eyes with the back of his hand, blew his nose, cleaned his fingers on the blanket, and muttered, "One may mourn a death or two or three, and organise elaborate funerals for every one of them, but when death becomes so massive, and men, women and children fall and die like cockroaches poisoned by a potent insecticide, it ceases to be an emotional thing, because it doesn't make sense any more. It refuses to be the bad dream which people would like to believe it is."

He blew his nose again, then added thoughtfully, "That's why, I think, Mr Tangh-e-keh burst into hysterical laughter this evening, like a deranged fool. He didn't cry just then because what he heard was too much for tears. His laughter was one of deep pain, not of profound joy, which is why when he got home and locked himself in this bedroom, he did weep like an infant. And he looked so worn out and dishevelled afterwards that he had to take a bath and tidy up before his appointment with the nurse at his cozy den."

Kwanga turned over to lie on his back, closed his eyes and imagined arriving at Abehema, disbelieving the devastation that the mysterious gas had caused. The stories he had just relived were far too horrifying. Again, with a shudder, he remembered what Tam and the rider said about their struggle through carcasses and corpses in Abehema, which, it would appear, was at the very heart of the mysterious killer gas.

"Should this be true," he muttered, shivering like a rain-soaked chick, "then I'm a lost man. It can't be true, it just can't be!" he protested.

The smiling faces he had gone home to see and play with throughout the years gone for good? The little children of Abehema whose innocent charm and cheerful poverty had forced many a tourist from Tougaland, Muzunguland and elsewhere to dip their hands into their pockets, how could it be true that they were no more? What crime had they committed to deserve a fate that brutal? Ngonsu his mother and the women of Abehema, who had toiled under the scorching sun and scourging rain to keep body and soul together, had failed in their mission? These women who had defied hardship with happiness and hope would sing and dance no more under the gentle light of the moon? How could he believe that Chief Ngain, Peaphweng Mukong and the other notables, who bridged the gap between the community of the living and the ancestors, had been ignored by the god of harmony and continuity? How could the villagers of Abehema vanish without his having fulfilled their dreams and craving for a better life, a modern life? Was it fair for them to perish so shabbily without a taste of the *Kwang* they had yearned and toiled for all their lives? Had they named him Kwanga in vain?

He hated to listen to the other voice in him, because it narrated a forbidden tale. It stroked the sad chord of realism, urging him with brutal callousness to accept the devastation of his people as a *fait accompli*. It told him to see things the way they had been narrated by Mathias, Tam and the rider.

"All this is true, willy-nilly," said the frightening voice of doom. "Life's clock has made a complete circle, and there is no turning it back, not even for the sake of a persistent fool like you!" It roared with delight like a lion after a good meal, its mocking tone piercing through his heart like a witch's words.

"Your peasant parents, sheepish in their tolerance like the donkey, having spent their last muscle, have got the last breath of air they deserve, and you must accept it, for they had little choice in anything they did all their lives," the voice clattered with laughter again, and he wished he could squeeze it out of him.

"Only one who has lost his freedom can accept to live a life that makes little sense to him," the voice went on. "Your folks did this for far too long. They carried their tolerance too far! That's why they've paid a price this big! Hope you learn from them, else–"

Kwanga suspected the voice was about to recommend suicide, and he was right, for it went on to do just that.

"You know you really ought to be ashamed of yourself," it moralised. "Why on earth are you still here, trying to catch your shadow like a mad dog? Who told you suicide isn't a noble thing? Better to die like a dog than live like a dog. Have you ever heard that saying? Suicides aren't spineless either. The cowards are those who like you, insist on living even this ugly and intolerable life, never seeming to question with decisive action the greed and selfishness of the vampires that feast on their lifeblood. Aren't you in fact saying you are too weak and incapable, when you condemn others for taking their own lives, yet shudder at the mere thought of confronting these vampires?

"Look at you," the voice went on, "a coward who has spent his entire life running. You run away from soldiers in Nyamandem, you run away from lecturers who make nonsense of your education and future, you run away from your responsibilities vis-à-vis your parents and people, you run away... you run away... And you only flex your muscles with women. See how tortured you've made Patience feel with your dependency. And now you proceed to make her pregnant without a source of income. How do you expect to feed your baby? How can a man fall so low? How can you accept a life of shame and call yourself a man?... Oumarou the meat roaster of Nyamandem, a mere refugee from beleaguered Warzone, is a thousand times more man than you can ever aspire to be. Shame.... Shame on..."

This voice, like someone speaking through him, tried to incite him to take his own life. He could bear it no longer. He opened his eyes, switched on the lights and sat up in bed, shaken and confused. Just as he searched under the pillow for his little watch, the clock chimed the hour of two. Seconds later, he heard the door open and Mr Tangh-e-keh walk in and slump himself into a chair. Emmanuel joined him in the parlour, to purge his mind of frightful thoughts

239

for a while, and perhaps, calm down enough to get a bit of sleep.

Mr Tangh-e-keh was tipsy but not drunk. From the exceptional radiance and sparkle in his eyes, Kwanga could guess he had just come from making passionate love. He didn't feel like going to bed just yet. There was too much on his mind, too much for him to get any sleep even if he went to bed. He told Kwanga he was waiting or rather, hoping, that Kwah, his younger brother, would return from Hiseng (the tributary village to the chiefdom of Abehema), with news about his cattle. Kwah had left for Hiseng a week ago, via Meng, to inspect the cattle, supply salt and modern medicines for their welfare, and pay the herdboys their wages. He had been expected back long before now, and Mr Tangh-e-keh was getting very worried.

"Everything seems to be dead or dying," he murmured repeatedly, more to himself than to Kwanga who was sitting opposite him with folded arms. "My cattle have died or are dying. Maybe my brother is dead or dying. What is the world coming to?" He looked at Kwanga, clearly downcast, as if he would break into tears the next moment.

Kwanga could see that the nurse hadn't succeeded in turning Mr Tangh-e-keh's mind away from his problems more than was necessary for a single session of passionate love. He thought Mr Tangh-e-keh was being exceedingly selfish: "He seems to forget I'm in a similar predicament. To hear him go on and on about his cattle one might think there are no human victims involved. Even Kwah, his brother, seems to be an afterthought, or just the key to resolving the incertitude about the fate of his cattle. What a greedy man!"

Not knowing how to reply, Kwanga said simply, "I don't know," with a heavy sigh.

This evening Mr. Tangh-e-keh had witnessed mass hysteria among the forsaken Fulanis at the market square and at the hospital. He saw and heard how they rubbed themselves in mud like pigs and screamed and wailed, inviting Allah to end their lives rather than put them through the ordeal of loss. They were terrified at the prospect of losing their kin and herds. Some of them had left their families as far back as Kakakum River and Yenseh, to sell a few cattle and pay their jangali taxes or buy provisions for their families and salt for their animals. Some had come to settle farmer-grazer land disputes in the modern court, leaving behind the bulk of their families and the cattle that gave meaning to their lives. Others had just come because it was their habit to visit the town every now and again to drink beer, get drunk, negotiate with free women on spending the night together, and take them to one of the only two hotels – Chuma Falls and Lake Kaizerbosch.

He knew that, like him, the Fulanis' concern for their cattle was well founded, for breeding these animals was no easy task. It entailed a lifelong commitment to roaming the hills, mountains and valleys in search of green pastures. Few people had such patience. The Fulanis lived for their cattle and were involved neither in farming nor in any other business. Their herds made life make sense to them.

"And suppose," Mr Tangh-e-keh thought aloud, "suppose those Fulanis I saw at the market square were to lose both their cattle and people back in Yenseh, Abehema or Tchang, what good would life be anymore?"

Kwanga, who must have thought the question addressed to him, refused to be drawn into any discussion of the very matter that chased him out of bed. He felt drained by his own thoughts and feelings and indisposed to contemplate Mr Tangh-e-keh's misfortunes with him. Instead, he suggested they stop torturing themselves with painful thoughts and futile speculations.

"At least, we must stay alive to discover the truth behind this mystery," he qualified, regretting the travel ban imposed by the District Officer. "Up to this point, we still can't say for sure what is actually happening in those forsaken villages. All we've gathered is the existence of an invisible killer who smells like rotten eggs or gunpowder, makes breathing difficult, and appears to be extremely poisonous and lethal. There is a lot more to know. Let's not lose our composure." He stopped briefly to blow his nose, using some of the toilet paper reserved for Mr Tangh-e-keh.

"I know it's difficult," he continued, aware he had captured Mr Tangh-e-keh's attention, "but let this bizarre occurrence not stop us from snatching a nap whenever we can, for no amount of hardship we inflict on ourselves right now will give us the information we desperately need, or change what has happened. No amount of weeping or going without sleep can alter a thing now! It's like singing and wailing at a funeral with full knowledge that no matter how hard and long we sing and wail, the person we are mourning is dead and gone for good. What we ought to be doing is seeking to convince the District Officer to allow us to go to the affected region and save lives when we still can." Kwanga was secretly planning his second attempt at slipping through the ban – in the dead of night, a time he hoped the gendarmes and soldiers would be too tired and sleepy to chase him.

Mr Tangh-e-keh nodded several times. If Kwanga, a mere boy, was capable of such courage, it was shameful of him to show less manliness. He warned himself not to forget that he was the elder, the father, the accomplished manhood!

On his part, Kwanga knew the philosopher speaking in him was a spectator scared to death when it came to concrete action, to beheading the vampires. He knew he wasn't being honest with his own feelings, that in truth he was too worried about his family and people, which was why he himself had tried and failed to fall asleep. Since his host appeared to listen to him, he wanted to carry through.

"You must be tired," he said, standing up and going across to Mr Tangh-e-keh. "Please, allow me to take you to bed," he added, and offered his hand. Impressed, Mr Tangh-e-keh obliged and followed Kwanga to the bedroom where

Kwanga took off his embroidered jacket and helped him into bed beside his snoring senior wife.

19

Kwah returned early in the morning on Saturday, August 23. His homecoming did little to reassure his brother, who had expected him to bring back precise information on the situation of his cattle in Abehema and thereabouts. Even the news that his cattle in Hiseng and beyond (an admittedly much much smaller herd than what he had at Abehema) were safe did not seem to delight Mr Tangh-e-keh in the least. Kwah knew his brother inside out. He knew him to be absolute and difficult to please, someone who hated half measures and who was quite capable of grieving for the loss of a single calf. Only such deep understanding had made living and working with his brother less intolerable. One of the herdboys, who knew Mr Tangh-e-keh less well, would have felt terribly insulted after a narrow escape from death, to be welcomed with a question on whether or not the cattle were okay.

When the brief wrangle over cattle had subsided, leaving Mr Tangh-e-keh clearly dissatisfied, Kwah proceeded to tell what he had seen and heard. He told his brother how he was at Hiseng on the night of Thursday, August 21, when something strange occurred. At exactly 1 a.m. that night, there was the most deafening explosion he had ever heard – "like the firing of a thousand dane guns all at once". At first the villagers of Hiseng didn't know what to make of the sound. None of them had ever heard anything so loud before, not even the oldest man in the village who claimed to have fought in Burma during World War II, to know the sound of fighter planes brought down by enemy fire, and to have witnessed several bombings. The only thing they could guess was that perhaps a lorry had ran into complications and exploded. This was rather farfetched, since the Ring Road, the only road motorable in the vicinity, was right down the distant valleys in Abehema, and no explosion from a lorry, no matter how great, could have been heard with such a loud boom in Hiseng, which was way up in the mountains.

The truth remained a matter for conjecture only until the following morning. As Kwah and other villagers came out of their houses and threw their eyes as far down the valley as these could see, they noticed that the mysterious Lake Abehema had grown bigger overnight, and that its water had turned muddy brown. So they took this as evidence linking the explosion with the lake. Kwah said that everyone in Hiseng was waiting to learn more from their sub-chief who had gone down to Abehema the morning of that same Thursday, to attend the market and join other notables in appeasing the ancestors with sacrifices. The sub-chief had still not returned when Kwah left Hiseng on foot for Kaizerbosch through Meng, a village in the opposite direction of Abehema and the Ring Road. Everyone in the village had their heart in their mouth. As long as the notable was away in Abehema, it was difficult for them to take the initiative and decide upon a rapid line of action.

When Kwanga was told Kwah's story later in the day, he immediately saw a connection between it and the horrifying dreams both Patience and he had dreamt. He couldn't help feeling that these dreams might indeed have been premonitions, warnings of some kind from the ancestors or from God. One thing troubled him though: If it were true that this was a warning and he the intended messenger, why then did the ancestors or God not make it possible for him to warn the villagers in time? Why had they provided the message and the messenger, yet allowed the audience to be victimised?

He hated the D.O., along with his gendarmes and soldiers, for barring his way to urgent answers for burning questions of the moment. He had tried two more times in vain to force his way through the human wall they had built round Kaizerbosch to prevent the living from attending to the dead and dying. Their insensitivity was unpardonable.

20

This was the first real meal they were having together for two days, Kwanga and Mr Tangh-e-keh. The older man was forcing the little balls of fufu down his throat as if they were smeared with quinine. The unusualness of the past three days had affected his appetite and instituted an uncharacteristic apathy even for the rarest delicacies. The only thing that seemed not to have been affected was his raw and brutish appetite for women outside of his own immediate wives, though even there he had assumed the rather sharp precision of a hypodermic needle and the summary haste of a village cock.

Kwanga was doing his utmost to swallow as many balls as he could, not so much because he felt hungry (although he had rarely eaten anything substantial since leaving Nyamandem), but because, like Mr Tangh-e-keh, he had been advised to fill his stomach in preparation for their journey to the affected area, at long last. They had also been advised to drink lots of palm oil and to carry some of it along, just in case the alleged gas was still very concentrated and lethal. The assumption was that if palm oil appeared to have protected Mathias, and a few others, it could help keep them alive too on their discovery mission.

"If the D.O. had dispatched soldiers to the area as soon as that dubious Ravageur and Vanunu brought word that their risky experiments were about to cause havoc, much might have been done to relieve the villagers, and perhaps a great loss of lives would have been prevented," he speculated as he swallowed his balls, grinding his teeth with bitterness, his face distorted by hatred and prejudice.

He wished the authorities could "track down these villains who featured in the nightmare I had, throwing hand grenades at my people! They must not be allowed to leave Mimboland before they've accounted for their shady activities around Lake Abehema."

His thoughts betrayed a total conviction in what he had dreamt, and a passionate distaste for Ravageur and Vanunu, whom he considered as terrorists. He had always mistrusted Ravageur, however much Ravageur tried to prove he meant no harm. Notwithstanding, Kwanga was well aware that these two could not be arrested on the basis of his dreams, and that there was no concrete evidence yet to link them with what had happened, apart, of course, from the purely circumstantial evidence that they were the first with word of a lethal gas. It could have been due simply to the fact that they were the most mobile, and were thus able to drive themselves out of Abehema in time. Yet Kwanga couldn't understand why Ravageur hadn't evacuated his father at least, if his alleged friendship with Peaphweng Mukong meant anything.

When they had both finished eating, they collected their bags and went to the District Office, where the official team they had asked to accompany them was taking their final instructions from the District Officer himself.

The D.O.'s instructions were clear: the team was under no circumstances to venture beyond the first village, Tchang, until there was every reason to suppose the poisonous gas had subsided.

To Kwanga, this was bad news indeed, for it meant that although Tchang was quite near Abehema, he wouldn't be able to know what the situation in his own village was. In any case, the state of Tchang would give him a rough idea of what things could be like in Abehema. The latest information about the gas – that is, Kwah's story of an explosion and of the sudden increase in size of Lake

Abehema – was passed on to the D.O. by Mr Tangh-e-keh, who apologised for not doing so earlier.

"I thought that by telling him it had to do with Lake Abehema," said Mr Tangh-e-keh, looking disappointed, "he would ask his team of fact-finders to proceed beyond Tchang to Abehema, and we might thus benefit from it. Instead, my information only hardened his stance against any visits to Abehema for the time being." He sighed as they climbed into the back of the army lorry. As usual when disappointed, he buried his face in his palms and shook his head sideways.

"Don't worry," Kwanga tried to console him. "Maybe we will learn about the situation in Abehema while in Tchang. Don't you think we might meet someone there that knows my parents, who might even have attended the Abehema market Thursday last, and can give us a firsthand account of what the hell is going on?"

Mr Tangh-e-keh shook his head vigorously in negation, then added, "No hope, Kwanga, no hope at all. I'm hardly pessimistic, but something in me is telling me strongly that there is every reason for pessimism now. I think the situation is disastrous, far worse than we are aware of at the moment."

"Cheer up, let's cheer up," Kwanga said, turning his face away to hide the tears in his eyes.

21

The night was particularly dark. There were perpetual strokes of lightning and thunderous roars in the skies, as the heavens examined the application for rain by the concerned people of Kaizerbosch. Mr Tangh-e-keh and Kwanga needed rain desperately, as did the District Officer and his team of fact-finders. Indeed, everyone needed rain as a matter of life and death. Only rain could limit the damaging effect of the killer gas. As the devil would have it, it hadn't rained seriously for three days. If it failed to rain tonight, then the lethal gas, carried by the wind, could eventually reach even Kaizerbosch, a hundred kilometres or so away from the affected area. This prospect made everyone panic, especially the suggestion that should it not rain tonight the town might be affected by midday tomorrow. Widespread panic had led to impromptu masses being organised by Christians, convening of nocturnal prayer sessions by Muslims, and the consultation of ancestors in shrines by those who believed in everything and more.

As far as Mr Tangh-e-keh and Kwanga were concerned, their trip to Tchang this afternoon had left them in no doubt about the gravity of the situation. What they saw was ghastly, larger than their emotions could sustain and more than words could describe. They found corpses along the road, across footpaths and in the bushes. The houses they forced open were full of dead bodies too. Sometimes they didn't succeed in opening a door, and had to get in through the roof. The discovery was always a foregone conclusion. Death was everywhere: in the bushes, on the Ring Road, along the footpaths, and in the houses and huts.

Many were those who had been taken quite by surprise and struck dead in their sleep or on their way back from Abehema where they had gone to attend the market on Thursday.

Strangely enough, not all they found were quite dead yet. Some people, mostly little children, were fighting hard to stay alive, to keep death away. Oscillating between life and death, their bruises, burns, and foaming mouths were there to catalogue the suffering they had endured. Their courage and determination touched the team profoundly, and forced tears out of even the most hard-hearted gendarmes. Two gendarmes were ordered by the captain to evacuate them to Kaizerbosch General Hospital, while the rest of the team stayed behind to bury the dead they could afford to bury.

The corpses, particularly those found by the roadside and in the bushes, were decaying already, as migrant flies and their maggots feasted on them. Others hidden away in the warmth of the houses were still recognisable, though these were all swollen and nigh bursting too. It wasn't at all easy to carry them to the shallow graves the team managed to dig in a hurry. The dripping puss and thickened blood, the flies and maggots swimming in liquid flesh, the repulsive stench, and sinister silence in the vicinity disgusted and nauseated the entire team and pushed them into discontinuing their attempts to do the dead a last service. They had come prepared to help if they could, but they hadn't come prepared for what they saw.

Among those fortunate enough to be buried was Peaphweng Ndyu, the diviner-healer from Abehema. Kwanga identified his corpse when the team broke into one of the houses. Peaphweng Ndyu's swollen body was found on the floor, close to the chair on which he had sat before death struck. Also on the floor was his famous raffia bag, in which he kept his divination kit, and which he carried around with him to save the people from every kind of mental and physical worry. On the bed was the body of a young woman, who must have invited Peaphweng Ndyu to divine for her, and to free her from the chains of sorcery at *Msa*, the mystical world of the spirits. Most unfortunately, they had both died during a divining session. The diviner had lost his life in an effort to make life better for someone else.

What Kwanga could not understand was how a man like Peaphweng Ndyu, believed to have supernatural powers and potency, could be whisked to death like a vulnerable fly.

"If it can happen to this potent diviner-healer familiar with the worlds of the living and the dead," Kwanga pondered in tears, "then whom did I expect to find safe in Abehema? What was this strange gas that could dare defy even the supernatural powers of Peaphweng Ndyu? And where were the ancestors whose order he had served all his life when this killer gas took hold of him?"

Among the dying survivors evacuated to Kaizerbosch were two children of Mr Tangh-e-keh's half-sister, about whom he was telling Kwanga for the first time. All these feeble children managed to tell him was that their mother had left on Wednesday to Abehema where she intended to visit her friends and attend the market the following day, but that she never returned. It was a real miracle how they, aged four and seven, had survived the poisonous gas and the hunger. Their father had died instead, leaving them behind.

Mr Tangh-e-keh and Kwanga made several attempts to persuade the D.O.'s men to allow them to proceed to Abehema, but to no avail. The gendarmes, whose overwhelming fear of death made them drink oil like beer, vehemently refused, saying they weren't even sure the team was going to survive after venturing as far as Tchang.

"Drink more oil, instead of going to die in Abehema," they told the disappointed Tangh-e-keh and Kwanga.

"If you like to die so much," said the team captain, "wait until we have safely taken you back to Kaizerbosch and told our boss you are okay. Then you can go and put a rope round your neck and die. For now, you are strictly under our custody."

As the team drove back to Kaizerbosch, they continued to see people, mostly Fulani, escaping from the valley of death into the hills and mountains of Kumbong and Wahing. A few of them still had cattle and sheep, but the majority had just a few possessions on their head, mostly kitchen utensils, a blanket and perhaps a torch. They looked desperate, indeed, with no precise idea where they were heading. A strange phenomenon had occurred in and around their neighbourhood, taking them entirely by surprise, and chasing them out of the homes and land that was theirs, that had been theirs for years. Today they were homeless, but a day or two ago, they had seemed so secure, going about their pastoral activities with rustic confidence and certitude, anticipating nothing like what was happening.

The sight of them escaping made Kwanga think of his family. He wished they might have sensed the danger coming and escaped. He remembered what his father used to tell him, that no one can die before his time.

"Should this be true," he reasoned, "then my family must be alive somewhere, at least part of it. For in Abehema, it was unheard of for an entire family to perish under the same blow, no matter how fatal and evil the blow. Should such an impossible thing happen, and none has been reported for generations, then the family in question is most likely to have committed an abomination in the eyes of the ancestors. What abomination could my poor parents have committed, serious enough to condemn the entire family?"

Like all other proverbs and sayings which his father had taught him, the one that no person can die before his time was based on the shared experiences of the people of

Abehema. With the help of the world hereafter, the people had collectively made sense of their world. Kwanga was aware that no proverb or saying suddenly sprang to life like a mushroom. Because these usually came to stay with the people, and outlive them, all proverbs and sayings took long to come to life. First they were conceived, then allowed to mature, and finally presented to the community to be seasoned and reseasoned. Then and only then did proverbs and sayings become part of a people, with a life of their own, longer and richer than that of anyone in the society.

His father had told him that no one could die before his time. He believed him, and knew this left every member of his family with two alternatives: dying when it was their time, or dying after their time. Although he couldn't say what their time was, he was convinced it couldn't be all at once for all of them. Thus, he hoped to find at least some members of his family alive. Yet his fear for the worst lingered, especially after the miserable spectacle of the dead Peaphweng Ndyu, the most able bridge between the ancestors and Abehema. If even he could die a miserable death, and a sudden one at that, wasn't this a sign that the ancestors had turned a blind eye on their most faithful servant? And who was safe, if this could happen to him?

The District Officer looked very worried when Mr Tangh-e-keh and Kwanga called to thank him for allowing them to accompany the fact-finders to Tchang. He declined to accept the bottle of whisky which Mr Tangh-e-keh insisted was only a show of gratitude, saying, "Hot drinks make sense when life is sweet, not when things are so tragic and death smells everywhere. Please Mr Tangh-e-keh, take it back with you. You can bring it again when our trials and tribulations of the moment are over and we have cause to celebrate."

What he said impressed Kwanga immensely, who had thought the District Officer was simply going to snatch the whisky and store it away in a cupboard full of many others, as did the bulk of his counterparts who justified bribery and corruption on the belief that a goat eats where it is tethered. Here was a goat, giving the impression that such vices were not as infectious as Kwanga had been led to believe, and that it was perfectly possible to curb them.

After Mr Tang-e-keh withdrew his tempting gift from the table around which the three of them sat, the D.O. told them why he was worried.

"I'm worried about what is happening in those remote villages of Tchang, Abehema, Yenseh and beyond. No administrator wants a tragedy in his area of jurisdiction. We administrators have always preferred attaining heroism through avoiding, not overcoming challenges. Man is delicate by nature, and can become even more vulnerable in the face of unpredictable occurrences such as this.

"I'm also worried about the telegram I sent to Nyamandem yesterday morning. So far there is no answer from there. Even the Governor's office in Zingraftstown, a stone's throw away from here, has not acknowledged receipt of a similar telegram. Nor has the provincial or national radio mentioned a word of what is going on here, despite the announcement I personally asked my press officer to draft and fax to both radio stations. I fear something is wrong with everything! What do you think, Mr Tang-e-keh? What do I do? I need your advice," he sounded really desperate. There was anxiety on his face, the fear of being embarrassed even further by what was already an embarrassment of unfathomable magnitude.

"The fault can't be the telecommunication system, sir," replied Mr Tangh-e-keh, sounding like his outspoken late father. "Personally, I think your messages have reached the right quarters. The government is like my late father who was so clever and experienced that he never reacted until he had considered all possible implications of his intended action. I think you should be calm, sir. Your message has reached the right ears, and as long as you don't receive an answer, consider it still under digestion."

"People are dying in great numbers. You saw it with your own eyes, didn't you? You brought back reports of horrific sights and rotting corpses, didn't you?" the D.O. asked Mr Tangh-e-keh, who nodded.

"Then how much longer can we wait? I fear that if we fail to act soon, we may have a serious epidemic in our hands, one worse than the cholera epidemic that took certain cities hostage a few years back. The more we delay, the more gas will continue to spread and kill innocent people." He paused to light a cigarette, the only vice he could stomach at a time like this.

He offered his guests cigarettes, but they both declined, Mr Tangh-e-keh reminding him that he didn't smoke.

"I understand what you mean about the government taking its time, but the situation is urgent," he repeated, banging on the table with a clinched fist.

"Yes, sir," replied Mr Tangh-e-keh, slightly amused by the D.O.'s show of anger. "Somehow you forget one thing. It might appear as if I'm trying to teach you what you should know. That's not the idea by any means. I think that like my late father, every complaint that comes to the government is said to be 'Very Urgent', 'Top Priority'. The government doesn't necessarily take things as defined by its local representatives. So it draws up a list of priorities of all the 'Very Urgent' and 'Top Priority' issues. Perhaps your message failed to sound urgent enough to attract priority response. And I don't think you expect a different reply from the Governor's office. I should think that being only a branch of the huge tree of government, the Governor and his team are equally waiting for instructions from the top of the central trunk. That is the way things work, isn't it? Just like everyone in our extensive family had to look up to my father to take all the important decisions. I remember the chaos that resulted from his death, as we his dependents had been cultivated to steer clear of initiative, and to follow even when we claimed to be leading. That was another matter."

"You are right, Mr Tangh-e-keh," said the D.O. "If I don't receive a message by midday tomorrow, I will have to go to the Governor's office myself, and possibly to Nyamandem if things don't work out satisfactorily at the provincial level. For you must agree with me that I can't, or rather shouldn't, malinger while the situation worsens."

"Do as you judge right, sir," said Mr Tangh-e-keh, in a politely sympathetic voice, not entirely free of cynicism.

The two of them talked on for a little longer about other matters, and then Kwanga and Mr Tangh-e-keh left, wishing the D.O. goodnight and good luck with the bureaucracy.

22

This morning's rainfall was brief but heavy. It moderated the temperatures and brought great sighs of relief. It looked as if this was the rain Kaizerbosch bargained for. It stopped just in time to permit Christians to go to their various places of worship to pray to God and ask him to be a father in this time of need. Kwanga went to the Church of the Poor, the Meek and the Innocent situated way out of town on the road to the forsaken villages of Tchang, Abehema and Yenseh.

In his sermon, the preacher stressed the need for calm and undying trust in the Lord. Events like this tested the faith of God's flock, but it was also at times like this that the good Lord knew the few to pick for heavenly glory from the many he had called. It was true that the authorities had delayed too much, and that lives perished unduly as a result. The God of unquestionable wisdom, mercy and hope, the God of life, was overseeing all actions, all thoughts, all aspirations in this beloved country and district. He would take care of everything, as he had always done. Things would come to pass just as the God of the living and the dead had planned, and he would never abandon his people in their hour of need. The sermon was infused with hope, and it reassured the congregation.

For his part, Mr Tangh-e-keh refused to go to church. When Kwanga made the suggestion that he should come along, the former replied most cynically that it wasn't by going to church that the dead would rise again and cattle would mow in the hills. His feeling of loss had penetrated him and profoundly affected his faith and hope. Not that he was one who ordinarily would be going to church, being more of a traditionalist in his beliefs and a regular consulter of medicine men and diviner-healers for protective portions of various kinds.

The first nationwide radio broadcast concerning the killer gas was made on Sunday morning by Radio Mimboland International station situated in Nyamandem. The broadcast was four days too late. Such armchair wait-and-see journalism of indifference was much to blame for massive loss of life. Why had it taken them four days to respond to the announcement the D.O. had dutifully telexed, drawing the attention of the nation and the world to the traumas and travails of Kaizerbosch and beyond? And even when they did get round to making a broadcast, couldn't they have thought of something better than the banality of "a volcanic explosion that emitted toxic gas and had reportedly claimed forty lives"? Which lives were they counting? Livestock or human? Kwanga was contemptuous yet relieved.

The lateness of the broadcast notwithstanding, Kwanga was pleased the whole nation was now aware of the tribulations of his people and was optimistic that soon the entire world would learn of it. There would be an influx of investigators and assistance, and before long he would know the fate of his family and people, and if he were lucky, might even get reunited with them, all of them. The prospect excited him and dappled his spirit with sparkles of hope.

He wondered where the broadcaster got his figure of forty deaths, though, when at Tchang alone they had counted more than double that figure. Could the District Officer have sent a false figure? He doubted that the D.O., whom he had come to recognise as a straightforward, clean-handed public servant, would doctor the figures. Maybe the Governor's office did. In any case, that wasn't too bad, as long as it didn't happen again. He would rather the entire truth was broadcast, so the victims might have the assistance they deserved. He feared that doctoring the figures might affect the amount of assistance by the rest of the world, and make countries and international agencies less enthusiastic to assist in a disaster presented as local and minor. Moreover, any attempt to doctor the figures might be treated with suspicion, for only those who know themselves to be sinners would seek to avoid the eyes of those they've sinned against.

Travellers from Zingraftstown also claimed they knew of the explosion as early as Friday night. The Governor was reported to have issued a local radio communiqué requesting the inhabitants of Chuma to remain calm, and warning them not to venture into the affected areas. He was also said to have assured them that the authorities were taking steps to cope with the situation and come to the aid of the affected. Why wasn't this message received in Kaizerbosch, Kwanga wondered, unaware of the fact that the 1kw MW radio station in Zingraftstown was too weak to be received beyond the immediate vicinity, although it was pompously referred to as "the provincial radio station". He was certain that if the District Officer had received any such message, he wouldn't have appeared so worried and desperate when he told them about his unanswered telegrams last night. It was unfortunate that a disaster of such magnitude had chosen to occur in a district as remote from the province, country and outside world as Chuma. A region that could neither be accessed easily by car, nor by radio was truly God-forsaken, and fate should not have compounded their predicament by landing such a disaster on them.

Kwanga wasn't afraid that the brief visit to Tchang might have endangered their lives. He was confident that the dark concoction given to them by the nurse on their return from Tchang, together with the volume of palm oil they had drunk, would ensure that nothing happened to them. That is, if Mathias's experience so far was anything to go by. His situation had not deteriorated as anticipated.

Kwanga advised Mr Tangh-e-keh to keep his radio permanently tuned to the national station, convinced that henceforth they would have to look up to Nyamandem for an account of what was happening around them. Though nearest to the affected area, they were not well informed about what was going on. So far, apart from their trip to Tchang where they saw things for themselves, all their knowledge had been based on hearsay. Without a radio station in Kaizerbosch, and with the travel ban imposed by the D.O., there was a total blackout on Abehema, Yenseh and the villages beyond, and even the broadcast about a volcanic explosion was mere conjecture at this stage. "Until journalists and the army are dispatched to over fly the region and report back," Kwanga concluded, "the primacy of hearsay and rumour is bound to stay the case." He was sure that unless the government sent helicopters to survey the area, the real origin and nature of the killer gas would remain a mystery, and the District Officer would continue to disallow concerned relatives from going to find out what had befallen their kin and kith in those remote villages. The District Officer had intensified the policing with gendarmes permanently stationed at Wahing as well, with strict instructions to send back everyone travelling to Tchang and beyond.

The streets of Kaizerbosch were in chaos, invaded by miserable mourners from all over the country, desperate for information about relatives and friends. Concerned relatives were breaking down emotionally. If tears could form a lake, those shed by the mourners would have created one twice the size of the mysterious Lake Abehema, but a thousand times holier and more respectful of life. This unusual occurrence had shaken their faith and awakened their distrust for everything around them, immediate or distant, natural or manmade. This explained their tears of concern for life, peace and justice, tears of love and humility, tears in respect of humanity. Theirs were not tears of ambition or

261

pretence, terror or devastation. Rather, they wept that the world of the innocents may not be torn asunder by the conflagrations and obstinacy of the arrogant and the greedy, whoever these were. That was why they wailed, against the pains of dying before one's time, for one reason or another, manmade or natural. Yes, that was why they wailed, nothing more. They mourned because they knew the jungle had room enough for the elephants to fight their battles for supremacy without crushing the ants.

23

There was a new development on Sunday afternoon, a tragedy within a tragedy. It came from an unexpected direction, and took Kwanga quite by surprise.

Mr Tangh-e-keh returned from a meeting with the unfortunate news that Chief Ngain had died under police custody. He explained to Kwanga how the chief had been arrested and detained, accused of murdering Ardo Buba. The Chief had resisted his detention until his death by a mysterious stroke of lightning, this Sunday afternoon. The policeman who had guarded his cell until his death recounted wild stories of mystical battles the Chief had engaged himself in with invisible forces. Chief Ngain would scream, swear and curse, and then attack violently with his hands, bite into invisible flesh, and cry out in pain when apparently beaten in return.

When the policeman brought him news of what had happened, and reports that his chiefdom of Abehema was afflicted by a mysterious gas that was causing lots of deaths, he celebrated in the following words: "I warned them, didn't I?" He shouted. "You don't strip your chief of the dignity of his office and find that nothing happens."

Then he spoke for long in Abehema, a language the policeman did not understand. When he was through, he turned to the Policeman and said: "The mosquito that gets entangled in a spider's web pays for all the blood it has sucked. He who invites the devil home must be ready to sacrifice his soul. No one provokes a python who does not know how to contain its venom."

When the policeman asked him for the meaning of all this, he laughed a wild dry laugh, and said: "Those who know shall understand, but the sufferings of those who have to suffer are just beginning."

Perplexed, the policeman asked in what way he could be of assistance.

"Nothing," the chief replied, adding, as if to himself, "The tortoise, for lack of relatives, carries its own coffin wherever it goes."

No sooner did the chief pronounce these words than he was struck by lightning, from which he died protesting: "I sent you to go and kill, to finish them who had wronged me, and not to come back to me."

Those who know the science of lightning claim it can never kill anyone unjustly. Those who summon its powers unjustly must pay with their own lives, for it comes back to finish them when it has found their target to be without guilt. The policeman said Chief Ngain's corpse was a pitiful sight after the lightning struck, as his pieces were minced and scattered and his blood splashed about.

Kwanga remembered some of the amazing and marvelous stories he had heard about lightning, believed to be an extremely powerful weapon to those who possess the ability to summon it. From what he had heard, lightning was effective only in the rain, as those who sent it had to stand in the rain next to a fresh banana tree until the lightning had gone, executed its mission and returned to be lodged under the banana tree. How then had Chief Ngain managed it from his detention cell, and how had he expected his lightning to deliver when he was not standing in the rain by a banana tree as expected? It is common knowledge that lightning would comb the world for its victims, and when angry, would flash away anything and anyone on its path, until the person targeted by its venom had been smoked out and hurt or killed. Sometimes it misses its target and falls on a tree, causing the tree to wither and dry off. When this happens, everyone is forbidden to move around, climb, or use the tree as firewood until the tree has been 'treated' by a diviner-healer. Usually, a calabash of medicinal concoctions and sacrifice is put under the tree. Sometimes, it is not the lightning that misses its route, but the victim who is more powerful and has an antidote against the lightning. Stories are told about clairvoyant or fortified persons who are capable of catching, diverting or throwing lightning back at the sender. Given how rampant lightning is used to settle scores, people plant cactuses in their compounds to protect themselves and their property from lightning. Peaphweng Mukong had gone the extra mile when he built the modern house that had infused him with so much pride: he had crowned the roof with a modern lightning conductor rod that was the talk of Abehema and the villages beyond. Perhaps because the rod was not planted on her own house as well, the extra protection did not stop lightning from savaging one of Peaphweng Mukong's wives seven seasons ago. She had been weeding her garden behind her house when lightning struck, breaking the earth on which she stood, then the wall of the house, lifting her off her feet and burning her body, to leave her unconscious until the timely intervention of Wabuah of Kakakum to save her life. She had had a bitter conflict over farmland with another woman who had threatened her with the ominous words: "you go see".

In Abehema, the chameleon was frequently associated with lightning. It was believed to be a messenger sent ahead to warn the victim and prepare the way for lightning to strike. As a child, Kwanga's parents had warned him not to play with the chameleon and to never dare kill it. Quite often adults would frighten children with threats of vengeful death from the chameleon or the person who had sent it on mission to occasion a lightning strike. Also associated with lightning was the axe, said to be the most potent weapon of the authors of lightning. The axe was what struck the victim when lightning fell. People would talk about the axe they saw when lightning struck. And the magnitude of the flash and intensity of sound produced usually informed people about the magnitude of the destruction lightning had occasioned. The flashes usually came before the thunderous blasts. Whenever the lightning was intense, people would fall on the ground and cover their heads with their hands, waiting for it to strike. Everyone related to someone somehow was a potential victim, although it was widely believed that lightning only struck the guilty. The sender had to be certain the victim was indeed guilty before sending. For if the lightning found the intended target innocent, it returned as a giant axe to strike the sender for wanting to harm an innocent. This, Kwanga reckoned, must have been what happened to Chief Ngain, if the strange tale of his mysterious death by lightning were to make sense. He had summoned lightning for an unjust cause, and had had to pay with his own life. From the mincemeat that had been made of him the unjustness of his cause must have been overwhelming.

The Chief Ngain connection came as a great shock to Kwanga, who hadn't heard any of it before, and who found it a difficult tale to swallow. It was a strange happening indeed, and he wondered why on earth Chief Ngain would want to kill Ardo Buba. As Mr Tangh-e-keh said, this was the question to which the police themselves had failed to extract an answer. During his custody, Chief Ngain had refused to say a thing to anyone on this particular matter, and had stubbornly defied torture and intimidation by the police. Kwanga feared the worst, following how Chief Ngain had been treated, and how he had died in detention. He feared the ancestors might react with violence, outraged by the ignominious and unprecedented detention of their representative amongst the living. The ancestors, he was convinced, would not forgive the modern forces of law and order for depriving Abehema of the leadership it needed at its most ominous hour.

"What are the authorities going to do with his corpse, or what is left of him, the bits and pieces, I mean?" he asked, emotional and concerned.

"Take whatever they can assemble of him home for burial," replied Mr Tangh-e-keh, crushing a fly against his trousers.

Kwanga was thankful the answer wasn't what he feared. It would have been a dangerous decision to take. To bury a leader apart from his people was to invite a curse upon them, to tear them into bits and pieces, to break down their social structure. The imprisonment of Chief Ngain was trauma enough for the people and their system. In the past, who would have heard of so abominable a deed as the detention or imprisonment of a chief? Things had changed drastically, and the people had tried to adapt, but still, to treat their chief in this way!

He was, however, grateful that tomorrow or the day after, Mr Tangh-e-keh and he would see the state of affairs in Abehema, when they accompanied another team appointed to take Chief Ngain's remains home for a decent burial. The chief may have died like a rat assaulted by a cat, but was glad the authorities had had the good sense not to decide otherwise about his final resting place. The deputy District Officer had told them and others to be patient and wait for his boss to return from Zingraftstown with the permission he had gone to seek.

When Kwanga had had the opportunity to think things through, he was not so sure what his attitude towards Chief Ngain should be. He had dreamt of him bringing disaster to the village, back in Nyamandem, and disaster had indeed struck his village and people. What should be his attitude towards a leader who had connived with evil forces to bring death upon his own people? Should such a person be buried in dignity, with full honours? Should he even be buried at all? The more he thought back on his dream, the less he cared for Chief Ngain, the leader who had sacrificed his own people and plunged the entire country into a mournful gloom. What greed could have pushed Chief Ngain to commit such an abomination as killing Ardo Buba, another people's chief? Kwanga recalled, his hair standing on end just as it had done in the dream, repeating again and again to himself: "What could have pushed this masked spirit to kill so sacred an animal as a black cat?" And as if killing Ardo Buba wasn't strange enough, Chief Ngain, whom the masked spirit in question had now turned out to be, had fished out the dead body and eaten it raw, growling and grunting as some of the thick dark red blood dripped in to colour the lake.

It was all clear to him now. Things were falling into place. Although Kwanga still couldn't say what the connection was, Ravageur and Vanunu, it was clear to him, must have been the two white men disguised as Kakakum warriors who had appeared in his dream, and who had charged towards the crowd with hand grenades. Whatever his liaisons with them, Chief Ngain had brought grief without measure to his land and people.

Kwanga put the pieces of the jigsaw together. Peaphweng Mukong was the taller of the masked spirits of his dream, who together with his supporters had stood for peace and order while Chief Ngain and his mercenary friends sought to plunge the village into chaos. Had his father and supporters survived? Was it they whom Chief Ngain had sought to eliminate with lightning? They had sided with virtue, and the ancestors should at least have saved them. "My father had tried to appease the ancestors, hadn't he? Perhaps they heard my scream after all, and sought safety before Ravageur and Vanunu exploded their grenades." Kwanga wasn't sure, but he was hopeful. The truth was just a day or two away.

Mr Tangh-e-keh and Kwanga were so involved in their speculation about a possible visit to Abehema on Monday or Tuesday that they missed the 10 p.m. news bulletin in Tougalish. As Kwanga was too tired and drowsy to wait for the news in Muzungulandish at 11 p.m., they both went to bed.

Kwanga's sleep was interrupted by the sound of flying aeroplanes. He listened to the zooming noises they made with excitement and hope. "They must be military planes transporting troops to the disaster zone," he thought. He was so excited and sure of his guess that he thought of waking Mr Tangh-e-keh. He didn't know that the latter was up already, listening keenly with equal excitement and hope, until Mr Tangh-e-keh called out to him from his room.

"Maybe we are going to Abehema tomorrow," he shouted, quite excited.

"Yes, maybe luck has smiled on us at long last," replied Kwanga.

And they both went back to sleep.

24

It was early Monday morning, and Kwanga was contemplating having his first thorough bath for several days. Going for days without a bath was like hell under such humid conditions, and the fact that flies were threatening to make a meal of him was indicative of just how bad his situation was. If he were in Nyamandem, Patience would say he smelt like a pig bred in Sopposburg, and would do her best for him to have a wash, which would entail going to negotiate for water from the neighbours who had a tap and a well of their own, or fetching from the filthy, excreta-happy brook in a valley a couple kilometres from where they lived, and boiling it to kill the germs and temper the stench. Kaizerbosch was quite unlike Nyamandem. Here water was no problem, and if Kwanga hadn't had a wash, it was because, following what had happened, he had decided to mourn for the dead in a typically traditional fashion – that is, by abstaining from washing for the duration of the mourning.

Until he took this decision, Kwanga was unaware just how much of a sacrifice mourning for the dead in Abehema was. Now that he knew, he couldn't imagine how in the past his parents had managed to go without a wash for weeks of mourning. In Abehema mourning the dead has always been a cultural thing, expected to be taken seriously by all and sundry. Like all other social functions, it has a set of rules, which are rigorously enforced by the chief and his notables. The period of mourning is usually determined by the social status of the dead person. Accordingly, babies and infants would be mourned for a week, young men and women of age for two weeks, adults for three weeks, notables for a month, and the chief for a month and a half.

During the period of mourning, people are supposed to stay indoors and meditate and weep for the dead, to the satisfaction of the ancestors whose invisible and scrutinising presence is (usually) assumed. The women must not go to their farms to work, though they may make a brief visit there from time to time to harvest enough food to take them through the period of mourning. Men mustn't hunt or split firewood with an axe for the first three days of mourning. Children shouldn't play about and be noisy – as care is taken not to disturb the tranquillity of the ancestors, and everyone must look gloomy and truly sorry to have lost someone. The only noise allowed is the sound of gunshots, an obligation that all close male relations of the dead person are expected to fulfil as the ultimate honour and farewell. Also as a sign of honour and farewell, the female relations of the dead are expected to stay in the compound of the deceased, where they must sleep on the floor, and not in bed. At the end of the mourning, everyone must shave their hair, which is all collected and thrown into the lake as a sign that the dead have been well mourned and respectfully escorted to the world of the ancestors. In the case of a chief, the whole village is involved, because the chief is there for all of Abehema, not just the royal family. With Chief Ngain dead, Kwanga would normally have to shave his head completely, but Chief Ngain having shaken hands with the devil, Kwanga was not too sure if he was still worth mourning for. For those who deserved to be mourned, Kwanga must find out who had died, so he could invoke the ancestors to welcome them all, when he shaved his head to the skull with a razor blade.

For now, if Kwanga had decided to temporarily suspend mourning the traditional way, it was because he truly smelt like a pig bred in the notorious backyards of the mountainside town of Sopposburg. As he picked up the relevant items for a thorough wash, he realised it was a minute to the news bulletin in Tougalish. He gave priority to the news, and postponed his wash for a while.

Mr Tangh-e-keh joined him in the parlour, equally thirsty for information. Everyone was beside a radio set these days, given that the country's TV station had so far remained silent on the afflictions of the villagers of Tchang and beyond. Kwanga strongly suspected, or rather, hoped, that some of last night's planes carried TV cameras and journalists to bring the disaster home to the affected here in Kaizerbosch and beyond.

The news was almost entirely devoted to what the broadcaster termed the Lake Abehema disaster, an appellation Kwanga found particularly satisfying. His village had at long last caught the attention of Kwang and its innovations, but no community in its right mind would pay such a price for such attention. Kwanga feared imprecision in the reporting of what had happened and what was unfolding. It was all too common for journalists to talk in vague broad terms, to say Chuma when they meant Kaizerbosch or Kaizerbosch when they meant Tchang, Abehema and Yenseh, thereby enhancing the obscurity of the obscured, the forgottenness of the forgotten. Journalism in Mimboland often attracted those who had failed to arrive in other courses of life they had ran, but that didn't keep their news stories from arriving.

They were delighted to learn from the newscast of President Longstay's abrupt visit to Zingraftstown yesterday. The District Officer's urgent mission there as well must have been connected to this. President Longstay must have needed some on-the-spot information about the situation. The newscaster dwelt at length on the presidential visit. Longstay was said to be deeply aggrieved and to have extended his personal condolences, and those of his wife, government and the nation to the affected families. He had also announced plans to rescue the situation. A team of responsible administrative, military and medical officers had been dispatched to the affected zone, the newscaster said. The president had also decided to make assistance available in the form of blankets, beds, clothing, and food to the survivors of the 'Lake Abehema Disaster'. The newscast ended with the president's regret for being unable to visit the scene of calamity because of the inaccessibility of the area, and his promise to improve the road network and make life more palatable to the people of the region. President Longstay returned to Nyamandem at nightfall, mission accomplished.

Kwanga was not amused. "He should have used a helicopter to over fly the disaster zone to know the magnitude of the affliction," he castigated President Longstay, determined to teach the president a lesson the day Mimboland is ready to surprise the world with a free and fair election. "That day," he swore, addressing the president directly, as if he were listening to him, "your name shall cease to be Longstay!"

As for Mr Tangh-e-keh, his hopes were restored by the news. He was glad they weren't entirely abandoned to themselves. To him a man of experience who had grown not to expect the impossible, President Longstay had demonstrated spectacular show of patriotic care and republican concern, which was reassuring.

"May the gods of power grease his aging elbows," Mr Tangh-e-keh whispered in Kaizerbosch.

Turning to Kwanga, he added in Abehema that in a world of despair, misery and disaster, grains of hope like the president must be protected. And Kwanga resisted an urge to counter him for he had never looked more serious.

Pretty certain their trip to Abehema was now only a matter of time, Kwanga went for his bath, a light one, careful not to be seen by the ancestors to be washing away the dead too soon.

The newscast was an indication that, sooner or later, the barriers would have to come down for concerned relations to rescue survivors and bury the decayed. It was clear that fears of an epidemic would push the authorities to allow access to the zone as early as they could. Now that TV cameras were penetrating the zone, the concerned would no longer be treated with indifference or lied to. That was Kwanga's uncertain hope.

"What stops it from being today?" Kwanga enthused, impatient to be on the road to Abehema.

If only this disaster had occurred in Nyamandem or elsewhere more modern and more equipped, all this question of roadblocks and inaccessibility would not arise, and most lives would certainly be saved. The very thought made Kwanga wonder why a thing like the killer gas should happen at all among peasants least competent in dealing with it.

"Why Abehema of all places in Mimboland, just why Abehema?" he muttered, puzzled as ever. "This could have happened elsewhere, somewhere less remote. Why did the gases settle on my poor village, on the devastation of the faceless, the voiceless, the unknown? The kwang-forsaken?"

He shook his head in sadness and dejection, his eyes clouded with fresh tears. His only consolation was that he would soon know the truth about his people, good or bad, shattering or reassuring. For neither the District Officer nor President Longstay ignored how emotionally frustrating was the prevention of relatives from going to find out about loved ones. So the sooner the barriers were lifted, the better for everyone.

After his light wash, as he came back to the house to apply some oil to his skin, Kwanga realised that Mr Tangh-e-keh had already assembled all he thought they might need in Abehema. These included two spades, two machetes and two raincoats.

"Would we need these tools to bury my family, or would we be much more fortunate?" Kwanga wondered, as he passed through the parlour into his room.

25

Driving to Abehema was a tug-of-war. They were at it all night, yet didn't seem to be getting anywhere. They had pushed, pulled and lifted all along, even getting stuck in the mud themselves, every now and again, but to little avail. When Mr Tangh-e-keh and Kwanga set out with the team on Monday afternoon, none of them thought they wouldn't be in Abehema by dusk. It was dawn on Tuesday already, and they were still on the meandering and difficult hills of Kumbong, struggling to keep the trucks on their wheels. The road was in a most deplorable state. It had greatly deteriorated since their first visit to Tchang on Saturday. It had rained thrice since then, and the wheels of the lorries were finding the muddy road too slippery for them to perform. Worse still, it started to drizzle at midnight, and had continued non-stop. Furthermore, the trucks that preceded them with troops and military equipment from Zingraftstown had actually aggravated the situation. Military drivers were never careful road users, and would find a quarrel even with a modern top quality road like the Express that linked Zingraftstown and Nyamandem.

Chief Ngain's wooden coffin was all mud. It had fallen off the lorry a countless number of times. If a minced corpse had feelings, his would have suffered enough to warrant a second death. All seven passengers but one felt sorry about this, but there wasn't much they could do.

Had Kwanga not linked Chief Ngain to the evil smell of death in the air, he might have been on his knees to the ancestors, asking for understanding, that they would not blame the forces of Kwang for carrying their representative in a muddy coffin, since things had become too unusual for anything to be done the normal way any more. Given what he now knew, the coffin could be fed to the dogs. He didn't care.

The strategy of the driver carrying the coffin, Kwanga and Mr Tangh-e-keh so far was to keep well ahead of all the other lorries, and it paid off quite well. Keeping one step ahead of everyone enabled the driver and his passengers to be helped out of their difficult entanglements in the mud, without giving others the chance to make things worse for them. Kwanga knew it was callous of them to treat others in this way, but he couldn't think of anything more realistic. For as he said, "It is only reasonable that if just one lorry has to arrive Abehema safely, it should be the one transporting Chief Ngain's remains, Mr Tangh-e-keh and me."

They knew the important thing was to keep the tussle going. As long as some progress was being made, they had to keep trying. Their driver knew the road better than all the others. He was very used to it, and had plied it for a decade and a half. His nickname was Okeleke because he was fond of saying 'He-life-no-straight', and he was the more experienced of the two drivers who plied the road commercially. He was very used to Kwanga as a holiday-period customer, was a good friend of Peaphweng Mukong's, and often acted as messenger and postman to people in the heart of the periphery.

In a remote region like this, where communication with the rest of Mimboland was more by foot than by wheel, drivers like Okeleke were God-sent messiahs. For a very long time, he had performed a praiseworthy service to the peasant farmers and breeders of the area, and to status-seekers from the region who had made it to the cities, but who still wanted to keep in touch with their places of birth. Were it not for Okeleke and Ndiko – the other driver – the peoples of Tchang, Abehema, and Yenseh and beyond, would have been virtually cut off from the rest of the world for the past decade and half. Apart from the occasional 4x4 car of a Muzungulander tourist or researcher like Ravageur, or the lorry of an administrator, the only other vehicles the people ever saw were the battered lorries of Okeleke and Ndiko.

Very few people knew Okeleke by his real name, and neither Kwanga nor Mr Tangh-e-keh was one of them. Few knew how he came by his nickname either, although he had had it for fifteen years. The Fulani could not articulate the nickname properly, so they called him Keleke instead. He was a most popular man among the folks, who all regarded him as their God-sent saviour. And he might have saved quite a few of them, had he attended the Abehema market of Thursday last. As fate would have it, his lorry had suffered a severe breakdown that same day.

The drizzles gradually became more intense, Tuesday promising to be a dull chilly day. They were thankful when they finished descending the hill just above the village of Tchang, for thenceforth, the road passed through a broad plain, with only an occasional hill to climb or descend. Now that they were in Tchang, Kwanga and Mr Tangh-e-keh were confident they would be in Abehema by the end of the morning, and that even in the case of a breakdown, they could still make there on foot.

As on Saturday when they first visited, Tchang smelled of death. The smell had intensified. Though the pungency of the gas had greatly diminished with the rainfall, the repulsive stench of more decaying bodies remained strong in the air. There were no human remains by the roadside to account for this, but there were bound to be some rotting away in the houses they couldn't visit last time, as well as in the bushes. As before, they had all been advised to drink palm oil, and to bring along with them scarves to cover their nostrils and mouths, to limit the inhalation of the gas and to break the stench. It certainly rendered breathing difficult, but it made them safe. At least, so they hoped.

Equally awful was the sight of dead cattle and sheep scattered all over the hills that punctuated the plains after Tchang. Some of the carcasses looked inflated, with their tongues hanging out, caught between their teeth. Others seemed to have exploded, exposing their entrails as havens to the multiplying flies and maggots. While many more flies had migrated from Kumbong and beyond to feast on the dead bodies, the early maggots had already matured into adult flies and were now sharing in the festivities. The whole scene looked ghastly and gloomy, and promised nothing but more scenes of ghastliness and gloom.

To Mr Tangh-e-keh, it was horrendous. He had every reason to be as silent as he had become. He had seen what everyone in the lorry saw, and knew that only a raving fool could continue to hope in such circumstances. If Tchang, peripheral to Abehema where rumour held the killer gas had originated by way of an explosion, could have suffered such severe losses in cattle and sheep, what hope was there that he would find his cattle alive in Abehema? Disappointment was written in the wrinkles of his face.

The powerful, repulsive stench intensified as the lorry approached Abehema. The rain became heavier, and the weather chillier. The smell of death remained thick in the air.

Soon Okeleke began to struggle with the rainwater. It prevented him from identifying and avoiding the puddles on the road. Like the passengers, he had remarked something unusual about the rainwater that flew down from the hills. It was thick red in colour, like a mixture of camwood and muddied water, or of animal blood and laterite. None of them had seen rainwater quite like this before. They ignored it and drove on, after a few initial worrying comments.

At the Hausa Quarters, the little stranger-settlement of Abehema, Okeleke came to a halt upon seeing a group of soldiers standing on the veranda of the now dilapidated building of the incomplete Government School, where Kwanga had done his first three years of primary education before moving onto a bigger school at Yenseh.

The soldiers, who appeared to be taking shelter under the leaking roof of the neglected building, beckoned, and Okeleke drove through the overgrown playground to meet them. It was still raining cats and dogs, and blood-soaked rainwater everywhere. The soldiers had particles of red soil all over their heads and hands, and their uniforms were spotted with red mud. They looked exhausted, overwhelmed. They had worked relentlessly since Sunday night, burying the dead.

As they explained, the corpses were so many that even with the assistance of the villagers whom they had asked to come down from the mountain settlements of Hiseng and Meng, they had still not been able to bury more than half the corpses. Following the instructions of their Captain who was actively involved as well, the soldiers had given priority to decaying bodies, and to corpses with gruesome burns. The burying had been done largely in mass graves, though there were a few exceptions where villagers had insisted that their relations be buried separately in graves of their own, and with as much dignity as was possible under the circumstances. Such cases of identification had been minimal.

It was most disheartening, what the soldiers said. They hadn't all been to the lake, but their more daring counterparts had reported that the lake's water was indeed muddy just as Kwah had observed, like a swamp stampeded by a thousand cattle.

The bodies of ten elderly men, whom the villagers from Hiseng and Meng identified as the notables of Abehema, had been found floating on the lake, along with the carcasses of two goats and two cocks, and also a big lump of camwood, and calabashes of raffia wine. They had died doing their bit to appease the ancestors in order to avert the worst for Abehema.

Even the Captain had recognised the importance of these men, and had insisted they be buried in individual graves, and according to tradition. This was what the soldiers had been doing since morning, assisted by the villagers of Hiseng and Meng. Just when they were through, it started to rain in Abehema. While the villagers rejoiced for the rain, which they saw as a sign that the ancestors had accepted the notables into the world hereafter, the soldiers had rushed for shelter.

Listening to the soldiers, Kwanga had no hope of burying his own father. Peaphweng Mukong had always been a notable, and there was every reason to consider him one of the ten buried already. Kwanga was grateful that Peaphweng Mukong had been buried in dignity, at least within the circumstance. Maybe he was still in time to bury his mother, stepmothers, brothers and sisters. He wished he would be lucky enough to find their corpses, and do them the honour of a final farewell in accordance with the customs of Abehema.

Lost for words, his heart bleeding with grief, all Kwanga could say was: "What a tragedy! What a world!" He was bitter.

"That I should not only have my father snatched away from me, but even be deprived of the opportunity to bury him, is a punishment that supercedes any crime I could possibly have committed," he burst out, making everyone feel deeply sorry for him. "Just what have I done to deserve being tossed about by the thorny hostility of contrived misfortune? Why should the cold hand of death fart lethally in the company of struggling villagers it knows are blind, dumb and deaf? What have a people done to merit devastation on such a savage scale? Were the ancestors asleep when this happened? Where was the God of the poor, the meek, the forgotten, when disaster struck?"

There was nothing anyone could say to console Kwanga, but everyone shared his feelings, for they all understood what it meant to lose all the members of one's family and village. As the soldiers had said, there wasn't as much as a fowl alive when they parachuted themselves into Abehema on Sunday night. The extermination had been massive and total. It had claimed humans and animals – both domesticated and wild – but strangely enough, it had left the vegetation intact, green and fresh.

One soldier, who had visited the lake and remarked the increase in its size resulting from what they had confirmed was an explosion, described the situation as "second only to the Hiroshima devastation".

"Perhaps the only difference between Hiroshima and Abehema," another soldier qualified, "is that while the atomic bomb which destroyed Hiroshima was manmade, the killer gas explosion of Abehema appears to be entirely the result of nature's creative mischief."

However, while he agreed with the comparison, Kwanga thought it was much too soon for the second soldier to rule out a human cause to the Lake Abehema explosion. There was, for example, Chief Ngain and that sneaky Ravageur and his friend the Vanunu fellow. What hand did they have in this? What sinister scheme had they plotted that even the efforts of his father and nine other notables had failed to stop through sacrifices of appeasement? Kwanga's mind was racing after the second soldier's comment, but his notorious fear of soldiers prevented him from voicing his opinion. He wished events would prove right this expert in the art of war, but he also prayed that no effort should be spared in satisfying relations who doubted that their kith and kin had died a natural death. Only in this way, he thought, could God, the ancestors and the dead forgive the living.

To Kwanga, it was moving to see someone almost the age of his own father weep like a little child. It didn't happen often, but when it did, this meant the man had reached his elastic limit, that he had cracked. Over the past six days, he had seen several men weep like babies, in public. Mr Tangh-e-keh had cried before, but in his bedroom. Now, he had broken openly into tears, in front of everyone. Kwanga tipped his head back in search of relief only to feel submerged by the grey sky, which seemed to be joining Mr Tangh-e-keh in losing count of tears.

The soldiers were not surprised when Kwanga cried but felt a man like Mr Tangh-e-keh ought to be able to control his emotions. They criticised him for being weak at heart, and worse still, in public. Given their training, Kwanga found their attitude perfectly understandable, although he didn't approve of it in the least. To him, it was in their training to be callous and ruthless. They were trained to kill every civilised emotion, to be fearless of death and hazards, to risk their lives and the lives of others, just that wars may be fought and won. He imagined: "Suppose, just suppose that these soldiers had been given some nuclear or chemical weapons to throw into Lake Abehema and then observe the reaction, would they have stopped to think of the disaster that could have resulted therefrom, or would they have gone right ahead and done it, like technicians of murder trained to despise emotion and to obey without questioning?"

No, he knew they couldn't understand. They no longer felt what it meant to be human, because they had lost their civilised emotions. They could bury masses and masses of bodies, yet at the same time chat and laugh over cards and cigarettes, as if this was all some kind of a joke, or a task like any other. However, he also knew that they weren't entirely to blame for their dehumanisation, but that their profession and those who saw it as indispensable were the real enemies of humanity. The states that moulded them into war machines propelled by a craving to destroy everyone it labelled 'enemy', was of course to blame. What he condemned were thus not the soldiers as such, but the perpetrators of a profession that turned humans into heartless, thoughtless harbingers of massive death for the innocent and the forgotten.

His criticism notwithstanding, Kwanga was thankful to the soldiers for burying his people. Even if they had done so almost without exception in mass graves, and in his absence, it was a service all the same, and he could afford to thank them heartily.

Mr Tangh-e-keh ignored the soldiers and wept on, and on. His tears joined the rain and created a mud puddle around his feet. The rain was still heavy, but he had run out of patience. He had to know the truth about his cattle now or never. There was no question of waiting for the rain to subside. He had reached his limit, and could wait no more. So he put on his raincoat, and walked off towards the distant hills, without saying a word, not even to Kwanga, who considered it most unkind of Mr Tangh-e-keh to abandon him to search for his family alone.

"We came all the way together from Kaizerbosch," he reminded himself in shocked embitterment. "And we've been through thick and thin together. Why should he suddenly abandon me like this? How does he expect me to bury my mothers, sisters and brothers alone, if I should find them?" He paused, his eyes contemplating the grass.

"No, it is too unkind of him, and I will never ever forgive him for it! Why should he openly prefer his cattle to the family of the very Peaphweng Mukong whom he claims was his best friend, and who had spent years catering for his interests in Abehema and the neighbourhood? Why has he suddenly ceased to care about me? And about all the people we set out to bury? Why? Why? Why! Is cattle any worth without people to give them value?"

He couldn't stop the tears that rolled out of his eyes and down his cheeks. He felt a sudden upsurge of bitterness and intense hatred for Mr Tangh-e-keh, and doubted whether he could ever talk to him again. To him, Mr Tangh-e-keh had finally come out of the cocoon of pretence to show the true magnitude of his inhumanity.

"If I have sympathised with him, it is because I believe it is possible for one to regret the loss of his people, and also the loss of his property. When one values property more than his fellow humans, it no longer is the same thing to me. Mr Tangh-e-keh has painted his face with the charcoal of greed. He has abandoned me with death to chase after material wealth. How does he expect me to remain his friend, to speak to him ever again?"

The rain persisted, but Kwanga wouldn't wait for it to subside either. He wanted to know the fate of the other members of his family. Peaphweng Mukong might have been buried already, but what about Ngonsu his mother? What about his step-mothers, his brothers and sisters? He had to find out about them, and perhaps do them a last service. He didn't want them to be turned back by the ancestors because of improper burial.

He couldn't bear to think of the disappointment he had been to them. He just couldn't bear to. He had told them lies, and had kept away from them for a year, because he would not face up to the truth about his failures at the University of Asieyam.

"Had I really been the good son they had always wanted me to be," he continued his self-persecution, "I would have told them long ago, that the university was not what they thought, that it was merely one of the many illusions of the Great City whose allure they had internalised. And perhaps they might have been purged of their delusions about *Kwang*, before this disaster struck."

He blamed himself for pretending all along that he was good enough to be sown as the seed of hope for his village. "I haven't lived up to my name – Kwanga. I have deceived and betrayed the whole of Abehema, and now it appears there is no one left to hear my confession."

As Kwanga went to the back of the lorry, Okeleke, who was watching the rain with thoughtful eyes, asked what he was doing.

"I'm going to my father's compound, to find out what there is to find out," he replied without looking back, knowing that even Okeleke would not come with him in the rain.

He didn't care. Accompanied or alone, he was determined to bury the dead, if only he could find them. He opened the back of the lorry and took out the tools he thought he might need. He could see Chief Ngain's molested coffin, but didn't care how it ended up. To be in a coffin was already more than Chief Ngain deserved, given what he had done to Abehema.

Kwanga failed to recall how his father never tired of saying that a leader, no matter how grave his atrocities, can always be forgiven by the people he has wronged, who must give him a decent burial however their differences with him. For to treat a corpse with contempt is to be ignorant of the humanity in us, good or bad, wrong or right.

This was not the time when anything was anything anymore.

Abehema didn't resemble the village Kwanga had known all his life. How could he believe that the exciting mixture of native settlers, the Fulanis and the Hausas, who constituted the integrated community – a laboratory of conviviality admired by all – had disappeared into thin air? Why was he being forced to believe that nature could be much more wicked than mankind? He knew God would not destroy the innocent, the pure of heart, the simple and the ignorant. Only man was wolfish with man. God would always forgive the ignorant, but man would capitalize on the ignorance of his fellows, use it as a ladder to climb up and sit on them, then hit them mercilessly like a drum, and force-feed them with the stench of his farts. Sincerely he didn't know why he was being forced to see God and his ancestors as guilty of human weaknesses. He just didn't see how that was possible.

From the Hausa Quarters to the main village all was deserted, but for groups of soldiers who were taking shelter on the verandas of the thatched houses and huts on both sides of the road. Apart from these men in uniform, there was no sign of life, human or animal. The picture was that of a village captured by enemy troops, with everyone in it either executed or imprisoned.

He ignored the soldiers shouting to find out where he was going, knowing that none of them would come after him in the heavy rain. At the point where the footpath to their compound branched off the main road, he saw the giant caterpillar that was doing the digging and burying of the decaying bodies, which the soldiers were evacuating from the houses, footpaths and bushes.

With a heavy sigh of grief he branched off, his heart thumping as anxiety seized him. Every step he took brought him closer to the compound. He tried to give himself courage, but couldn't. All that came instead were wild thoughts difficult to describe.

At last he came to the compound. All was quiet. The only familiar sound came from the river behind his mother's house, the river where he had fetched water and fished as a child learning to be useful to his family and the community, learning to be more than one person's child. Apart from that nothing stirred. Silence reigned.

On a bamboo pole to his left, he noticed his father's baggy pair of trousers and winter coat. His father's house was locked from without, as he could see from the padlock that hung over the wooden door. The houses of his mother and step-mothers were wide open, forcibly opened.

"The soldiers have been here." He was too late.

As he stepped into his mother's house, a repulsive stench greeted him. A combination of abandonment, death and familiarity made it unique. He inhaled the stench, desperate for reconnection with his loved ones. There were patches of human blood on the floor and the bamboo beds, and little bits and pieces of human flesh on the floor as well. He couldn't say whether it was the flesh of his mother, or of one of his brothers or sisters, or of all of them minced together by the vicious killer.

Over the fireplace stood a pot of coco-yams, half cooked. A bowl of fufu-corn lay open on the grinding stone against the wall. Next to it was a basket of vegetables now turned yellow. Still hanging on his mother's bedpost was the topless hurricane lamp of which she was so proud. There was no fuel left in it any more.

As he stood in the middle of the room completely weakened by what he had seen, the whole idea of a toxic gas began to puzzle him anew, from a different angle altogether. When this idea of a poisonous gas first cropped up in Kaizerbosch, he accepted it uncritically, because there was no reason to be critical then. The first survivors may well have been victims of a toxic gas, he reasoned. The whole issue of blood, of severe burns, and of bits and pieces of minced human flesh here and there, made him wonder what manner of gas this could have been. He knew next to nothing about gases, but he had the strong feeling that, should the violent killer be a gas as rumour had so far claimed it was, it may well be one whose nature expert scientists the world over were still to discover. Whoever's evil scheme it was to deal his folks a fatal blow, the choice of a mysterious weapon had been ingenious, a weapon that seemed to have taken even God and the ancestors of Abehema by surprise.

"With more investigation," he speculated, the picture of Ravageur and the anonymous Vanunu strongly on his mind, "our new gas might turn out to be even more useful to nuclear and chemical warriors than any of their weapons has so far proven to be."

He gritted his teeth in anger.

"For a gas which destroys only people and animals, but not plants, a gas which chooses to experiment itself on poor innocent peasants, such a gas is bound to attract scientific and military curiosity. And God bless the day my folks will go down in the history of scientific discovery, as the martyrs that marked a new era in the race for military superiority."

Kwanga was cynical, but with no one in particular, except that his suspicious mind kept trying to link Ravageur and Vanunu with what had happened.

He rushed out into the house of one of his stepmothers. The story there was the same. So was the story in the other houses. What was there for him but to conclude that the rest of his family must belong to the group of priority cases described to him by the soldiers at the Hausa Quarters? Cases disposed of in a hurry en masse in shallow graves dug in a rush by the caterpillar, to avoid an epidemic or to conceal the gruesomeness? The soldiers had done their less than thorough bit. It was up to him to collect for proper burial the remaining pieces of human flesh they had left behind in their haste to do the essential.

Just as he came out of the last house and started to walk across the courtyard towards his father's, a sudden storm began to blow strongly from across the hills. The avocado tree that stood in the middle of the compound swayed violently under the force of the storm. And as he ran across under the tree to his father's house, a huge avocado fell on his head, making him perplexed for quite some time. Still dazed, he picked up the fruit, discovered it was ripe. Then something strange happened. He could swear Peaphweng Mukong was urging him: "Eat Kwanga, eat the avocado and hold our dream." There was a sudden feeling of hunger in him, and before he could think twice, he was eating the avocado already. When he had finished eating, Kwanga felt someone walking away, looked up, and thought he saw the mocking face of Chief Ngain, wearing his father's favourite winter coat, the gift from Ravageur. What could this mean? Peaphweng Mukong's voice? Chief Ngain's mocking face in his father's attire? Had the dead now turned upon him to feed their unsettled scores? Perplexed, he scooped his hands and collected some of the rainwater, which he drank.

Soon he began to feel weak and drowsy, and to experience severe stomach-aches. He sat down, even tried to lie down on his back, but his situation only grew worse. He attempted to stand up and see if he could walk to the main road to alert the soldiers that something was the matter with him. He couldn't. He felt weaker and drowsier, an urge to vomit and more stomach-aches. Then he lost total control of himself, and couldn't even sit upright any more. His bones seemed crushed, and his flesh appeared to melt away. He believed he was dying, dead. Had his father come to show him the way to the ancestors?

26

Mr Tangh-e-keh hurried up the hills, half walking, half running. The rain meant nothing to him, and his raincoat was of little use. His clothes were soaked, but it didn't bother him. He wanted to find out whether he wasn't dreaming when he imagined he might have lost his cattle. Such a loss would be a great blow to him, more than he could stand. He had spent his entire life trying to accumulate the little he could, in an effort to build on solid ground, to be a rich and powerful figure someday. He had made his mark locally already and was well on course to turning provincial in a matter of years, but then here was this disaster from nowhere, threatening him with the poverty he had sought to avoid like a plague. He was lost in his thoughts and fears, and the more he thought and felt worried, the more he ran up the hills, where his herdboys lived. He was bound to grow tired soon, despite his enthusiasm and anxiety.

When he came to the huts his herdboys occupied, what he saw was beyond credulity. He just couldn't believe that these were his cattle, spread out on the extensive hillside in front of him and in the valley below, providing food for vultures, flies and other scavengers. He threw his eyes down the valley and beyond. The same sad story reverberated everywhere. There was no hope for him anywhere. His future was shattered. He was a dead man.

"How can God do this to me?" he asked, as if expecting an answer. Just how could this happen? Why him?

"Of all the people in this vast Mimboland," he cried, "why has God singled me out to punish in this manner?"

Mystified and dazed, he grasped his head, then thrust his arms upward and screamed, "What have I done wrong? Tell me!"

There was no answer for Mr Tangh-e-keh, no answer for anybody, including the thousands who had been deprived of life. The less fortunate were those who had died, and whose cattle and sheep, fowls and pigs, children, wives, and husbands had died with them. They were the ones who would never have the opportunity to ask what they had done wrong.

Mr Tangh-e-keh turned round, completely numb inside. He started his journey back to the village, thinking of his cattle and his doom.

When he came to the Ring Road again, he recalled that he had travelled from Kaizerbosch together with Kwanga. He was immediately seized by a feeling of guilt. Why had he abandoned the young man without a word about where he was going, or when he would return? He knew he must have been out of his mind to do a thing like that. So he hurried to Peaphweng Mukong's compound where he hoped to find Kwanga, burying the dead if they were still there to be buried.

Peaphweng Mukong's compound was empty. There was no one in any of the three wide open houses. He looked round the whole compound, the surroundings, and at the river. No sign of Kwanga. All he saw were some of the tools they had brought with them, and an avocado seed and peelings, which he guessed must have been left by Kwanga.

"Where is he then?" he wondered.

He stood on an elevation and shouted into the distance. There was no answer. He picked up the tools and went back to the dilapidated school where he had left Kwanga, the soldiers and the others when he went up into the hills to check on his cattle.

The soldiers were there, playing cards. They had just finished burying Chief Ngain. When they saw Mr Tangh-e-keh, they started scolding him.

"Look at that heartless fool who abandoned a young man to die," some accused.

"Because he has lost a few cows," others mocked.

"What will you do now that he is dead, or rather, dying?"

Though they treated Mr Tangh-e-keh with such contempt that they refused to inform him directly, he was able to deduce a lot from their insults. He learnt that Kwanga had fainted and was carried away to the Health Centre in Yenseh. He guessed that Okeleke had taken him there, because he and his lorry were absent. That was all he needed in terms of information. So he ignored the soldiers who were getting more and more aggressive. Had he stayed on a little longer, he might have been beaten up even. For they were clearly disgusted with the way he had behaved towards Kwanga.

The portion of the Ring Road to Yenseh was familiar, but it was frightful and gloomy as night was fast approaching. Mr Tangh-e-keh saw tents on both sides of the road as he trekked down to Yenseh.

"These must belong to the soldiers that have been doing the burying," he thought.

He was against the idea of passing the night in a tent with any soldier, no matter how kind and unlike the others the soldier was prepared to be. So he hurried, half running and half walking, to reach Yenseh before darkness overcome him. He couldn't imagine himself alone on this road at night, surrounded by the smell of death, and haunted by thoughts and beliefs associated with death. Luckily for him, Yenseh wasn't as far away from Abehema as he had always imagined, and all he really had to do was to keep descending.

As he walked into the premises of the Health Centre, a soldier armed with a machine gun ordered him to stop. Mr Tangh-e-keh stopped and gave an elaborate self-introduction, as commanded. Then came the question he had expected from the outset.

"What are you going in there for?" asked the soldier, with professional sternness.

He told the soldier about Kwanga, and how he had been told to check for him at the Yenseh Health Centre.

"I know the young man you are talking about," replied the soldier in a softer, almost gentle tone. "His case was serious, so we asked the driver to take him straight to Alfredsburg."

Mr Tangh-e-keh had not expected to hear that. He shook his head in disappointment. Unable to say what was becoming of the world, he asked the soldier, "Is there any place in the village where I can stay for the night? It's too late for me to continue to Alfredsburg tonight." He stated his case in impeccable Pidgin-Tougalish.

The soldier informed him that there were some natives who had come back to bury their dead relations, and advised him to go into the village and look for where to stay the night.

"If you still can't find where to sleep, you can come back and keep guard here with me," the soldier added with a grin.

Mr Tangh-e-keh was luckier than that, and didn't have to return to keep guard. On his way to the village, he met two relations he knew of the late Captain Tsemsi. They had just arrived from other regions of the vast Kingdom of Kakakum to bury their kinsman. Because it was late and dark when they arrived in Yenseh, they had decided to keep everything till the morning. So Mr Tangh-e-keh stayed the night with them.

Mr Tangh-e-keh woke up barely in time for the burial of the late Captain Tsemsi. The funeral was so heavily attended that he wondered if the attendance would have been any better had Tsemsi died a normal death. The fact that not only Kakakum people had defied the dangers of the gas to pay Captain Tsemsi their last respects attested to the captain's popularity beyond tribal boundaries. Many people came from as far away as Nyamandem where he had worked until his untimely death. His coffin was one of four specially made by government carpenters in Zingraftstown to bury four important individuals.

"It would appear even the modern authorities believe that the state in which someone arrives in the world hereafter matters a great deal," Mr Tangh-e-keh observed reflectively. If it were really true that the exuberance and elaborateness of one's funeral influenced the way God and the ancestors examined his file, he thought, then Captain Tsemsi was one of the four with a good case, a perfect passport for the life hereafter. He noticed the sun coming through the clouds. Then, thinking of himself, he wondered where he would go after his own death.

Among those who came to bury Captain Tsemsi were journalists and reporters from all over the world, armed with cameras, tape recorders, pens and notebooks, and determined to miss no detail. They came from Muzunguland, Kaizerland, Tougaland and from elsewhere in the world, Africa, and Mimboland. Few of them were journalists only. Most were also highly qualified scientists who had come to establish the scientific causes of the disaster. They worked round the clock, journalists and scientists, determined to leave no stone unturned, to dig into the bottom of the lake and uncover the geochemistry of the lethal explosion.

Now that his mind had cleared a bit, Mr Tangh-e-keh recalled seeing some of these journalists and scientists when he went up the hills to find out about his cattle. He wasn't in the mood to look at anything twice. When the funeral was over, some of these men and women of the press and science approached him. There were many things they wanted to know from him about what had happened, but his tongue was still heavy over the loss of his cattle. However, when one of the reporters promised him a lift in his jeep to Alfredsburg, Mr Tangh-e-keh became responsive.

The journalists were interested in all sorts of things, ranging from the shared socio-cultural beliefs of the devastated peoples, to the geology of the lake. All these questions he found pretty easy, and responded to each and every one. The more he seemed to know the answers, the more they were encouraged to ask. When after an hour and half they at last ran out of questions, they all thanked him and turned to other people, asking the same questions.

"What is the point of this?" Mr Tangh-e-keh wondered. He felt hurt. "Do they mean to say what I've been telling them is false?"

He didn't know that was simply the way journalists and scientists functioned, that they found it useful to listen to as many versions as possible of the same story, before trying to squeeze their own truth out of all the truths they had gathered.

The gentleman who had promised him a lift kept his word, and soon Mr Tangh-e-keh was sitting with him in the jeep, on the way to see Kwanga, the young man who, like himself, had lost virtually all that mattered in the world.

Mr Tangh-e-keh's companion, a most talkative journalist, forced him into the role of passive listener, as soon as he had sucked out all the information he wanted. The journalist's name was Fardeau, and he was from Muzunguland. He told Mr Tangh-e-keh how the president of Mimboland had done the right thing by appealing to the international community for aid and assistance.

"The response is tremendous because your president is a good one," Fardeau echoed his point. "When someone respects human rights here in Africa the way your President does, we out there in the free white world love and respect him," he went on, Mr Tangh-e-keh listening despite himself.

"There is nothing as sacred as human rights and freedoms. A father might abuse his daughter and be forgiven, but a politician who rapes a people's liberty deserves the death penalty!"

Though Mr Tangh-e-keh didn't quite understand this racy brand of Tougalish, Fardeau continued to babble, as if all he wanted was an opportunity to air his views on freedom and democracy.

"According to your national radio, which you should listen to because it is one of the freest in black Africa," Fardeau told him, as if he had a super indicator of freedom better than any Mr Tangh-e-keh had known, "the first spontaneous response came from the Muzunguland government. You know why, don't you?" he asked.

Mr Tangh-e-keh shook his head to show he was ignorant.

"Because this disaster coincided with the visit of the Muzunguland Prime Minister to your country, to cement relations strained of late. Do you listen to the radio often? Radio Mimboland International, it is called, isn't it?"

Mr Tangh-e-keh shook his head again, to indicate that he sometimes listened to the radio, and that the name was what Fardeau said it was.

"There is already a team of seventeen medical experts at Alfredsburg where we are heading. So you don't have to worry because your young friend is in very good hands." Fardeau gave him taps of reassurance on the shoulder.

"I was dispatched here immediately by the Muzungu International News Services for which I work. I didn't even have the time to put my things together. This is all what it means to respond to an emergency. We are there for that.

"Muzunguland has flown in two plane loads of 20 tonnes of disinfectant, medical equipment and transport vehicles as well as two volcanologists, two medical doctors and seven chemical experts. Other big big countries have provided big big money for immediate assistance, and have despatched assessment teams as well. Tougaland, for example, has donated millions for emergency relief, while pledging further assistance. Kaizerland, as well, has sent in big money, blankets and tents. And so on and so forth. It's raining aid in Mimboland. Do try to listen to the radio for the latest information," he advised.

Although Fardeau babbled on and on, he remained in perfect control of the steering on a section of the Ring Road that was a hundred times better than the belaboured stretch between Kaizerbosch and Abehema.

"Na all that?" Mr Tangh-e-keh managed to ask in Pidgin-Tougalish. "No Africa country, no send aid too?" He was quite surprised that in the whole list, Fardeau had said nothing about Mimboland's neighbours like Kuti, Mamawese, and Warzone.

"I'm sorry about that," Fardeau apologised, thinly. "There have been some gestures from Mamawese, Kuti and others. Of course there have been. I was talking of the major donors with the big big money. If you want, everyone is going to send letters of condolence bleating their sympathies with your country for what has happened. Some are going to offer to join you in prayer and so on. Does that solve the problem? Can they put their money where their mouths are? What you need at a time like this is a major relief operation, and there aren't many countries capable of assistance of such magnitude! It is true you Mimbolanders are fond of saying 'small-no-be-sick', but you also say that 'A rat however well fed can never compete with an elephant however starved'."

Mr Tangh-e-keh was tired of listening to this fellow, though he knew he would have to listen willy-nilly, until they came to Alfredsburg. When Fardeau changed the topic of his monologue, however, from aid and assistance to the burying of the dead, Mr Tangh-e-keh became a bit more interested.

He listened to Fardeau's impressions of the goings-on at the scene of the disaster. Fardeau was satisfied with the idea of mass graves, which he thought had greatly facilitated the burying of the dead. With the help of caterpillars, the digging had gone at a faster rate. What would have taken weeks or months was likely to be completed in a matter of days. The only thing the hardworking soldiers still had to do was dispose of the stinking carcasses. Deciding upon how best to do this wasn't really within their competence. The soldiers were waiting for orders from above, and the sooner they came, the better.

"Those of them who have talked with me say they want to be through with the nightmare and gone as soon as possible," he told Mr Tangh-e-keh, whose interest was revived by the mention of carcasses. "And some of them recount being unable to stand the place for much longer because of the many ghosts roaming the afflicted villages at night, like souls trapped in limbo," he added, a note of scepticism in his voice.

Mr. Tangh-e-keh had visions of them wondering the streets chanting, "Where have our souls gone."

"Such figments are understandable. It isn't easy living in tents exposed to the revolting stench of decomposing bodies. The authorities are quite unlikely to come out with a final decision in the next day or two," he yawned. "So I'm afraid they are stuck with the ghosts for now," he sounded mocking. "They've got a point," he said, on second thought. "It is important for them to know whether an epidemic can best be avoided by burying the cattle in mass graves or by burning them with the help of chemicals. They should appreciate that this is a difficult decision, involving more than just bureaucratic whim and caprice. It involves expert advice which takes time to come by."

An idea had cropped up in Mr Tangh-e-keh's mind in the course of Fardeau's exposé on aid, which was now reinforced by his reference to carcasses and how to dispose of them. Mr Tangh-e-keh wanted to find out from this youthful journalist who appeared to be so informed, whether or not some of the aid received would trickle down to survivors as compensation for the death of relatives and livestock. He didn't quite know how or when to ask, as he waited for Fardeau to finish speaking.

"When these soldiers eventually leave the disaster zone," Fardeau continued, "it's unlikely they will forget their ordeals easily, which have been quite traumatic, to be honest. They recounted how they saw dead mothers with babies on their backs, and how in one particular case, a mother died while in labour, the head of a baby between her thighs! To some, what they've been through is nothing short of hell. As someone so aptly put it, the death of one person can be understood, that of a family attributed to witchcraft, that of a whole village to God. That which even the soldiers cannot understand is death in thousands. Like the village folks they all want to put their finger on the hidden hand behind this disaster that defies logic and witchcraft combined.

"It is easy to detect that Mimboland soldiers haven't fought many wars, unlike their counterparts in the warzones of Africa, where mass fratricides and genocides are an ordinary part of daily life. However, they've marvelled at and contemplated what has happened. Some told me the story of a five-day-old baby girl found near her dead mother at the Yenseh Health Centre. What fascinated them isn't only that the baby survived the poisoned fumes, but that it ate nothing for five days. Apart from the miraculous survival of the baby girl, the soldiers have been touched by the death of the captain you buried this morning. He was such a nice guy, they all say."

"Yes," Mr Tangh-e-keh agreed. "Captain Tsemsi yi die don make all people dem cry." His mind went back to poor young Tam, Tsemsi's son and sole survivor of the gas that claimed his entire family, whom he pictured narrating his ordeal at the Kaizerbosch General Hospital. Like Kwanga and the Mukong family, Tam would have to start from scratch to keep the Tsemsi family name from dying out completely.

Judging the moment ripe for his question, he cleared his throat and went ahead.

"Tell me Fardeau, you think say government fit use some dat aid for helep we who loss all we people and cattle?" he asked, uncertain if Fardeau would understand his less than elementary version of Tougalish.

Fardeau found difficulty understanding Pidgin-Tougalish, but with a lot of mutual effort, he eventually did.

"It is up to your government to decide," said Fardeau. "We are there to make this aid available. Your government decides how best to use it. It is our duty to take the horse to the river, but it isn't our place to force it drink, even if that were possible," he added diplomatically.

Just then the jeep pulled to a stop at the checkpoint a little outside the town of Alfredsburg, manned by the local gendarmes and police complemented by soldiers. Fardeau proudly presented his Muzungulander press card, and was allowed to proceed. When he came to the Alfredsburg General Hospital, which was two kilometres away from the checkpoint, he dropped off his passenger at a second checkpoint at the entrance and proceeded to the Tunga Hotel at the town centre, to cable his report. It was his very first, and he had taken care to craft it in tune with the palates of his Muzungulander readers, knowing that the rest to follow would have to build off it.

Titled "Socio-cultural Beliefs of Victims of the Killer Gas Disaster", the report read:

It is hardly surprising that the survivors of the afflicted villages of Tchang, Abehema and Yenseh are asking journalists and scientists what causes we are investigating when the answer is so obvious. Most

301

believe that a local chief who killed the chief of another village has attracted the wrath of the spirits, resulting in the killer gas devastation of humans and livestock. The chief himself has died in police detention at the district headquarters of Kaizerbosch, and the survivors say that was to be expected, for no one wins a fight against the spirits of the living-dead who oversee the world of the living. Though dead, the chief is somehow still considered dangerous, so survivors are keen to seek whatever protection they can against his formidable magic and witchcraft. As Toubegh, son of a highly regarded witchdoctor by the name of Wabuah has told me, "Chief Ngain shall not be considered vanquished, much as he has died physically, until he has been subdued as well in Msa, the invisible world of the spirits."

This explains why in the region and throughout Mimboland, few fights make sense, without co-optation of supernatural powers with the help of personal witchcraft, witchdoctors, cult membership and magic. A person who desires to hurt or influence another by witchcraft or occult means does not need to bother with the physical presence of the enemy if something of that enemy (hair, cloth or whatever) is there to serve as substitute. One may be visible and physically present, at the same time that one's spirit has temporarily evacuated one's body to go preying on game, committing mischief, or wreaking havoc on others and their property. This speaks not only of the fact that life is seen and lived as multi-dimensional, but also of the fact that life's multiple dimensions are both visible and invisible.

A hunter comes across a leopard preying on an antelope it has stalked, and the leopard walks away upon seeing him. Back home, the hunter meets the chief of the village who asks: "Did you collect the game I left for you?" A mother on her farm weeding is extra careful not to hurt a particular kind of snake, since this could be the baby she left back home with her babysitter. Someone dies and is duly buried, but reports continue to circulate that he or she was spotted here and there, doing this or that, and has refused to disappear with death. Or, as happens often, relatives wanting to know more than the physical causes of death of their loved ones may visit Wabuah of Kakakum, a renowned diviner-healer who has a proven track record of summoning the dead to speak.

You visit a local market that seems particularly poorly attended that market day, but a well respected notable tells you the market was bustling with people from far and wide, and that the crowd was so thick there was hardly room for one to walk freely. He is talking about the invisible buyers and sellers from Msa, the mystical land of the spirits. It is election time, and ordinary politicians are busy with campaigns among ordinary voters. The big fish are less bothered with actual voters. They are busier consulting diviner-healers in remote villages, inner cities or prestigious hotels where these privileged guests have been invited and lodged. Winning or losing elections is not a simple matter of the ballot. How well one harnesses spiritual or mystical powers to this end will determine to a large extent how much political power one wields and for how long. There is always the hidden hand ready to make or mar.

A powerful person, successful politician or village chief is thus one who is able to convince others of being in control of a complex array of visible and invisible forces. In a context where wealth, prestige and power are in limited supply, it pays to be ingenious in one's quest for these in the face of stiff competition. And acquiring the strength of others through eating their vital organs or drinking their blood after ritual killings could be a sure technique of acquiring or maintaining all three. My informants say this was what the village chief of Abehema attempted to do when he killed the chief of another village.

Appearances can indeed be deceptive.

In Mimboland, newspapers are the prerogative of the urbanites. Like the city dwellers, they are a product of Muzungulanderisation. Or are they? A casual visit to the news kiosk treats you to a rich menu of fascinating accounts on witchcraft and the occult. And if you were to collect such newspaper accounts over the years as my assistant Kimbi, a young Mimbolander journalist, has done, you would be amazed by how much witchcraft and the occult animate life and discussion in urban spaces and among elite Mimbolanders. In Mimboland, witchcraft has no sacred spaces. It touches on all aspects of urban and rural life. The emphasis on the mystical or mysterious is striking, and the fact that such stories make it to the papers at all speaks volumes of how African journalism in practice is at variance with the professional cannons of objectivity and empirical evidence that characterise our Muzungulander journalism. Few in the readership ever write back asking for proof, because most readers subscribe to the same popular beliefs as the journalists, one that sees the visible and the invisible as two sides of the same reality. In our Muzungulander context such stories would be dismissed offhand by editors and readers alike, as figments of the imagination, clearly lacking in logic and evidence as they are.

Fardeau Westview,
African Correspondent,
Muzungu International News Services

304

27

The hospital was packed full of people who had come to visit victims of the disaster. Most of them were sobbing, but no one was allowed to wail. The authorities had sent away quite a few who had failed to heed the warning. Mr Tangh-e-keh made his way through the crowd, telling everyone who protested that his case was a very urgent one.

"There is a dying young man lying in there, whom I must see," he repeated in Abehema.

And because he spoke Abehema, he got his way easily. People sympathised with him because they were all aware of the damage the disaster had caused Abehema in particular. Unlike the villages of Tchang and Yenseh, Abehema was at the centre of the disaster, and as such, had lost everybody who was in the village that fateful Thursday night. Of a village with over a thousand villagers, everyone had died. So they sympathised with him because they knew he had a point to be concerned with the only living kin he had left in the world.

Once he had gained access to the first of the four danger wards, Mr Tangh-e-keh started his tiresome search for Kwanga. It wasn't at all easy because the wards were equally packed full of patients. The sights he saw were more ghastly than anything he had seen in Tchang. Unlike Tchang where he had seen only corpses, here in the hospital, hardly able to lie in bed because of horrendous burns, were living beings, all half dead. He just couldn't believe his eyes. What had happened to produce children with charred lips, unable to suck the milk from their mothers' breasts? What gas was it that crept up people's laps to roast their private parts so gruesomely? Just what manner of gas was this that had barbecued people to a point where they looked no different from grilled beef? He could not answer any of these questions, which raced in his head and puzzled him more than anything ever had.

As he stood absent-mindedly gazing at a roasted woman (who had lost both breasts), a white doctor walked up behind him, making him startle.

"What do you want?" the doctor asked in seeming disapproval of his presence. "May I help you?" the doctor added with a little more politeness, after a quick summing-up look at him.

It took Mr Tangh-e-keh time to recover from the ghastliness. When his voice returned, he narrated his story to the doctor who was rather impatient with details. After hearing the essential, the doctor asked Mr Tangh-e-keh to follow him. Together, both men went out of the ward and walked across the yard to another ward, quite isolated from the others. There the doctor called the attention of yet another Muzungulander doctor whom he asked to attend to Mr Tangh-e-keh, in Muzungulandish, a language that the latter did not understand. Then he withdrew, just as his counterpart beckoned to Mr Tangh-e-keh.

Once inside the ward, Mr Tangh-e-keh remarked that the patients looked less ghastly. Unlike those in the danger wards, these patients had little or no burns at all, looked physically normal, and reminded him more of Mathias, the first survivor who brought news of the disaster to Kaizerbosch. He took a quick glance through the triangular room, but there was no sight of Kwanga, whom the doctor said was receiving treatment at that very moment.

"His isn't a critical case," the doctor told Mr Tangh-e-keh, who looked disturbed. "It could have led to death if he wasn't brought in yesterday. That driver did a good thing to rush him here. We found Emmanuel Kwanga to be suffering from food poisoning, and when he recovered this morning, he admitted to having eaten an avocado fruit and drunk water while in Abehema. It was a most unwise thing to do, but he is fortunate to be alive. We have just sent word asking Radio Mimboland International to broadcast that no one must risk his life by eating or drinking anything from the affected area. Every food there must be treated as poisonous, until we have examined and established otherwise," said the doctor, most emphatically.

"You look strained and tired, gentleman," he told Mr Tangh-e-keh, examining the latter's eyes and feeling his body. "You wouldn't mind if I ask you to take a bed and be examined, would you?"

Mr Tangh-e-keh was only too ready. He wouldn't like to miss a lifetime opportunity to be examined by a medical practitioner who sounded like he knew his job well. He nodded his head in the affirmative, unwilling to start struggling to make his Pidgin-Tougalish understood.

"You follow me then, and occupy that bed in the corner," the doctor pointed to the bed in question.

"Mr Wabuah is a friendly person whom you are surely going to like." He was talking about the diviner-healer from Yenseh, who seemed to be sound asleep. "Just lie down and relax, sleep if you can," the cheerful doctor told him. "I will come back to you as soon as I'm ready," he said, and left the room.

Mr Tangh-e-keh took off his shoes and climbed into bed.

28

K wanga lay on his bed staring into space. There was a major issue on his mind, the reconciliation Mr Tangh-e-keh had been seeking since he came to the hospital four days ago. Even though Mr Tangh-e-keh had apologised profusely for his behaviour at Abehema, Kwanga still didn't know whether to forgive him. He felt strongly that someone who chose to let people die because he must pursue his wealth was not worth the love of the community. He had had his mind on this same issue for the past three days, yet he was far from reaching a firm conclusion. At last, he decided to give himself more time to ponder the issue over.

"After all, that Muzungulander doctor made it clear to me that both Mr Tangh-e-keh and I still have a week to be here," he told himself. "By that time, I will have made up my mind."

The day before, with a feeling of nostalgia, Kwanga watched Wabuah leave the hospital. The diviner-healer had provided him with a detailed account of the strange turn things had taken in Abehema while he had been away. Although he had divined it himself already, hearing the real story of Chief Ngain's involvement with the forces of evil left him spellbound. Wabuah had confirmed that the nightmares he and Patience had had about Abehema in Nyamandem had not been baseless.

He recalled Wabuah's concluding words: "When I predicted disaster for Abehema a week or so ago, I didn't know the burden was going to be larger than Abehema could bear. Naturally, Abehema turned to its neighbours in Tchang and Yenseh to help, because we still stick to the belief that our brother's burden is our burden. We have always stood firm that society can stand together when one person's child is only in the womb."

Then Wabuah had gone on to reveal why he was and would remain, for as long as he lived, the greatest diviner of all times. "Sleeping here at the hospital, I saw what happened to you when you went to the compound in Abehema to check on your family. It must have been the ring I had prepared for your father, a ring that had served him well but that he had forgotten to wear when it mattered most the day he and his fellow notables fell victim to the wizardry of Chief Ngain. At the compound in Abehema, the voice that invited you to eat the avocado, that was not my friend Peaphweng Mukong's voice. It was Chief Ngain, with whom you had travelled to Abehema from Kaizerbosch, making a desperate attempt to have the last laugh. It is common with dangerous witches to borrow the faces and clothes of people intimate to you, in a bid to sow the seeds of confusion within your family and close circles. Fortunately, the ancestors were with you and had Okeleke handy to rescue you."

Kwanga was stunned by Wabuah's interpretation of what to him would just have passed for a natural occurrence. If he had found Wabuah credible, it was because the divine-healer was able to access knowledge that Kwanga did not remember sharing with him. Wabuah was truly the greatest, and there was certainly a lot more to life than nature and logic. The supernatural was part and parcel of everything.

Kwanga was now wearing the ring Wabuah had given him yesterday, with solemn promises of future protection against evil and dangers of all kinds. "You must remember," said Wabuah, putting the ring on his finger. "It is not because Chief Ngain is dead that we should assume his battles with the living are over. Stubborn witches

310

continue to function even from the world hereafter, from *Msa*, which I visit regularly. So you must watch out. As the living eye and ear of what is left of Abehema and your own family, you are going to be targeted, so be very careful." This was a warning Kwanga was determined to heed.

Then they had separated, with Kwanga promising to keep in touch, and Wabuah, to monitor the ring to steer him free of all evil.

The more Kwanga thought over the whole issue of the disaster, the more confused he became. He had reached a stage in the story where he didn't know what to believe and what not to believe. Perhaps it was no use trying to think in linear terms about what had happened, what had caused what, and what made or didn't make sense. Perhaps the more down-to-earth and inclusive he was in seeking to understand the disaster the easier things would be for him. If probing into the depth of issues was meant to produce final and absolute answers, he was bound to be disappointed for the more one dug the more there seemed to be to dig. It was gradually dawning on him that life did not lend itself to simple, unequivocal truths.

He took his eyes off the ceiling by turning round and lying on his belly. Remembering the newspapers, which the Tougalander volcanologist who came around to the hospital in the morning had brought him, he decided to have a look at them. He got up and collected the papers from the cupboard on the other side of the triangular room. He was pleased to remark that his stomach no longer pained as it had the previous days – a sign that the poison was growing weaker. He feared less for his life.

He returned to the bed and began to scan through the papers. The first article which caught his eye included a list of international leaders who had sent their condolences to President Longstay of Mimboland. It was extensive and included many prominent figures, an indication that the international community was as touched by what had happened as were Mimbolanders. He read of the aid in cash and kind that continued to pour into Mimboland. It was so great that President Longstay had appointed a National Coordination Committee headed by Minister Tchopbrokpot, which he charged with its reception, storage and distribution. He also read how the committee had opened an account, which was known as 'The Disaster Account' – without the word 'Abehema', "for the sake of brevity", the paper quoted Tchopbrokpot's response to critics. The committee – working round the clock – had calculated the amount of aid in cash received thus far. Kwanga couldn't read the figure because it was so large. Added to the drugs, food, tents, blankets, all-weather trucks, and scientific expertise, Mimboland had surely received more than triple what the surviving victims of the disaster alone could ever need for their rehabilitation.

However, as the author of this particular article argued, it all depended on whether or not the committee and its subsidiaries were ready to be honest. The note of warning was timely, and Kwanga read it several times, agreeing with everything it said. As the international community "sent in scientists, food, drugs and equipment," the article read, "national concern should be focused on their optimal use." It pointed out that the assistance was intended for the victims of the disaster in question, and that "it will be dangerous for anyone to misuse, divert overtly or covertly, by omission or commission" anything received as aid for the survivors of the Lake Abehema Disaster.

In the same *Mimboland Tribune*, he found two other articles, just as relevant to the whole issue of aid. The first echoed fears expressed in the preceding article, fears shared by the majority of Mimbolanders. To him these fears were justified by the fact that civil servants and politicians tended to presuppose that a goat should eat where tethered, without ever stopping to think that some goats were forever tethered in areas of rich and abundant pastures, while others were tethered to nothing but abject aridity and barrenness.

"Perhaps a good solution would be to let loose all goats to fend for themselves in genuine freedom and fairness," Kwanga thought. "Even this is liable to criticism, since it presupposes that all goats are equal in strength and intelligence, and that they are all honest and considerate," he countered.

As one whose pessimism seldom allowed him to trust people the way they normally expected to be trusted, Kwanga tended to admire any article that was in any way critical of established practice and things often taken for granted. His appreciation of a second article was equally good, because he had the habit of reading more into a piece of writing than the writer's timidity ever allowed him the freedom to express without inhibition. He branded the article "pragmatic and creative", convinced that its author was a master of the art of biting and blowing. He saw it as presenting in a nutshell the problems of a country where some individuals wholeheartedly believed that in order for them to laugh, others must weep.

He heaved a sigh and put down the *Tribune*. There was no doubt that he shared the mixed feelings of the authors, but unlike them, he had come to the sad conclusion that most barking dogs in Mimboland couldn't bite and that those who could had chosen not to, lest they attracted attention and were deprived of their catch.

He picked up another edition of the *Mimboland Tribune* at random. The front page contained statistics about the affected and the aid, which continued to flow in. He didn't want to see any more numbers, and he remained dubious about the omission of the word Abehema in the name of the account opened by the presidential commission. Why only 'The Disaster Account'? he questioned. "For brevity," he whispered with a sarcastic smile. "Brevity indeed!"

Kwanga remembered wordings from the first article: "It will be dangerous for anyone to misuse, divert overtly or covertly, by omission or commission anything we receive..." and forced a cynical smile again. He failed to see the danger the author was prophesying. Moral danger? Perhaps. Legal danger? Perhaps, but then... And if it was on the ancestors of the afflicted villages that he was counting for retribution, perhaps he needed reminding that the moral authority of ancestors never crosses the frontiers of the home village.

Another portion of the paper caught his attention. It said the affected area had a population of some 10000 to 12000 people. The victims (the dead) were somewhere between 1500 and 1700 people, while some 4500 people had been displaced. Among the displaced were some 2500 children with ages varying from four days to 15 years. Many were of school-going age. The demographic statistics were informative. Even though he had grown up in this area, he didn't know with exactitude the region's population. And he couldn't say if the figures being produced now were political figures of convenience, or the real thing. That wasn't his problem.

Rather, he was concerned with the death toll and what the papers and the radio all tended to give as the cause of the disaster. According to him, even though there was talk everywhere of over 1700 deaths and of thousands of livestock gone, no one had yet come out with any clear answer as to why these people and animals had been raped of life. Although not seeking simple, straightforward answers himself, he hated the sort of answers the media had tended to bleat out effortlessly.

At one level, he could say he was satisfied with the cause of death, at least, as confirmed to him by Wabuah the diviner-healer. Chief Ngain and his evil deeds had brought death in bulk to wipe out Abehema, death that had spilt over to affect the neighbouring villages of Tchang and Yenseh. That, the respected Wabuah of Kakakum had established.

He had gone further to offer him a protective ring against such evil in future. The world was larger than Abehema and its beliefs, and since the cultural beliefs of some are the cultural poison of others, the authorities were yet to come up with convincing answers for the wider Mimboland community.

So Kwanga was interested in the second level of explanation as well, where the cause of death was still the crucial unanswered question. To the best of his knowledge, even experts had accepted the rumour that a volcanic eruption had emitted a poisonous gas. The commentators had tended to insist on the naturalness of the disaster as if they feared being challenged to prove the contrary. He was yet to see a paper that had mentioned Ravageur, Vanunu, their shady experiments at Lake Abehema, and possibly dangerous liaisons with the evil Chief Ngain. Had their fellow scientists and journalists been bribed into doublespeak or silence? Time would tell.

"I only wish this initial inclination of theirs doesn't prejudice their final findings," he expressed his concern, finding the modern ways of finding out far more convoluted and less convincing than the practised and tested methods of diviner-healers like Wabuah. "It's essential that the right cause be established. Only then can any headway be made in the question of resettlement or rehabilitation of victims, which seems to preoccupy the authorities at the moment."

Unlike traditional divination where the experts were few and well known, so-called scientific methods of finding out were poisoned with perpetual disagreements over expertise. There were too many cooks struggling to make the same sauce, each with wild recipes of their own, and as could be expected, stood a good chance of spoiling the sauce. Kwanga turned himself over to lie on his back again. He had remarked that the experts, instead of pooling their resources together to work as a team, cherished individual prognosis and single-handed guesses. This had in fact taken none of them anywhere. Though he felt drowsy, he continued to run his eyes over all the papers.

The last paper he scanned before sleep finally overcame him was the latest edition of the *Tribune*. He wasn't aware that his Tougalander friend had brought the day's issue as well.

"Why does this volcanologist fellow insist on keeping me informed?" he wondered, amused.

Nothing in the edition was new, except for an article by an Agence Muzunguland Presse (AMP) reporter. It was a pleasant surprise for him to read something written by a foreigner. There was a feeling of *déjà vu* that pushed him to read the article, though he detested the sensationalism and exaggerations.

"What I should read if I'm interested in such distortions are the foreign papers themselves, not reports of what they publish in *Mimboland Tribune*," he stifled a smile. "*Mimboland Tribune* would certainly not go out of its way to reprint something considered harmful to national prestige," he chuckled, and ran his eyes through the article.

The paradox of paradoxes the *Mimboland Tribune* certainly was.

"Not bad, not bad at all," he remarked. "For a journalist, I must say that his senses are quite alert. Naturally, there are certain minor details he should get right," Kwanga appreciated the article.

"As far as I know my people, none of them would come back for any utensils – no matter how destitute they got. If the custom is to be respected, Abehema remains abandoned until the time that we the survivors are able to come together and offer purification sacrifices to our ancestors. Until then, Abehema remains a desecrated land. From what Wabuah the diviner-healer recounted to me before he was discharged yesterday, and from what the soldiers told us in Abehema, I know that Peaphweng Mukong and the other notables – may their souls rest in perfect peace – didn't succeed in getting the land purified before disaster struck. Chief Ngain's handshake with the devil proved too much for them."

Struggling to stay awake, Kwanga's mind went back to one particular sentence in the article: "Sometimes, horrifyingly, a hand or a face emerges from the soil, the shallow graves eroded by a heavy rain shower." It was as if the land itself had refused the hastily buried bodies. Or as if the bodies were still trying to defy death and cling to life on earth. This confirmed his fears and scepticism about mass and shallow graves. He wondered whether it wasn't advisable to start all over again, and do the burying thoroughly and with dignity.

"Certainly, it is more painful to die than to stay behind to do the burying," he asserted, and was overcome by sleep.

29

When Radio Mimboland International made its first broadcast of the Lake Abehema disaster, Patience was attending a party at her boss' residence, organised in honour of the newly appointed Director of National Development. She, like every other person, was too hilarious and too involved with having a good time to care about turning on the radio for news. Only the Honourable Minister's nine-year-old son was more conscientious, and followed the devastating newscast. Who was he to interrupt a whole party with news of forty deaths in a remote village, which even his father had probably never heard of before? Having learnt from previous mistakes, the kid dutifully kept his trap shut. Thus Patience didn't learn of the disaster until later, when the situation had become much worse.

On Tuesday morning she went to the office, still ignorant of what had happened. No sooner had she settled down than Betty (alias 'weaver bird'), her friend and colleague, came in with the bad news.

"Have you heard?" asked Betty, even before she could close the door behind her.

"What!" said Patience, quite startled. She detested Betty's dramatic fashion of starting a conversation.

"That an explosion has killed everyone at your boyfriend's home village of Abehema!"

Betty might have been light-hearted when she said what she said, and might have expected her friend and colleague to take the news light-heartedly too, but Patience's reaction was more than anything she might have anticipated. Even before Betty had pronounced the words 'home village of Abehema', Patience fell from her chair.

Not believing her eyes, Betty dashed out of the room and bumped into the Minister's office to report what had happened. It was only 10 a.m. and the Minister had not yet arrived, so she dashed out again. Desperate, she knocked at the office of the newly appointed Director of National Development, but he wasn't in either.

"Still suffering from the hangovers of last night's party," she thought, with a grain of jealousy – not having attended the party herself, because her fiancé wouldn't let her. At last she thought of calling an ambulance, so she dashed into the office again to make the call.

An hour and a half later, Patience was admitted into L'Hôpital Central following her fainting.

For a week and more, Patience was lying in hospital, cut off from the truth about the disaster, and falsely fed with a more palatable version contrived by the doctor who took care of her, following strict instructions from the Minister not to divulge the truth about Abehema to her. Though she eventually recovered and felt strong enough to go back home, the doctor would not discharge her, neither would the Minister who visited her regularly to do more than pay lip service to intervene on her behalf.

Patience became dubious of what her doctor told her was the truth about Abehema. She wondered, "Why does he never bring me the papers I keep asking him to bring? Is it possible for a man of his intelligence to be so forgetful? How come he remembers his appointments with me?" Incredulous, she finally made up her mind to take matters into her own hands, but she kept it her secret.

When Betty next paid her a visit and asked to be forgiven for her tactlessness the day she had reported the disaster, Patience was more ready to listen.

"Do you really think you ought to be forgiven, after all you have done?" she asked Betty who was sitting by her sickbed.

"I have told you that I meant no harm," Betty sobbed. "I definitely didn't mean to hurt you," she insisted, blowing her nose with a handkerchief. "Why should I want to? Why should I want to hurt you? Tell me." She was as apologetic as she had been for the past week. In fact, since the episode at the office, everyone seemed to be criticising her for doing what she did, so much so that she had grown quite pale and had even lost her appetite.

"Okay," Patience agreed at last, "I forgive you."

Betty couldn't believe her ears, but she was sure of what she had heard. This was the moment she had prayed and hoped for over the past week. She gave Patience a long and warm embrace, and felt her body and psychology re-establish their equilibrium. She felt truly happy and was grateful to Patience.

"Would you do me a favour, Betty?" Patience asked, staring imploringly into her friend's eyes.

"Of course!" shouted Betty, delighted to be of help. "What's a friend for?" she asked eagerly. "Say what you want me to do, and I'll do it right away!" She sounded ready for anything.

"I want you to go to my place in Quartier Kongosa," Patience began, pausing to clear her throat, and to spit out the lump into the handkerchief Betty had brought her as a present. "I want you to go to my place, pack some dresses into my travelling bag and bring it to me together with some money."

"Where am I going to find the money?" asked Betty. "You know how tough the going is for me moneywise. Charlie and I are going to marry soon, remember? We are both saving towards that," she confessed.

"No," said Patience, smiling. "No, Betty, I'm not asking you to pay me money. How can I?"

Betty gave a sigh of relief. She didn't want to lose what she had just gained, the reconciliation.

"You will find the money in my wardrobe," Patience told her. "You can't miss it. Make sure you pack enough dresses," she stressed. "And don't come back till dusk," she warned. "Please remember not to, because the success of my plan depends on what you do."

Betty went away, wondering what Patience was up to and never stopping to ask herself whether what she was doing was right. There was every indication she was about to help Patience escape from the hospital. This hardly bothered her. All she wanted was to prove to her friend that she truly regretted the awkward manner in which she had introduced the news about the disaster. As long as she succeeded in doing this, the law could go to rest. "After all, who respects the law anymore in Mimboland?" she rationalised.

30

Patience was just in time for the last bus to Zingraftstown. She was certainly the luckiest passenger that day. Once on her seat, she felt a bit relieved. She knew she wouldn't be totally out of danger until they had actually driven a hundred kilometres or more away from Nyamandem. Until then, she knew anything could happen. The night watchman, though accepting her bribe to pretend not to have noticed her leave, had declined any responsibility if she was caught. Also, there was the possibility that Weaver Bird might not keep quiet for long enough. So when the bus finally started off, Patience anxiously counted every blessed kilometre accomplished. It wasn't until they had crossed le Pont de Maturité over the Nagasang that she relaxed a bit and started to focus on what was really bringing her to these parts for the first time.

It was also at this point that she realised all the other passengers were dozing. That was what she hated in night journeys. Apart from the fact that the driver himself could doze off at any minute or another, the absence of liveliness in the bus made the surrounding darkness creepy. She wished she could fall asleep as well, and wake up to find herself in Zingraftstown. The burden on her mind had chased sleep away.

Patience didn't know what to think or believe. She knew the doctor had hidden the truth from her and that Emmanuel may well be dead. She was going to Abehema to find him alive, not dead! In hospital, she had suffered from constant bouts of migraine, because she strained and stressed her brains to do the impossible: tell her for sure whether or not Emmanuel had survived the catastrophe.

"Why Abehema, of all places, and why Emmanuel?" Patience kept asking herself as the driver faltered along with the bus. She couldn't understand just why it had to be her boyfriend's village and why her dream had occurred when it did, and not when Emmanuel would have visited a safer Abehema. Why did things always happen the way they did? Why had she not encouraged him to stay back with her in Nyamandem for a little longer?

The more Patience thought about the disaster, the greater her feeling of guilt. The driver of the bus had tried more than twice to start a chat with her, but failed. The only thing which could keep her away from her worries was the sleep that she couldn't get. Her insomnia was total.

The bus arrived in Zingraftstown at 3 a.m., but Patience refused to leave the station despite the fact that it was too early to catch a lorry for Kaizerbosch, and staying around was a dangerous alternative. The driver tried to speak sense into her, but her aggressive persistence forced him to abandon his attempts.

"Dat girl yi heart black pass Satan yi own," he told the other passengers, and drove his empty bus away.

Patience sat in the deserted bus station in defiance of all the warnings about the risks involved. What the driver and the other passengers didn't know was that Patience wasn't exactly in the same world as they. Her thoughts were far away, speculating about Abehema, where she had never been, and where it seemed she was going just to mourn. Even the criminals of the night seemed to have understood her burdens, for none dared attack her.

As early as 6 o'clock, Patience was on the first bus for Kaizerbosch, the morning paper in her hands. She skimmed through it with expectancy, but there were only two articles about the disaster, which, it was clear, had lost most of its appeal to newsmen already. It surprised her that there should be only two articles on the disaster, but it also showed for how long she had been kept in the dark about what was actually going on.

She read the first article voraciously. Some volcanologists, a Muzungulander and a Tougalander, argued that the disaster had resulted from a volcanic explosion, explaining that volcanic gas had accumulated to saturation point under Lake Abehema and erupted. If no debris had been projected, it was because "une éruption phréatique" or the meeting of magma or hot vapour with water did not always result in the projection of debris. They also maintained that this particular explosion was the first of its kind in the world, and that this made it difficult to outline ways of preventing reoccurrences. They were optimistic that, because gas accumulations of this type usually took very long to attain a point of saturation, there was no immediate danger in having the affected populations return to their abandoned villages.

Others, including Mimbolander scientists such as Kwankwang, Njumbeng and Shyntamu, and the Muzungulander team, rejected the hypothesis of a volcanic eruption. If there had been any such eruption, they maintained, debris would have been spotted, and the bed of the lake would have shown signs of this having taken place. Their examinations had revealed no such evidence. They didn't doubt the fact that the gas emitted was volcanic, but they refuted the idea of an eruption.

The Mimbolander team argued that an external factor had provoked the gas emission, although they couldn't say for sure what this external factor might have been. Given their conclusion, they strongly advised against the immediate return of the victims to their villages, and urged for caution and further investigation.

Thus, while some argued that the gas came from the ground beneath the lake and resulted in an eruption, others affirmed that the gas had accumulated at the bottom of the lake and been forced out either by external provocation, or by natural movements in the lake. Both schools of thought agreed that the gas was of a volcanic nature, and that carbon dioxide was its main component.

However, when it came to determining the cause of the gruesome burns observed on certain victims both dead and alive, the scientists could only speculate. It was out of the question that carbon dioxide could have caused the burns, given its nature and qualities. What, then, had caused the first, second and third degree burns on some of the victims?

A few scientists suggested the burns might have been caused by fire, and still fewer thought water might have caused them, but the majority were convinced the victims had been burnt by gas. They argued that if the burns had been caused by fire, the victims' clothes should have been burnt as well. As it happened, some of them were severely burnt on their stomachs, around their genitals and on their legs, yet the clothes they wore had stayed intact.

Inspired by the experiences of the survivors who compared the smell of the killer gas to that of rotten eggs and gunpowder, some medical doctors, notably Bismarck of Kaizerland and Ngalle Ngalle of Mimboland, had found traces of sulphur in burns on the victims and concluded that a high concentration of sulphuric acid vapours in the gas had caused the burns. The origins of these acid vapours remained a mystery.

Replying to the question why this sulphuric acid had burnt people, but not the vegetation or the victim's clothes, Dr Ngalle Ngalle argued that it all depended on the resistivity of the material attacked. If acid is poured on a table, he explained, nothing would probably happen. Such might have been the case for the clothes and vegetation in question, depending on the type and concentration of acid. The human body is more sensitive because it is constituted of living tissues, thus the immediate reaction on the body, if one mistakenly overturns a jar of sulphuric acid in the laboratory for example.

The second and much shorter article focused particularly on the views of a certain Dr F. Y. Freebomb, a leading geologist-volcanologist working on the staff of the Muzunguland Geological Survey. He "dismissed the popular hypothesis" that there had been a volcanic explosion and argued that the gas emitted was carbon dioxide. If people had been killed, it was because this particular gas, by nature suffocating, had been emitted in large quantities. Why such an enormous concentration of carbon dioxide without evidence of an explosion remained a mystery to Dr Freebomb. He also conjectured that the carbon dioxide must have blended at one level with sulphur to produce sulphuric acid, thus accounting for the gruesome grilling, roasting and burning of certain victims. All this he hoped to be able to prove with the specimens – leaves, grasses, stones, rocks – which he had collected for laboratory analysis back in Muzunguland. Dr Freebomb, the article reported, had flown to Mimboland at the head of a four-man team of Muzungulander scientists.

Although not a scientist, Patience thought the bickering by the various experts beside the point. The fundamental question, as far as she was concerned, wasn't the nature of the gas, whether it had erupted or exploded, and why it had affected humans, livestock and vegetation differently. To her, the most important question which the scientists were yet to address was WHY the disaster at all, and why in the entire world and Mimboland, the village of Abehema, of all places, had been singled out by the disaster as the place to manifest itself. This was the question to answer, not the secondary concerns of the nature, activities and effects of gases.

To Patience, this showed the limits of science too narrowly confined to the realm of the observable, which she had always known could not explain everything.

According to the popular traditions in which she had been raised, reality is more than meets the eye. It is larger than logic. The real is not only what is observable or what makes cognitive sense. It is also the invisible, the emotional, the sentimental or the apparently inexplicable. Hence to understand happenings like the Lake Abehema disaster, it was important to look beyond the senses, to reach out to the supernatural, from which ordinary folks, Patience and Emmanuel included, drew daily to bridge their visible and invisible worlds.

In this way, even if the scientists were to agree amongst themselves about the gas, its origins, actions and effects, they would still not have answered the fundamental question of WHY – a valid question as far as most Mimbolanders were concerned. In Mimboland, the belief was strong that no truth is complete that fails to capture the complexity of phenomena beyond the immediate and the apparent. For, it is not because something is certified absent by the senses that that thing does not exist. The scientists who were working round the clock to explain the Lake Abehema disaster would yield little until they understood that the opposite or complement of presence is not necessarily absence, but invisibility. And that understanding the visible is hardly complete without investigating the invisible.

The newspaper also announced that the disaster had claimed over 1700 lives. On seeing the figure, Patience exclaimed. Her doctor had told her all along that only 40 had died.

"If the figures are this high, then what hope is there for me?" she started to weep.

It didn't take the driver and the other passengers long to discover that she was a victim of the tragedy. And once they did, they tried to console her as much as they could. When she collected herself again, she read on, despite her tears.

She didn't know what to make of all she read. She was at a loss, overtaken by events because the doctor had not ceased to lie to her. Why Dr Minko had told her of a minor volcanic discharge of gas that killed a handful of people only was quite baffling. If 1700 deaths were only a handful, then Dr Minko was a misanthropic maniac.

Also, she was angry about these so-called specialists who had had to wait for the disaster to occur before rushing in with belated, even if shallow, expertise. Why couldn't they have surveyed the area long before then? Why must it be disasters that forced scientists to use their minds? What use was a doctor who always came after a death for post-mortems, but hardly ever in time to save lives? So she went on, asking one impossible question after another.

She prayed and hoped to find Emmanuel alive, burnt and handicapped maybe, as long as he was alive! He had come to mean more to her than anyone else, and she just wasn't prepared to lose him when she needed him most.

"Lord God, why me? Why me? Help... please God. Help me out of this entanglement, Almighty Father! You know I need him Lord, you know how much he means to me, don't you? Please... Plea-sse... Plea-ssssse let him see his child, a survivor of Abehema."

Her mind kept going back to the terrible dream she had had before the disaster, a dream that had shocked both Emmanuel and her, and that now seemed to have come to pass. She relived the dream over and over, making her all the more nervous and confused. In her desperation, she seemed to blame herself for the dream. If only she hadn't told Emmanuel. If only she hadn't accepted to follow him to Abehema in the dream, the disaster might not have befallen him and his people. She blamed herself for everything.

"Why had I yielded after my initial hesitation? I should have allowed him to go alone, and perhaps his ancestors would have forgiven him and averted the disaster. My recklessness and lack of tact devoured the very people I was so eager to earn approval from. Whom would I turn to now to endorse me as wife and in-law?"

She would simply not stop blaming herself as if she had willed the dream. Her tears flowed and made banks of her makeup.

"Where do I now deliver the presents of soap, kerosene, and cooking utensils, which I brought along in my bad dream? And the baby, our baby, for whom we carried essentials to the village that is no more, who shall take care of it now that you and yours are gone forever? Emmanuel, please forgive me for bringing this nightmare upon you and your people."

She could still recall Emmanuel's reaction to her recounting when she reached the point of the disaster that had come to pass: "What! Did I hear you well?" he had asked, disbelieving his ears. And her answer had been slow and deliberate, spelling out every single word of doom, tears in her eyes: "Em-m-a... Emm-a, Emmanuel. T-h-e-r-e w-a-s n-o A-b-e-h-e-m-a t-o b-e f-o-u-n-d." And now to read and hear that his parents, his people and perhaps himself had vanished along with it, was something she couldn't bear, let alone forgive herself for willing it on them in a dream.

Pulling herself out of her world of recrimination, she would face reality for a while, still on terms dictated by her dream. "I hope I find you and your village intact. Driver, please deliver me to Emmanuel and Abehema. Assure me that nothing I read and hear is true. Please tell me I am dreaming."

All that the driver or anyone could do or say was to comfort her with reassuring words ... that brought little reassurance.

In a bid to soothe her, a fellow passenger told a story that only brought her more gloom. The story had come his way through the grapevine, like most things true about people in high office. Apparently, the person appointed by

President Longstay to manage a newly created disaster fund for the victims, a fund into which millions had already been poured by benevolent sympathisers at home and abroad, was his right-hand man and neighbour from the same village. Tchopbrokpot needed no introduction as a man rendered bald by years of public service in all capacities, including as *ministre plénipotentiaire* for 20 years.

"You can't go further to look for someone to trust," the narrator commented, noticing that even Patience was paying attention, and refusing to disclose his real identity. Could he be a spy testing the waters on behalf of the ruling clan? There was too much disaster in the air for this to cross anyone's mind. As the saying goes, *à Mimboland on ne sait jamais à qui on a affaire.*

"More like ensuring that no survivor shall bring disaster to the funds," someone interrupted, but was ignored by the storyteller who seemed confident of having the last laugh.

"It is said that once the appointment came through by presidential decree," the rumour-monger continued, his sophisticated Tougalish and accent betraying a prolonged stay in Tougaland, "Tchopbrokpot called a party at his home village to celebrate the windfall. A critical and very artistic musician, who apparently did not take kindly to those who would scavenge for fortune even amongst the dead, but whose name I can't remember, has criticised the celebrations in a big hit, which seems to be doing the rounds in bars throughout Nyamandem."

Just then another passenger lent the storyteller credence by claiming he had heard the song in a bar at Zingraftstown and that the musician in question was a certain Donny something.

The storyteller hated interruptions, so he ignored this intervention just like he had the first.

"The song is about a young man who is throwing parties everywhere in the village because his brother has been appointed to a very high post. As you know, given the rarity of such appointments, relations, friends and village communities do not hesitate to join in the celebrations," the storyteller commented, sounding very much like one of those disgruntled overly educated people one meets every so often, especially in West Mimboland.

"'Au village on va fêter, on va bouger, on va boire, on va manger'," the song goes, "'because my brother has been appointed to very high office'," he continued, commenting, "leaving one to wonder why on earth someone called upon to manage a disaster fund should be celebrating at his home village, instead of getting into transparent emergency humanitarian relief."

Others shouted "Sasse", asking him to tone down his big Tougalish.

He got the message, it seemed.

"The young man in the song sings that the appointment did not come cheap. His brother had to sacrifice virtually everything to be appointed, first as minister plenipotentiary, and then as manager of the disaster fund. He has been to see renowned pygmy diviner-healers to grease his way and fortify against jealousy and shame, and has gone through most trying experiences such as crossing dangerous rivers and sleeping for days with his nose in water. He even danced their village dance naked, feet in fire, with old baboons, not to mention the bark of trees, herbs and bitter concoctions which he has eaten and drunk, in order to be magnified in the presidential eye. Now that the appointment has come his brother's way at last, there is no reason why his life shouldn't change for the better – 'Mon frère est en haut, du coup ma vie va changer.'" The storyteller bent over backwards to demonstrate his mastery of Muzungulandish through such interjections.

People were listening. His story was all too familiar, and yet another example of how rotten power had become in Mimboland.

"The young man envisions his brother's appointment changing his life in a big way: 'my life is going to change', 'at last I am going to relax like a baobab of achievement and power', 'from small die fowl to suffer don finish'. The days of trekking, sandwiches, and struggle in overloaded taxis are over. He anticipates riding in his own car, an air-conditioned Mercedes, going into the inner cities to fetch vulnerable girls – especially those who turned him down when he was nobody – who can't resist anyone with a car. He also looks forward to winning tenders to supply tents, blankets, water or whatever, which he has no intention to honour, given the protection he is sure to receive from his brother in high office. He would move up to live with those in beautiful residential areas, keeping his old friends and relations at a distance, by limiting access to him, and employing a stern guard to keep visitors out of sight with false accounts of his whereabouts. At last he would be able to travel abroad to Muzunguland, to see beautiful sights, indulge in delicacies such as smoked salmon, and shop in hard currency. It's going to be hectic, as he spoils himself with power, privilege and comfort, thanks to his brother in high office. The song is a real celebration of the power, privilege and comfort of the chosen and insensitive few in the political landscape of Mimboland." The storyteller ended his paraphrasing of the song, oblivious of the grandiloquence that had stood in the way of comprehension for some passengers.

Patience understood him, even if his story had left her all the more beleaguered. With such corruption and insensitivity even to emergencies, what chance was there that she would find Emmanuel alive?

Once at the Kaizerbosch bus station, the driver asked all the other passengers to get down, and he drove Patience straight to the General Hospital where, in the absence of crisis centres, the critically affected and afflicted were rushed in chaos and hopelessness for whatever attention could be mustered. Patience was hoping to find Emmanuel there. The driver dropped her off at the main entrance and tipped two young men to help her in, then returned to continue with his own affairs.

The young men supported Patience to the waiting room where a nurse immediately came up to her.

"What is wrong with the young woman?" the middle-aged nurse asked, taking Patience by the hand. She could feel that Patience's temperature was high, and that she shivered all over. "We don't know," replied one of the young men.

"The bus driver who brought her just asked us to help her in," said the other.

The nurse asked the young men to bring Patience to a seat, which she indicated to them. Once she was seated, the nurse started to interview her, to find out what was wrong.

"What is your name, young woman?" asked the nurse, ready to write it down in her green notebook.

By then Patience was collected enough to tell the nurse her name. She realised that if she wasn't careful, she might be hospitalised for being unwell. And what if it turned out that Emmanuel wasn't there in the hospital? What if he were elsewhere or even dead? What would she be doing there in the Kaizerbosch General Hospital? So she tried to be calm and to answer the nurse's questions in a way that would not make the nurse conclude that she needed a bed in the hospital.

There was one thing Patience didn't know. The hospital was so full of patients that some of the less critical cases had been evacuated to a nearby college, and the nurses had been strictly instructed against admitting any new patients, unless the case was truly critical. She didn't know how delighted the nurse was when she said, "No, please, I'm not ill, but I'm looking for my boyfriend who was involved in the disaster. I've come all the way from Nyamandem to find out if he is here in the hospital."

"What is he called?" asked the nurse, pleased to discover that true love was still possible among the materialistic youth of today. "What is your boyfriend's name, my dear?"

Just when Patience was about to call the name, a middle-aged man came into the waiting room and engaged the nurse in a lengthy conversation. He was Okeleke the driver, who had come to inquire whether the hospital had any more people going to visit their relatives hospitalised in Alfredsburg, where he was about to go. Ever since the District Officer authorised visits to the disaster zone, Okeleke had been transporting people to and from Alfredsburg on almost a daily basis, except, of course, when it rained and the road was impassable.

The nurse asked him to wait a minute while she finished with "my beautiful daughter".

"Yes, my dear?" She turned back to Patience, gentle as a dove.

"Emmanuel Kwanga Mukong," said Patience, a slight tremor in her voice.

"Wait a moment," said the nurse, going to her table to consult the register. Okeleke interrupted her.

"Tell me Madam, wetti dis young woman want?" he asked the nurse.

"She want find out about her boyfriend," the nurse replied.

"De boy yi name na Emmanuel Kwanga Mukong?" asked Okeleke, full of interest.

"Yes," replied the nurse, turning to Patience for confirmation. "Isn't that so, my daughter?" she asked.

"Yes, his name is Emmanuel Kwanga Mukong," Patience confirmed enthusiastically, her heart thumping.

"Den tell'am make she come with me," replied Okeleke, jingling his keys and pleased to be useful.

"Why, you know whosai yi deh?" asked Patience, jumping up, and embracing Okeleke.

"Yes," replied Okeleke. "Your boyfriend deh for Alfredsburg Hospital. If I be correct, he get for come out today sep sep. I be di go so for bring he back with Mr Tangh-e-keh, he papa he friend," Okeleke told Patience who still clung to his chest.

"He well? – He papa well? – All man for he family well?" Patience asked him in jerks, and each time she felt better as the tension oozed out of her.

"No, I sorry plenty," Okeleke told her. "All person for yi family don die na dasso yi one lef for dis ground."

"He deh! You talk true say he deh?"

"Yes, he deh fine," replied Okeleke, offering her a handkerchief to wipe away her tears. Then he supported her out of the waiting room and into his battered lorry at the entrance.

The nurse watched them drive away with great admiration for Patience, who to her was a real reason for hope. For in a society where materialism and the love of money had corrupted every young woman, it was quite reassuring to meet someone like Patience, who reminded one of the good old days when love used to be love and girls lived the life of grace and virtue mapped out by their parents. She shook her head approvingly and resumed her routine work, wondering how long it would take before a young woman like Patience came up again.

31

Kwanga was pleased. He congratulated himself for what had just taken place. To have accepted to reconcile with Mr Tangh-e-keh was not an easy decision to take. Neither was it a sign of weakness on his part, though he had tended to think so. How could he refuse to forgive simply because he had vowed never to? He had been converted, much to his own surprise, to believing that the true men of principles were those who knew just when to bend their principles, and when to straighten them again, not those who clung to principles as determined blockheads. The world wasn't a place for rigid intransigence or fanatical extremism, but one of compromise and moderation, one where because everyone had a part to play and something to aspire to, it was absolutely unrealistic to insist on always having things one's own way. Those who did were sure to encounter a lot of awkward situations, and to cause their fellows lots of headaches as well. He was thrilled to have just proven himself not to belong to this degree of intolerance.

Now that he had accepted Mr Tangh-e-keh's conciliatory handshake, he felt at peace with his conscience, pleased, reassured and complete. He was glad he had abandoned his adamant stupidity at last, and that he had replaced it with realism. For how could one who had lost every relation in the world continue to reject overtures of friendship (even if these were made by former enemies), except if he wanted to follow his kin to the world of oblivion where they had all been forced? The world was simply not the type of place where one could afford to fall out with others just anyhow. If one did that, one was bound to run out of friends sooner or later, and to become everyone else's enemy. The complex nature of the world made diplomacy everyone's necessity, and not just the privileged activity of politicians.

The two of them had just been discharged from the hospital. Mr Tangh-e-keh, whose lungs had been diagnosed as contaminated by the dangerous gas, was declared fit to return home. Same with Kwanga, who in addition to contaminated lungs, had poisoned his bowels with the avocado and water.

The doctor told them they were to come back every two months for further checkups.

"Remember that we can't really be sure of anything at this stage because we've never seen anything quite like this before," he told them. "During your stay, you've witnessed the high incidence of stillbirths and miscarriages we've had in this hospital alone as a result of the gas, not to mention in Kaizerbosch, where they say it is much higher. All these things are strange and unprecedented – except of course the Japanese experience, which had quite a different cause altogether. So make sure you do as we tell you, just to be on the safe side."

So they gave the doctor their word, and signed the paper indicating the time of their discharge, which was 3 p.m. They shook hands with the doctor and with the other patients, and left the C Ward. Then they went round the Danger Wards biding farewell to some of the critical patients with whom they had become friendly. They sympathised abundantly with some of them for whom there was clearly very little hope of survival. For others, there were glimmers of hope, but life after treatment was bound to be a real tussle. There were some who would look so much like ghosts and zombies ever after. So though they felt lucky to be going away, Mr Tangh-e-keh and Kwanga were not unaware of the tribulations of those they were about to leave behind.

After their farewells, they went out of the hospital to the bus station where Okeleke had asked them to wait for him if they happened to be discharged before he came from Kaizerbosch. At the station, they would buy some food to eat while waiting for Okeleke.

Kwanga ate absent-mindedly, his thoughts all of Patience and Nyamandem. He wondered what she could be thinking. Where did she think he was? Dead? Alive? How he wished he could call and reassure her! All the time he was in the hospital, he had hoped she would suddenly appear like a miracle, a pleasant, curative surprise. All his hopes and expectations had been in vain. He couldn't understand why she hadn't come looking for him all this while. Perhaps she had tried and failed, he thought. Maybe she had come as far as Kaizerbosch, had asked around in vain, concluded he was dead, and returned to Nyamandem disappointed. He wondered what she would do if indeed he was dead. Would she kill herself, or would she just cry and stay? Would she remain faithful to him, or would she forget him soon afterwards? How would she and her new love treat his child? If well, just how well? Would she ever look at the child and think of him? Would she...?

He was so deep in thought that he didn't notice Okeleke's lorry pull to a halt just where Mr Tangh-e-keh and he sat eating. He also didn't notice when Patience jumped out of the lorry and raced towards him. He was taken completely by surprise, but what a pleasant surprise it was!

"EEEEMMMMann-uuuel!" Patience screamed at the top of her voice. And before he had time to see who the owner of the familiar voice was, she had pulled him out of his seat and begun to embrace him vigorously.

When Kwanga realised who it was, he was beyond words. At first his reaction was disbelief, then happiness, joy and excitement, then a mixture of all these emotions. And finally words were too weak to express his feelings. So like Patience, all he kept murmuring was: "I can't believe it! I just

338

can't believe it. Impossible... incredible. Can this be true? Is this really true? Incredible... just incredible. Is it you or is it your ghost?"

Mr Tangh-e-keh and Okeleke watched the moving display of emotion with paternal admiration. They were in no doubt about the strength of the youngsters' feelings for each other. The emotion with which Emmanuel and Patience greeted each other said it all.

Emmanuel and Patience reached a stage when all they were able to do was whisper each other's name. "Emmanuel... Patience... Emmanuel... Patience...." It became a melody. They could not believe they were really together, they who thought they might never set eyes on each other again.

"De girl tell me say dem go marry," commented Okeleke.

"Na so Kwanga don tell me too," replied Mr Tangh-e-keh. "I no be don yet see the girl, but now I know say yi be fine girl, yi get good heart."

When they had recovered from their surprise, Kwanga introduced Patience to Mr Tangh-e-keh.

"This is the girl I have talked to you about," Kwanga told him in Abehema. "She is the one I was coming to tell Peaphweng Mukong and Mama Ngonsu about. You know what has happened. My father was your friend and that is why I introduce Patience to you. Since one person's child is only in the womb, you are now like my father, and if you say that you approve of her, she will be my wife, but if you don't, I will do as you bid." He spoke the solemn language of the adult and the wise, which Peaphweng Mukong had always wanted him to learn to speak. He had come of age, and his father, watching from beyond in the company of the living-dead, would certainly be pleased to know.

Mr Tangh-e-keh was more than flattered. He looked at Patience over and over again, and the atmosphere was tense as he made his detailed evaluation. At last he spoke, this time in Pidgin-Tougalish, so that everyone could understand him.

"My friend yi pikin na my pikin," he said, looking at Patience and Okeleke, then at Kwanga who listened keenly. "We all know wetti yi don happen, but life must go dasso for before. Kwanga don loss yi family, all yi family. Na dasso yi one deh for dis ground now. Like he papa, I go say make yi and Patience marry, and make wena born dasso twin, so dat wena go build dis family back again, quick, quick." And with these words, he promised to make time and go to Camp-Kupeh to meet and discuss the issue with Patience's parents.

Emmanuel and Patience were ecstatic. Without the tragedy, things couldn't have ended better. As Mama Ngonsu had told her son the day he was leaving to study in the Great City, things weren't always going to be normal. "Normally, a child grew up and stayed around to help his parents," she had told him. "The world has changed, and things are no longer as they used to be." Then upon reflection, she had added: "Things must not be normal all the time, otherwise life would not be life."

Clearly, truly, things weren't always the way people would like to have them. Normally, Patience's and Emmanuel's joy would have continued unabated. Because things were not normal, they found themselves reminded of the tragedy, as Okeleke's battered lorry struggled through the valleys of death.

32

Four years have gone by since disaster struck the villages of Abehema, Tchang and Yenseh, killing over 2000 peasants and tens of thousands of livestock. Life has not returned to normal for most of the survivors now scattered all over Chuma Division and beyond, but they all seem resigned to their abnormal way of life. They are resigned to being ignored when they complain of heartburn, eye lesions, nerve problems, dying muscles, and paralysis. They have waited long for resettlement, rehabilitation or return from living and partly living, but they have waited in vain.

Four years ago when disaster struck, their fellow Mimbolanders came to their rescue, and so did the outside world. Then, although charred and burnt and roasted, even the most desperate of them found reason and determination to keep hope alive, which they did exceptionally well. This hope started fading only weeks after the immediate flare and universal gestures of solidarity and concern had died down.

The bulk of the victims were temporarily accommodated in camps and tents in Abeghabegh, Kakakum River, Pukafong and Hepalem, while men of science competed with one another to divine the causes of the disaster, ignoring whatever diviner-healers like Wabuah had had to say on the matter. They were determined to force feed Mimbolanders with their conviction that they knew best, and that only their 'scientific' opinion would have to count at the end of the day. To them, Wabuah and his likes were simply much too superstitious and illiterate to have anything to contribute. How could they be so insensitive as to deprive Science of the opportunity to be baffled by the fact

341

that it was not in the nature of lakes to simply rise up and wipe out thousands of people and tens of thousands of livestock?

That was four years ago. Today they are still waiting, waiting with fading hope for the scientists' famous master verdict. The diviner-healers pronounced theirs a long time ago, but no one in high office would listen to them, being schooled in science as modern politicians and civil servants all pretended they were. Waiting for the scientists seems like waiting for eternity. Three years ago, international experts in matters of gases, lakes and volcanoes met, deliberated and separated without agreeing on the causes. Wabuah and his fellow diviner-healers did not meet the criteria for invitation to participate in the conference, which was held under their very noses. The government of enlightened politicians and bureaucrats has repeatedly rejected the verdict of the diviner-healers for being "primitive and superstitious, and for taking Mimboland back to the dark ages prior to colonisation," but their hopes for "more scientific explanations" are yet to be fulfilled by the high priests of modern science. Yet Wabuah and his fellow diviner-healers are perplexed by the contradictions of the men and women of Kwang: "How can the same politicians, civil servants and intellectuals who consult them daily in private and at night for solutions to the challenges of modern city life, not want to acknowledge them and their expertise in broad daylight?" Many diviner-healers, shaking their heads in perplexion, have asked themselves this question, wondering how such a crop of dishonest elite can be trusted with the affairs of the land of Mimbo.

Survivors continue to live half a life as scientists, politicians, civil servants and intellectuals play games of hierarchy of cultures, civilisations and knowledge systems with their future, their very existence.

Suffering has not placed itself on hold as power elites debate themselves and their contradictions. At the temporary camps in Abeghabegh, Kakakum River, Pukafong and Hepalem, children have died of chronic diarrhoea, cough, fever, vomiting and infections. Some have been born with nervous and genetic disorders, some with lung and heart infections, while others have become epileptic and paralytic. Abortions, stillbirths and premature deliveries have increased, and certain children with good school performance prior to the disaster have degenerated remarkably.

Cases of madness and loss of memory amongst adult survivors have multiplied. Mr Tangh-e-keh is one of the latest victims. After waiting in vain for four years to be compensated for his cattle – his life essence –, he has taken to the streets of Kaizerbosch. From sunrise to sunset he roams about in nakedness, making strange noises and absurd accusations, defying attempts by his family to re-domesticate him, and by the police to shackle him. Some have heard him accuse the government of recruiting mercenaries to dispossess harmless villagers. The mysterious Ravageur and Vanunu are his favourite scapegoats, for the story has spread, since it was first featured in the critical *West Mimboland Post*, that Ravageur and Vanunu had been agents testing nuclear and chemical weapons for foreign governments too powerful to name. Wabuah has tried in vain to bring Mr Tangh-e-keh back to normal, which is understandable, as Mr Tangh-e-keh's madness is not caused by witches extracting his heart to be eaten at *Msa*. His madness has been induced by government's failure to fulfil its own pledges of rehabilitation and compensation, thereby denying him reconnection with the soul of his existence.

Most cases of madness are among the Fulani who have lost their lifeways. Unable to bear the loss of their herds and families, most of the survivors have felt derooted, dispossessed. After a long time of waiting in vain for something to happen, for the rays of the sun to smile again, many of them are out of their minds. They can be seen

343

wandering up and down the hills and mountains, chasing after and herding imaginary cattle. Day and night, under the sun and in the rain, they re-enact this same old ritual in honour of the herds, family, peace and life of relative quiet they once enjoyed. The cement of their lives is gone, the centre can no longer hold: "Isn't it time we went back to our herds?"

Once in a while the man specially appointed by the District Officer to oversee life in the camps leaves Kaizerbosch with a lorry of assorted foodstuffs. His destinations are the temporary camps of Abeghabegh, Kakakum River, Pukafong and Hepalem, where the victims have their eyes on the road always looking in the direction of Kaizerbosch, full of expectations of survival. He distributes the food for which they are thankful, but there is seldom enough. That is not their major concern now. Before disaster struck they were self-sufficient peasants, even exporting most of their harvest to the towns and cities, and paying various types of taxes to the government. No, their problem isn't exactly food. It's something quite different, something they've wanted to know from the overseer for the past four years.

Each time he visits, they want to know when this will all be over. "When shall we stop living in tents and go back home to start life again? Isn't it time we went back to life as normal? When shall we say farewell to the farms imposed on us? We want to live like people once more. We want to reconnect with our land, our shrines and our ancestors. *We want our souls back.* So please tell us. When shall we be home again?"

When he tells them he doesn't know either, that the answer lies somewhere well above him, they think he is mocking them.

"What do you mean 'government'?" they would retort. "Aren't you the government? Do you expect us to believe that? Please sir, try something else. All we want is to be able to farm again, to be able to feed ourselves so that you can stop wasting your money trying to get us food. All we want is to live a full life in tune with our values, which is not possible disconnected as we are from where our forefathers, parents, brothers, sisters, wives and husbands are buried. Or should we say rotting away? Please, please, understand us. We beg you."

"If only they knew that I would readily help if I could," the overseer laments, getting into the lorry, sorrow in his eyes. And as he drives away, he can hear them curse and call him witch. He cannot blame them, knowing what they've been through. "If only I could help," he mutters, heaving a sigh of regret. "Life is larger than logic," he tells himself, as if hit by the veracity of the statement for the first time.

Little wonder that a newly launched unauthorised political party promises to bring misery to a halt, to imprison all the architects of sorrows, and deliver all those confined to the margins of existence. Little wonder that this party has been warmly embraced by survivors determined to give the insensitive government of Mimboland a piece of their peasant mind.

Meanwhile in Nyamandem, Emmanuel and Patience have been married for four years. Their first son and daughter – a set of twins just as Mr Tangh-e-keh had wished when he permitted them to marry four years back – are called Mukong and Ngonsu respectively, after Emmanuel's late parents. They both adore the mischievous little things, as Patience chooses to call them. They keep intending to move house, but Patience's meagre salary cannot afford a bigger and better accommodation just yet. When Mukong and Ngonsu have grown bigger and ripe for school, Emmanuel hopes to find a job to supplement his wife's efforts. Until then, they are both satisfied with his current role as stay-home father.

Officially, Emmanuel Kwanga Mukong is not a recognised victim of the Lake Abehema disaster, because he failed to register as one before the deadline set by the National Coordination Commission. He had been in Camp-Kupeh when the announcement was made and hadn't felt like abandoning his wedding halfway through, to certify himself as a victim. He wasn't alone in failing to meet the deadline. Others, mostly illiterate farmers and breeders, had simply not heard the announcement on radio. Radio was captured with difficulty even at the best of times in Kaizerbosch, and announcements were made in Muzungulandish and Tougalish, languages the farmers and breeders neither spoke nor understood.

Not being thus recognised, Emmanuel harbours no illusions concerning the funds in the famous Disaster Account created by the commission four years ago. Not that those duly registered would benefit from the funds in any case. It is rumoured that Mr Tchopbrokpot, *ministre plénipotentiaire* and director of The Disaster Fund, is contemplating retirement to a quiet life in Muzunguland, where he has bought a whole street in an upper-class residential area of the capital city, for himself and his childhood friend and kinsman, President Longstay. A recent song by a once renowned musician is rumoured to have been paid for by Tchopbrokpot. It hails his patriotism and selflessness in public service, and has taken Radio Mimboland International by storm. Mimbolanders are dancing to it with their feet, their hearts and their minds, as Tchopbrokpot laughs all the way to bank in hard currency.

This doesn't worry Emmanuel as much as the fact that four years after the disaster no conclusion about its so-called 'scientific' causes has been reached. The deaths of more than two thousand people are now history, forgotten under duress even by those who should actively be praying to the ancestors through sacrifices to cleanse and admit them into their ranks. Few survivors have fully recovered from the impact of the disaster. The nature and origin of their tragedy has been deliberately made a mystery by the authorities, even as obvious culprits remain at large. For how much longer this mystery would continue to defy the collective wish of Mimbolanders to know the whole truth remains an unanswered question by scientists and a government who claim more than they can deliver.

In the meantime, Emmanuel has become active in the newly created popular political party, promising to bring an end to misery in the lives of ordinary Mimbolanders trapped in victimhood. The party leaders seem to enjoy his total confidence, especially as they are armed with the right slogans and rhetoric and have even rewarded his intellectual abilities by appointing him to the party's think tank. Reason enough to hope, won't you say?

Emmanuel isn't so hopeful. Two days ago he dreamt again.

Patience came to his rescue when he woke up sweating in the heart of the night as if bitten by a poisonous snake.

He shared his dream with her. He dreamt about an election, a second and third.

"My party, popular though it was, lost all three."

Patience could see he was perplexed.

"We had campaigned and campaigned, and had been reassured by people big and small, high and low, in villages and in towns. Each time the results were released, we couldn't believe what we saw and heard. President Longstay was always the winner, even though he never went out to campaign. We couldn't understand a thing. How could that be?" he asked, a worried look on his face.

Patience was quiet. He should finish his story before asking her for answers.

"How could President Longstay win an election when he never went out to campaign? When he wasn't even popular in his own home village?"

Emmanuel told her of a rally at President Longstay's home village. Their new party had organised the rally with the intention of using it as a red card, knowing that massive attendance would send shock waves through the ruling clan with a clear message: "Pack and go. Your time is up."

The attendance was indeed massive, and the chairman of his party had spoken the language of ordinary people, a language of the right to dream. He had been hailed. A messiah had come, and hope had been born again. Never again shall a chief take Mimboland for a ride with greed as creed.

Even more, village musicians who had come from all over President Longstay's home area had animated the rally. The villagers had turned out to share their plight with the chairman of the new party, by asking President Longstay, a son of the soil in absentia, some pertinent questions in music.

The first group of musicians, singing in the president's native tongue mixed with Muzungulandish, lamented and called him a liar. He was like the person in folklore who had cried wolf time and again in vain, to the point that his people had lost faith only to fall prey to him as the real wolf. Men and women alike had given up their farms for the day, to share their disillusionment with a son of the soil who had promised without fulfilling, and who had used them to fight his sterile battles for selfish power. They stated their case in enchanting music, and left the scene, still heavy with the disappointment that had poisoned their blood and turned their music bitter.

The Chairman, dressed strangely in white calico gown, hat and gloves, and white shoes like a ghost at night, told them: "I've heard your plight. The resources are yours. The country is yours. The power should be yours. There is no reason to suffer with so much in abundance."

Emmanuel continued recounting the dream while Patience listened patiently, "The Chairman, who was sitting on a kingly throne elevated by a specially constructed platform to welcome him, had, to my surprise, seated our little Mukong on his right lap, and little Ngonsu on his left. Like him, the twins were enjoying the music, and shaking their heads in sympathy with the villagers who had had enough of President Longstay. How our children came to be with him, I couldn't say. And how they felt at ease with his white calico gown, even playing with it, when ordinarily they would be running to hide from a ghost, was beyond my comprehension."

A second group took over, using the same musical instruments to play a different tune. The tarred roads, electrification and other development initiatives President Longstay had promised his own people upon assuming office decades ago were still to be delivered. "Papa Longstay, why have you abandoned your promise of hope? It is important that we live a decent life Papa Longstay. We need funds. We are suffering, and our crops sell poorly, but we work very hard. You've abandoned us, Papa Longstay, and we are not happy about it. " In return for their support, the president had simply compounded their hardships with his callous indifference to their plight and the bleakness of the future of their children.

The Chairman, echoed by Mukong and Ngonsu, greeted them with hope: "I've heard your plight. The resources are yours. The country is yours. The power should be yours. There is no reason to suffer with so much in abundance."

In a moving song, a third group comprising mostly young men and women, rejected the god-like status President Longstay had assumed based on false promises and the torture his insensitive regime had imposed even on them, his own supporters of the same ethnic origin. Their disappointment and frustrations were such that their music was no longer enveloped in metaphors. It would have pierced directly into the president's heart, had he been present.

To them, the Chairman, still echoed by Mukong and Ngonsu, repeated his message: "I've heard your plight. The resources are yours. The country is yours. The power should be yours. There is no reason to suffer with so much in abundance."

The fourth group was also direct and clear and without fear. Their song was critical of the economic crisis. It denounced surging social injustices and the slow pace of development, and condemned government inaction and complicity in the face of corruption and misappropriation. President Longstay was even compared unfavourably to his predecessor, President Habas, during whose leadership money was available, and peasants were at least sure to sell their crops, feed themselves and keep their children in school. In angry tempo, they invited the people to meet President Longstay with pertinent questions and demands. He should have foreseen the economic crises, and assumed his responsibility "to save them from death and not let them perish". Schools are without teachers, hospitals without drugs, and harvests have ceased to fetch money, yet the president was insensitive to all this. He must be reminded that it is his duty to bring things back to normal, for "your team is working without output", and many seem to have been born to watch a few enjoy the country's resources. President Longstay, they concluded, through the excesses and indifference of his gang to their plight, was presiding over a sorcerer state that delighted in sucking the blood of innocent folks.

Applauding, the Chairman, echoed by Mukong and Ngonsu, told them: "I've heard your plight. The resources are yours. The country is yours. The power should be yours. There is no reason to suffer with so much in abundance."

The fifth and final group was made up of elderly women, who came up to the Chairman and asked Ngonsu and Mukong to join them in their music, which they did. The women sang with dignity. They invited the other groups to join in, for theirs was a popular tune known throughout the region. In their song, they asked President Longstay to tell them where he had kept the money of the country for life to become so expensive. Their farm products sold poorly, but the price of meat, salt and other essential items had skyrocketed. Life in the village and in the city had become unbearably expensive, and President Longstay must say what he had done with the country's money. It cannot be true, the women sang, that Longstay knew what was going on in his country and decided to sit quiet: "Longstay do you know where it hurts? Out here it hurts, out here things are bad. Do you have a heart, Longstay, to feel our hurt?"

Then the strangest thing happened. Mukong and Ngonsu, all of a sudden, became my late parents – Peaphweng Mukong and Mama Ngonsu. Singing along with the women, they shared with them the stories of Chief Ndze of Tchang, who for years had bamboo-holed the commonwealth, only to die and be kept in *Msa* until he had repented through a diviner-healer he sent back with word on where to look for the money he had stashed away in bamboos and pleads to his people to be forgiven. They also shared with the women the story of Ngain, the chief who had connived with the devil to bring death and untold suffering upon Abehema and beyond. Upon hearing the stories, the village women composed an instant song: "President Longstay. Or is it President Ndze? Or shall we say Ngain? Your sterile love of bamboo-holes has drained our resources and lifeblood. Your greed is suffocating us. You have forgotten your own. You have sold your soul to the devil to feast on the blood of your forgotten kinswomen. And the children – can't you at least be good to children: our future, our hope?" At the mention of the word children, Peaphweng Mukong and Mama Ngonsu became little twins again and were returned to the Chairman.

Then, accompanied by Mukong and Ngonsu, the Chairman went down to the women and shook hands, saying: "I've heard your plight. The resources are yours. The country is yours. The power should be yours. There is no reason to suffer with so much in abundance. Together we must fight for the dignity that was once the pride of Mimboland."

Then with one voice, all the villagers who had assembled at President Longstay's home village to welcome their new hope gave the Chairman their vote of confidence: "He is not a listening president, he is not informed, and he does not care even for those who have sacrificed so his unproductive reign may keep power. We do not know him any more. Go ahead and chart out a new course for us and for people where you come from."

"We danced and celebrated, thinking the election results a foregone conclusion," Emmanuel shook his head, still unable to make head or tail of the dream. "We were mistaken."

Patience became more attentive.

"When President Longstay was told about the rally, how successful it had been, he is reported to have said: 'Ils ne savent pas à qui ils ont affaire.' In an interview with Radio Mimboland International he went on: 'Vandals cannot build the country, thieves and those who burn down banks are incapable of building the country, those who destroy roads are uninformed of what it takes to build the country. We want a country that is strong, rich and united, and there are no two people in Mimboland who can ensure that. So what change are they plotting?' The radio interview was followed by a menacing declaration in a newspaper published by Tchopbrokpot of the Disaster Account, his best friend and right-hand man, and consumed exclusively by his ethnic kin: 'Traîtres. Vous allez me sentir!'

"The interviews were followed by the first snap election, which we lost. The second and third elections, we lost as well. What does this mean, Patience? I'm lost for an explanation." Emmanuel was desperate for reassurance from his wife.

"I can't say fortunately it's only a dream, since I know better," Patience told him. "You mustn't share your dream with anyone else. I don't want you inflaming sensitivities in high places," she cautioned.

"We can't go on like this. Things must change in this country," he protested.

"You must be patient. Why are you in such a hurry? Your party isn't even legal yet."

"You sound just like President Longstay in his victory speeches. He made the same promises he had made twenty years ago, and when confronted by a journalist, he said Mimbolanders must be patient for Rome was not built in a day: His exact words were: 'Il faut attendre. Tu es pressé pour aller où?' Am I to believe that you and President Longstay think alike?"

"Of course not, but we've lost too many people already, and I'm too young to be a widow. And my children aren't going to start life as orphans."

Emmanuel gave up on her. He would have to decipher the head and tail of his dream himself. It was out of the question to simply wait and see.

Two days later Emmanuel came back to her.

"I've decided to give up on the state," he told Patience.

"What does that mean?"

"That it isn't through problematic state structures that change shall see the light of day in Mimboland," he explained.

Still Patience failed to understand what he was driving at.

"What I'm saying is that if we wait for the government to change our lives, we shall have to wait forever. There is no hope from that direction. That I gathered from my dream."

"So what do you intend to do?" Patience asked,

preparing Mukong and Ngonsu for church, for it was the morning of August 21, fourth anniversary of the Lake Abehema disaster. She and Emmanuel had offered a special mass for the victims of the disaster, and had to be in church in time to take the readings.

"I have decided to start an NGO to do for my dead and alive what the government and Tchopbrokpot have failed to do with its Disaster Account."

Patience was interested. "Tell me more," she said, combing Mukong's hair.

"It is all planned out," Emmanuel began. "It shall be called 'Foundation for the Forgotten Victims of the Lake Abehema Disaster – FOVILAD'. It shall be totally owned and controlled by the victims themselves, with a steering committee and technical committees comprised of persons from their own ranks elected on a rotating basis for specified periods of time. FOVILAD shall have its headquarters in Kaizerbosch, and branches throughout Mimboland and wherever sons and daughters and well-wishers of the region are found in the world. FOVILAD's principal role shall be to raise funds within and outside of Mimboland and shall directly manage the use of these funds in the interest of survivors of the Lake Abehema disaster seeking rehabilitation and a future of hope."

"And what role shall you play in the management of FOVILAD?" asked Patience, passing Emmanuel a white shirt to wear for church.

"No managerial or executive role in particular," he answered, not sure, as he hadn't quite expected this question. "The idea is to initiate it, raise enough funds at the beginning, and allow the villagers themselves to run the show."

"Excellent idea," Patience congratulated her husband. "I see it working!" She meant it. Structured in this way, FOVILAD was unlikely to pass for the type of NGO that the late Professor Moses Mahogany had termed: 'Nothing Going

On'.

Emmanuel thanked Patience for her understanding and encouragement, and told her he would need to travel to Kaizerbosch to start work on the project immediately and intended to stay there until FOVILAD was up and running.

"Go for it, my husband," said Patience, proudly. "This is a good initiative. I'm sure Peaphweng Mukong, Mama Ngonsu and all the forgotten souls of Abehema and beyond would be proud of their son and kinsman – Kwanga."

Emmanuel embraced her, tears of appreciation in his eyes.

"Let's hurry," said Patience, pretending not to notice the tears. "We mustn't be late for mass." Then, pointing at the children, she said: "Look. Your parents are waiting for us."

"May their souls rest in perfect peace," said he, in between tears.